MARY
HIGGINS
CLARK

We'll Meet Again

Simon & Schuster

SIMON & SCHUSTER
Rockefeller Center
1230 Avenue of the Americas
New York, NY 10020

ISBN 0-684-83597-5

Acknowledgments

"Once upon a time" is the way most of us start to tell a story. It is the beginning of a journey. We seek out the people who have begun to form in our minds. We examine their problems. We tell their tales. And we need all the help we can get along the way.

May the stars shine brightly on my editors, Michael Korda and Chuck Adams, for their unfailing guidance, editing, and encouragement. They are the best. One hundred thousand thanks, guys.

Copy Supervisor Gypsy da Silva, copy editor Carol Catt, proofreader Barbara Raynor, assistants Carol Bowie and Rebecca Head continue to surpass themselves in their generosity of time and concern. Bless You and Thank You.

A grateful tribute to my publicist, Lisl Cade, always my loyal friend, rooter, and sounding board.

Kudos and gratitude to my agents, Gene Winick and Sam Pinkus, for their sound advice and encouragement.

Profound thanks to my friends who so generously shared their medical, legal, and technical expertise with me: psychiatrist Dr. Richard Roukema, psychologist Dr. Ina Winick, plastic and reconstructive surgeon Dr. Bennett Rothenberg, criminal attorney Mickey Sherman, writers Lindy Washburn and Judith Kelman, producer Leigh Ann Winick.

Merci and Grazie to my family for all the help and rooting along the way: the Clarks, Marilyn, Warren and Sharon, David, Carol, and Pat; the Conheeneys, John and Debby, Barbara, Trish,

Nancy and David. A tip of the hat to my work-in-progress reading friends, Agnes Newton, Irene Clark, and Nadine Petry.

And of course love and bouquets to "Himself," my husband, John Conheeney, who is truly a model of patience, sympathy, and wit.

Now once again to joyfully quote my fifteenth-century monk, "The book is finished. Let the writer play."

FOR MARILYN,

My firstborn child

With love

Prologue _____

The State of Connecticut will prove that Molly Carpenter Lasch, with the intent to cause the death of her husband, Dr. Gary Lasch, did in fact cause his death; that as he sat at his desk, his back to her, she shattered his skull with a heavy bronze sculpture; that she then left him to bleed to death as she went upstairs to their bedroom and fell asleep. . . .

The reporters seated behind the defendant scribbled furiously, roughing out the articles they would have to file in just a couple of hours if they were to meet their deadlines. The veteran columnist from *Women's News Weekly* began inking her usual gushing prose: "The trial of Molly Carpenter Lasch, charged with the murder of her husband, Gary, opened this morning in the mellow dignity of the courtroom in historic Stamford, Connecticut."

Media from all over the country were covering the trial. The *New York Post* reporter was jotting down a description of Molly's appearance, noting in particular how she had dressed for her first day in court. What a knockout, he thought, a remarkable blend of classy and gorgeous. It was not a combination that he often saw— especially at the defense table. He noticed how she sat, tall, almost regal. No doubt some would say "defiant." He knew she was twenty-six. He could see that she was slender. Had collar-length, dark blond hair. That she wore a blue suit and small gold earrings. He craned his neck until he could see that she was still wearing her wedding band. He made note of it.

As he watched, Molly Lasch turned and looked around the

courtroom as though searching for familiar faces. For a moment their eyes met, and he noted that hers were blue; and her lashes, long and dark.

The *Observer* reporter was writing down his impressions of the defendant and the proceedings. Since his paper was a weekly, he could take more time in actually composing his article. "Molly Carpenter Lasch would look more at home in a country club than in a courtroom," he wrote. He glanced across the aisle at Gary Lasch's family.

Molly's mother-in-law, the widow of the legendary Dr. Jonathan Lasch, was sitting with her sister and brother. A thin woman in her sixties, she had an expression that was stony and unforgiving. Clearly, if given the chance, she'd gladly plunge the needle with the lethal dose into Molly, the *Observer* reporter thought.

He turned and peered around. Molly's parents, a handsome couple in their late fifties, looked strained, anxious, and heartsick. He noted those words on his pad.

At 10:30 the defense began its opening statement.

"The Prosecutor has just told you that he will prove Molly Lasch guilty beyond a reasonable doubt. Ladies and Gentlemen, I submit to you that the evidence will show that Molly Lasch is not a murderer. She is, in fact, as much a victim of this terrible tragedy as was her husband.

"When you have heard all of the evidence in this case, you will conclude that Molly Carpenter Lasch returned on Sunday evening last April 8th, shortly after 8 P.M., from a week in her Cape Cod home; that she found her husband, Gary, sprawled over his desk; that she put her mouth to his to try to resuscitate him, heard his final gasps, then, realizing he was dead, went upstairs and, totally traumatized, fell unconscious on the bed."

Quiet and attentive, Molly sat at the defense table. They're only words, she thought, they can't hurt me. She was aware of the eyes on her, curious and judgmental. Some of the people she had known best and longest had come up to her in the corridor, kissing her cheek, squeezing her hand. Jenna Whitehall, her best friend since their high school years at Cranden Academy, was one of them. Jenna was a corporate lawyer now. Her husband, Cal, was chairman of the board of Lasch Hospital and of the HMO Gary had founded with Dr. Peter Black.

They've both been wonderful, Molly thought. Needing to get

away from everything, she had sometimes stayed with Jen in New York during the past months, and it had helped tremendously. Jenna and Cal still lived in Greenwich, but during the week, Jenna frequently overnighted at a Manhattan apartment they kept near U.N. Plaza.

Molly had seen Peter Black in the corridor as well. Dr. Peter Black—he always had been so pleasant to her, but like Gary's mother, he ignored her now. The friendship between him and Gary dated from their days in medical school. Molly wondered if Peter would be able to fill Gary's shoes as head of the hospital and the HMO. Shortly after Gary's death, he'd been elected by the board to take over as chief executive officer, with Cal Whitehall as chairman.

She sat numbly as the trial actually began. The prosecutor began calling witnesses. As they came and went, they seemed to Molly to be just blurred faces and voices. Then Edna Barry, the plump sixty-year-old woman who had been their part-time housekeeper, was on the stand. "I came in at eight o'clock on Monday morning, as usual," she stated.

"Monday morning, April 9th?"

"Yes."

"How long had you been working for Gary and Molly Lasch?"

"Four years. But I'd worked for Molly's mother from the time Molly was a little girl. She was always so gentle."

Molly caught the sympathetic look Mrs. Barry cast toward her. She doesn't want to hurt me, she thought, but she's going to tell how she found me, and she knows how it will sound.

"I was surprised because the lights were on inside the house," Mrs. Barry was saying. "Molly's suitcase was in the foyer, so I knew she was back from the Cape."

"Mrs. Barry, please describe the layout of the first floor of the house."

"The foyer is large—it's really more of a reception area. When they had large parties they would serve cocktails there before dinner. The living room is directly beyond the foyer and faces the front door. The dining room is to the left, down a wide hallway and past a service bar. The kitchen and family room are in that wing as well, while the library and Dr. Lasch's study are in the wing to the right of the entrance."

I got home early, Molly thought. There hadn't been much traffic on I-95, and I was earlier than I'd expected to be. I only had one bag with me, and I brought it in and put it down. Then I locked the door and called Gary's name. I went directly to the study to look for him.

"I went into the kitchen," Mrs. Barry told the prosecutor. "There were wine glasses and a tray of leftover cheese and crackers on the counter."

"Was there anything unusual about that?"

"Yes. Molly always tidied up when they had company."

"What about Dr. Lasch?" the prosecutor asked. Edna Barry smiled indulgently. "Well, you know men. He wasn't much for picking up after himself." She paused and frowned. "But that was when I knew something was wrong. I thought that Molly must have come and gone."

"Why would she have done that?"

Molly saw the hesitance in Mrs. Barry's face as once again she looked over at her. Mother was always a little annoyed that Mrs. Barry called me Molly and I called her Mrs. Barry. But I didn't care, she thought. She's known me since I was a child.

"Molly hadn't been home when I went in on Friday. The Monday before that, while I was there, she'd left for the Cape. She seemed terribly upset."

"Upset, how?"

The question came quickly and abruptly. Molly was aware of the hostility the prosecutor felt for her, but for some reason it didn't worry her.

"She was crying as she packed her bag, and I could see that she was very angry. Molly's an easygoing person. It takes a lot to ruffle her. In all the years I'd worked there, I'd never once seen her so upset. She kept saying, 'How could he? How could he?' I asked her if there was anything I could do."

"What did she say?"

"She said, 'You can kill my husband.' "

" *'You can kill my husband!'* "

"I knew she didn't mean it. I just thought they'd probably had an argument, and I figured she was leaving for the Cape to cool down."

"Did she often go off like that? Just pack up and leave?"

"Well, Molly likes the Cape; says she can clear her head there. But this was different—I'd never seen her leave like this, so upset." She looked at Molly, sympathy in her eyes.

"All right, Mrs. Barry, let's go back to that Monday morning, April 9th. What did you do after you'd seen the condition of the kitchen?"

"I went to see if Dr. Lasch was in the study. The door was closed. I knocked, and there was no answer. I turned the knob and noticed it felt sticky. Then I pushed open the door and saw him." Edna Barry's voice quivered. "He was slumped over in his chair at the desk. His head was caked with dried blood. There was blood all over him and the desk and the chair and the carpet. I knew right away he was dead."

Listening to the housekeeper's testimony, Molly thought back to that Sunday night. *I came home, let myself in, locked the front door, and went down to the study. I was sure Gary would be there. The door was closed. I opened it. . . . I don't remember what happened after that.*

"What did you do then, Mrs. Barry?" the prosecutor asked.

"I dialed 9-1-1 right away. Then I thought about Molly, that maybe she was hurt. I ran upstairs to her bedroom. When I saw her in there, on the bed, I thought she was dead too."

"Why did you think that?"

"Because her face was crusted with blood. But then she opened her eyes and smiled and said, 'Hi, Mrs. Barry, I guess I overslept.' "

I looked up, Molly thought as she sat at the defense table, and then realized I still had my clothes on. For a moment I thought I'd been in an accident. My clothes were soiled, and my hands felt all sticky. I felt groggy and disoriented and wondered if maybe I was in a hospital instead of my own room. I remember wondering if Gary had been hurt too. Then there was a pounding at the door downstairs, and the police were there.

All about her, people were talking, but the voices of the witnesses were blurring again. Molly was vaguely aware of the days of the trial passing, of going in and out of the courtroom, of watching people coming and going on the witness stand.

She heard Cal and Peter Black and then Jenna testify. Cal and Peter told how on Sunday afternoon they had called Gary and said they were coming over, that they knew something was wrong.

They said they found Gary terribly upset because Molly had learned he was having an affair with Annamarie Scalli.

Cal said that Gary told him that Molly had been at their home in Cape Cod all week and wouldn't talk to him when he called, that she slammed down the phone when she heard his voice.

The prosecutor asked, "What was your reaction to Dr. Lasch's confession of this affair?"

Cal said they were deeply concerned, both for their friends' marriage and also for the potential damage to the hospital of a scandal involving Dr. Lasch and a young nurse. Gary had assured them there would be no scandal. Annamarie was leaving town. She was planning to give up the baby for adoption. His lawyer had arranged a $75,000 settlement and confidentiality statement that she had already signed.

Annamarie Scalli, Molly thought, that pretty, dark-haired, sexy-looking young nurse. She remembered meeting her at the hospital. Had Gary been in love with her, or was it just a casual affair that got out of hand when Annamarie became pregnant? Now she'd never know. There were so many unanswered questions. Did Gary really love me? she wondered. Or was our life together a sham? She shook her head. No. It hurt too much to think like that.

Then Jenna had taken the stand. I know it hurts her to testify, Molly thought, but the prosecutor had subpoenaed her, and she had no choice.

"Yes," Jenna had acknowledged, her voice low and halting, "I did call Molly at the Cape on the day that Gary died. She told me that he had been involved with Annamarie and that Annamarie was pregnant. Molly was totally devastated." Vaguely she heard what they were saying. The prosecutor asking if Molly was angry. Jenna saying Molly was hurt. Jenna finally admitted that Molly was very angry with Gary.

"Molly, get up. The judge is leaving."

Philip Matthews, her lawyer, was holding her elbow, urging her to stand. He kept his hand under her arm, steadying her as they exited the courtroom. Outside, flashbulbs exploded in her face. He made her hurry through the crowd, propelling her into a waiting car. "We'll meet your mother and father at the house," he said as they drove away.

Her parents had come up from Florida to be with her. They wanted her to move, to get out of the house where Gary had died, but she couldn't do that. It was her grandmother's present to her and she loved it. At her father's insistence, she had agreed to at least redecorate the study. All the furniture was given away, and the room was redone from top to bottom. The heavy mahogany paneling had been stripped off, and Gary's treasured collection of early-American furniture and art had been removed. His paintings, sculptures, carpets, oil lamps, and Wells Fargo desk along with his maroon leather couch and chairs had been replaced with a brightly patterned chintz sofa and matching love seat and bleached oak tables. Even then, the door to the study was always kept closed.

One most valued piece in his collection, a thirty-inch-high sculpture of a horse and rider, an original Remington bronze, was still in the custody of the prosecutor's office. That was what they said she had used to smash the back of Gary's head.

Sometimes, when she was sure her parents were asleep, Molly would tiptoe downstairs and stand in the doorway of the study and try to remember every detail of finding Gary.

Finding Gary. No matter how hard she tried, when she thought back to that night, there was no single moment when she remembered talking to him or approaching him as he sat at his desk. She had no memory of picking up that sculpture, of grasping the front legs of the horse and swinging it with enough force to cave in his skull. But that's what they said she had done.

At home now, after another day in court, she could see the growing concern on her parents' faces, and she could feel the increased protectiveness with which they hugged her. She stood stiffly inside their embraces, then stepped away and looked at them dispassionately.

Yes, a handsome couple—everyone called them that. Molly knew she looked like Ann, her mother. Walter Carpenter, her father, towered over both of them. His hair was silver now. It used to be blond. He called it his Viking streak. His grandmother had been Danish.

"I'm sure we'd all welcome a cocktail," her father said as he led the way to the service bar.

Molly and her mother had a glass of wine, Philip requested a martini. As her father handed it to him, he said, "Philip, how damaging was Black's testimony today?"

Molly could hear the forced, too-hearty tone of Philip Matthews's answer: "I think we'll be able to neutralize it when I get a crack at him."

Philip Matthews, powerful thirty-eight-year-old defense lawyer, had become a kind of media star. Molly's father had sworn he would get Molly the best money could buy, and that comparatively young as he was, Matthews was it. Hadn't he gotten an acquittal for that broadcasting executive whose wife was murdered? Yes, Molly thought, but they didn't find him covered with her blood.

She could feel the cloudiness in her head clearing a little, although she knew it would come back. It always did. But at this moment she could understand the way everything must seem to the people in the courtroom, especially to the jurors. "How much longer will the trial last?" she asked.

"About another three weeks," Matthews told her.

"And then I'll be found guilty," she said matter-of-factly. "Do you think I am? I know that everybody else thinks I did it because I was so angry at him." She sighed wearily. "Ninety percent of them think I'm lying about not remembering anything, and the other ten percent think I can't remember that night because I'm crazy."

Aware that they were following her, she walked down the hall to the study and pushed open the door. The sense of unreality was already closing in again. "Maybe I did do it," she said, her voice expressionless. "That week at the Cape. I remember walking on the beach and thinking how unfair it all was. How after five years of marriage and losing the first baby and wanting another one so terribly, I'd finally gotten pregnant again, then had a miscarriage at four months. Remember? You came up from Florida, Mom and Dad, because you were worried that I was so heartbroken. Then only a month after losing my child, I picked up the phone and heard Annamarie Scalli talking to Gary, and I realized she was pregnant with his child. I was so angry, and so hurt. I remember thinking that God had punished the wrong person by taking my baby."

Ann Carpenter put her arms around her daughter. This time Molly did not resist the embrace. "I'm so scared," she whispered. "I'm so scared."

Philip Matthews took Walter Carpenter's arm. "Let's go into the library," he said. "I think we'd better face reality here. I think we're going to have to consider a plea bargain."

Molly stood before the judge and tried to concentrate as the prosecutor spoke. Philip Matthews had told her the prosecutor reluctantly agreed to allow her to plead guilty to manslaughter, which carried a ten year sentence, because the one weakness in his case was Annamarie Scalli, Gary Lasch's pregnant mistress, who had not yet testified. Annamarie had told investigators that she was home alone that Sunday night.

"The prosecutor knows I'll try to throw suspicion on Annamarie," Matthews had explained to her. "She was angry and bitter at Gary, too. We might have had a crack at a hung jury, but if you were convicted, you'd be facing a life sentence. This way you'll be out in as little as five."

It was her turn to say the words that were expected of her. "Your Honor, while I cannot remember that horrible night, I acknowledge that the state's evidence is strong and points to me. I accept that the evidence has shown that I killed my husband." It's a nightmare, Molly thought. I will wake up soon and be home and safe.

Fifteen minutes later after the Judge had imposed the ten year sentence she was led away in handcuffs toward the van that would transport her to Niantic Prison, the State Women's Correctional Center.

Five and a Half Years Later

1 _____

Gus Brandt, executive producer for the NAF Cable Network, looked up from his desk at 30 Rockefeller Plaza in Manhattan. Fran Simmons, whom he'd recently hired as an investigative reporter for the six o'clock news hour and for regular assignments to his hot new *True Crime* program, had just entered his office.

"The word's in," he said excitedly. "Molly Carpenter Lasch is being paroled from prison. She gets out next week."

"She *did* get parole!" Fran exclaimed. "I'm so glad."

"I wasn't sure you'd remember the case. You were living in California six years ago. Do you know much about it?"

"Everything, actually. Don't forget, I went to Cranden Academy in Greenwich, with Molly. I had the local papers sent to me throughout the trial."

"You went to school with her? That's great. I want to schedule a full background story on her for the series as soon as possible."

"Sure. But Gus, don't think I have an inside track with Molly," Fran warned. "I haven't laid eyes on her since the summer we graduated, and that was fourteen years ago. At the same time I began U. Cal, my mother moved to Santa Barbara, and I lost touch with just about everybody in Greenwich."

There'd actually been many reasons for both her and her mother relocating to California, leaving Connecticut as far behind as memory would allow. On the day of Fran's graduation from the academy, her father had taken her and her mother out for a festive dinner of celebration. At the end of the meal he had toasted Fran's future at his alma mater, kissed both of them, and then, saying that he'd left his wallet in the car, he had gone out to the parking lot and shot himself. In the next few days the reason for his suicide became apparent. An investigation quickly determined that he'd embezzled $400,000 from the Greenwich Library Building Fund drive he'd volunteered to chair.

Gus Brandt knew that story already, of course. He'd brought it up when he came to Los Angeles to offer her the job at NAF-TV. "Look, that's in the past. You don't need to hide away out here in California, and besides, coming with us is the right career move for you," he'd said. "Everyone who makes it in this business has to move around. Our six o'clock news hour is beating the local network stations, and the *True Crime* program is in the top ten in the ratings. Besides, admit it: you've missed New York."

Fran almost had expected him to quote the old chestnut that outside New York it's all Bridgeport, but he hadn't gone that far. With thinning gray hair and sloping shoulders, Gus looked every second of his fifty-five years, and his countenance carried permanently the expression of someone who had just missed the last bus on a snowy night.

The look was deceptive, however, and Fran knew it. In fact, he had a razor-sharp mind, a proven track record for creating new shows, and a competitive streak second to none in the industry. With hardly a second thought, she'd taken the job. Working for Gus meant being on the fast track.

"You never saw or heard from Molly after you graduated?" he asked.

"Nope. I wrote her at the time of the trial, offering my sympathy and support, and got a form letter from her lawyer saying that while she appreciated my concern, she would not be corresponding with anyone. That was over five and a half years ago."

"What was she like? When she was young, I mean."

Fran tucked a strand of light brown hair behind her ear, an unconscious gesture that was an indication she was concentrating. An image flashed through her mind, and for an instant she could see Molly as she'd been at age sixteen, at Cranden Academy. "Molly was always special," she said after a moment. "You've seen her pictures. She was always a beauty. Even when the rest of us were still gawky adolescents, she was already turning heads. She had the most incredible blue eyes, almost iridescent, plus a complexion models would kill for and shimmering blond hair. But what really impressed me was that she was always so composed. I remember thinking if she met the pope and the queen of England at the same party, she'd know how to address them and in what order. And yet, the funny part was that I always suspected that, inside, she was shy. Despite her remarkable composure, there was something tentative about her. Kind of like a beautiful bird perched at the end of a branch, poised but ready at any second to take flight."

She'd glide across the room, Fran thought, remembering seeing her once in an elegant gown. She looked even taller than five eight because she had such gorgeous carriage.

"How friendly were you two?" Gus queried.

"Oh, I wasn't really in her orbit. Molly was part of the money-eyed country club set. I was a good athlete and concentrated on sports more than on social activities. I can assure you my phone was never ringing off the hook on Friday night."

"As my mother would have put it, you grew up nice," Gus said dryly.

I was never at ease at the academy, Fran thought. There are plenty of middle-class families in Greenwich, but middle class wasn't good enough for Dad. He was always trying to ingratiate himself with wealthy people. He wanted me to be friends with the girls who came from money or who had family connections.

"Apart from her appearance, what was Molly like?"

"She was very sweet," Fran said. "When my father died and the news came out about what he had done—the embezzling and the suicide and everything—I was avoiding everyone. Molly knew I jogged every day, and early one morning she was waiting for me. She said she just wanted to keep me company for a while. Since her father had been one of the biggest donors to the library fund, you can imagine what her show of friendship meant to me."

"You had no reason to be ashamed because of what your father did," Gus snapped.

Fran's tone became crisp. "I wasn't *ashamed* of him. I was just so sorry for him—and angry too, I guess. Why did he think that my mother and I needed things? After he died, we realized how frantic he must have been in the days just before, because they were about to audit the library fund's books, and he knew he'd be found out." She paused, then added softly, "He was wrong to have done all that, of course. Wrong to have taken the money and wrong to think we needed it. He was weak also. I realize now he was terribly insecure. But at the same time, he was an awfully nice guy."

"So was Dr. Gary Lasch. He was a good administrator too. Lasch Hospital has a top-drawer reputation, and Remington Health Management isn't like so many of the cockamamie HMOs that are going bankrupt and leaving patients and doctors high and dry." Gus smiled briefly. "You knew Molly and you went to school with her, so that gives you some insight. Do you think she did it?"

"There's no question that she did it," Fran said promptly. "The evidence against her was overwhelming, and I've covered enough murder trials to understand that very unlikely people ruin their lives by losing control for that one split second. Still, unless Molly changed dramatically after the time I knew her, she'd be the last person in the world I would have said was likely to kill someone. But for that very reason, I can understand why she might have blocked it out."

"That's why this case is great for the program," Gus said. "Get on it. When Molly Lasch gets out of Niantic Prison next week, I want you to be part of the reception committee welcoming her."

2

A week later, the collar of her all-weather coat turned up to cover her neck, her hands shoved in her pockets, her hair covered by her favorite ski hat, Fran waited in the cluster of media people huddled at the gate of the prison on a raw March day. Her cameraman, Ed Ahearn, was beside her.

As usual, there was grumbling; today it was about the combination of the early hour and the weather—stinging sleet, driven by gusts of icy wind. Predictably there was also a rehashing of the case that five and a half years ago had made headlines across the country.

Fran already had taped several reports with the prison in the background. Earlier that morning she had done a live report, and as the station ran tape over her voice, she'd announced, "We are waiting outside the gate of Niantic Prison in upstate Connecticut, just a few miles from the Rhode Island border. Molly Carpenter Lasch will emerge shortly, after having spent five and a half years behind bars following her manslaughter plea in the death of her husband, Gary Lasch."

Now, waiting for Molly to appear, she listened to the opinions of the others there. The consensus was that Molly was guilty as sin, was damn lucky that she'd gotten out after only five and a half years, and who was she kidding that she couldn't remember bashing in the poor guy's skull?

Fran alerted the control room as she saw a dark blue sedan emerge from behind the main building of the prison. "Philip Matthews's car is starting to leave," she said. Molly's attorney had arrived to pick her up a half-hour earlier.

Ahearn turned on the camera.

The others had spotted it too. "It's a cinch we're wasting our time," the *Post* reporter commented. "Ten to one the minute that gate opens they'll burn rubber. Hey, wait a minute!"

Fran spoke quietly into her microphone. "The car carrying Molly Carpenter Lasch to freedom has just begun its journey." Then she stared in astonishment at the sight of the slim figure walking beside the dark blue sedan. "Charley," she said to the anchor at the morning news desk, "Molly Lasch is not in the car but walking beside it. I'll bet she's going to make a statement."

Strobe lights flashed on, tape rolled, microphones and cameras were jostled together as Molly Carpenter Lasch reached the gate, stopped, and watched as it swung open. She has the expression of a child seeing a mechanical toy operating for the first time, Fran thought. "It is as though Molly cannot believe what she is seeing," she reported.

When Molly stepped onto the road, she was immediately surrounded. She was jostled as questions were shouted at her. *"How does it feel? . . . Did you think this day would ever come? . . . Will you visit Gary's family? . . . Do you think your memory of that night will ever come back?"*

Like the others, Fran held out her microphone, but she deliberately stayed to one side. She was sure that whatever chance she might have for an interview in the future would be ruined if Molly perceived her as the enemy now.

Molly raised her hand in protest. "Please give me a chance to talk," she said quickly.

She's so pale and thin, Fran thought. She looks as though she's been sick. She's different, and it's not just about being older. Fran studied her appearance for clues. The once-golden hair was now as dark as Molly's eyebrows and lashes. Longer than Molly had worn it in school, it was caught with a clip at the nape of her neck. The fair complexion was this morning the shade of alabaster. The lips that Fran remembered as easily smiling were straight and somber, as though they had not smiled in a long time.

Gradually the questions being hurled at her stopped until finally there was silence.

Philip Matthews had left the car and was standing at her side. "Molly, don't do this. The parole board won't like it—" he urged, but she ignored him.

Fran studied the lawyer with interest. This generation's F. Lee Bailey, she thought. What's he like? Matthews was of average height, sandy haired, thin faced, intense. The image of a tiger protecting its young flashed through her mind. She realized she would not have been surprised if he physically dragged Molly into the car.

Molly cut him off. "I have no choice, Philip."

She looked directly into the cameras and spoke clearly into the microphones. "I am grateful to be going home. In order to be granted parole, I had to concede that I was the sole cause of my husband's death. I have admitted that the evidence is overwhelming. And having said that, I now tell all of you that, despite the evidence, I feel in my soul that I am incapable of taking another human being's life. I know that my innocence may never be proven, but I hope that when I am home, and there is some quiet in my life, maybe then a *full* memory of that terrible evening may come back. Until that time I'll never have peace, nor will I be able to start to rebuild my life."

She paused. When she spoke again, her voice had become firmer. "When my memory of that night finally began to return, even a little, what I recalled was that I found Gary dying in his study. Just lately, another distinct impression from that night has come to me. I believe there was someone else in that house when I arrived home, and I believe that person killed my husband. I do not believe that person is a figment of my imagination. That person is flesh and blood, and I will find him and make him pay for taking Gary's life and destroying mine."

Ignoring the shouted questions that followed her declaration, Molly turned and ducked into the car. Matthews closed her door, hurried around, and got into the driver's seat. Leaning her head back, Molly closed her eyes as Matthews, his hand resting on the horn, began to inch the car through the mob of reporters and photographers.

"There you have it, Charley," Fran said into the microphone. "Molly's statement, a protestation of innocence."

"A startling statement, Fran," the anchor replied. "We will follow this closely to see what, if anything, develops. Thank you."

"Okay, Fran, you're clear," the control room told her.

"What's your take on that speech, Fran?" Joe Hutnik, a veteran crime reporter for the *Greenwich Time,* asked.

Before Fran could answer, Paul Reilly from the *Observer* scoffed, "That lady's not so dumb. She's probably thinking about her book deal. No one wants a killer to profit from a crime, even if it *is* legal, and the bleeding hearts will love to believe that somebody else killed Gary Lasch and that Molly is a victim too."

Joe Hutnik raised an eyebrow. "Maybe, maybe not, but in my opinion, the next guy who marries Molly Lasch should be careful not to turn his back on her if she gets sore at him. What do you say, Fran?"

Fran's eyes narrowed in irritation as she looked at the two men. "No comment," she said crisply.

3

As they drove down from the prison, Molly watched the road signs. Finally they left the Merritt Parkway at the Lake Avenue exit. It's all familiar, of course, but I don't remember much about the drive *to* the prison, she thought. I only remember the weight of the chains, and that the handcuffs were digging into my wrists. As she sat in the car now, she looked straight ahead and felt rather than saw Philip Matthews's sideward glances at her.

She answered his unasked question. "I feel strange," she said slowly. "No—'empty' is a better word."

"I've told you this before: it was a mistake to keep the house, and a bigger one to go back to it," he said. "And it's also a mistake not to let your parents come up and be with you now."

Molly continued to stare straight ahead. The sleet was beginning to coat the windshield faster than the wipers could remove it. "I meant what I said to those reporters. I feel that now that this is over, living at home again I may recover my memory of every detail of that night. Philip, I didn't kill Gary—I just couldn't have. I know the psychiatrists think I'm in denial about what happened, but I'm certain they're wrong. But even if it turned out they are right, I'd find a way to live with it. Not knowing is the worst."

"Molly, just suppose your memory is accurate, that you found Gary injured and bleeding. That you went into shock, and that your memory of that night will eventually come back to you. Do you realize that if you are right, and you do remember, then you'll become a threat to the person who *did* kill him? And that the killer may even now view you as a very *real* threat, since you've just announced that you feel that once you're home you may remember more about another person being in the house that night?"

She sat in silence for a minute. Why do you think I told my parents to stay in Florida? Molly thought. If I'm wrong, nobody will bother me. If I'm right, then I'm leaving the door wide open for the real killer to come after me.

She glanced at Matthews. "Philip, my father took me duck hunting when I was little," she said. "I didn't like it a bit. It was early and cold and rainy, and I kept wishing I were home in bed. But I learned something that morning. *A decoy gets results.* You see, you, like everyone else in the world, believe I killed Gary in a moment of madness. And don't deny that that is what you believe. I heard you and my father discussing the fact that you had almost no hope of getting an acquittal by suggesting that Annamarie Scalli had done it. You said I had a good shot at a passion/provocation manslaughter conviction because the jury would probably believe I had killed Gary in a fit of rage. But you also said there was no guarantee that it wouldn't be a murder conviction and that I'd better grab the manslaughter plea if the prosecutor would allow it. You *did* discuss that, didn't you?"

"Yes," Matthews acknowledged.

"So if I killed Gary I'm very lucky to get off so easily. Now, if you and everyone else in the world—including my parents—are right, I'm absolutely safe in claiming that I believe I may have felt another presence in the house the night Gary died. Since you don't believe another person was there, then you don't really think anyone will come after me. That's correct, isn't it?"

"Yes, it is," he said reluctantly.

"Then no one has to worry about me. If, on the other hand, I'm right, and I do frighten someone enough, it could cost me my life. Well, believe it or not, I'd *like* that to happen. Because if I'm found murdered, somebody might actually open an investigation that *doesn't* automatically assume I killed my husband."

Philip Matthews did not answer.

"That *is* right, isn't it, Philip?" Molly asked, her tone almost cheerful. "If I die, then maybe someone will look closely enough into Gary's murder to actually find the real killer."

4

It's good to be back in New York, Fran thought as she looked down from her office onto Rockefeller Center. The bleak, sleet-filled morning had evolved into a cold, gray afternoon, but still she loved what she was seeing, loved watching the brightly dressed skaters, some so graceful, others barely able to stay upright. The peculiar mix of the gifted and the plodders, she thought. Then, looking beyond the skating rink toward Saks, she studied how the store windows on Fifth Avenue lighted the March gloom.

The five o'clock crowds pouring from office buildings were a reassurance to her that at the end of the day, New Yorkers, like people all over the world, hurried to go home.

I'm ready to go home too, she decided as she reached for her jacket. It's been a long day, and it isn't over yet. She was scheduled to be on air at 6:40 to give an updated report of Molly Lasch's release from prison. After that she could go home. She already loved her apartment on Second Avenue and Fifty-sixth Street with its views of both the midtown skyscrapers and the East River. But returning to the still-unpacked boxes and crates, knowing that eventually she had to sort out the contents, was disheartening.

At least her office was in order, she thought with some comfort. Her books were unpacked and within easy reach on the shelves behind her desk. Her plants relieved the monotony of the standard office furniture she'd been given. The insipid beige walls were brightened with colorful reproductions of Impressionist paintings.

When she and Ed Ahearn had arrived back at the office this morning, she'd checked in with Gus Brandt. "I'm going to give it a week or two, then try to set up a meeting with Molly," she'd explained after she discussed with him Molly Lasch's unexpected statement to the press.

Gus had chewed vigorously on the nicotine gum that was giving him absolutely no relief in his personal antismoking campaign. "What are the chances she'll open up to you?" he'd asked.

"I don't know. I stood to one side when Molly made her statement, but I'm pretty sure she saw me. Whether or not she recognized me is something else. It would be great to have her cooperation on the story. Otherwise I'll have to work around her."

"What did you think of that statement?"

"In person, I'd say Molly was very convincing when she suggested there was someone else in the house that night, but I think she's whistling in the dark," Fran said. "Of course, some people will believe her, and maybe her real need is to create that sense of doubt. Will she talk to me? I just don't know."

But I can hope, Fran thought, remembering that conversation as she raced down the hall to the makeup room.

Cara, the makeup artist, snapped a cape around her neck. Betts, the hairdresser, rolled her eyes. "Fran, give me a break. Did you sleep in your ski cap last night?"

Fran grinned. "No. Just wore it this morning. Perform a miracle, the two of you."

As Cara applied base makeup and Betts turned on the curling iron, Fran closed her eyes and thought of her lead sentence: "At 7:30 this morning, the doors of Niantic Prison opened and Molly

Carpenter Lasch walked down the driveway to make a brief but startling statement to the press."

Cara and Betts worked with lightning speed, and a few minutes later, Fran was deemed camera ready.

"A new me," she confirmed as she studied the mirror. "You've done it again."

"Fran, it's all there. It's just that your coloring is monochromatic," Cara told her patiently. "It needs accentuating."

Accentuating, Fran thought. That was the last thing I ever wanted. I was always accentuated. The shortest kid in kindergarten. The shortest kid in the eighth grade. The peanut. She'd finally grown all in a spurt, during her junior year at Cranden, and she'd managed to reach a respectable five five.

Cara was taking off the cape. "You look great," she pronounced. "Knock 'em dead."

Tom Ryan, a seasoned newsman, and Lee Manners, a brightly attractive former weather girl, were the anchors of the six o'clock news. At the end of the show, as they unsnapped their mikes and stood up, Ryan commented, "Good piece on Molly Lasch, Fran."

"Call for you, Fran; pick up on four," a voice from the control room directed.

To Fran's surprise, it was Molly Lasch. "Fran, I thought I recognized you at the prison this morning. I'm glad it was you. Thanks for the report you just did. At least you sound as though you may have an open mind about Gary's death."

"Well, I certainly *want* to believe you, Molly." Fran realized she was keeping her fingers crossed.

Molly Lasch's voice became hesitant. "I wonder, do you think you'd be interested in investigating Gary's death? In exchange, I'd be willing to let you make me a subject for one of the news feature programs on your network. My lawyer tells me that just about every one of the networks has called, but I'd rather go with someone I know and feel I can trust."

"You bet I'm interested, Molly," Fran said. "In fact, I was planning to call you about exactly that."

They agreed to meet the next morning at Molly's house in Greenwich. When Fran replaced the receiver, she raised her eyebrows at Tom Ryan. "Class reunion tomorrow," she said. "This should be interesting."

5

The corporate headquarters of Remington Health Management Organization was located on the grounds of Lasch Hospital in Greenwich. Chief Executive Officer Dr. Peter Black always arrived at his office there at 7 A.M. sharp. He claimed that the two hours of work he got in before the staff arrived were the most productive of his day.

Uncharacteristically on that Tuesday morning, Black had turned on the television to NAF.

His secretary, who had been with him for years now, had told him that Fran Simmons had just started working for the network, and she had reminded him of who Fran was. Even so, it had been a surprise to see that she was the reporter covering Molly's release from prison. Fran's father's suicide had occurred only weeks after Black accepted Gary Lasch's offer to join the hospital, and for months the scandal had been the big story in town. He doubted that anyone who had lived in Greenwich at the time had forgotten it.

Peter Black had been watching the news program this morning because he'd wanted to see his former partner's widow.

Frequent glances at the screen to be sure he did not miss the segment he was awaiting had finally forced him to put down his pen and take off his reading glasses. Black had a thick head of dark brown hair, prematurely gray at the temples, and large gray eyes, and conveyed a friendly demeanor that newly hired members of his staff found comforting—that is, until they made the serious mistake of crossing him.

At 7:32, the event he'd been anticipating began. With somber gaze he watched Molly walk beside her lawyer's car to the gate of the prison. When she spoke into the microphones, he pulled his chair closer to the set and leaned forward, intent on taking in every nuance of her voice and expression.

As soon as she began to speak, he raised the volume on the set, even though he could hear her words perfectly. When she was finished, he leaned back in his chair and folded his hands. An instant later he picked up the phone and dialed.

"Whitehall residence."

The maid's slight English accent always annoyed Black. "Put me through to Mr. Whitehall, Rita." He deliberately did not give his name, but there was no need to—she knew his voice. He heard the phone being picked up.

Calvin Whitehall did not waste time in greetings. "I saw it. At least she's consistent about denying she killed Gary."

"That's not what worries me."

"I know. I don't like having the Simmons woman in the picture either. If necessary, we'll deal with it," Whitehall said, then paused. "I'll see you at ten."

Peter Black hung up without saying good-bye. The prospect of something going wrong haunted him for the remainder of the day as he attended a series of high-level meetings concerning Remington's proposed acquisition of four other HMOs, a deal that would make Remington one of the major players in the remarkably lucrative health maintenance field.

6

When Philip Matthews had driven Molly home from prison, he'd wanted to go into the house with her, but she wouldn't allow it. "Please, Philip, just leave my bag at the door," she'd directed. Then she'd added wryly, "You've heard that old Greta Garbo line, 'I vant to be alone'? Well, that's me."

She'd looked thin and frail, standing on the porch of the handsome home she'd shared with Gary Lasch. In the two years since the inevitable break with his wife, who was now remarried, Philip Matthews had come to realize that his visits to Niantic Prison had become perhaps more frequent than was professionally appropriate.

"Molly, did you arrange for anyone to shop for you?" he'd asked. "I mean, do you even have any food in the house?"

"Mrs. Barry was to take care of that."

"Mrs. Barry!" He knew his voice had risen two decibels. "What's she got to do with it?"

"She's going to start working for me again," Molly had told him. "The couple who have been checking on the house are gone now. As soon as I knew I was getting out, my parents contacted Mrs. Barry, and she came over and supervised sprucing up the house and stocked the kitchen. She'll begin coming in three days a week again."

"That woman helped to put you in prison!"

"No, she told the truth."

All through the rest of the day, even when he was in conferences with the prosecutor about his newest client, a prominent real estate dealer accused of vehicular homicide, Philip could not shake off his growing sense of apprehension over knowing that Molly was alone in that house.

At seven o'clock, as he was locking his desk and debating whether or not to call Molly, his private phone rang. His secretary was gone. It rang several times before curiosity overcame his initial inclination to let the answering machine pick up.

It was Molly. "Philip, good news. Do you remember my telling you that Fran Simmons, who was at the prison this morning, went to school with me?"

"Yes, I do. Are you okay, Molly? Do you need anything?"

"I'm fine. Philip, Fran Simmons is coming over tomorrow. She's willing to do an investigation into Gary's death for a show she works on called *True Crime*. Wouldn't it be wonderful if by some miracle she can help me prove there was someone else in the house that night?"

"Molly, let go of it. Please."

A moment of silence followed. When she spoke again, the tone of Molly's voice had changed. "I knew I shouldn't have expected you to understand. But that's okay. 'Bye."

Philip Matthews felt as well as heard the click in his ear. As he lowered the receiver, he remembered how, years ago, a Green Beret captain had cooperated with a writer who he thought would prove he was innocent of murdering his wife and children, only to have the writer later emerge as his chief accuser.

He walked to the window. His office was situated in Lower Manhattan's Battery Park and overlooked New York's Upper Bay and the Statue of Liberty.

Molly, if I'd been prosecuting you, I'd have convicted you of deliberate murder, he told himself. This program will destroy you if that reporter starts digging; what she'll find is that you got off easy.

Oh God, he thought, why can't she just *admit* she was under terrible stress and lost control that night?

7

Molly found it difficult to believe that she finally was home, harder still to realize she'd been away over five and a half years. When she'd first gotten there, Molly had waited until Philip's car disappeared down the road before she opened her purse and took out the key that would unlock her house.

The front door was handsome dark mahogany with a stained-glass side panel. Once inside she'd dropped her bag, closed the door, and in a reflex gesture, pushed her heel down on the floor bolt. Then she'd walked slowly through every room of the house, running her hand along the back of the couch in the living room, touching her grandmother's ornate silver tea service in the dining room while willing herself not to think of the prison dining room, the coarse plates, the meals that had been like ashes in her mouth. Everything seemed familiar; yet she couldn't help feeling herself to be an intruder.

She'd lingered at the door of the study, looking inside, still surprised that it was not exactly as Gary had known it, with its mahogany paneling and oversized furniture and the artifacts he'd so painstakingly acquired. The chintz sofa and love seat seemed out of place, intrusive, too feminine.

Then Molly did what she'd dreamt of doing for five and a half years. She went upstairs to the master bedroom, undressed, reached into her closet for the fleecy robe she loved, went into the bathroom, and turned on the taps in the Jacuzzi.

She'd lingered in the steaming, scented water while it foamed and swirled around her, washing over her skin until it felt clean again. She'd sighed in relief as tension began to seep from her bones and muscles. Then she'd taken a towel from the heated towel rack and wrapped herself in it, reveling in its warmth.

After that she'd drawn the drapes and gone to bed. Lying there, she had closed her eyes, listening to the insistent rapping of the sleet against the windows; gradually she had fallen asleep, remembering all the nights when she'd promised herself that this moment would come, when once more she'd be in the privacy of her own room, under the down comforter, her head sinking into the softness of the pillow.

It had been late afternoon when she awoke, and immediately she'd put on her robe and slippers and gone down to the kitchen. Tea and toast now, she'd thought. That will tide me over until dinner.

Steaming tea cup in hand, she'd made the promised call to her parents: "I'm fine," she'd said firmly. "Yes, it's good to be home. No, I honestly need to be alone for a while. Not too long, but for a while."

Then she listened to the messages on the answering machine. Jenna Whitehall, her best friend, the only person other than her parents and Philip whom she'd allowed to visit her in prison, had left a message. She said she wanted to stop by for a minute that evening, just to welcome Molly home. She asked that Molly give her a quick call if that was okay.

No, Molly thought. Not tonight. I don't want to see anyone, not even Jenna.

She watched the six o'clock news on NAF, hoping to see Fran Simmons.

When the program ended, she had called the studio and reached Fran, asking that she make her a subject for a special investigation.

Then she had called Philip. His obvious disapproval was exactly what she knew to expect from him, and she tried not to let it bother her.

After talking to him, she had gone upstairs, dressed in a sweater and slacks, and slipped her feet back into her old slippers. For a few minutes she sat at her dressing table, studying her reflection in the mirror. Her hair was too long; it needed shaping. Should she lighten it a little? she wondered. It used to be fair; it had darkened over the last years. Gary used to joke that her hair was so golden blond that half the women in town were sure she was helping it along.

She'd pushed back the vanity bench and crossed to her walk-in closet. For the next hour she'd systematically examined everything in it, switching to one side the clothes she knew she would never wear again. Some outfits brought an unconscious smile, like the pale gold gown and jacket she'd worn to the New Year's Eve party at the country club that last year, and the black velvet suit Gary had seen in the window of Bergdorf's and had insisted she try on.

When she knew she was going to be released from prison,

she'd sent Mrs. Barry a shopping list of groceries. At eight o'clock, Molly went back downstairs and began to prepare the supper she had planned and had been looking forward to for weeks now: a green salad with a balsamic-vinegar dressing; crisp Italian bread, heated in the oven; a light tomato sauce that she made from scratch, served over linguine cooked al dente; a glass of Chianti Riservo.

When it was prepared, she sat in the breakfast nook, a cozy spot that overlooked the backyard. She ate slowly, savoring the spicy pasta and crunchy bread and tangy salad, enjoying the velvety warmth of the wine, looking out into the dark yard, enjoying the anticipation of spring, only weeks away.

The flowers will be late, she thought, but soon things would be blooming again. That was another of the promises she had made to herself—to dig in the garden again, to feel the earth, warm and moist, to watch for the tulips as they sprang up with their potpourri of color, to once again plant impatiens along the borders of the flag-stone walk.

She ate slowly, reveling in the silence, so different from the constant, mind-numbing noise at the prison. After tidying the kitchen, she went into the study. There she sat in the darkness, her hands wrapped around her knees. As she sat, she listened for the sound that had suggested to her there was someone else in the house that night Gary had died, the sound, familiar yet unfamiliar, that had been slipping in and out of her fragmented nightmares for nearly six long years. There was nothing but the wind outside and, nearby, the ticking of a clock.

8

When Fran left the studio, she walked across town to the four-room apartment she'd rented on Second Avenue and Fifty-sixth Street. It had been a jolt to sell her Los Angeles condo, but now that she was here, she realized that, as Gus had perceived, New York was indeed in her blood.

After all, I did live in Manhattan until I was thirteen, she thought as she walked up Madison Avenue and passed Le Cirque 2000, casting an admiring glance at the lighted courtyard that led to the entrance. Then Dad made a killing in the stock market and decided to be a country gentleman.

That was when they'd moved to Greenwich and bought a house only a short distance from where Molly lived now. The house was in an exclusive Lake Avenue neighborhood. It turned out, of course, that they couldn't afford it, and the house was followed by a car they couldn't afford and clothes they couldn't afford. Maybe it was because he panicked that Dad couldn't make money in the market again, Fran thought.

He loved being active in town affairs and getting to know people. He believed that volunteers make friends, and he was a dream volunteer. At least until he "borrowed" donations to the library fund.

She had been dreading the thought of sorting through the boxes she had shipped East, but the sleet had let up, and the cold was bracing. By the time she'd put the key in the lock of her apartment, 21E, she'd developed a second wind.

At least the living room is in pretty decent shape, she told herself as she switched on the light and looked around the cheerful room with its moss-green velvet couch and chairs, its red and ivory and green Persian carpet.

The sight of the still almost-empty bookshelves galvanized her into action. She changed into an old sweater and slacks and got to work. Putting some lively music on the stereo helped relieve the monotony of emptying boxes and sorting books and tapes. The box with the kitchen equipment was the easiest to go through. Not that much in it, she thought wryly. Shows what kind of cook I am.

At quarter of nine she sighed a fervent amen and dragged the last of the empty boxes out to the disposal closet. It takes a lot of loving to make a house a home, she thought with satisfaction as she walked through the apartment, which at last did seem like home.

Framed snapshots of her mother and stepfather and of her stepbrothers and their families made them feel closer. I'm going to miss you guys, she thought. Coming to New York on a fast visit had been one thing, but actually moving here and knowing she wouldn't be seeing any of them regularly was much more difficult. Her mother had put Greenwich behind her. She never mentioned having lived there, and when she remarried, she urged Fran to assume her stepfather's name.

No way, Fran thought.

Pleased with all she'd accomplished, she debated going out for dinner, but then settled for a grilled cheese sandwich. She ate sitting at the tiny wrought-iron table in front of the kitchen window that offered a generous view of the East River.

Molly is having her first night home after five and a half years in prison, she thought. When I see her I'll ask for a list of people I can talk to, people who'll be willing to talk to me about her. But I have some questions of my own that I'll try to get answered along the way, not all of them about Molly.

Some of these were questions that had been bothering her for a long time. No record had ever been found of the $400,000 her father had taken from the library fund. Given his history of betting on risky stocks, it was assumed that he had lost the money that way, but after his death not a single scrap of paper had turned up to show where he had made an investment of that size.

I was eighteen years old when we left Greenwich, Fran thought. That was fourteen years ago. But I'm back now, and I'll be seeing a lot of people I used to know, talking to a lot of people in Greenwich about Molly and Gary Lasch.

She got up and reached for the coffeepot. As she poured, she thought of her father, and of what the lure of a hot tip would do to him. She remembered how anxious he had been to be invited to join the country club, to become one of the in crowd of men who regularly teed off together on the golf course.

The suspicion had begun to rise unbidden. Given their failure to find any record of the sum of money Dad had embezzled, she had to have doubts. Was it possible that someone in Greenwich, someone her father had been trying to impress, had given him a hot tip and then taken but never invested the $400,000 Dad had so foolishly "borrowed" from the library fund?

9

"Why don't you give Molly a call?"

Jenna Whitehall looked across the table at her husband. Dressed in a comfortable loose silk shirt and black silk slacks, she appeared dramatically attractive, an impression enhanced by her charcoal-brown hair and hazel eyes. She had arrived home at six o'clock and checked her messages. There had been no call from Molly.

Trying not to let her irritation show, she said calmly, "Cal, you know I left a message on Molly's answering machine. If she wanted company, she'd have gotten back to me. Clearly she doesn't want company tonight."

"I still can't figure why she'd want to go back to that house," he said. "I mean, how can she go into that study without remembering that night, without thinking about picking up that sculpture and smashing it into poor Gary's head? It would give me the creeps."

"Cal, I've asked you before, please don't talk about it. Molly's my closest friend, and I love her. She doesn't remember a thing about Gary's death."

"That's her story."

"And I believe it. Now that she's home, I intend to be with her whenever she wants me. And when she doesn't want me, I'll give her space. Okay?"

"You're very attractive when you're mad and trying not to show it, Jen. Let it out. You'll feel better."

Calvin Whitehall pushed back the chair from the dining room table and crossed to his wife. He was a formidable-looking, broad-shouldered, broad-chested, heavy-featured man in his mid-forties, with thinning light red hair. Thick eyebrows over ice-blue eyes enhanced the aura of authority that emanated from him even in his home.

There was nothing in Cal's presence or bearing to suggest his humble beginnings. He'd put a lot of distance between himself and the two-family frame house in Elmira, New York, in which he'd been raised.

A scholarship to Yale, and the ability to quickly mimic the manners and bearing of his more highborn schoolmates, had led to a spectacular rise in the business world. His private joke was that the only useful thing his parents had ever given him was a name that at least sounded classy.

Now, comfortably settled in an exquisitely furnished twelve-room mansion in Greenwich, Cal was living the life he had dreamed about for himself years ago in the tiny, spartan bedroom that had been his retreat from his parents, who had spent their evenings drinking cheap wine and quarreling. When the quarrels got too loud or became violent, the neighbors had called the police. Cal learned to dread the sound of the police siren, the contempt in the eyes of the neighbors, the snickers of his classmates, the comments around town about his trashy parents.

He was very smart, certainly smart enough to know that the only road out for him was education, and in fact, his teachers in school soon realized he'd been blessed with near-genius intelligence. In his bedroom with its sagging floor, peeling walls, and single, dim overhead light, he'd studied and read voraciously, concentrating particularly on learning everything he could about the possibilities for and future of the computer.

At twenty-four, after getting an MBA, he went to work at a struggling computer company. At thirty, shortly after his move to Greenwich, he wrenched control of the company from the bewildered owner. It was his first opportunity to play cat and mouse, to toy with his prey while knowing all the time that it was a game he would win. The satisfaction of the kill appeased in him the lingering anger at his father's bullying, the subsequent necessity of toadying to a variety of employers.

A few years later he sold the company for a fortune, and now he spent his time handling his myriad business enterprises.

His marriage had not produced children, and he was grateful that instead of becoming obsessed over that lack, as Molly Lasch had done, Jenna devoted her energies instead to her Manhattan law practice. She, too, had been part of his plan. The move to Greenwich. The choice of Jenna—a stunningly attractive, smart young woman from a good family of limited means. He knew very well that the life he could give Jenna was a big attraction to her. Like him, she enjoyed power.

He enjoyed toying with her too. Now, he smiled down on her benignly and ran his hand over her hair. "I'm sorry," he said contritely. "It's just that I think Molly would have welcomed a visit from you even if she didn't call. It's a big change to come home to that empty house, and it's got to be pretty damn lonely for her there. She had plenty of company in prison, even if it was company she didn't appreciate."

Jenna lifted her husband's hand from her head. "Stop it. You know that mussing my hair annoys me." Abruptly she announced, "I have a brief I want to go over for a meeting tomorrow."

"Always be prepared. That's being a good lawyer. You haven't asked about our meetings today."

Cal was chairman of the board of Lasch Hospital and Remington Health Management. With a satisfied smile, he added, "It's still a little tricky. American National Insurance wants those HMOs as much as we do, but we'll get them. And when we do, we'll be the biggest HMO in the East."

Jenna looked at her husband with grudging admiration. "You always get what you want, don't you?"

He nodded. "I got *you,* didn't I?"

Jenna pressed the button under the table to signal the maid to clear. "Yes," she said quietly, "I guess you *did.*"

10

The traffic on I-95 is getting into the California freeway class, Fran thought as she craned her neck, looking for a chance to change lanes. Almost immediately she had regretted not taking the Merritt Parkway. The semitrailer ahead of her was rumbling so loudly that it sounded like a bombing attack was underway, but it was traveling ten miles below the speed limit, making the experience of being stuck behind it doubly irritating.

Overnight, the skies had cleared, and as the noncommittal weatherman on CBS put it, "Today will be partly sunny and partly cloudy, with a chance of rain."

That covers just about every possible situation, Fran decided, then realized she was concentrating on the weather and the driving conditions because she was nervous.

As every rotation of the tires brought her nearer to Greenwich and her meeting with Molly Carpenter Lasch, she felt her thoughts insistently returning to the night her father shot himself. She knew why. On the way to Molly's house she would be passing Barley Arms, the restaurant to which he'd taken her mother and her for what turned out to be their final family dinner together.

Details she had not thought of in years came back to her, odd little facts that for some reason stuck in her memory. She thought of the tie her father had been wearing—blue background with a small green check pattern. She remembered that it had been very expensive—her mother had commented on it when the bill came in. "Is it sewn with gold thread, Frank? That's a crazy price to pay for a tiny strip of cloth."

He wore that tie for the first time that last day, Fran thought. At dinner, Mom had teased him about saving it for my graduation. Had there been anything symbolic about his wearing something so extravagantly expensive when he knew he was going to kill himself because of money problems?

The exit for Greenwich was coming up. Fran left I-95, reminding herself again that the Merritt would be a more direct route; then she began watching for the local streets that after two miles would lead her to the neighborhood where she had spent four years of her life. She found herself shivering, despite the warmth in the car.

Four formative years, she told herself. And they certainly were.

When she drove past Barley Arms, she resolutely kept her eyes on the road, not permitting herself even a glance at the partially concealed parking lot where her father had sat in the backseat of the family car and fatally shot himself.

She deliberately avoided as well the street on which she had lived those four years. There'll be another time for that, she thought. A few minutes later she was pulling up to Molly's house, a two-story ivory stucco with dark brown shutters.

A plump woman in her sixties with a cap of gray hair and bright birdlike eyes opened the door almost before Fran's finger left the doorbell. Fran recognized her face from the newspaper clippings of the trial. She was Edna Barry, the housekeeper who had given such damaging evidence against Molly. Why would Molly rehire her? Fran wondered in astonishment.

As she was taking off her coat, steps sounded on the stairs. A moment later, Molly came into view and hurried across the foyer to greet her.

For a moment they studied each other. Molly was wearing denim jeans and a blue shirt with the sleeves rolled to her elbows. Her hair was twisted up and casually pinned so that tendrils fell around her face. As Fran had noticed at the prison, Molly looked too thin, and fine lines were starting to show around her eyes.

Fran had worn her favorite daytime outfit, a well-cut pin-striped pants suit, and she felt suddenly overdressed. Then she brusquely reminded herself that if she was to do a good job on this assignment, she had to separate her present self from the insecure adolescent she'd been all those years ago at Cranden.

Molly was the first to speak: "Fran, I was afraid you'd change your mind. I was so surprised to see you at the prison yesterday and so impressed when I saw you on the news last night. That's when I got this crazy idea that maybe you could help me."

"Why would I have changed my mind, Molly?" Fran asked.

"I've seen the *True Crime* program. In prison it was very popular with all of us, and I could tell they don't do many open-and-shut cases. But obviously my fears were unfounded—you're here. Let's get started. Mrs. Barry made coffee. Would you like some?"

"I'd love a cup."

Dutifully, Fran followed Molly down a hallway on the right. She managed to get a good look at the living room, noticing the quiet, tasteful, and obviously expensive furnishings.

At the door of the study, Molly stopped. "Fran, this was Gary's study. It's where he was found. It just occurred to me that before we sit down, I'd like you to see something."

She walked into the study and stood beside the couch. "Gary's desk was here," she explained. "It was facing the front windows, which means his back was to the door. They say that I came in, grabbed a sculpture from the side table that was there"—again she pointed—"and smashed Gary's head with it."

"And you agreed to a plea bargain because you and your lawyer felt a jury would convict you of doing just that," Fran said quietly.

"Fran, stand here where the desk used to be. I'm going to the foyer. I'm going to open and close the front door. I'm going to call your name. Then I'm going to come back here. Please, just bear with me."

Fran nodded and walked into the room, stopping at the spot Molly had indicated.

The hallway was not carpeted, and she could hear Molly's steps as she went down the hall, and a moment later she heard Molly calling her name.

What she's saying is that if Gary had been alive, he should have heard her, Fran thought.

Molly was back. "You could hear me calling, couldn't you, Fran?"

"Yes."

"Gary phoned me at the Cape. He begged me to forgive him. I wouldn't talk to him then, though. I said I'd see him Sunday night at about eight. I was a little early, but even so he would have been waiting for me. Don't you think if he had been able, he would have gotten up or at least turned his head when he heard me? It doesn't make sense that he would have ignored me. The floor wasn't covered with wall-to-wall carpeting the way it is now. Even if he hadn't heard me call his name, he absolutely would have heard me once I was in the room. And he would have turned around. I mean, who *wouldn't?*"

"What did your lawyer say when you told him that?" Fran asked.

"He said that Gary might simply have dozed off sitting at his desk. Philip even suggested that that story could work against me, that it could look as though I came home and was infuriated that Gary wasn't anxiously watching for me."

Molly shrugged. "All right, I've done my bit. Now I'll let you ask the questions. Shall we stay in here, or would you be more comfortable in another room?"

"I think that's your decision, Molly," Fran said.

"Then let's stay here. The scene of the crime." She said it matter-of-factly, without a smile.

They sat together on the couch. Fran took out her tape machine and put it on the table. "I hope you don't mind, but I have to record this."

"I expected it."

"Please keep this in mind, Molly—the only way I can hurt you when we do this program is by concluding it with a statement like, 'The overwhelming evidence suggests that even though Molly Lasch claims she cannot remember causing the death of her husband, there seems to be no other possible explanation.'"

For an instant, Molly's eyes brightened with tears. "That wouldn't shock anyone," she said flatly. "It's what they all believe now."

"But if there *is* another answer, Molly, I'll only be able to help you find it if you're absolutely candid with me every step of the way. Please don't hedge or hold back, no matter how uncomfortable you may feel about a question."

Molly nodded. "After five and a half years in prison, I've learned what total lack of privacy is all about. If I could survive that, I can handle your questions."

Mrs. Barry brought in coffee. Fran could see by the set of her mouth that the woman disapproved of their staying in this room. She had the sense that the housekeeper was protective of Molly; yet at the trial she had given damaging evidence against her. Mrs. Barry is *definitely* on the list of people I want to interview, she thought.

For the next two hours, Molly Lasch answered Fran's questions, seemingly without hesitation. From Molly's responses, Fran learned that the girl she had known mostly from a distance had become a woman who shortly after graduating from college had fallen in love with and married a handsome doctor ten years her senior.

"I was working at an entry-level job at *Vogue,*" Molly said. "I loved it and began moving up pretty fast. But then, when I got pregnant, I had a miscarriage. I thought maybe the tight schedules and the commuting had something to do with it, so I quit the job."

She paused. "I wanted a baby so much," she continued, her voice soft. "I tried to get pregnant for another four years, and then when I finally did, I lost that baby too."

"Molly, what was your relationship with your husband like?"

"Once, I would have said perfect. Gary was so supportive after I had the second miscarriage. He always spoke about what an asset I was to him, that he couldn't have launched Remington Health Management without my help."

"What did he mean by that?"

"My connections, I guess. My father's connections. Jenna Whitehall was a big help. She was Jenna Graham—you probably remember her from Cranden."

"I remember Jenna." Another member of the in crowd, Fran thought. "She was president of our class in the senior year."

"That's right. We were always best friends. Jenna introduced Gary and Cal to me at a reception at the country club. Later Cal joined Gary and Peter Black as a business partner. Cal's a financial wizard and was able to steer some important companies into signing up with Remington." She smiled. "My dad was a big help, too."

"I'll want to talk to both the Whitehalls," Fran said. "Will you help me arrange it?"

"Yes, I want you to talk to them."

Fran hesitated. "Molly, let's talk about Annamarie Scalli. Where is she now?"

"I have no idea. I understand the baby was born that summer after Gary died, and I understand it was put up for adoption."

"Did you suspect that Gary was involved with another woman?"

"Never. I trusted him absolutely. The day I found out, I was upstairs and picked up the phone to make a call. Gary was talking, and I would have hung up, but then I heard him say, 'Annamarie, you're being hysterical. I'll take care of you, and if you decide to keep the baby, I'll support it.' "

"How did he sound?"

"Angry and nervous. Almost panicky."

"How did Annamarie respond?"

"She said something like, 'How could I have been such a fool?' and hung up."

"What did you do, Molly?"

"I was shocked, stunned. I came racing downstairs. Gary was here at his desk, just about to leave for work. I'd met Annamarie at the hospital. I confronted him with what I had overheard. He readily admitted that he'd gotten involved with her, but he said it was a crazy, foolhardy thing to do and he regretted it bitterly. He was almost in tears and begged me to forgive him. I was furious. Then he had to leave for the hospital. The last time I saw him alive was when I slammed the door after him. Terrific memory to keep for the rest of my life, isn't it?"

"You loved him, didn't you?" Fran asked.

"I loved him and trusted him and believed in him, or at least I told myself I did. Now I'm not so sure; sometimes I wonder." She sighed and shook her head. "Anyway, I *am* sure that the night I came back from the Cape, I was much more hurt and sad than angry." As Fran watched, an expression of utter, profound sadness filled Molly's eyes. She hugged her arms across her chest and sobbed, "Don't you see why I have to prove I didn't kill him?"

Fran left a few minutes later. Every instinct told her that Molly's outburst was the key to her search for exoneration. This is slam-dunk, she thought. She loved her husband, and she'll do anything to get someone to tell her that there's a possibility she didn't kill him. I think she probably genuinely doesn't remember, but I still think she did it. It's a waste of time and money for NAF-TV to try to raise even a serious doubt about her guilt.

I'll tell Gus that, she thought, but before I do, I'm going to find out everything I can about Gary Lasch.

On impulse she detoured on the way to the Merritt Parkway to drive past Lasch Hospital, which had replaced the private clinic founded by Jonathan Lasch, Gary's father. This was where her father had been taken after he shot himself and where he died seven hours later.

She was astonished to see that the hospital was now twice the size that she remembered. There was a traffic light outside the main entrance, and she slowed the car enough to miss the green light. As she waited at the red signal, she studied the facility, noting the wings that had been added to the main structure, the new building on the righthand side of the property, the elevated parking garage.

With a stab of pain she searched out the window of the waiting room on the third floor where she remembered standing while she waited for news about her father, knowing instinctively that he was beyond help.

This will be a good place to come and talk to people, Fran thought. The light changed, and five minutes later she was on the approach to the Merritt Parkway. As she drove south through the swiftly flowing traffic, she mulled over the fact that Gary Lasch had met and become involved with Annamarie Scalli, a young nurse at the hospital, and that reckless indiscretion had cost him his life.

But was that his only indiscretion? she wondered suddenly.

Chances were, it would probably turn out that he'd made one colossal mistake, like her father, but otherwise was the upstanding citizen, fine doctor, and devoted health-care provider that people knew and remembered.

But maybe not, Fran reminded herself as she passed the state line between Connecticut and New York. I've been in this business long enough to expect the unexpected.

11

After she saw Fran Simmons to the door, Molly returned to the study. Edna Barry looked in on her at 1:30. "Molly, unless there's something else you want me to do, I'll be leaving now."

"Nothing else, thank you, Mrs. Barry."

Edna Barry stood uncertainly at the door. "I wish you'd let me get you some lunch before I go."

"I'm not hungry yet, really."

Molly's voice was muffled. Edna could tell she had been crying. The guilt and fear that had haunted Edna Barry every waking hour for nearly six years suddenly deepened. Oh God, she begged. Please understand. I couldn't do anything else.

In the kitchen she put on her parka and fastened a scarf under her chin. From the counter she picked up her key ring, stared at it for a moment, and with a convulsive gesture, folded her fist around it.

Not twenty minutes later she was in her modest Cape Cod–style home in Glenville. Her thirty-year-old son, Wally, was watching television in the living room. He did not take his eyes off the set when she came in, but at least he seemed calm. Some days, even when he's on the medicine, he can be so agitated, she thought.

Like that terrible Sunday when Dr. Lasch had died. Wally had been so angry that day because Dr. Lasch had scolded him earlier in the week when he came to the house, went into the study, and picked up the Remington sculpture.

Edna Barry had omitted one detail from her account of what had happened that Monday morning. She had not told the police that her key to the Lasch house was not on her key ring where it belonged, that she had had to let herself in with the key Molly kept hidden in the garden, and that later she had found the missing key in Wally's pocket.

When she asked him about it, he started to cry and ran into his room, slamming the door. "Don't talk about it, Mama," he had sobbed.

"We must *never, never* talk about this to anybody," she had told him firmly, and had made him promise that he wouldn't. And he never had, not to this day.

She always had tried to convince herself it probably had been just a coincidence. After all, she had found Molly covered with blood. Molly's fingerprints *were* on the sculpture.

But suppose Molly *did* start to remember details of that night? Suppose she really *had* seen someone in the house?

Had Wally been there? How could she ever be sure? Mrs. Barry wondered.

12

Peter Black drove through the darkened streets to his home on Old Church Road. Once it had been the carriage house of a large estate. He had bought it during his second marriage, which, like his first, had ended within a few years. His second wife, however, unlike his first, had had exquisite taste, and after she left him, he had made no effort to change the decor. His only alteration was to add a bar and stock it plentifully. His second wife had been a teetotaler.

Peter had met his late partner, Gary Lasch, at medical school, and they had become friends. It was after the death of Gary's father, Dr. Jonathan Lasch, that Gary had come to Peter with a proposition.

"Health management is the new wave of medicine," he had said. "The nonprofit clinic my father opened can't go on like this. We'll expand it, make it profitable, start our own HMO."

Gary, blessed with a distinguished name in medicine, had taken his father's place as head of the clinic, which later became Lasch Hospital. The third partner, Cal Whitehall, came on board when together they founded the Remington Health Management Organization.

Now the state was on the verge of approving Remington's acquisition of a number of smaller HMOs. Everything was going well, but it wasn't a done deal yet. They had reached the last step on the tightrope. The only problem they could see was that American National Insurance was fighting to acquire the companies too.

But everything still could go wrong, Peter reminded himself as he parked at his front door. He knew he had no intention of going out again tonight, but it was cold, and he wanted a drink. Pedro, his longtime live-in cook and housekeeper, would put the car away later.

Peter let himself in and went directly to the library. The room was always welcoming, with the fire burning and the television set tuned to the news station. Pedro appeared immediately, asking the nightly question: "The usual, sir?"

The usual was scotch on the rocks, except when Peter decided on a change of pace and asked for bourbon or vodka.

The first scotch, sipped slowly and appreciatively, began to calm Peter's nerves. A small plate of smoked salmon likewise appeased his slight feeling of hunger. He did not like to dine for at least an hour after reaching home.

He took the second scotch with him while he showered. Carrying the rest of the drink into the bedroom, he dressed in chinos and a long-sleeved cashmere shirt. Finally, almost relaxed, and with the worrisome sense that something was going wrong somewhat abated, he went back downstairs.

Peter Black frequently dined with friends. In his renewed status as a single man, he was showered with invitations from attractive and socially desirable women. The evenings he was at home he usually brought a book or magazine to the table. Tonight, though, was an exception. As he ate baked swordfish and steamed asparagus and sipped a glass of Saint Emilion, he sat in silent reflection, thinking through the meetings that were still to come concerning the mergers.

The ring of the telephone in the library did not interrupt his thought process. Pedro knew enough to tell whoever it was that he would return the call later. That was why, when Pedro came into the dining room, the cell phone in his hand, Peter Black raised his eyebrows in annoyance.

Pedro covered the mouthpiece and whispered, "Excuse me, Doctor, but I thought you might want to take this call. It is Mrs. Lasch. Mrs. Molly Lasch."

Peter Black paused, then downed his glass of wine in a single gulp—allowing himself none of the customary time to savor the delicate taste—and reached for the phone. His hand was trembling.

13 _____

Molly had given Fran a list of people she might want to begin inter-viewing. First on the list was Gary's partner, Dr. Peter Black. "He never said a word to me after Gary's death," she'd told her.

Then Jenna Whitehall: "You'll remember her from Cranden, Fran."

Jenna's husband, Cal: "When they needed a cash reserve to start Remington, Cal arranged the financing," she explained.

Molly's lawyer, Philip Matthews: "Everyone thinks he was wonderful because he got me a light sentence and then fought for early parole. I'd like him better if I thought he had even an ounce of doubt about my guilt," she'd said.

Edna Barry: "Everything was in perfect order when I got home yesterday. It was almost as though the past five and a half years hadn't even happened."

Fran had asked Molly to speak to each of them and let them know she would be calling. But when Edna Barry looked in on her before she left, Molly did not feel like mentioning it to her.

Eventually Molly had gone into the kitchen and looked in the refrigerator. She saw that Mrs. Barry had stopped at the delicatessen on her way in. The rye bread with caraway seeds, Virginia ham, and Swiss cheese she had requested were there. She took them out and with careful pleasure made a sandwich, then opened the refrigerator again and found the spicy mustard she loved.

And a pickle, she thought. I haven't wanted to eat a pickle in years. Smiling unconsciously, she brought the plate to the table, made a cup of tea, then looked around for the local newspaper she had not bothered to open earlier.

She flinched when she saw a picture of herself on the front page. The caption read "Molly Carpenter Lasch released after five and a half years in prison." The account rehashed the details of Gary's death, the plea bargain, and her declaration of innocence at the prison gate.

Hardest to read was the coverage given to the background of her family. The article included a profile of her grandparents, long-time pillars of Greenwich and Palm Beach society, listing their achievements and charities. It also discussed her father's sterling business career, Gary's father's distinguished history in medicine, and the model health maintenance organization Gary had cofounded with Dr. Peter Black.

All of them good people, their accomplishments impressive, but everything is turned into juicy gossip because of me, Molly thought. No longer hungry, she pushed away the sandwich. As it had earlier in the day, the feeling of fatigue and sleepiness was overwhelming her. The psychiatrist at the prison had treated her for depression and had urged her to see the doctor who had treated her while she was awaiting trial.

"You told me you liked Dr. Daniels, Molly. You said you felt comfortable with him because he believed you when you said you had no memory of Gary's death. Remember, extreme fatigue can be a sign of depression."

As Molly rubbed her forehead in an effort to ward off the beginning of a headache, she remembered that she liked Dr. Daniels very much and that she should have included his name with those she had given Fran. Maybe she would try to get an appointment with him. More important, she'd phone and tell him that if Fran Simmons called, he had permission to speak freely about her.

Molly got up from the table, dumped the rest of the sandwich in the compactor, and started upstairs, carrying her tea. The ringer on the phone was turned off, but she decided she should check the answering machine for messages.

She now had a new unlisted phone number, so only a few people knew it. They included her parents, Philip Matthews, and Jenna. Jenna had called twice. "Moll, I don't care what you say, I'm coming over tonight," her message said. "I'm bringing dinner over at eight."

Once she's here, I'll be glad to see her, Molly acknowledged to herself as she started up the stairs again. In the bedroom, she finished the tea, kicked off her shoes, lay down on top of the coverlet, and pulled it around her. She fell asleep immediately.

Her dreams were fragmented. In them, she was in the house. She was trying to talk to Gary, but he wouldn't acknowledge her. Then there was a sound—what was it? If she could only recognize it, then everything would be clear. That sound. *That sound.* What *was* it?

She woke at 6:30 to find tears running down her cheeks. Maybe it's a good sign, she thought. This morning, when she spoke to Fran, had been the first time she had cried since that week she spent on Cape Cod nearly six years ago, when she'd done nothing *except* cry. When she first learned that Gary was dead, it was as though something inside her dried up, became permanently arid. From that day to this one, she had been tearless.

Reluctantly she got up, splashed water on her face, brushed her hair, and changed from the jeans and cotton shirt to a beige sweater and slacks. As an afterthought she put on earrings and light makeup. When Jenna had visited her in prison, she had prodded her to wear makeup in the visiting room. "Best foot forward, Moll; remember our motto."

Downstairs again, Molly lit the gas fire in the family room off the kitchen. Family room for the family of one, she thought. On the evenings they had been home, Gary and she had loved watching old movies together. His collection of classic films still filled the shelves.

She thought of the people she had to call to ask them to cooperate with Fran Simmons. She was unsure of one of them. She did not want to call Peter Black in his office, but she *did* want him to agree to talk to Fran, so she decided to call him at home. And rather than putting it off, she'd do it tonight. No, she'd do it right now.

She had scarcely thought of Pedro in nearly six years, but when she heard his voice, memories of the small dinner parties Peter used to have came rushing back. Often they included just the six of them—Jenna and Cal, Peter and his current wife or date, herself and Gary.

She didn't blame Peter for wanting nothing to do with her. She knew she probably would feel that way if someone hurt Jenna. Old friend, best friend. That was the litany they used to singsong to each other.

She half expected to be told that Peter was not available and was surprised when he did take her call. Hesitantly, then quickly, Molly said what she needed to say: "Tomorrow, Fran Simmons from NAF-TV is going to call to make an appointment with you. She's doing a piece for the *True Crime* program, on Gary's death. I don't care what you say about me, Peter, but *please* see her. I'd better warn you that Fran said it would be much better if she had your cooperation, but if not, she'd find a way to work around you."

She waited. After a long pause, Peter Black said quietly, "I would think you would have the decency to leave well enough alone, Molly." His voice was tight, though his words were ever so slightly slurred. "Don't you think Gary's reputation deserves better than to have the Annamarie Scalli story revived? You paid a very small price for what you did. I warn you, you will be the ultimate loser if a cheap television show reenacts your crime for a national audience . . ."

The click of the receiver as he hung up was almost drowned out by the ringing of the front doorbell.

For the next two hours, Molly felt as though life was almost normal again. Jenna had brought not only dinner but a bottle of Cal's best Montrachet. They sipped wine in the family room, then ate their meal at the coffee table there. Jenna dominated the conversation as she mapped out the plans she had made for her friend. Molly was to come in to New York, spend a few days in the apartment, go shopping and to the hot new salon Jenna had discovered, where she could have a complete one-stop makeover. "Hair, face, nails, the bod, the works," Jenna said triumphantly. "I've already planned to take time off to be with you." She grinned at Molly. "Tell the truth. I look pretty good, don't you think?"

"You're a walking ad for whatever regimen you're on," Molly agreed. "At some point I'll take you up on that. But for now, no."

She put down her demitasse cup. "Jen, Fran Simmons was here today. You probably remember her. She went to Cranden with us."

"Her father shot himself, right? He was the guy who embezzled all that money from the library."

"That's right. She's an investigative reporter now, for NAF-TV. She's going to do a show about Gary's death for the network's *True Crime* program."

Jenna Whitehall did not attempt to hide her dismay: "Molly, no!"

Molly shrugged. "I didn't expect even you to understand, so I know you won't understand this next thing either. Jenna, I need to see Annamarie Scalli. Do you know where she is?"

"Molly, you're crazy! Why in God's name would you want to see that woman? When you think . . ." Jenna's voice trailed off.

"When you think that if she hadn't fooled around with my husband, he might still be alive today? That's what you mean—right? I agree, but I simply must see her. Does she still live in town?"

"I haven't a clue where she is. From what I understand, she

accepted that settlement from Gary, got out of town, and hasn't been heard from since. She would have been called as a witness at the trial, but that wasn't necessary after the plea bargain."

"Jen, I want you to ask Cal to get his people onto finding her. We all know Cal can do anything, or at least get someone to do it for him."

Cal's "can do" attitude had been a kind of running joke between them for years. Jenna, however, didn't laugh.

"I'd rather not," she said, her voice suddenly strained.

Molly thought she understood the reason for Jenna's reluctance. "Jenna, you've got to understand something. I've paid the price for Gary's death, whether I was responsible for it or not. I believe that at this point I have earned the right to know what really happened that night and why. I need to try to understand my own actions and reactions. Maybe after that I'll be able to go on. I have to try to put together for myself something that will resemble a normal life."

Molly got up, went into the kitchen, and returned with the morning paper. "Maybe you've seen this. It's the kind of thing that will follow me throughout my life."

"I've seen it." Jenna pushed the paper aside and took Molly's hands. "Molly, a hospital, like a person, can lose its reputation because of a scandal. All the stories about Gary's death, including disclosure of his affair with a young nurse, followed by your trial, hurt Lasch Hospital *badly.* It's doing a good job for the community, and Remington Health Management is flourishing at a time when a lot of other HMOs are in deep trouble. Please, for your sake, for the sake of the hospital, call off Fran Simmons and forget about finding Annamarie Scalli."

Molly shook her head.

"Just *consider* it, Molly," Jenna urged. "Look, you know I'll back you up no matter what, but please at least *consider* Plan A."

"We go in to the city, and I get a makeover. Right?"

Jenna smiled. "You bet." She stood. "Okay, I'd better be on my way. Cal will be looking for me."

Arm in arm they walked to the front door. With her hand on the knob, Jenna hesitated, then said, "Sometimes I wish we could go back to Cranden and start all over, Moll. Life was a lot easier then. Cal is different from you and me. He doesn't play by the same rules.

Anything or anyone that causes him to lose money becomes the enemy."

"Including *me?*" Molly asked.

"I'm afraid so." Jenna opened the door. "Love you, Molly. Be sure to lock up and turn the security system on."

14

Tim Mason, the thirty-six-year-old sports announcer for NAF-TV, had been on vacation when Fran first started at the network. Raised in Greenwich, he had lived there briefly after college, while he worked for a year as a cub reporter for the *Greenwich Time*. It was at that point that he realized that the sports pages were where he wanted to be, and so he switched to a sports-reporter job at a newspaper in upstate New York.

Broadcasting for the local station there followed a year later, and over the next dozen years, a progression of stepping-stone jobs brought him to his big break, the sports desk at NAF. In the tristate area, its hour-long evening news program was already making impressive dents in the ratings of the three major networks, and Tim Mason soon became known as the best of the best of the new generation of sports commentators.

Rangy and with uneven features that gave him a boyish appeal, affable and easygoing by nature, Tim turned into a type-A personality when observing or discussing a sports event, which created a bond with ardent sports fans everywhere.

When he dropped into Gus Brandt's office the afternoon he came back from vacation, he met Fran Simmons for the first time. She still had her coat on and was filling Gus in on her visit that morning with Molly Lasch.

I *know* her, Tim thought, but from where?

His prodigious memory bank instantly furnished the facts he was seeking. He had started working at the *Time* in Greenwich the same summer that Fran Simmons's father, Frank Simmons, faced with the disclosure that he had embezzled library funds, shot himself. The gossip in Greenwich was that he'd been a social-climbing bootlicker who used the money trying to make a killing in the market. The scandal died down quickly, however, once Simmons's wife and daughter moved out of Greenwich almost immediately thereafter.

Looking at the attractive woman she had become, Tim was sure Fran wouldn't know him from a hole in the ground, as his grandmother used to put it, but he found himself curious as to what kind of person she'd turned out to be. Working as investigative reporter on the Molly Lasch case in Greenwich wasn't exactly a job he would have chosen if he had been in her shoes. But of course he wasn't, and he had no idea how Fran Simmons felt about her father's suicide.

That louse left his wife and teenage daughter to face the music, Tim thought. Simmons took the coward's way out. Tim was confident it was not something he would have done. If *he* had been in that situation, he'd have gotten his wife and daughter out of town, then faced the consequences of his actions himself.

He'd covered the funeral for the *Time,* and he remembered seeing Fran and her mother coming out of the church after the Mass. She'd been a kid then, with downcast eyes and long hair that fell over her face. Now Fran Simmons was extremely attractive, and he found that she had a direct handshake, a warm smile, and a way of looking straight into his eyes. He knew she couldn't read his thoughts, couldn't know that he'd been mentally rehashing the scandal surrounding her father, but for the brief moment of the handshake, Tim felt guilty and awkward.

He apologized for bursting in on them. "Usually Gus is by himself at this hour, trying to decide what will go wrong with the newscast." He turned to go, but Fran stopped him.

"Gus told me that your family lived in Greenwich and that you grew up there," she said. "Did you know the Lasches?"

In other words, Tim thought, she's saying I know you know who I am and all about my father, so let's skip that. "Dr. Lasch, I mean Gary's father, was our family doctor," he said. "A nice man and a good physician."

"How about Gary?" Fran asked swiftly.

Tim's eyes hardened. "A dedicated doctor," he said flatly. "He took wonderful care of my grandmother before she died at Lasch Hospital. That was only weeks before his own death."

Tim did not add that when his grandmother had been ill, the special-duty nurse who frequently attended her was Annamarie Scalli.

Annamarie, a pretty young woman, had been a terrific nurse and a nice, if rather unsophisticated, kid, he remembered. Gran had been crazy about her. In fact, Annamarie had been in the room with his grandmother when she died. By the time I got there, Tim thought, Gran was gone, and Annamarie was sitting by her bed, crying. How many nurses would react like that? he wondered.

"I've got to see what's going on at my desk," he announced. "Talk to you later, Gus. Nice to meet you, Fran." With a wave he left the office and headed down the corridor. He did not think it fair to tell Fran how totally his opinion of Gary Lasch had changed after he heard about his involvement with Annamarie Scalli.

She'd been only a kid, Tim thought angrily, and in a way she was not unlike Fran Simmons, the victim of someone else's selfishness. She'd been forced to give up her job and move out of town. The murder trial brought national attention, and for a time she was in every gossip column.

He wondered where Annamarie was now and worried briefly if Fran Simmons's investigation would hurt the new life she might have built for herself.

15

Annamarie Scalli walked briskly down the block to the modest home in Yonkers where she began her daily rounds of home care for the elderly. After more than five years of working for the visiting nurse service, she had made her peace with life, at least to a degree. She no longer missed the hospital nursing she once had loved. She no longer looked every day at the pictures of the child she had borne. After five years it had been agreed that the adoptive parents were no longer required to send her an annual picture. It had been months since she received the last photo of the little boy who was growing up to be the image of his father, Gary Lasch.

She used her mother's maiden name now, Sangelo. Her body had filled out and, like her mother and sister, she was now a size 14. The dark hair that used to bounce on her shoulders was a trim, curly cap around her heart-shaped face. At twenty-nine, she looked to be what she in fact was—competent, practical, kindhearted. Nothing in her appearance resembled the curvaceous "other woman" in the Dr. Gary Lasch murder case.

The night before last, Annamarie had caught on the evening news the clip of Molly Lasch making her statement to the media. The sight of Niantic Prison in the background had made her almost physically ill. Since then she had been haunted by the memory of the day three years ago when a desperate need made her drive past the prison. She'd tried to visualize herself in there as well.

It's where I *belong,* she whispered fiercely to herself as she made her way up the cracked concrete steps to Mr. Olsen's home. But driving past the prison that day, her courage had failed her, and she'd gone directly home to her little apartment in Yonkers. It was the only time she had come close to calling that fatherly lawyer who'd been her patient at Lasch Hospital to ask him to help her turn herself in to the state's attorney.

As she rang Mr. Olsen's bell, then let herself in with her key and called a cheery "Good morning," Annamarie had the ominous feeling that the renewed interest in the Lasch murder would inevitably bring renewed interest in finding her. And she didn't want that to happen.

She was *afraid* to have that happen.

16

Calvin Whitehall ignored Peter Black's secretary as he walked past her desk and opened the door to Peter's lavishly appointed corner office.

Black looked up from the reports he was reading. "You're early."

"No I'm not," Whitehall snapped. "Jenna saw Molly last night."

"Molly had the nerve to phone and warn me I'd better be available to Fran Simmons, that reporter on NAF. Did Jenna tell you about the *True Crime* show the Simmons woman is doing on Gary?"

Calvin Whitehall nodded. The two men stared across the desk at each other. "There's worse," Whitehall said flatly. "Molly seems to be determined to locate Annamarie Scalli."

Black paled. "Then I suggest you find a way to send her on a wild goose chase," he said quietly. "The ball is in your court on this one. And you'd better handle it carefully. I don't need to remind you of what this can mean to both of us."

Angrily he tossed the reports he had been studying across the desk. "All these are new potential malpractice suits."

"Squash them."

"I intend to."

Cal Whitehall studied his partner, observing the slight tremor in Peter Black's hand, the broken capillaries on his cheeks and chin. Cold distaste evident in his tone, he said, "We've got to stop that reporter and keep Molly away from Annamarie. In the meantime you'd better have a drink."

17

Fran knew the instant she met Tim Mason that he was aware of her background. I might as well get used to it, she thought. I'll see that reaction again and again from people in Greenwich. All they have to do is put two and two together. Fran Simmons? Wait a minute. *Simmons.* The speculative look. *Why does that name sound familiar? Oh, of course. Her father was the one who . . .*

She did not sleep well that night and was feeling less than chipper when she reached the office the next morning. An immediate reminder of her troubled dreams was waiting on her desk—a message from Molly Lasch, giving the name of the psychiatrist who had treated her pending the trial: "I called Dr. Daniels. He's semiretired now but would be happy to see you. His office is on Greenwich Avenue," her message said.

Dr. Daniels; Molly's lawyer, Philip Matthews; Dr. Peter Black; Calvin and Jenna Whitehall; Edna Barry, the housekeeper Molly had rehired—these were the people Molly suggested she see as a starting point in her investigation, but Fran had other people in mind too. Annamarie Scalli, for one.

She picked up Molly's message and studied it. I'll start with Dr. Daniels, she decided.

John Daniels had been contacted by Molly Lasch and was expecting Fran's call. He readily suggested that if she wanted to come up that afternoon, he would be able to see her. Although seventy-five on his last birthday, and semiretired, he had not been able to completely give up his practice, despite the coaxing of his wife. There were too many people who still depended on him and whom he could help.

One of the few he felt he had failed was Molly Carpenter Lasch. He had known her since she was a child and would sometimes come to dinner at the club with her parents. She had been a beautiful little girl, unfailingly polite, and composed beyond her years. Nothing in either her makeup or in the battery of tests he conducted after her arrest suggested she might be capable of the violent outburst that had resulted in Gary Lasch's death.

His receptionist, Ruthie Roitenberg, had been with him

twenty-five years and, with the privilege of longevity in a job, was not above stating her frank opinions and passing along gossip. It was she who, after being told Fran Simmons was expected at two o'clock, said, "Doctor, you do know whose daughter she is?"

"Am I supposed to know?" Daniels asked mildly.

"Remember that man who stole all the money from the library fund, then shot himself? Fran Simmons is his daughter. She went to Cranden Academy with Molly Carpenter."

John Daniels did not allow her to see how startled he was at her news. He remembered Frank Simmons all too well. He himself had donated ten thousand dollars to the library fund drive. Money down the drain, as it turned out, thanks to Simmons. "Molly didn't go into that. I guess she felt it wasn't important."

His mild reproof went unnoticed. "If I were in her boots I'd have changed my name," Ruthie said. "As a matter of fact, I think Molly would be smart to change *her* name, move away from here and make a fresh start. You know, Doctor, everybody thinks it would be a lot better if, instead of stirring everyone up again, she'd just come out and say how much she regrets having killed that poor man."

"Suppose there is another explanation for his death?"

"Doctor, anyone who believes that still looks under the pillow for a dime from the tooth fairy."

Fran was not scheduled to appear on the news broadcast until that evening, so she was able to spend the morning in her office, lining up interviews. Once she was done, she bought a sandwich and soda to eat in the car and set off for Greenwich at 12:15. She left early so that she would have time before her appointment with Dr. Daniels to drive around the town and reacquaint herself with the places she had known when she lived there.

In less than an hour she arrived at the outskirts of Greenwich. During the night, a light dusting of snow had fallen, and the trees and bushes and lawns were shimmering under the late winter sun.

It *is* a lovely place, Fran thought. I can't blame Dad for wanting to be part of it. Bridgeport, where her father had been raised, was only half an hour farther north, but there was a world of difference in the lifestyles of the two places.

Cranden Academy was located on Round Hill Road. She drove past the campus slowly, admiring its mellow stone buildings, remembering the years she had spent there, thinking about the girls she had known best, and those she'd known only at a distance. One was Jenna Graham, who was now Jenna Whitehall. She and Molly were always close, Fran thought, even though they were very different. Jenna was much more take-charge and affirmative, while Molly was really quite reserved.

With sudden warmth she thought of Bobbitt Williams, who had been on the basketball team with her. Is it possible that she still lives around here? Fran wondered. She was a good musician too, she recalled—she tried to make me take piano lessons with her, but I told her I was hopeless. The Lord left musical talent out of my genes.

As she turned the car toward Greenwich Avenue, Fran realized with a pang that she genuinely *wanted* to look up some of her old school friends, at least the ones she remembered fondly, like Bobbitt. Mother and I never talked about those four years we lived here, but they *did* exist, and maybe it's time I acknowledged them, she thought. There were a lot of people here I honestly cared about; maybe seeing some of them will be therapeutic for me.

Who knows? she thought as she glanced at her notebook to check Dr. Daniels's address, someday I might actually come into this town and not relive the terrible anger and embarrassment I've felt ever since I realized my father was a crook.

Dr. John Daniels escorted Fran past Ruthie's observant eyes and into his private office. He immediately liked what he saw in Fran Simmons—a poised, soft-spoken young woman, well dressed in a casual way.

Underneath her all-weather coat she was wearing a brown tweed jacket and camel slacks. Her light brown hair, with its natural wave, skimmed her jacket collar. Dr. Daniels watched her closely as she settled into the chair facing him. She really was very attractive. It was her eyes, though, that really intrigued him—they were such an unusual shade of blue gray. They get bluer when she's happy, then turn gray when she's retreating, he thought. Realizing suddenly that he was getting a little too fanciful, he shook his head. He could not help admitting to himself that he was scrutinizing Fran Simmons so thoroughly because of what Ruthie had revealed about Fran's father. He hoped she hadn't noticed.

"Doctor, you know I'm planning to do a program about Molly

Lasch and her husband's death," Fran said almost immediately, getting directly to the point. "I understand Molly has given you permission to speak openly to me."

"That's right."

"Was she your patient before her husband's death?"

"No, she was not. I knew her parents, principally through the country club. I saw Molly there from the time she was a child."

"Did you at any point observe any aggressive behavior from her?"

"Never."

"Do you believe her when she says that she is unable to remember the details of her husband's death? Let me rephrase that, please. Do you believe that she cannot remember the details of her husband's death or of finding him when he was dying or dead?"

"I believe that Molly is telling the truth as she knows it."

"Which means?"

"Which means that whatever happened that night is so painful that she has pushed it deep into her subconscious. Will she ever retrieve it? I don't know."

"If she *does* recover some memory of that night—for example, about her sensation that there may have been someone else in the house when she returned home—will that be an accurate memory?"

John Daniels took off his glasses and wiped them. He put them back on, realizing as he did so that, ludicrous as it was, he had become so dependent on them that to speak without them made him feel vulnerable.

"Molly Lasch is suffering from dissociative amnesia. This involves gaps in memory that are related to extremely stressful and traumatic events. Obviously, the death of her husband, however that may have occurred, fits into that category.

"Some people who suffer from this condition respond well to hypnosis and are able to regain significant and often trustworthy memory of the event. Molly agreed willingly to submit to hypnosis before the trial, but it just didn't work. Think about it. She was emotionally devastated by her husband's death and terrified of her upcoming trial, much too distraught and fragile to be successfully hypnotized."

"Does she have a chance of gradually recovering accurate memory, Doctor?"

"I wish I could say that Molly has a good chance of recovering her memory and of clearing her name. To be honest, I feel that whatever she may eventually believe she remembers will not necessarily be trustworthy. If Molly seems to regain some sense of what happened that night, it's very possible she will be filling in with what she wishes had happened. She may honestly believe that she is really remembering what happened, but that won't necessarily mean that it actually *did* happen that way. It's called 'retrospective memory falsification.' "

Back in her car outside Dr. Daniels's office, Fran sat for several minutes, trying to decide her next move. It was quarter of three. The offices of the *Greenwich Time* were only a few blocks away. She thought suddenly of Joe Hutnik. He worked there; he had covered Molly's release from prison. He'd been adamant in stating he believed her guilty. Had he covered her trial too? she wondered.

He seemed like a stand-up guy, Fran thought, and clearly he's been around for a while.

Maybe too long? a voice whispered. Maybe he covered your father's story as well. Do you really want to deal with that?

Outside, the late winter sun was fading as thick, gray clouds moved in. March, the unpredictable month, Fran thought as she continued to debate what to do next. Why not take a chance, she decided finally, reaching for her cell phone.

Fifteen minutes later she was shaking Joe Hutnik's hand. He was in his cubbyhole off the computer-filled *Greenwich Time*'s newsroom. About fifty years old, with broad, dark eyebrows and alert, intelligent eyes, he waved her to the mini-sized love seat, half of which was piled with books.

"What brings you to 'The Gateway to New England,' as our fair town is known, Fran?" He did not wait for an answer. "No, let me guess. Molly Lasch. The word is that you're doing a program on her for *True Crime.*"

"The word moves too fast for my taste," Fran told him. "Joe, can we level with each other?"

"Of course. Provided it doesn't cost me a headline." Fran raised her eyebrows. "You're my kind of guy. Question: Did you cover Molly's trial?"

"Who didn't? It was a slow news time, and she filled it for us."

"Joe, I can pull all the information I need from the Internet, but no matter how much testimony you read, it's a lot easier to judge truth when you get to see the demeanor of the witnesses, especially under cross-examination. You obviously think Molly Lasch killed her husband."

"Absolutely."

"Next question. What did you think of Dr. Gary Lasch?"

Joe Hutnik leaned back in his desk chair, swiveling from side to side as he considered his answer. Then he said slowly, "Fran, I've lived around Greenwich all my life. My mother is seventy-six years old. She tells the story of when my sister had pneumonia forty years ago. She was three months old. In those days doctors came to the house. It was known as a house call. You weren't told to bundle up sick kids and take them to an emergency room, right?"

Hutnik stopped swiveling the chair and folded his hands on the desk. "We lived at the top of a pretty steep hill. Dr. Lasch, Jonathan Lasch, I mean, Gary's father, couldn't get his car up the hill. The wheels kept spinning. He left it and climbed through snow up to his knees to our house. That was at eleven o'clock at night. I can remember seeing him standing over my sister. He had her under a strong light, lying on blankets on the kitchen table. He stayed with her for three hours. He gave her a double penicillin shot and made sure she was breathing comfortably and her temperature was down before he'd go home. In the morning he was back again to check on her."

"Was Gary Lasch that kind of doctor?" Fran asked.

Hutnik thought for a moment before responding. "There are still plenty of dedicated physicians in Greenwich, and everywhere else, I assume. Was Gary Lasch one of them? I honestly don't know the answer to that, Fran, but from what I hear, he and his partner, Dr. Peter Black, were more into the business end of medicine and perhaps a little less into the actual care giving."

"It looks like they've been successful. Lasch Hospital has doubled in size since I saw it last," Fran commented. She hoped her voice sounded steady.

"Since your father died there," Hutnik said quickly. "Look, Fran, I've been around a long time. I knew your father. He was a nice man. Needless to say, like a lot of other residents, I wasn't thrilled to see all the donations disappear the way they did. That money was going to build a library in one of our less classy sections of town, so that kids could walk to it easily."

Fran winced and looked away.

"Sorry," Hutnik said. "I shouldn't bring that up. Let's stick to Gary Lasch. After his father died, he brought in his medical school buddy, Dr. Peter Black, from Chicago. They turned the Jonathan Lasch Clinic into Lasch Hospital. They began the Remington Health Management Organization, which has been one of the really successful HMOs."

"What do you think of health maintenance organizations in general?" Fran asked.

"What most people do. They stink. Even the best of them—and I think Remington may be in that category—are putting doctors between a rock and a hard place. Most doctors have to belong to one or maybe even a number of health maintenance plans, which means, of course, that their diagnoses are subject to review, and that if they feel a patient needs to see a specialist, their judgment may be overridden. In addition, doctors are forced to wait for their money—I mean to a point where many of them are placed in a tight financial position. Patients are being sent to out-of-the-way facilities just to discourage them from having too many visits. And at the very time when drugs and treatments are available to make people's lives easier, the guys who decide whether you get a treatment are the ones who make the money if you don't. Great progress, wouldn't you say?"

Joe shook his head indignantly. "Right now Remington Health Management, meaning CEO Dr. Peter Black and Chairman Cal Whitehall, our resident tycoon, are negotiating with the state for permission to take over four smaller HMOs. If that happens, the company stock will fly like a birdie. Is there a problem with that? Not really. Except that American National Insurance would also like to take over the smaller HMOs, and there's talk they may attempt a hostile takeover of Remington as well."

"Is that likely to happen?"

"Who knows? Probably not. Remington Health Management and Lasch Hospital have a good reputation. They've rebounded from the scandal revolving around the murder of Dr. Gary Lasch and the revelation that he was fooling around with a young nurse, but I'm sure Peter Black and Cal Whitehall would have liked to have had the new deal completed before Molly Lasch arrived back in town with her suggestion there was more to the story of the doctor's murder than came out initially."

"What kind of 'more to the story' could possibly affect a merger?" Fran asked.

Joe shrugged. "Honey, quaint as it may seem, sleaze is on the way out, at least temporarily. American National is headed by a former surgeon general who vows he's going to reform health maintenance organizations. Remington still has the inside track on the acquisition, but in this crazy world, any cold wind can freeze the harvest. And any hint of scandal could squelch the deal."

18

There is no one I can count on, was Molly's first waking thought. She glanced at the clock. Ten past six. Not bad, she decided. She had gone to bed shortly after Jenna left, so that meant she'd slept seven hours.

In prison there were many nights when she didn't sleep at all, when sleep was like a chunk of ice pressing between her eyes as she willed it to melt and flow through her.

She stretched, and her left arm touched the empty pillow beside her. She had never visualized Gary next to her on the narrow prison bed, but now she was constantly aware of his absence, even after all these years. It was as though the entire time had been simply a dream sequence. Dream? No—*nightmare!*

She had felt so totally one with him; "We're joined at the hip" had been her favorite expression in those days. Had she been deluding herself?

I sounded smug and self-satisfied back then, Molly thought, *and perhaps I was. Obviously I was stupid as well.* She sat up, fully awake now. *I've got to know,* she thought. *How long did that affair with the nurse go on? How long was my life with Gary a lie?*

Annamarie Scalli was the only person who could give her the answers she needed.

At nine she phoned Fran Simmons's office and left Dr.

Daniels's name. At ten she phoned Philip Matthews. She had only been in his office a few times, but she could visualize it clearly. He had a view of the Statue of Liberty from his World Trade Center office. When she had been there, listening to him plan her defense, it had seemed incongruous to her—clients in danger of going to prison, observing the symbol of liberty.

Molly remembered telling Philip that, and he'd said that he considered the view of the statue to be a harbinger: when he took on a client, his goal was liberty for them.

Philip might very well have Annamarie Scalli's last address because she'd been scheduled to testify at the trial, Molly reasoned. At least it would be a place for her to start.

Philip Matthews had been debating whether or not to phone Molly, so when his secretary announced her call, he quickly reached for the receiver. From the moment she walked out of prison she had consumed his thoughts. It had not helped that two nights ago he'd been at a dinner party where the entertainment was to have your fortune told. As a guest there was no way he could avoid going along with the games, even though he lumped all fortune-telling—palmistry, astrology, tarot cards, Ouija boards—in the same category: hocus-pocus.

But the fortune-teller actually had made him uneasy. She had studied the cards he selected, frowned, reshuffled, and had him pick others, then flatly said, "Someone close to you, a woman I think, is in grave danger. Do you know who that could be?"

Philip tried to tell himself the woman was referring to a client who was charged with vehicular homicide and would undoubtedly serve some time, but every instinct in his bones told him that the fortune-teller was talking about Molly.

Now, Molly confirmed his fears that she had no intention of letting her parents come back to Greenwich to stay with her.

"Not yet, anyway," she said firmly. "Philip, I want to find Annamarie Scalli. Do you have her last address?"

"Molly, let all this go. Please. It's over. You need to get on with your life."

"That's what I'm trying to do. And that's why I've got to talk to her."

Philip sighed. "Her last known address was the apartment she lived in at the time of Gary's death. I have no idea where she is now."

He could tell that she was about to hang up, and he was anxious to keep her on the phone. "Molly, I'm coming up. If you don't agree to go out to dinner with me, I'll just stand there and knock on your door until the neighbors get annoyed."

Somehow Molly could visualize him doing just that. The same intensity that she had seen at her trial when he was cross-examining witnesses was in his voice now. He was obviously a determined man, used to getting his way. Still, she did not want to see him yet. "Philip, I need a little more time to myself. Look, it's Thursday. Why don't you come to dinner on Saturday? I don't want to go out. I'll cook something."

After a moment he accepted her invitation, deciding to be satisfied with that for now.

19

Edna Barry was in the process of basting a chicken. It was one of Wally's favorite dinners, especially when she made her own stuffing. The truth was she used prepared stuffing mix, but the secret was to add sautéed onions and celery and extra poultry seasoning.

The inviting fragrance filled the house, and the act of cooking calmed Edna. It reminded her of the years when her husband, Martin, was alive and Wally was a bright, normal little boy. The doctors said that Martin's death was not what triggered the change in her son. They said that schizophrenia was a mental illness that frequently surfaced in teenage years or early adulthood.

Edna didn't believe that was the answer. "Wally has always been lonely for his dad," she would tell people.

Sometimes Wally talked about getting married and having a family, but she knew now that probably wasn't going to happen. People didn't want to be around him. He was too touchy, lost his temper too easily.

What would happen to Wally after she died was a ceaseless worry for Edna. But at least while she was around she could take care of him, this son of hers who had been so badly treated by life. She could make him take his medicine, although she knew he sometimes would spit it out.

Wally had been so responsive to Dr. Morrow—if only he were still alive.

As Edna closed the oven door, she thought of Jack Morrow, the dynamo young doctor who had been so good with people like Wally. He'd been a GP and had his office on the ground floor of his modest home only three blocks from here. He had been found shot to death just two weeks before Dr. Lasch died.

Of course the circumstances were totally different. Dr. Morrow's medicine cabinet had been broken into and emptied. The police were sure it was a drug-related crime. They had questioned all his patients. Edna always told herself that it was a funny thing to be grateful that your son had broken his ankle shortly before that. She had made him put his walking cast back on before the police came to talk to him.

She knew after only one day that she should never have gone back to work for Molly Lasch. It was too dangerous. There was always the chance that Wally would find his way over to Molly's house, as he had a few days before Dr. Lasch died. She'd told him to wait in the kitchen, but then he'd gone into Dr. Lasch's study and picked up the Remington sculpture.

Was there any end to worrying? Edna wondered. Never, she told herself as she sighed and began to set the table.

"Mama, Molly's home, isn't she?"

Edna looked up. Wally stood in the doorway, his hands in his pockets, his dark hair falling forward over his forehead. "Why do you want to know, Wally?" she asked sharply.

"Because I want to see her."

"You must not go over to her house, ever."

"I like her, Mama." Wally's eyes narrowed as though trying to remember something. As he gazed over Edna's shoulder, he said, "She wouldn't yell at me like Dr. Lasch did, would she?"

Edna felt a chill go through her. Wally hadn't brought up that incident in years, not since she forbade him to talk about Dr. Lasch or the house key she'd found in Wally's pocket the day after the murder.

"Molly is very kind to *everyone,*" she said firmly. "Now, we're not going to talk about Dr. Lasch ever again, are we?"

"All right, Mama. I'm glad Dr. Lasch is dead, though. He won't yell at me anymore." His voice was without emotion.

The phone rang. Nervously, Edna picked it up. Her hello was delivered in a voice that quivered with anxiety.

"Mrs. Barry, I hope I'm not disturbing you. This is Fran Simmons. We met yesterday at Molly Lasch's home."

"Yes. I remember." Edna Barry realized suddenly how abrupt she sounded. "Of course, I remember," she said, her voice warmer.

"I'm wondering if I could come by and spend a little time with you on Saturday."

"Saturday?" Edna Barry frantically searched for a reason to refuse to see Fran.

"Yes. Unless Sunday or Monday would be better."

Why bother to postpone it? she decided. Clearly there would be no putting the woman off. "Saturday will be all right," Edna said stiffly.

"Is eleven too early?"

"No."

"Fine, let me just be sure I have the right address."

When Fran hung up the phone, she thought, That woman is a nervous wreck. I could hear the tension in her voice. She was on edge yesterday too, when I was at Molly's house. What has she got to be so nervous about? she wondered.

Edna Barry was the person who had found Gary Lasch's body. Was it possible that Molly's decision to rehire her was tied into some vague intuition Molly had about the housekeeper's version of events?

Interesting prospect, Fran thought as, after checking the refrigerator, she put on her coat again with the idea of walking down the block to P. J. Clarke's to get a hamburger.

As she moved briskly along Fifty-sixth Street, she thought of the interesting possibility that perhaps Molly might not be the *only* one suffering from retrospective memory falsification.

20

"Jenna, I know you're an intelligent woman. So I should think therefore that you could understand that I mean what I say when I tell you that Annamarie Scalli has for all intents and purposes dropped off the face of the earth. And even if I *could* locate her, which I cannot, I assure you I would not furnish information on her whereabouts to Molly Lasch, of all people!"

The spots of red on Calvin Whitehall's cheekbones were a warning to his wife of his growing impatience, but Jenna chose to ignore them. "Cal, what possible objection could you have to Molly trying to get in touch with that woman? It might help her, might give her some sort of closure."

They were having coffee and juice in the sitting room off their bedroom. Jenna was ready to leave for work, her coat and bag on a nearby chair. Calvin slammed down his coffee cup. "I don't care about Molly. What needs closure is the negotiations I have been working on for three years for the benefit of *both* of us." He took a deep breath. "Now you'd better catch your train. Even Lou won't be able to get you to the station in time if you wait much longer."

Jenna got up. "I think I'll stay over in the apartment tonight."

"As you wish."

They stared at each other for a moment, then Calvin Whitehall's expression changed, and he smiled. "Darling girl, I wish you could see your expression. I'll bet if you had that horse-and-cowboy sculpture at hand you'd do the same thing to me that Molly did to Gary. You girls from Cranden Academy certainly have strong feelings."

Jenna paled. "You really *are* worried about your negotiations, aren't you, Cal? You're not usually that cruel."

"I'm not usually in danger of having a multibillion-dollar deal slip through my fingers either. Jen, you're the *one* person who seems to have Molly's ear. As soon as possible, persuade her to go in to New York with you. Talk *sense* to her. Remind her that in trying to convince herself and the world that she didn't kill Gary, she's only besmirching his memory further and probably further harming herself in the process."

Without responding, Jenna put on her coat and picked up her

purse. As she walked toward the staircase, her husband called, "Multibillion-dollar deal, Jen. Admit it. You don't want it messed up either."

Lou Knox, Cal's longtime chauffeur and aide-de-camp, jumped out of the car when he saw Jenna emerge from the house. He held the car door open, closed it behind her, and was back behind the wheel in seconds.

"Good morning, Ms. Whitehall. Looks as if we're cutting it close today. Well, I can always drive you in if we miss the train."

"No, Cal wants the car, and I don't want the traffic," Jenna said sharply. Sometimes Lou's cheery observations grated on her, but he had come with the territory. He had been a classmate of Cal's at the godforsaken high school they'd attended, and Cal had brought him with him when he arrived in Greenwich fifteen years ago.

Jenna was the only one who knew about the beginning of their relationship. "Needless to say, Lou understands that it need not be general knowledge that we sang school songs together," was the way Cal put it.

She had to give Lou credit. He responded to her moods. He immediately sensed that she did not want to talk and quickly tuned the radio to her favorite classical music station, keeping the volume low. That was her standard request, unless for some reason she wanted to listen to the all-news station.

Lou was Cal's age, forty-six, and even though he was in good physical shape, Jenna had always felt there was something unhealthy about him. He was a little too subservient for her taste, a little too anxious to please. She didn't trust him. Even now, during the short ride to the station, she had the feeling that his eyes were studying her in the rearview mirror, gauging her mood.

I did my best, she told herself, thinking about her discussion with her husband. There's no way Cal will help Molly locate Annamarie Scalli. Instead of feeling anger, however, she realized that underneath her resentment at his tone, her usual grudging admiration for him was setting in.

Cal was a powerful man, and he had the charisma that went with it. He had built himself up from that first computer company, which he referred to as a mom-and-pop-candy-store operation, to a man whose name commanded respect. Unlike the showy entrepreneurs who grabbed headlines as they made and lost fortunes, Cal preferred to remain essentially in the background, though known and respected as a major figure of the financial world, and feared by anyone who got in his way.

Power—it was what had attracted Jenna to him in the first place. It also was what continued to enthrall her. She enjoyed her job as a partner in a prestigious law firm. It was something she had achieved on her own. If Cal had never come along, she still would have had a successful career, and that knowledge gave her a feeling of having her private territory. "Jenna's little acre," Cal called it, but she knew he respected her for it.

At the same time, however, she loved being Mrs. Calvin Whitehall, with all the prestige that continued to accumulate around that name. Unlike Molly, she had never yearned for children or the elitist suburban life her mother and Molly's mother had always enjoyed.

They were approaching the station. The train was sounding its horn. "Just in time," Lou said pleasantly as he stopped, jumped out, and opened her door. "Shall I pick you up this evening, Ms. Whitehall?"

Jenna hesitated, then said, "Yes, I'll be in at the regular time. You can tell my husband to expect me."

21

"Good morning, Doctor."

Peter Black looked up from his desk. The uncertainty on his secretary's face warned him that whatever she was about to say would not be welcome. As a person, Louise Unger was timid, but as a secretary she was extremely efficient. Her timidity annoyed him; her efficiency, he valued. His eyes flickered to the clock on the wall. It was only 8:30. She had arrived at work early, as she often did.

He murmured a greeting and waited.

"Mr. Whitehall was on the phone, Doctor. He had to take another call but asks you to be available." Louise Unger hesitated. "I think he's very upset."

Peter Black had long ago learned to control his facial muscles so that his emotions were not reflected in his expression. With a faint smile, he said, "Thanks for the warning, Louise. Mr. Whitehall is often upset. We know that, don't we?"

The woman nodded eagerly, her birdlike eyes shining as she bobbed her head. "Just wanted to give you advance warning, Doctor."

For her, this was a bold statement. Peter Black chose to ignore it. "Thank you, Louise," he said smoothly.

The phone on his desk rang. He nodded, indicating that she should pick up the receiver.

She began to say, "Dr. Black's office," but got no further than "Doctor—" "It's Mr. Whitehall, Doctor," she said, putting the phone on hold. She knew enough to scurry out and close the door.

Peter Black knew that to show weakness to Calvin Whitehall was to be doomed. He had taught himself to ignore Cal's references to his drinking and was convinced that the only reason Whitehall restricted himself to one glass of wine was to prove his superiority of will.

He picked up the phone and spoke immediately.

"Cal, how goes the empire?" Peter Black enjoyed asking that question. He knew it irritated Whitehall.

"It would go a lot better if Molly Lasch weren't out there making waves."

Peter Black felt as though the resonant tone of Calvin Whitehall's voice was making the receiver tingle. Holding the phone with his left hand, Black deliberately stretched the fingers of his right hand, a trick he had picked up to relieve tension. "I thought we'd already established that she was making waves," he responded.

"Yes, after Jenna saw her night before last. Molly wants me to locate Annamarie Scalli. She insists she has to see her, and obviously she doesn't intend to be put off. Jenna was hammering at me about it again this morning. I told her I had no idea where Scalli is."

"Nor do I." Black knew his tone was even, his words precise. He remembered the panic in Gary Lasch's voice: *"Annamarie, for the sake of the hospital. You've got to help."*

I didn't know at the time she was involved with Gary, Peter Black thought. What if Molly *did* get to her now? he wondered. Suppose Annamarie decided to tell what she knew. What then?

He became aware that Cal was still talking. What was he asking?

". . . is there anyone at the hospital who might have stayed in touch with her?"

"I have no idea."

After he put the receiver down a minute later, Dr. Peter Black spoke into the intercom. "Hold my calls, Louise." He put his elbows on the desk and pressed his forehead with his palms.

The tightrope was fraying. How could he stop it from breaking and sending him hurtling to the ground?

22

"She didn't want to worry you, Billy."

Billy Gallo stared across his mother's bed at his father as they stood in the intensive care unit at Lasch Hospital. Tony Gallo's eyes were welling with tears. His sparse gray hair was disheveled, and the hand that patted his wife's arm was trembling.

There was no mistaking the kinship of the two men. They had strikingly similar features—dark brown eyes, full lips, square jaw lines.

Sixty-six-year-old semiretired Tony Gallo, a former corporate security officer, was a school crossing guard in the town of Cos Cob, a stern and trusted fixture at the intersection of Willow and Pine. His son, Billy, thirty-five, a trombonist in the orchestra of the road company of a Broadway musical, had flown in from Detroit.

"It wasn't Mom who didn't want to worry me," Billy said, his tone angry. "You wouldn't *let* her call me, would you?"

"Billy, you were out of work for six months. We didn't want you to lose this job."

"To hell with the job. You should have called me—I would have stood up to them. When they refused her permission to go to a specialist, I wouldn't have let them get away with it."

"Billy, you don't understand; Dr. Kirkwood fought to get her to a specialist. Now they've okayed surgery. She'll be fine."

"He *still* didn't send her to a specialist soon enough."

Josephine Gallo stirred. She could hear her husband and son arguing, and she had a vague awareness that it was over her. She felt sleepy and weightless. In some ways it was a nice sensation, to lie there and almost float, to not have to be a part of their argument. She was tired of begging Tony to help Billy when he was between jobs. Billy was a fine musician, and he wasn't cut out for a nine-to-five job. Tony just didn't understand that.

She kept hearing their angry voices. She didn't want them to argue anymore. Josephine remembered the pain that had yanked her from her sleep this morning; it was the same pain that she'd been telling Dr. Kirkwood, her primary care physician, about.

They were still arguing; their voices seemed to be getting louder, and she wanted to tell them to please, please stop. Then somewhere off in the distance she heard bells clanging. She heard running feet. And a pain like the one that had awakened her that morning came rushing back. A tidal wave of pain. She tried to reach out to them: "Tony . . . Billy . . ."

As she drew in her last breath, she heard their voices, in unison, urgent, filled with fear, edged with grief: "Mommmmmmmmm," "Josieeeeeeeee." Then she heard nothing.

23

At quarter of twelve, Fran walked into the lobby of Lasch Hospital. Pushing back the memories of that same place years earlier, memories of stumbling, and of her mother's arms around her, she forced herself to stop and to look about the space.

The reception/information desk was on the far wall, opposite the entrance. That's good, she thought. She didn't want a solicitous volunteer or guard offering to help direct her to a patient. If that were to happen, she had a story ready: she was picking up a friend who was visiting a patient.

Any patient, she thought.

She studied the area. The furniture—couches and individual chairs—was upholstered in green imitation leather and had plastic arms and legs in a faux maple finish. Less than half the seats were occupied. A corridor to the left of the reception desk had an arrow and a sign that read ELEVATORS. Then Fran found what she was looking for—the sign on the other side of the lobby that read COFFEE SHOP. As she headed for it, she passed the newspaper rack. The weekly community paper was displayed in it, and a picture showing Molly at the prison gate was on page one. Fran fished in her pocket for two quarters.

She deliberately had arrived before the lunch-hour rush began, and she stood at the entrance to the coffee shop for a moment as she looked around, trying to choose the most advantageous seat. There were about twenty tables in the restaurant, as well as a counter with a dozen stools. The two women behind the counter, wearing candy-striped aprons, were hospital volunteers.

There were four people sitting at the counter; about ten others were scattered at tables. Three men in standard white jackets, obviously doctors, were deep in conversation by the window. There was a small empty table next to them. For a moment Fran debated whether or not to ask for that table, as the hostess, also wearing a candy-striped apron, bore down on her.

"I'll go to the counter," Fran said quickly. Over coffee she might be able to strike up a conversation with one of the volunteers working there. Both women looked to be in their mid-sixties. Perhaps one or both of them had been volunteers there six years ago, when Gary Lasch was running the hospital.

The woman who served her coffee and a bagel was wearing a smiley-face name tag that read, "Hello, I'm Susan Branagan." A pleasant-faced woman, with white hair and a bustling manner, she clearly felt that part of her job was to draw people out. "Can you believe that spring is less than two weeks away?" she asked.

It gave Fran the opening she wanted. "I've been living in California, so it's hard to get used to the East Coast weather again."

"Visiting someone in the hospital?"

"Just waiting for a friend who's visiting. Have you been a volunteer long?"

Susan Branagan beamed. "Just got my ten-year pin."

"I think it's wonderful that you volunteer to help out here," Fran said sincerely.

"I'd be lost if I didn't come to the hospital three times a week. I'm a widow, and my kids are married and busy with their own lives. What would I do with myself, I ask you?"

Clearly it was a rhetorical question.

"I guess it must be pretty fulfilling," Fran said. Trying to appear casual as she did it, she laid the community paper on the counter, placing it so that Susan Branagan could not miss seeing Molly's picture and the headline above it: WIDOW OF DR. LASCH PROTESTS HER INNOCENCE.

Mrs. Branagan shook her head. "You may not realize, being that you're from California, but Dr. Lasch used to be the head of this hospital. It was a terrible scandal when he died. Only thirty-six, and such a handsome man."

"What happened?" Fran asked.

"Oh, he got involved with a young nurse here, and his wife—well, I guess the poor woman went into temporary insanity, or something. Claimed she didn't remember killing him, although nobody really believes that, of course. What a tragedy and loss it was. And the sad thing is that the nurse, Annamarie, was the sweetest girl. Why, she was just about the last person in the world you'd think would carry on with a married man."

"It happens all the time," Fran commented.

"Isn't that the truth? But still, it was something of a surprise, since there was this other young doctor—just the nicest man—who really *liked* her. We all thought that romance would blossom, but I guess she just got her head turned by Dr. Lasch. Anyway, poor Dr. Morrow was left out in the cold, may he rest in peace."

Dr. Morrow. Rest in peace.

"You don't mean Dr. Jack Morrow, do you?"

"Oh, did you know him?"

"I met him once, years ago, when I was here for a while." Fran thought of the kind face of the young doctor who had tried to comfort her that terrible evening fourteen years ago, when she and her mother had followed her dying father to this hospital.

"He was shot in his office, only two weeks before Dr. Lasch was murdered. His medicine cabinet had been broken into." Susan Branagan sighed, remembering that time. "Two young doctors, both dying so violently. I know the deaths were unrelated, but it seemed like such a terrible coincidence."

Coincidence? Fran thought, and both of them involved with Annamarie Scalli. Was there any such thing as coincidence when it came to murder?

24

Three nights at home, Molly thought. Three mornings of waking up in my own bed, in my own room.

Today she'd awakened a few minutes before seven, gone down to the kitchen, made coffee, poured it into her favorite mug, and returned upstairs, the coffee fragrant and steaming. She'd propped up the pillows, gotten back into bed, and slowly sipped the coffee. She looked about the room, freshly aware of a space that for the five years of her marriage she had taken for granted.

During sleepless nights in prison she had thought about her bedroom, thought about her feet touching the plush ivory carpeting, thought about the feel of the satin quilt against her skin, thought about her head sinking into the deep, soft pillows, thought of leaving the shades up so that she could look out into the night sky, something she often had done with her husband sleeping quietly beside her.

As she sipped the coffee, Molly reflected on the months and then years of those long prison nights. As her mind had slowly started to clear, she'd begun to formulate the questions that now almost obsessed her. Questions such as, if Gary had been able to dupe her so completely about their intimate relationship, was it possible that he was dishonest as well in other areas of his life?

She was on her way to take a shower when she stopped to look out the window. It was so simple a thing to do, yet it was something that had been denied her for five and a half years, and the freedom of it still amazed her. It was another cloudy day, and she could see patches of ice in the driveway; even so, she impulsively decided to put on her sweats and go for a run.

Run free, she thought as she began to quickly don her jogging clothes. And I am free—to go out without asking permission and without waiting for doors to be unlocked. She felt a sudden exhilaration. Ten minutes later she was jogging along the old, familiar streets that suddenly seemed unfamiliar.

Please don't let me meet anyone I know, she prayed. Don't let me be recognized by someone driving by. She passed Kathryn Busch's house, a lovely old colonial that sat at the corner of Lake Avenue. She remembered that Kathryn had been on the board of the Philharmonic Society and had been very much involved in trying to develop a local chamber group.

As had Bobbitt Williams, Molly thought, picturing the face of an old schoolmate who almost had faded from memory. Bobbitt was in class at Cranden with Jenna and Fran and me, but she and I never socialized that much, and then she moved to Darien.

As Molly ran, her head seemed to clear, and people and houses and streets were coming into focus. The Browns had added a wing. The Cateses had repainted. Suddenly she realized that this was the first time she had been outside, on her own like this, since the day just over five and a half years ago when she had been handcuffed and chained and locked in the van for the drive to Niantic Prison.

The wind this morning was chilling, but invigorating—fresh, clean air that swept through her hair and filled her lungs and body, making Molly feel as though, inch by inch, her senses were coming alive.

She was breathing heavily and already beginning to ache when, after a two-mile round-trip, she ran back up her driveway. She was headed toward the kitchen door when a sudden impulse caused her to cut across the frozen lawn and walk almost the length of the house until she was facing the window of the room that had been Gary's study. She stopped, went up to the window, pushed aside the shrubbery, and looked in.

For a brief instant she expected to see Gary's handsome Wells Fargo desk still there, walls covered with mahogany paneling, bookcases filled with medical texts, the sculptures and paintings that Gary had collected with so much enthusiasm. Instead, she saw a room that was just another room in a house far too big for one person. The impersonal chintz-covered furniture and bleached oak tables looked suddenly very unattractive.

I was standing in the doorway, looking out.

It was a random thought that suddenly entered her mind and just as quickly disappeared.

Suddenly self-conscious at the possibility of being observed peering into the window of her own home, Molly retraced her steps and let herself in through the kitchen door. As she pulled off her sneakers, she realized that she had time for another cup of coffee and an English muffin before Mrs. Barry arrived.

Mrs. Barry.

Wally.

Now why would I suddenly think about *him?* Molly wondered, as she headed back upstairs, this time finally to take her shower.

Fran called her in the late afternoon, from her office where she was getting ready for the evening news broadcast. "Molly, a quick question," she said. "Did you know Dr. Jack Morrow?"

Molly's mind was wrenched back over a span of forgotten years to that morning when a phone call interrupted their breakfast. She had known immediately that it was bad news. Gary's face had turned a sickly gray color as he listened silently. Then, after he hung up, he spoke, almost in a whisper: "Jack Morrow was found shot to death in his office. It happened sometime last evening."

"I hardly knew him," Molly told Fran. "He was on staff at the hospital, and I'd met him at a few Christmas parties, that kind of thing. He and Gary were killed within two weeks of each other."

Suddenly aware of her own words, she could imagine how that statement must sound to Fran. "Were killed." Something that had happened to two men, but had nothing to do with any act she committed. At least no one can say that I was involved with Jack Morrow's death, she thought. Gary and I were at a dinner party that night. She told that to Fran.

"Molly, you must know I wasn't suggesting that you had anything to do with Dr. Morrow's death," Fran said. "I mention him only because I've uncovered an interesting bit of information. Did you know that he was in love with Annamarie Scalli?"

"No, I did not."

"It's becoming obvious that I have to talk to Annamarie. Do you know anyone who might know where to find her?"

"I've already asked Jenna to have Cal's people try to find her, but Jen says that Cal doesn't want to get involved."

There was a moment of silence before Fran responded. "You didn't tell me *you* were trying to locate Annamarie, Molly."

Molly could hear the startled tone in Fran's voice. "Fran," she said, "my desire to talk personally to Annamarie has nothing to do with your investigation. The five and a half years I spent in prison were directly connected to the fact that my husband was having an affair with her. It seems so odd that someone I don't know at all could have had such a powerful impact in my life. Let's make a deal—if I locate her, or even get a lead, I'll tell you. Likewise, if *you* find her, you let me know, okay?"

"I'll have to think about that," Fran said. "I will tell you that I'm going to call your lawyer and ask him about her. Annamarie was on the list of scheduled witnesses at your trial, and because of that, he should have had her last address in the file."

"I spoke to Philip about that already, and he swears he doesn't have it."

"I'll try him anyway, just in case. I've got to run." Fran paused. "Molly, be careful."

"Funny. Jenna said the same thing to me just the other night."

Molly replaced the receiver and thought of what she had told Philip Matthews—that if anything happened to her, at least it would prove that someone out there had reason to be afraid of Fran's investigation into Gary's death.

The phone rang again. Instinctively she knew that it was her mother and father calling from Florida. They talked of the usual inconsequential things before the subject of how she was faring "alone in that house" was broached. After reassuring them that she was doing well, she asked, "What happened to everything that was in Gary's desk after he died?"

"The prosecutor's office took just about everything except the furniture from Gary's study," her mother said. "After the trial, whatever they returned, I put in boxes in the attic."

The answer made Molly anxious to end the conversation and sent her up to the attic as soon as she was off the phone. There she found the neatly packed boxes her mother had told her would be on the storage shelves. She pushed aside the ones containing books and sculptures, pictures and magazines, and reached for the two labeled DESK. She knew what she was looking for: the daily reminder diary

Gary always carried and the appointment book he kept in the top desk drawer.

Maybe there are some kind of notations that will give me at least some idea of what else was going on in Gary's life, Molly thought.

She opened the first box with a sense of dread, afraid of what she might find, yet determined to learn whatever she could.

25

Seven years ago our lives were so different, Barbara Colbert thought as she watched the familiar landscape roll by. As he did each week, her chauffeur, Dan, was driving her from the apartment on Fifth Avenue to the Natasha Colbert Long-Term Care Residence on the grounds of Lasch Hospital in Greenwich. When they arrived in front of the residence, she sat for several minutes, bracing herself, knowing that for the next hour her heart would twist and break as she held Tasha's hand and said words that Tasha probably didn't hear and was no doubt beyond understanding.

A straight-backed, white-haired woman in her mid-seventies, Barbara Colbert knew that in the years since the accident, she seemed to have aged twenty. The Bible refers to cyclical events in terms of seven years of plenty, seven years of famine, she thought as she fastened the top button of her mink jacket. Cyclical events implied that something might change, but she knew that there was no change possible for Tasha, who was in the seventh year of unconscious life.

Tasha, who gave us so much joy, Barbara Colbert agonized— our beautiful, unexpected gift. Barbara had been forty-five, her husband, Charles, fifty, when she realized she was pregnant. With their sons in college, they had assumed they were done with raising a family.

Each time she reached this point, as she braced herself to get out of the car, the same memory always came to her. They were living in Greenwich then. Tasha, home from law school, had popped into the dining room. She was dressed in her running togs, her red hair twisted in a ponytail, her dark blue eyes warm and alive and intelligent. Her twenty-fourth birthday was only a week away. "See you guys," she had said, and then she was gone.

Those were the last words they ever heard her utter.

An hour later they had gotten the call that sent them rushing to Lasch Hospital. There had been an accident, they were told, and that was where Tasha had been taken. Barbara remembered the short ride to the hospital and the terror she felt. She remembered the incoherent prayer she uttered over and over: "Please, dear God, please."

Jonathan Lasch had been Barbara's family doctor when the children were little, so she took some comfort in the thought that Gary Lasch, Jonathan's son, would be taking care of Tasha. As soon as she saw him in the emergency room, however, she knew from the expression on Gary's face that something was terribly wrong.

He told them that, while she was running, Tasha had fallen and hit her head on the curb. The injury itself hadn't been serious, but before reaching the hospital she'd developed a cardiac arrhythmia. "We're doing everything we can," he promised, but it soon became evident that there really was nothing they could do. A seizure had cut off the supply of oxygen to Tasha's brain, destroying it. Except for the ability to breathe on her own, Tasha was, for all intents and purposes, gone.

All the money in the world, the most powerful newspaper family in the country, and still we couldn't help our only daughter, Barbara thought as she nodded to Dan that she was ready to get out of the car.

Noticing how stiffly she moved today, he put his hand under her arm. "There may be a bit of ice, Mrs. Colbert," he said. "Let me help you to the door."

After she and her husband were finally resigned to the fact that there was no hope Tasha would ever recover, Gary Lasch had urged them to consider placing her eventually in the long-term nursing facility being built adjacent to the hospital.

He had shown them the plans for the modest structure, and it had proved to be a blessed diversion for them to call in the architect and to make the donation that totally changed and expanded the residence so that every room was bright and airy, with a private bath and comfortable homelike furniture and state-of-the-art medical equipment. Now all the residents, who, like Tasha, had had their lives unexpectedly, inexplicably shattered, were receiving whatever comfort money and care could provide.

A special, three-room apartment had been designed for Tasha, an exact replica of her suite at home. A nurse and an aide were in constant attendance. The classical music Tasha loved played softly day and night. She was moved every day from the bedroom to the sitting room, which faced a private garden.

Passive exercises and facials and massages and pedicures and manicures kept her body beautiful and supple. Her hair, still flame red, was washed and brushed daily and worn loose about her shoulders. She was dressed in silk pajamas and robes. The nurses were instructed to talk to her as if she could understand every word.

Barbara thought of the months when she and Charles had come to see Tasha almost every day. But the months soon became years. Worn out with emotional and physical exhaustion, they eventually reduced the number of visits to twice a week. When Charles died, she had, with great reluctance, heeded the advice of her sons and given up the house in Greenwich and set up permanent residence in the New York apartment. Now she made the trip only once each week.

Today as always, Barbara walked through the reception area and down the corridor to her daughter's suite. The nurses had Tasha propped up on the couch in the sitting room. Barbara knew that under the coverlet there were safety straps that held her rigidly in place and kept her from slipping, a precaution against injury caused by the involuntary jerking movements Tasha's muscles sometimes made.

With familiar pain, Barbara studied the calmly serene expression on Tasha's face. Sometimes she thought she could detect eye movement, or perhaps hear a sigh, and would have the impossible, wild thought that maybe Tasha was not beyond hope after all.

She sat by the couch and took her daughter's hand. For the next hour she talked to her about the family. "Amy is starting college, Tasha, can you believe that? She was only ten when you had the accident. She looks a lot like you. She could almost be your daughter, not just your niece. George Jr. is a bit homesick but otherwise enjoys prep school."

At the end of the hour, weary but at peace, Barbara kissed

Tasha on the forehead and signaled the nurse to come back into the room.

When she reached the reception area she found Dr. Peter Black waiting for her. When Gary Lasch had been murdered, the Colberts had debated moving Tasha to another facility, but Dr. Black had convinced them to leave her there.

"How did you find Tasha today, Mrs. Colbert?"

"The same, Doctor. It's about the best I can expect, isn't it?" Barbara Colbert knew that she was unreasonable in her ambiguous feelings about Peter Black. Gary Lasch had chosen him to be his partner, and she had no reason to feel that Tasha's care was lacking in any way. Still, she just couldn't warm to him. Maybe it was because of his close association with Calvin Whitehall, whom Charles had derisively dubbed a "would-be robber baron." On those occasions when she got back to Greenwich and dined at the club with her friends, she often saw Black and Whitehall together there.

As she bid Peter Black good night and walked to the door, Barbara could not know that the doctor was staring intently at her, or that he was remembering the terrible moment when her daughter had been catastrophically damaged, and that he was remembering as well the words a traumatized Annamarie Scalli had screamed at Gary: "That girl came in here with nothing worse than a mild concussion. *Now the two of you have destroyed her!*"

26

For almost six years Philip Matthews had believed that he had done the best job a trial lawyer could to get Molly Lasch a light sentence. Five and a half years for the murder of a doctor with a thirty-five-year life expectancy was practically a free ride.

As Philip had often told Molly on his visits to her in prison, "When you get out, you can put all this behind you."

But now Molly was out of prison and was doing exactly the

opposite of that. It was clear that she did *not* think she had gotten off easily.

Philip knew that, more than anything else, he wanted to protect Molly from the people who inevitably would attempt to exploit her.

People such as that Fran Simmons.

Late on Friday afternoon, just as he was about to leave for the weekend, his secretary announced a call from Simmons.

Philip considered not taking the call, but then decided he might as well speak to her. His greeting, however, was cool.

Fran got right to the point: "Mr. Matthews, you must have a transcript of Molly Lasch's trial. I'd like to have a copy of it as soon as possible."

"Ms. Simmons, I understand you went to school with Molly. So as an old friend, I wish you would consider calling off this program. We both know it can only hurt Molly."

"Would it be possible to have a copy of the transcript on Monday, Mr. Matthews?" Fran asked crisply, then added, "You must know that I am planning this program with Molly's complete cooperation. In fact, it's even at her request that I undertook it in the first place."

Philip decided to try a different approach. "I can do better than Monday. I'll have a copy run off and delivered to you tomorrow, but I'm going to ask you to consider something. I believe Molly is much more fragile than anyone realizes. If during the course of your investigation, you become convinced of her guilt, then I ask you to give her a break and cancel this program. Molly is not going to get the public vindication she wants. Don't destroy her with a guilty-as-charged verdict just so you can get higher ratings from the mindless couch potatoes out there who want to see someone eviscerated."

"Let me give you my address for your messenger," Fran said, biting off her words, hoping she sounded as furious as she felt.

"I'll put my secretary on. Good-bye, Ms. Simmons."

Once Fran had replaced the receiver, she got up and walked to the window. She was due in makeup right now but knew she needed to take a moment to calm down first. Without having met him, she thoroughly disliked Philip Matthews, although she could not help feeling that he was passionately sincere in his desire to shield Molly.

She found herself wondering suddenly if anyone had ever considered searching for another explanation for Gary Lasch's death.

Molly's parents and friends, Philip Matthews, the Greenwich police, and the state attorney who prosecuted her—all of them must have begun with the presumption of her guilt.

Which is exactly what I've been doing as well, Fran thought. Maybe it's time to start with the opposite approach.

Molly Carpenter Lasch did not *kill her husband, Gary Lasch,* she said to herself, considering the sound of it, and wondering where it would lead.

27

On Friday afternoon, Annamarie Scalli went straight home after taking care of her last patient. The weekend loomed ahead of her, and already she knew it was going to be a difficult one. Since Tuesday morning, when Molly Lasch's release from prison had received so much television coverage, half of Annamarie's patients had mentioned the case to her.

She understood that it was only coincidence, that they had no awareness of her connection to the case. Her patients were homebound, and they saw the same repetitious programs, mostly soap operas, all the time. Having a more-or-less-local crime like this was simply something new and different to mull over—a privileged young woman claiming that she didn't believe she murdered her husband, even though she had plea-bargained to a lesser charge and had spent time in prison for his death.

The comments varied from crusty old Mrs. O'Brien saying that he got what any husband who cheated deserved, to Mr. Kunzman's comment that if Molly Lasch had been black and poor, she'd be serving twenty years.

Gary Lasch wasn't worth having her serve even one day in prison, Annamarie thought as she opened the door of her garden apartment. Too bad I was too much of a fool to realize it then.

Her kitchen was so tiny that she always said it made the galley of an airplane look roomy. But she had made the most of it by painting the ceiling a sky blue and sketching a lattice with flowers on the walls; as a result the meager space became her indoor garden.

This evening, however, it failed to raise her spirits. Having to revisit painful old memories had made her feel depressed and lonely, and she knew she had to get away. There was one place she could go that would help. Her older sister, Lucy, lived in Buffalo, in the home where they had been raised. Annamarie did not visit there regularly since her mother's death, but this weekend she would make the trek. After she put away the last of the groceries she reached for the phone.

Forty-five minutes later she threw a hastily packed duffel bag in the backseat of her car and, with brightened spirits, turned on the ignition. It was a long trip, but she didn't mind. Driving gave her a chance to think. Much of the time was spent regretting. Regretting not listening to her mother. Regretting being so foolish. Definitely despising herself for her affair with Gary Lasch. If only she could have willed herself into really loving Jack Morrow. If only she had realized how much she had begun to care for him.

She remembered with renewed shame the trust and love she had seen in his eyes. She had fooled Jack Morrow like everyone else, and he neither knew nor suspected that she was involved with Gary Lasch.

Even though it was past midnight when she arrived, her sister Lucy had heard the car when it drove up and was opening the door. With a rush of renewed joy, Annamarie reached into the back for her bag. A moment later she was hugging her sister, glad to be where, at least for the weekend, she would be able to force away the distressing thoughts of what might have been.

28

On Saturday morning, Edna Barry awoke with a nervous start. Today that reporter was coming to see her, and she had to make sure Wally wasn't around when Fran Simmons got there. He had been moody for several days, and since seeing Molly on television had kept talking about wanting to visit her. Last night he'd announced that he wasn't going to the club, where he usually spent Saturday mornings. The club, run by Fairfield County for outpatients like Wally, was usually one of his favorite places to go.

I'll ask Marta to keep him at her place, Edna thought. Marta Gustafson Jones had been her neighbor for thirty years. They'd seen each other through illness and widowhood, and Marta doted on Wally. She was one of the few people who could handle him and calm him down when he became upset.

When Fran rang Edna's bell at eleven o'clock, Wally was safely out of the way, and Edna was able to manage a reasonably pleasant greeting and even offered her coffee, which Fran accepted. "Why don't we just sit in the kitchen?" she suggested, as she unbuttoned her coat.

"If you like." Edna was justifiably proud of her spotless kitchen, with its brand-new maple dinette set she'd bought on sale.

At the table, Fran fished her recorder out of her shoulder bag. Casually she laid it on the tabletop. "You know, Mrs. Barry, I'm here because I want to help Molly, and I'm sure you do too. That's why, with your permission, I need to record you. There may just be something that will come up that might prove to be helpful to Molly. I'm sure that she's become more and more convinced she wasn't the one responsible for her husband's death. In fact, she's beginning to remember things about that night, and one of them is that there was someone else in the house when she arrived home from the Cape. If that could be proven, it might mean her conviction would be overturned, or at least that the investigation would be reopened. Wouldn't that be wonderful?"

Edna Barry was pouring water into the coffeemaker. "Yes, of course, it would," she said. Then, "Oh, dear."

Fran's eyes narrowed as she saw that Mrs. Barry had splashed water on the counter. Her hand is trembling, Fran thought. There's something about all this that's bothering her. I could tell she was nervous the other day when I met her at Molly's and she certainly was uptight when I talked to her on the phone to ask about coming here today.

As the aroma of coffee began to fill the room, Fran set about trying to get Edna Barry to relax and let down her guard. "I went to school with Molly at Cranden," she said. "Did she tell you that?"

"Yes, she did." Edna took cups and saucers from the cabinet and placed them on the table. She peered at Fran over her glasses for a moment before sitting down.

She's thinking about the library-fund scandal, Fran thought, then brushed her concern aside and went ahead with her interview. "But I understand you've known her even longer than that?"

"Oh, yes. I worked for her parents from the time she was little. Then they moved to Florida right after she got married, and that's when I started working for her."

"Then you knew Dr. Lasch very well also?"

Edna Barry considered the question. "I guess the answer to that one has to be yes and no. I was there three mornings a week. The doctor was always gone off to work when I got there at nine and seldom home at one o'clock when I left. But if Molly was giving a dinner party—which she did fairly often—then she'd have me in to serve and clean up. That's really the only time I saw the doctor and her together. When he was around, he was always very pleasant."

Fran noticed that Edna Barry's lips tightened into a straight line as though whatever she was thinking as she spoke was not very pleasant. "When you did see him and Molly together, did you get the feeling that they were happy?" she asked.

"Until that day I came in and Molly was so upset and packing to go to the Cape, I never saw even a hint of a quarrel. I will say that before that day, I had felt time hung a little heavy on her hands. She did a lot of volunteer work in town, and I know she's a very good golfer, but sometimes she'd tell me that she missed having a job. And, of course, she had some tough breaks too. She was so anxious to start a family, and then, when she had that last miscarriage, she seemed different, very quiet, very withdrawn."

Nothing Edna Barry was saying was really of any help to Molly, Fran thought, as a half-hour later she finished her second cup of coffee. She had only a few questions left to ask, and so far the woman hadn't been very forthcoming. "Mrs. Barry, the security system wasn't on when you got to work that Monday, was it?"

"No, it wasn't."

"Did you check to see if there might have been an unlocked door that an intruder might have used?"

"There was *no unlocked door.*" Edna Barry's voice turned suddenly antagonistic, and the pupils of her eyes widened.

I've hit a nerve, Fran thought, and there's something she's not telling me. "How many doors are there in the house?"

"Four," she answered without pausing to think. "The front door. The kitchen door. They had the same key. A door from the family room to the patio. That only opened from the inside. A basement door that was always locked and bolted."

"Did you check *all* of them yourself?"

"No, but the police did, Miss Simmons. Why don't you talk to them?"

"Mrs. Barry, I'm not questioning what you told me," Fran said, her tone conciliatory.

Seemingly mollified, Edna Barry said, "On that Friday afternoon, when I left, I checked all the doors to be sure that they were locked. Dr. Lasch always came in the front door. The floor bolt wasn't fastened that Monday morning, so that means over the weekend someone used that door."

"The floor bolt?"

"At night, Molly always put it on. The kitchen door was locked when I came in. I am positive about that."

Edna Barry's cheeks were flushed. Fran could see the woman was on the verge of tears. Is she afraid because she thinks she may have been careless and left the house unlocked? she wondered.

"Thank you for your help, Mrs. Barry, and your hospitality," Fran said. "I've taken enough of your time for now, but I may want to ask you a few more questions later, and possibly we'll ask you to be a guest on the program."

"I don't want to be a guest on the program."

"Of course. As you wish." Fran turned off the recorder and got up to leave. At the door she asked a final question: "Mrs. Barry, let's just assume the possibility that there *was* someone else in the house the night Dr. Lasch died. Do you know if the locks on any of the doors were ever changed?"

"Not to my knowledge."

"I'm going to suggest to Molly that they should be changed. Otherwise she might be in danger from an intruder. Don't you agree?"

Now the color drained from Edna Barry's face. "Miss Simmons," she said, "if you'd seen what I saw when I went upstairs— Molly lying in that bed, covered with crusted blood—you'd know that no intruder came into the house that night. Stop trying to make trouble for innocent people."

"What innocent people am I trying to make trouble for, Mrs. Barry?" Fran demanded. "I thought I was trying to help a young woman, someone you've known for years and say you care for, to perhaps prove herself innocent of this crime!"

Mrs. Barry said nothing, her lips a grim, straight line as she opened the door for Fran to leave. "We'll be talking again, Mrs. Barry," Fran said, unsmiling. "I have a feeling I still have a lot of questions for you that need to be answered."

29

As Molly suspected, when her phone rang on Saturday afternoon, it was Jenna calling.

"I was just talking to Phil Matthews," Jenna said. "I understand you're cooking dinner for him. I approve."

"Good Lord, don't even think in those terms," Molly protested. "I would have had him pounding on the door if I hadn't let him come over, and since I'm not ready to go to a restaurant, it just seemed like the logical thing to do."

"Well, we decided that, invited or not, we're coming over for a drink. Cal is anxious to see you."

"You're not invited," Molly said, "but come over around seven."

"Moll," Jenna said, then hesitated.

"Say it. It's okay."

"Oh, it's nothing dramatic, my friend. It's just that you sound like yourself again—and I love it."

Who is "myself"? Molly wondered. "Nothing like windows without bars and a satin quilt on the bed," she commented. "They do wonders for the soul."

"Wait till I get you in to Manhattan for the makeover. What are you up to today?" Molly hesitated, then decided that she was not ready to share, even with Jenna, the fact that she was going through Gary's daily reminder and appointment books, searching day by day for clues. She settled instead for a half-truth. "As long as I'm a hostess, however unwelcome that role, I'm getting a few things started in the kitchen. It's been a long time since I've done anything like that."

That much was true. The rest of the truth was that Gary's date books going back several years before his death were stacked on the kitchen table. Working backwards, starting with the date of his death, she had been going through them page by page, line by line.

Molly remembered that Gary's schedule always had been crowded, and that he was always jotting down reminders to himself. She already had come across several such notations, entries like "5 P.M. Call Molly at club."

She remembered with a pang that there were times he'd phone her and ask, "Why is it in my book that I'm supposed to call you now?"

At 5:30, just before she set the table for that night's dinner, Molly found the notation that she wanted. It was a phone number that showed up several times in Gary's last reminder diary. She checked with the information operator and learned that the area code for the number given was in Buffalo.

She dialed the number, and when a woman answered, Molly asked if Annamarie was there.

"Speaking," Annamarie Scalli said quietly.

30

When she left Edna Barry's house, Fran embarked on a pilgrimage through Greenwich, a further trip down memory lane. This time she drove to the Stationhouse Pub, with the idea of having lunch there. We used to come here for a quick dinner before going to the movies, she remembered nostalgically.

Turkey on rye was what Fran ordered. It used to be her mother's favorite. She looked about the dining room. It was unlikely that her mother ever would set foot in Greenwich again. The memories for her were just too painful. The joke that last summer had been that instead of a new library, the town was stuck with a different lending institution: "Simmons Trust." Some joke, she thought bitterly.

She had considered the possibility of driving past the house where they'd lived for those four years but realized she wasn't up to it. Not today, Fran thought, as she signaled for her check.

When she got back to the city and her apartment building, Fran saw that Philip Matthews had kept his word. A bulky package was waiting for her at the lobby desk. She opened it to find that it was the entire transcript of Molly Lasch's trial.

She looked at it longingly, anxious to get started, but she knew it would have to wait. Errands needed to be run first, she reminded herself. She simply had to do some food shopping, then get to the dry cleaner, then try to hit Bloomingdale's for hosiery and cosmetics.

It was 4:30 when she was finally able to put everything else aside and make a cup of tea, then settle into her deep club chair, prop her feet on the ottoman, and open the transcript.

The text did not make for pretty reading. The prosecutor presented a strong and chilling argument: *Is there evidence of a struggle? No. . . . gaping wound in the head of Dr. Gary Lasch . . . skull caved in. . . . He was bludgeoned while sitting at his desk, his back to his assailant . . . totally defenseless. . . . The evidence will show that Molly Lasch's fingerprints, clear and bloody, were on that sculpture, that Gary Lasch's blood was on her face and hands and clothing . . . that there was no sign of forced entry. . . .*

"No evidence of forced entry," Fran thought. Obviously the

police *did* check the doors. They don't say anything about them being unlocked, though. Did Philip Matthews follow up on that? she wondered. She highlighted that section of testimony with a yellow marker.

Molly Lasch did not kill her husband, Gary Lasch. I'm beginning to believe that could be true, Fran thought. Now let's take it one step further. Let's assume that someone else killed Gary Lasch and was lucky enough that when Molly came in and found her husband, she was so traumatized that inadvertently she did everything possible to incriminate herself. She handled the murder weapon that killed her husband, touched his face and head, splattered herself with his blood.

Splattered herself with his blood, Fran thought. If Gary Lasch was still alive when Molly found him, is it possible that he was able to say anything to her? If there was someone in the house, then Molly could have arrived home moments after Gary was attacked.

Did Molly come home, go to the study, find her husband mortally injured but still alive? Fran asked herself. It would explain why she would have been touching him, why her mouth and face were covered with blood. Did she try to resuscitate him when she found him?

Or had she tried to resuscitate him only after she realized what she had done to him?

If we go with the idea that she's innocent, then somebody right now is terribly, terribly nervous, Fran realized.

A certainty that Molly Lasch was in grave danger washed over Fran. If Gary Lasch had been alone in a house—a house that the evidence showed had been locked—and had not heard his assailant come into the study, as appearances would indicate, then the same thing could happen to Molly, Fran thought.

She reached for the phone. She'll think I'm crazy, but I'm going to call her.

Molly's greeting sounded hurried. "Fran. It seems to be reunion time," she explained. "Philip Matthews is coming to dinner, and Jenna and Cal insisted on stopping by for a cocktail. And I just got a call from Peter Black. He was not happy when I told him earlier that you wanted to see him, but he sounded quite civil just now. *He's* stopping over too."

"Then I won't keep you," Fran said, "but I had a quick thought.

I gathered from Mrs. Barry that the doors have the same locks they've had since you bought the house?"

"That's right."

"Look, I think it would be a great idea to change them."

"I hadn't thought about it."

"How many people have a set of keys?"

"It's not a set. Just one key, really. The front door and the kitchen door have the same lock. The patio and basement doors are always bolted from the inside. There were only four keys. Gary's. Mine. Mrs. Barry's. And the one we hide in the garden."

"Who knows about the one in the garden?"

"I don't think anyone knows. It was just for emergencies and never used. Gary never forgot his keys and neither did I. Mrs. Barry never forgets *anything*. Fran, you're going to have to forgive me, but I have to go."

"Molly, call a locksmith on Monday. Please."

"Fran, I'm not in danger, unless . . ."

"Unless you had the hard luck to arrive on a murder scene and become traumatized, and now someone could be afraid of what you'll remember."

Fran heard Molly's gasp. Then, with a catch in her voice, Molly said, "That's the first time in six years I've heard anyone suggest that I might be innocent."

"So you see why I want you to change your locks? Let's plan to get together on Monday."

"Yes, let's do. I may have some very interesting news for you," Molly said.

Now what did she mean by that? Fran wondered as she replaced the receiver.

31

Tim Mason had planned to get in one last weekend of skiing at Stowe in Vermont, but a call from his cousin Michael, who still lived in Greenwich, changed his plans. The mother of Billy Gallo, an old school friend of both men, had died of a heart attack, and Michael thought Tim might want to stop in at the wake.

That was why on Saturday evening Tim was on the Merritt Parkway, driving to southern Connecticut and thinking of the high school years when he and Billy Gallo had played together in the band. Billy was a real musician even then, Tim reflected. He remembered how they had tried to start their own group when they were seniors and how the group always practiced at Billy's house.

Mrs. Gallo, a warm, hospitable woman, was always urging them to stay for dinner, and it never took much persuasion. Her kitchen tantalized them with aromas of baking bread, garlic, and simmering tomato sauce. Tim remembered how Mr. Gallo would come home from work and go straight to the kitchen, as though he were afraid his wife wouldn't be there. The minute he spotted her, a big smile would come over his face and he'd say, "Josie, you're opening cans again."

Somewhat wistfully, Tim thought of his own parents and of the years before they divorced, when he had been glad to escape the escalating coolness between them.

Mr. Gallo never failed to deliver that corny line, he thought, and Mrs. Gallo would always laugh as though it were the first time she had heard it. They clearly were crazy about each other. Mr. Gallo, though, was never close to Billy. He thought Billy was wasting his time trying to be a musician.

As Tim drove and thought of those earlier days, he remembered another funeral he had gone to in Greenwich. He'd been out of school then, already working as a reporter.

He thought of Fran Simmons, how grief stricken she had been. In church her muffled sobs had been audible throughout the entire Mass. Then, as the casket was being lifted into the hearse, he had felt like a voyeur, jotting notes for his story while the cameraman took flash pictures.

Fourteen years had changed Fran Simmons. It wasn't just that she had grown up. There was a cool professionalism about her, like an invisible armor; he'd sensed it when they met in Gus's office. Tim was embarrassed to realize that when they were introduced he had been thinking about her father and how he had been a crook. Why did he have the uncomfortable feeling that he owed her an apology for that?

He was so deep in thought that he was at the North Street exit before he realized it, and he almost missed the turnoff. Three minutes later he was in the funeral home.

The place was filled with friends of the Gallo family. Tim saw a host of familiar faces, people he had lost touch with, a number of whom came up to him when he was waiting on line to speak to Mr. Gallo and Billy. Most of them made flattering comments about his reporting, but fast on the heels of those comments came references to Fran Simmons, because she was now on the program with him.

"That *is* the Fran Simmons whose father cleaned out the library fund, isn't it?" Mrs. Gallo's sister asked.

"My aunt thinks she saw her in the coffee shop at Lasch Hospital," someone else commented. "What on earth would she be doing there?"

That question was asked of Tim just as he came face to face with Billy Gallo, who obviously had overheard. His eyes swollen from crying, he shook Tim's hand. "If Fran Simmons is investigating something at the hospital, tell her to find out why patients are being allowed to die when they don't have to," he said bitterly.

Tony Gallo touched his son's sleeve. "Billy, Billy, it was God's will."

"No, Pop, it *wasn't*. A lot of people who are building up to heart attacks can be saved." Billy's voice, agitated and tense, rose in volume. He pointed to his mother's casket. "Mom shouldn't be *in* there, not for another twenty years. The doctors at Lasch didn't care—they just let her die." He was practically sobbing now. "Tim, you and Fran Simmons and all the reporters on your television show have got to look into this. You've got to find out why they waited so long, why she wasn't sent to a specialist in time."

With a strangled, choking groan, Billy Gallo covered his face with his hands and surrendered once more to the tears he had been fighting. Tim braced him with firm hands on both arms, holding him until Billy's sobs quieted and, in a voice calm and sad, he finally managed to ask, "Tim, tell the truth. Did you ever taste a better pasta sauce than my mother made?"

32

I don't know how I let this happen, Molly thought as she placed a tray of cheese and crackers on the table in the family room. Seeing Cal and Peter Black here, together, upset her in ways she had not anticipated. The serenity, the comfort she had found in being in her own house was suddenly gone. It was as though her privacy had been violated. Seeing these two men in here brought back the many times when they would meet with Gary in his study. The three of them would spend hours in conference there—the other Remington Health Management board members were only rubber stamps.

These past few days the house had felt different from the way she remembered it. It was as though the five and a half years she had been in prison had changed her perception of her life as she had known it.

Before Gary died, I believed I was happy, Molly thought. I believed that the gnawing restlessness I felt came from my frustration at not having a baby.

Now she could feel the old, familiar heaviness of spirit closing in around her. She could tell Jenna sensed her change of mood and was concerned. Jenna had trailed her out to the kitchen, had insisted on cutting the cheese into squares, had arranged the crackers neatly on the plate, had folded the napkins just so.

After being so curt on the phone, Peter Black seemed to be going out of his way tonight to be agreeable. When he came in, he had kissed her on the cheek and squeezed her hand. His message was clear: That terrible tragedy is behind us.

Is it? she wondered. Can we make something like that—the

murder, the years in prison—just disappear, as though they had never happened? I don't think so, she decided as she looked at these old friends—if indeed that's what they were—gathered together in this room.

She looked at Peter Black—he seemed tremendously uncomfortable. *Why* had he insisted on coming here?

Philip Matthews seemed to be the only one at ease. He had been the first to arrive, getting there promptly at seven, an amaryllis plant held in the crook of his arm. "I know you're looking forward to gardening," he'd said. "Maybe you'll find a corner for an amaryllis."

The huge, pale red blossoms were exquisite. "Be careful," she warned him. "The amaryllis is also called a belladonna lily, and belladonna is a poison."

The lightness she had felt then was gone. Now Molly felt that even the air was poisoned. Cal Whitehall and Peter Black were not here as a welcome-home committee—that was clear from the outset. They had a different agenda. That would also explain Jenna's nervousness, she decided. She was the one who had forced the meeting.

Molly wanted to tell Jenna that it was all right. She *understood* that Cal was a steamroller, that if he'd made up his mind to come, Jenna wouldn't have been able to stop him.

The reason behind their visit soon became apparent. It was Cal who first broached the subject. "Molly, yesterday that TV news reporter, Fran Simmons, was in the hospital coffee shop asking questions. Was she there at your suggestion?"

"No, I didn't know Fran was going there," she responded with a shrug of her shoulders, "but it's fine with me."

"Oh Molly, please," Jenna murmured. "Don't you understand what you're doing to yourself?"

"Yes, I do, Jen," Molly said quietly but firmly.

Cal set his glass on the table with unnecessary force, causing a few drops to splash from it.

Molly resisted the urge to immediately mop up the spill, part of her impulse to do anything to escape this nightmare. Instead, she looked at the two men who had been her husband's partners.

Cal was not ignoring the spill. He jumped up, muttering, "I'll get a paper towel." In the kitchen he looked around, found the towel rack. As he started back, his eyes diverted to the single notation on the wall calendar. Carefully he studied it.

Peter Black's cheeks were flushed; clearly this wasn't his first drink of the night. "Molly, you know that we're in discussion about the acquisition of several other health maintenance organizations. If you persist in allowing, much less encouraging, this program to proceed, could you at least ask Fran Simmons to hold off until after the merger is completed?"

So *that's* what this is all about, Molly thought. They're afraid that if I open old wounds, the infection could spread to them.

"Of course, there's nothing to hide," he added emphatically. "But talk and gossip and rumors have ruined plenty of important negotiations."

He was drinking scotch, and Molly watched as he drained his glass. She remembered that years ago he had been a heavy hitter when it came to booze. Obviously that hadn't changed.

"And Molly, *please* give up the idea of trying to locate Annamarie Scalli," Jen pleaded. "If *she* found out about a possible television program, she might sell her story to one of those scandal magazines."

Molly still sat unspeaking, staring at the three people, feeling her old fears and doubts bubbling just below the calm surface she had displayed so far tonight.

"I think the case has been presented," Philip Matthews said bluntly, breaking the awkward silence. "Why don't we give it a rest?"

Peter Black, Jenna, and Cal left a short time later. Philip Matthews waited until the door closed behind them, then he asked, "Molly, would you prefer that we skip dinner and I get out of your way?"

On the verge of tears, she nodded, then managed to say, "You can have a rain check if you want one."

"I *do* want one."

Molly had prepared coq au vin and wild rice. After Philip left, she covered the dishes and put them in the refrigerator, then checked the door locks and went into the study. Tonight, maybe because Cal and Peter Black had been there, she had a strong sense of something lurking at the edges of her conscious mind, trying to break through.

What was it? she wondered. Old memories, old fears that would drag her deeper into the depression she felt? Or would it provide answers, maybe even help her escape the darkness that threatened to envelop her? She would just have to wait and see.

She did not turn on a light but curled up on the sofa, her legs tucked under her.

What would Cal and Peter and Philip Matthews think, she wondered, if they suspected that tomorrow evening at eight o'clock, at a roadside diner in Rowayton, she was actually going to meet Annamarie Scalli?

33

There is nothing like Sunday morning in Manhattan, Fran decided as she opened the apartment door at 7:30 to find the Sunday *Times*, thick and inviting, awaiting her. She fixed juice and coffee and a muffin, settled in her big chair, planted her feet on the ottoman, and picked up the first section of the paper. A few minutes later she put it down, realizing she had absorbed very little of what she had read.

"I'm worried," she said aloud, then reminded herself that it was a bad habit to talk to yourself.

She had not slept well the night before and was sure that her restlessness had something to do with Molly's cryptic statement that she might have some very interesting news for her. What kind of news could be "very interesting"? she wondered.

If Molly is conducting some kind of private investigation of her own, she could be getting in over her head, Fran thought. Pushing aside the newspaper, she got up, poured a second cup of coffee, and returned to the chair, this time to read Molly's trial transcript.

For the next hour she went through the testimony, line by line. There was testimony from the first police officers to arrive on the scene, as well as from the medical examiner. That was followed by testimony from Peter Black and the Whitehalls, describing their final meeting with Gary Lasch, a few hours before he died.

Clearly it had been like pulling teeth to get Jenna to say anything negative, Fran thought, as she carefully studied her testimony.

PROSECUTOR: Did you speak to the defendant in the week before her husband's death, while she was at her home on Cape Cod?

JENNA: Yes, I did.

PROSECUTOR: How would you characterize her emotional side?

JENNA: Sad. She was very sad.

PROSECUTOR: Was she angry at her husband, Mrs. Whitehall?

JENNA: She was upset.

PROSECUTOR: You didn't answer my question. Was Molly Carpenter Lasch angry at her husband?

JENNA: Yes, I guess you would say so.

PROSECUTOR: Did she express *great* anger at her husband?

JENNA: Will you repeat the question?

PROSECUTOR: Surely, and will Your Honor direct the witness to answer without equivocation?

JUDGE: The witness is directed to answer the question.

PROSECUTOR: Mrs. Whitehall, during your telephone conversations with Molly Carpenter Lasch in that week before her husband's death, did she express great anger at him?

JENNA: Yes.

PROSECUTOR: Did you know the reason Molly Carpenter Lasch was angry at her husband?

JENNA: No, not initially. I asked her, but she wouldn't tell me at first. That Sunday afternoon she did.

When she read through Calvin Whitehall's testimony, Fran decided that, intentionally or otherwise, he had been an extremely damaging witness. The state attorney must have loved *him,* she thought.

PROSECUTOR: Mr. Whitehall, you and Dr. Peter Black visited Dr. Gary Lasch on Sunday afternoon, April 8th. Is that correct?

CALVIN WHITEHALL: Yes, we did.

PROSECUTOR: What was the purpose of your visit?

CALVIN WHITEHALL: Dr. Black had told me he was very concerned about Gary. He said it had been obvious to him all week that Gary was deeply worried, so we decided to go see him.

PROSECUTOR: By "we," you mean . . . ?

CALVIN WHITEHALL: Dr. Peter Black and myself.

PROSECUTOR: What happened when you got there?

CALVIN WHITEHALL: It was about five o'clock. Gary brought us into the family room. He had put out a plate of cheese and crackers and opened a bottle of wine. He poured a glass for each of us and said, "I'm sorry to say this, but it's time for true confessions." Then he admitted to us that he had been having an affair with a nurse at the hospital named Annamarie Scalli and that she was pregnant.

PROSECUTOR: Was Dr. Lasch concerned over your possible reaction?

CALVIN WHITEHALL: Of course. That nurse was only in her early twenties. We were afraid of the ramifications—a sexual harassment suit, for example. Gary was the head of the hospital, after all. The Lasch name, thanks to his father's legacy, is a symbol of integrity that, of course, spilled over to the hospital and then to Remington Health Management. We were deeply distressed at the prospect of that image changing because of a scandal.

Fran continued to read the trial transcript for another hour. When she put it down, she kneaded her forehead, hoping to prevent the beginning of a headache she could feel coming on.

Gary Lasch and Annamarie Scalli certainly seem to have managed to keep their affair under wraps, she thought. What jumps out of these pages is absolute shock on the part of Molly, Peter Black, and the Whitehalls, the people closest to him, when they learned about it.

She remembered the wide-eyed astonishment expressed by Susan Branagan, the volunteer at the hospital coffee shop. She had said that everyone had assumed Annamarie Scalli was falling for that nice Dr. Morrow.

Dr. Jack Morrow, who was murdered just a short time before Gary Lasch, Fran reminded herself.

It was ten o'clock. She debated going for a run but then decided she really didn't feel like doing that today. Maybe I'll see what's playing at the cinema, she thought. I'll take in a movie, as Dad would say.

The phone rang just as she had picked up the entertainment section of the newspaper to begin her search for the right film, at the right theater, at the right time.

It was Tim Mason. "Surprise," he said. "I hope you don't mind. I called Gus, and he gave me your phone number."

"Not at all. If this is a sports survey, even though I lived in California for fourteen years, the Yankees are my team. I also want

Ebbets Field to be rebuilt. And I have to say that between the Giants and Jets, it's close, but given a choice at the altar, I'd choose the Giants."

Mason laughed. "That's what I like—a woman who can make up her mind. Actually I called to see if, by any chance, you might have nothing better to do and would therefore consider meeting me for brunch at Neary's."

Neary's Restaurant was virtually around the corner from Fran's apartment, on Fifty-seventh Street.

Fran realized that she was not only surprised but pleased at the invitation. She had resented the way, when they met, Mason's eyes had reflected his awareness of who she was and who her father had been, but then she had told herself she had to expect that reaction. It wasn't *his* fault that he knew her father was a thief.

"Thank you. I'd like that," she said sincerely.

"Noon?"

"Great."

"Please don't dress up."

"I wasn't planning to dress up. Day of rest and all that."

After Fran hung up she talked aloud to herself for the second time that morning: "Now what is *this* all about?" she asked. "It sure as blazes isn't old-fashioned boy-meets-girl."

Fran arrived at Neary's to find Tim Mason deep in conversation with the bartender. He was wearing an open-necked sport shirt, dark green corduroy jacket, and tan slacks. His hair was rumpled, and his jacket felt cold when she touched his arm.

"I get the feeling you didn't take a cab," she said as he turned to look at her.

"I don't like all those reminders about buckling your seatbelt," he said. "So I walked. Good to see you, Fran." He smiled down at her.

Fran was wearing ankle boots with low heels and realized that she felt the way she had in the first grade—short.

A smiling Jimmy Neary gave them one of his four corner tables, which immediately signaled to Fran that Tim Mason must be a favorite regular patron. In the weeks since she had moved to New York, she had come here once before, with a couple from her apartment building. They'd been given a corner table then, too, and they had explained its significance to her.

Over bloody marys, Tim talked about himself. "My folks left

Greenwich when they got divorced," he told her. "It was the year after college, and I was working for the *Greenwich Time*. The editor called me a cub reporter, but actually I was mostly a gofer. That was the last time I lived there."

"How many years ago was that?" Fran asked.

"Fourteen."

She made a quick mental calculation. "That's why, when we met, you recognized my name. You knew about my father."

He shrugged. "Yes." His smile was apologetic.

The waitress handed them menus, but they both ordered eggs Benedict without even looking at the options. When the waitress was gone, Tim took a sip of his bloody mary, then said, "You haven't asked, but I'm going to give you the story of my life, which I think you'll find particularly enthralling since you obviously know your sports."

We're actually not too dissimilar, Fran thought as she listened to Tim talking about his early job, broadcasting the high school games in a small town she had never heard of in upstate New York. Then she told him about being an intern at a local cable system in a town located near San Diego, where the most exciting event was the town council meeting.

"Starting out, you take whatever job you can get," she said as he nodded in agreement.

He, too, was an only child, but unlike her, he did not have stepsiblings.

"After the divorce my mother moved to Bronxville," he explained. "That's where both she and my father had been raised. She bought a townhouse. Guess what? My father bought one in the same complex. They never got along when they were married, but now they go out on dates, and on holidays we go to his place for cocktails and hers for dinner. It confused me at first, but it seems to work for them."

"Well, I'm pleased to say my mother is very happy, and with good reason," Fran said. "She's been remarried for eight years. She figured that I'd be coming back to New York eventually and suggested I take my stepfather's name. You certainly know how much publicity there was about my father."

He nodded. "Yes, there was. Were you tempted to do that?"

Fran folded and unfolded her cocktail napkin. "No, never."

"Are you sure it's wise for you to be the one to research a program set in Greenwich?"

"Probably not wise, but why do you ask?"

"Fran, I was at a wake in Greenwich last night, for a woman I knew growing up. She died of a heart attack at Lasch Hospital. Her son is my friend, and he's terribly angry. Seems to feel more could have been done for her and thinks that, while you're at it, you should investigate the treatment they give patients at the hospital."

"Could more have been done for his mother?"

"I don't know. He may have been just crazy with grief, although I wouldn't be surprised if you hear from him. His name is Billy Gallo."

"Why would he call me?"

"Because he heard you were seen in the coffee shop at Lasch Hospital on Friday. I bet by now everyone in town has heard you were there."

Fran shook her head in disbelief. "I didn't think I'd been on air long enough for people to recognize me so easily. I'm sorry about that," she said with a shrug. "I did pick up an interesting piece of information though, just by chatting with a volunteer in the coffee shop. She probably would have clammed up if she had known I was a reporter."

"Was this visit connected to the program you're doing on Molly Lasch?" he asked.

"Yes, although mostly for background," she said, not anxious to go into the Molly Lasch investigation. "Tim, do you know Joe Hutnik at the *Greenwich Time?*"

"Yes. Joe was there when I was on the staff. A good guy. Why do you ask?"

"Joe doesn't think much of HMOs in general, but he seems to think that Remington Health Management is no worse than the rest of them."

"Well, Billy Gallo doesn't think so." He saw a look of concern on her face. "But don't worry. He's really a nice guy—just very upset right now."

As the table was cleared and coffee served, Fran looked around. Almost every table was taken now, and there was a cheerful bustle in the cozy pub. Tim Mason is a really nice guy, she thought. Maybe his friend is going to call me, and maybe he isn't. Tim's real message is that I'm in the spotlight in Greenwich, and that the old stories—and jokes—about my father's death are being revived.

As Fran looked around the room, she did not see Tim Mason's compassionate glance, nor did she realize that the expression in her eyes brought back to him vividly the image of the teenage girl mourning her father.

34

Annamarie Scalli had agreed to meet Molly at eight o'clock at a diner in Rowayton, a town ten miles northeast of Greenwich.

The location and the hour had been Annamarie's suggestion. "It's not fancy, and it's quiet on Sunday, especially that late," she had said. "And I'm sure neither one of us wants to bump into anyone we know."

At six o'clock—much too early, she knew—Molly was ready to leave. She had changed clothes twice, feeling too dressed up in the black suit she first put on, then too casual in denims. She finally settled on dark blue wool slacks and a white turtleneck sweater. She twisted her hair into a chignon and pinned it up, remembering how Gary had liked her to wear it that way, especially liked the tendrils that escaped and fell loosely on her neck and ears. He said it made her look real.

"You always look so perfect, Molly," he would tell her. "Perfect and elegant and well bred. You manage to make a pair of jeans and a sweatshirt look like formal dress."

At the time she thought he'd been teasing her. Now she wasn't sure. It was what she needed to find out. Husbands talk to their girlfriends about their wives, she thought. I need to know what Gary told Annamarie Scalli about me. And while I'm asking questions, there's something else I want to talk to her about: what she was doing the night Gary died. After all, she had a good reason to be very, very angry with him too. I heard the way she spoke to him on the phone.

At seven o'clock, Molly decided it finally was reasonable to leave for Rowayton. She took her Burberry from the downstairs closet and was headed toward the door when, as a last-minute thought, she went back up to her bedroom, took a plain blue scarf from the drawer, and searched until she found a pair of oversized Cartier sunglasses, a style that had been fashionable six years ago but probably was dated now. Well, at least they will give me a *sense* of being disguised, she decided.

At one time the three-car garage had held her BMW convertible, Gary's Mercedes sedan, and the black van he had bought two years before he died. Molly remembered how surprised she'd been when Gary showed up with it one day. "You don't fish, you don't hunt, you wouldn't be caught dead on a campground. You've got a big trunk in the Mercedes, easily big enough for your golf clubs. So what's with the van?"

It had not occurred to her at the time that, for his own purposes, Gary might have wanted a vehicle that looked exactly like dozens of other vans in the area.

After Gary's death, his cousin had arranged for his cars to be picked up. When Molly went to prison, she had asked her parents to sell hers. As soon as her parole was granted they had celebrated by buying her a new car, a dark blue sedan she'd selected from the sales brochures they sent.

She had looked at the car the day she came home, but now she got in it for the first time, enjoying the smell of the new leather. It had been nearly six years since she had driven, and suddenly she found the feel of the ignition key in her hand to be very liberating.

The last time she had been behind the steering wheel of a car was that Sunday she had returned from Cape Cod. With her hands on the wheel now, Molly could visualize that drive. I was gripping the wheel so tightly that my hands hurt, she remembered as she backed out of the garage, then used the remote to close the door. She drove slowly down the long driveway and onto the street. Normally I'd have put the car in the garage, but I remember that night I stopped right in front of the house and just left it there. Why did I do that? she wondered, straining to remember. Was it because I had the suitcase and, that way, wouldn't have to carry it as far?

No, it was because I was frantic to talk to Gary face to face. I was going to ask him then the same questions I'm going to ask Annamarie Scalli now. I needed to know how he felt about me, why he was away so much, why, if he wasn't happy in our marriage, he hadn't been honest and told me instead of letting me waste so much time and so much effort in trying to be a good wife to him.

Molly felt her lips tighten, felt the old anger and resentment surge through her body. Stop it! she told herself. Stop it right now, or turn around and go home!

Annamarie Scalli arrived at the Sea Lamp Diner at twenty after seven. She knew she was ridiculously early for her meeting with Molly Lasch, but she wanted very much to be the first to arrive. The shock of actually speaking to Molly, of having her actually track her down, had not set in until after she had agreed to the meeting.

Her sister Lucy had argued strenuously against keeping the date. "Annamarie, that woman was so upset about you that she bludgeoned her husband to death," she had said. "What makes you think she won't attack you? The very fact that she may be telling the truth when she says she doesn't remember killing him tells you she's a mental case. And you've always been afraid because you know too much about what was going on at the hospital. Don't meet her!"

The sisters had argued all evening, but Annamarie had been determined to go through with it. She had reasoned that since Molly Lasch had tracked her down, it would be better to go ahead and meet with her face to face at the diner rather than to risk having her show up at her home in Yonkers, maybe even stalking her as she tried to take care of her clients.

Once inside the diner, Annamarie had headed for a corner booth at the far end of the long, narrow room. A few people were sitting at the counter, their expressions glum. Equally malcontent was the waitress, who had become annoyed when Annamarie had refused the front table at which she'd tried to place her.

The gloom of the diner only added to the feeling of foreboding and despondency that had come over Annamarie on the long drive back from Buffalo. She could feel fatigue settling into her bones. I'm sure that's why I feel so low and depressed, she told herself without conviction, sipping the tepid coffee the waitress had slapped down in front of her.

She knew much of the problem stemmed from the argument that had raged between her and her sister. While she did love her sister dearly, Lucy was not shy about hitting her where it hurt most, and her litany of "if onlys" finally had gotten to her.

"Annamarie, if *only* you'd married Jack Morrow. As Mama used to say, he was one of the nicest men who ever walked in shoe leather. He was *crazy* about you. And he was a doctor, and a good one at that! Remember, Mrs. Monahan came in to say hello that weekend you brought him up here? Jack said he didn't like her color. If he hadn't persuaded her to go for those tests and that tumor hadn't been found, she wouldn't be alive today."

Annamarie had continued to give the same answer she'd been giving Lucille the past six years. "Look, Lucy, give it a rest. Jack knew that I wasn't in love with him. Maybe under other circumstances, I could've loved him. Maybe it would've worked out if things had been different, but they weren't. The fact was, I was only in my early twenties and on my first job. I was just starting to live. I wasn't *ready* for marriage. Jack understood that."

Annamarie remembered that the week before Jack was killed, he had quarreled with Gary. She'd been on her way to Gary's office but was stopped in the reception room by the sound of angry voices. The secretary had whispered, "Dr. Morrow is in there with Dr. Lasch. He's *terribly* upset. I haven't been able to make out what it's about, but I suppose it's the usual—a procedure he wanted done for a patient has been canceled."

I remember at the time being terrified that they might be arguing about me, Annamarie thought. I ran rather than risk having Jack confront me there; I was that sure Jack had found out.

But later, when Jack had stopped her in the corridor, he had given no indication of being angry with her. Instead, he had asked if she was going to visit her mother soon. When Annamarie told him she would be driving up the weekend after next, he said that he was going to copy a very important file he had compiled, and he asked if she please would keep the copy in her mother's attic. He'd get it from her later.

I was so relieved he hadn't found out about Gary and me and so tortured over what I knew about the hospital that I wasn't even curious about what was in the file, Annamarie thought. He said he'd give it to me soon and made me promise that I wouldn't tell anyone about it. But he never did give it to me, and a week later he was dead.

"Annamarie?"

Startled, Annamarie looked up. She'd been so immersed in thought that she had not seen Molly Lasch come in. One glance at the other woman and she suddenly felt heavy and unattractive. The oversized sunglasses could not hide Molly's exquisite features. The hands that untied the belt of her coat were long and slim. When she pulled the scarf from her head, her hair was darker than Annamarie remembered, but still fine and silky.

Molly studied Annamarie as she slid into the seat opposite her. She's not what I expected, Molly thought. She'd seen Annamarie Scalli in the hospital a few times and remembered her as being very pretty, with a provocative figure and a mass of dark hair.

There was nothing provocative about this plainly dressed woman across from her. Her hair was short now, and while her face was still pretty, it was somewhat puffy. She was heavier than Molly remembered. But her eyes were lovely, deep brown with dark lashes, although the expression Molly saw in them was one of unhappiness and fear.

She's afraid of me, Molly thought, amazed that she might have that effect on someone.

The waitress reappeared, friendlier now. Annamarie could see that she was impressed by Molly.

"Tea with lemon, please," Molly said.

"And more coffee for me, if it's not too much trouble," Annamarie added as the waitress turned away.

Molly waited until they were alone before she said, "I'm grateful you agreed to meet me. I know this is probably as awkward for you as it is for me, and I promise I won't keep you too long, but you can help me if you'll be honest with me."

Annamarie nodded.

"When did your relationship with Gary begin?"

"A year before he died. My car wouldn't start one day, and he gave me a ride home. He came in for a cup of coffee." Annamarie looked steadily at Molly. "I knew he was getting ready to hit on me. A woman can always tell, can't she?" She paused for a moment, looking down at her hands. "The truth is, I had a huge crush on him, and so I made it easy for him."

He was getting ready to hit on her, Molly thought. Was she the first? Probably not. The tenth? she wondered. She'd never know. "Was he involved with any other nurses?"

"None that I knew of, but then I'd only been working at the hospital a few months when I became involved with him. He *did* stress the need for absolute discretion, which suited me fine. I come from a strict Italian Catholic family, and my mother would have been heartbroken if she'd known I was carrying on with a married man.

"Mrs. Lasch, I want you to know—" Annamarie stopped as the waitress returned with the tea and more coffee. She didn't slam the cup down in front of Molly Lasch, Annamarie noticed.

When the waitress was out of earshot, she continued: "Mrs. Lasch, I want you to know that I absolutely, profoundly regret what happened. I know it destroyed your life. It ended Dr. Lasch's life. I gave up my baby because I wanted him to have a clean start with people who would give him a happy, two-parent home. Maybe someday, when he's an adult, he'll want to see me. If he does, I hope he'll be able to understand and even forgive me. You may have taken his father's life, but my actions set this entire tragedy in motion."

"Your actions?"

"If I hadn't gotten involved with Dr. Lasch, none of this ever would have happened. If I hadn't called him at home, you probably would never have known."

"Why *did* you call him at home?"

"Well, first of all, he told me that you and he had been discussing divorce, but that he didn't want you to know there was another woman in the picture. He said it would complicate things for him with the divorce, and it would just make you jealous and vindictive."

So that's what my husband was telling his girlfriend about me? Molly thought. He said that we were talking about divorce, and that I was jealous and vindictive? *That's* the man I went to prison for killing?

"He said it was just as well that you lost the baby; he said a baby would only have complicated the breakup."

Molly sat in stunned silence. Dear God, could Gary really have said that? she thought. *He said it was just as well I lost the baby.*

"But when I told him *I* was pregnant, he freaked out. Told me to get rid of it. He stopped coming to see me and even ignored me at the hospital. His lawyer phoned and offered a settlement, provided I signed a nondisclosure statement. I called your home because I had to talk to him, and he wouldn't see me at the hospital. I was desperate; I wanted to discuss with him whether or not he planned to be involved with his child. At that time I had no intention of giving it up for adoption."

"And I picked up the phone and overheard the call."

"Yes."

"Did my husband ever talk about me to you, Annamarie? I mean, other than to say we were talking about divorce?"

"Yes."

"Please, tell me what he said. I have to know."

"I realize now that anything he said to me about you then was because he thought it was what I wanted to hear."

"I'd still like to know exactly what that was."

Annamarie paused uncertainly, then looked directly at the woman across from her, a woman who at first she had disdained, then hated, and now, finally, was beginning to feel some compassion for. "He called you a boring Stepford wife."

A boring Stepford wife, Molly thought. For a moment it seemed to her that she was once more in prison, eating the tasteless food, hearing the click of locks, lying awake for sleepless night after sleepless night.

"As a husband—*and* as a doctor—he wasn't worth the price you paid for killing him, Mrs. Lasch," Annamarie said quietly.

"Annamarie, you've made it very clear that you believe I killed my husband, but, you see, I'm not so sure myself. I genuinely don't know what happened. I'm not convinced that I won't regain some memory of that night. At least, that's what I'm working toward. Tell me, where were you on that Sunday evening?"

"In my apartment, packing."

"Was anyone with you at the time?"

Annamarie's eyes widened. "Mrs. Lasch, you're wasting your time if you came here with the purpose of suggesting I had anything to do with your husband's death."

"Do you know of anyone who might have had a reason to kill him?" Molly could see the startled look in the eyes of the other woman. "Annamarie, you're afraid of something. What is it?"

"No I'm not. I don't know anything more. Look, I have to go now." Annamarie put her hand on the table, preparing to stand.

Molly reached over and grasped her wrist. "Annamarie, you were only in your early twenties then. Gary was a sophisticated man. He wronged both of us, and we both had reason to be angry.

But I don't think I killed him. If you have *any* reason to think there was someone else who might have had a grudge against him, please, *please,* tell me who it is. At least it would give me a starting point. Did he quarrel with anyone?"

"There was one quarrel I know of. With Dr. Jack Morrow."

"Dr. Morrow? But he died before Gary."

"Yes, and before he died, Dr. Morrow was acting strange and asked me to hold a copy of a file for him. But he was murdered before he gave it to me." Annamarie pulled her hand away from Molly's grasp. "Mrs. Lasch, I don't know whether you did or didn't kill your husband, but if you didn't, then you'd better be very careful how you go around asking questions."

Annamarie almost crashed into the waitress, who was returning to offer refills. Instead, Molly asked for the check and hastily paid it, hating the lively curiosity in the woman's eyes. Then she quickly grabbed her coat, anxious to catch up with Annamarie. Boring Stepford wife, she thought bitterly as she hurried from the diner.

As she drove back to Greenwich, Molly mentally reviewed the short talk with Annamarie Scalli. She knows something she's not telling me, Molly thought. It's almost as if she were afraid. But of what . . . ?

That night, Molly stared in shock at the breaking story on the CBS eleven o'clock news, of the just-discovered body of an unidentified woman who had been stabbed to death in her car in the parking lot of the Sea Lamp Diner in Rowayton.

35

Assistant State Attorney Tom Serrazzano had not been the one who prosecuted Molly Carpenter Lasch, but he'd always wished he'd had the chance. It was obvious to him that she'd been guilty of murder, and that because of who she was, she'd been given the sweetheart deal of all sweetheart deals—only five and a half years served for taking her husband's life.

Tom had been in the office when Molly had been prosecuted for Gary Lasch's death. He had been appalled when the trial prosecutor had allowed a plea to the manslaughter charge. He believed that any prosecutor worth his salt would have continued the trial and gone for the murder conviction.

It particularly bugged him when the perpetrators had money and connections, like Molly Carpenter Lasch.

In his late forties, Tom's entire legal career had been spent in law enforcement. After clerking for a judge, he had joined the state attorney's office and, over a period of time, had earned the reputation of being a tough prosecutor.

On Monday morning the stabbing of a young woman, first identified as Annamarie Sangelo, from Yonkers, took on new meaning when the investigation revealed that her real name was Annamarie Scalli, the "other woman" in the Dr. Gary Lasch murder case.

The statement given by the waitress from the Sea Lamp Diner, describing the woman Scalli had met there, sealed it for Serrazzano. He saw it already as an open-and-shut case.

"Only this time she won't plea-bargain," he said grimly to the detectives working on the case.

36

It's terribly important that I'm absolutely accurate in what I tell them, Molly said to herself over and over through the night.

Annamarie left the diner before me. I paid the check. When I was walking from the table to the door, it felt as though my head was spinning. All I could hear was Annamarie's voice, saying that Gary was relieved I'd lost my baby, that he thought of me as a boring Stepford wife. I suddenly felt as if I were suffocating.

There were only a few cars in the lot when I got to the diner. One of them was a Jeep. I noticed it was still there when I left. A car was pulling away as I came out. I *thought* it was Annamarie, and I called to her. I remember that I wanted to ask her something. *But what?* What could I have wanted to ask her?

The waitress will describe me. They'll know who I am. They'll ask questions. I've got to call Philip and explain to him what happened.

Philip thinks I killed Gary.

Did I?

Dear God, I know I didn't hurt Annamarie Scalli, Molly thought. Will they think that? No! Not again! I can't go through that again.

Fran. Fran will help me. She's starting to believe that I didn't kill Gary. I *know* she'll help me.

The news at 7 A.M. identified the victim of the stabbing in Rowayton as Annamarie Sangelo, an employee of the Visiting Nurse Service, from Yonkers. They don't know who she is yet, Molly thought. But they'll work it out soon.

She made herself wait until eight o'clock to call Fran, then cringed at the distress and disbelief in Fran's voice when she said, "Molly, are you telling me you met Annamarie Scalli last night, and now she's been murdered?"

"Yes."

"Have you called Philip Matthews?"

"Not yet. My God, he told me not to see her."

Fran quickly flashed on the trial transcript she had read, including the devastating testimony Calvin Whitehall had given. "Molly, I'll call Matthews right away." She paused, then continued with a new urgency in her voice. "Listen to me. Don't answer the phone. Don't answer the door. Don't talk to anyone, even Jenna, until Philip Matthews is with you. Swear that you won't."

"Fran, do you think I killed Annamarie?"

"No, Molly, I don't, but other people will think you did it. Now sit tight. I'll be there as soon as I can."

An hour later Fran was turning into Molly's driveway. Molly had been watching for her and opened the door before she could knock.

She looks as though she's in shock, Fran thought. Good God, is it possible that she really *is* guilty of two murders? Molly's complexion was ashen, as white as the chenille robe that seemed much too large for her slender frame.

"Fran, I can't go through this again. I'd rather kill myself," she whispered.

"Don't even think like that," Fran said, taking both her hands in her own. She felt how trembling and cold they were. "Philip Matthews was in the office when I called. He's on the way. Molly, go upstairs, take a hot shower and get dressed. I heard on the car radio that Annamarie has been identified. There's no question that the police will be looking to talk to you. I don't want them to see you looking like this."

Molly nodded and, like an obedient child, turned and started up the stairs.

Fran took off her coat and looked apprehensively out the window. She knew that as soon as the news was out that Molly had met Annamarie Scalli at the diner, the media would arrive like a pack of wolves.

Here comes the first one, she thought as a small red car turned in off the street. Fran was grateful when she saw Edna Barry behind the wheel. She hurried to the kitchen to meet her and noticed there was no sign that Molly had even made coffee. Ignoring the instant hostility that came over Barry's face when she let herself in, Fran said, "Mrs. Barry, would you please put on a pot of coffee right away and fix whatever Molly usually has for breakfast."

"Is anything wrong with—?"

The chimes of the front doorbell cut short the question.

"I'll get it," Fran said. Please, God, let it be Philip Matthews, she prayed.

She was relieved to find that it was Philip, although his worried expression told her even more forcibly than she already felt that there might easily be a rush to judgment.

He did not mince words: "Ms. Simmons, I appreciate your calling me, and I appreciate that you warned Molly not to talk to anyone until I got here. Nevertheless, this situation has to be grist for the mill for you and your program. I must warn you that I will not tolerate your questioning Molly or even being around when I talk to her."

He looks just the way he did when he tried to stop Molly from talking to the press outside the prison last week, Fran thought. He may believe that she killed Gary Lasch, but he's still the kind of lawyer Molly needs. He'll slay dragons for her if he has to.

It was a comforting thought. Keep your perspective, Fran

warned herself. "Mr. Matthews," she said, "I'm familiar enough with the law to know that your conversations with Molly are privileged and mine are not. I think you still are convinced that Molly killed Dr. Lasch. I started out believing that, but in the past few days I have developed some mighty serious doubts about her guilt. At the very least, I have a lot of questions I want to get answered."

Philip Matthews continued to look at her coldly.

"I suppose you think this is a media trick," Fran snapped. "It isn't. As someone who likes Molly very much and wants to help her, who wants to learn the truth, however hurtful that may be, I suggest you develop an open mind where Molly is concerned; otherwise you should get the hell out of her life."

She turned her back on him. I need a cup of coffee as much as Molly does, she decided.

Matthews followed her into the kitchen. "Look Fran . . . It *is* Fran, isn't it?" he asked. "I mean, that's what your friends call you?"

"Yes."

"I think we'd better get on a first-name basis. Obviously when I talk to Molly, you can't be in the room, but it would be helpful if you would fill me in on anything you know that might help her."

The antagonism was gone from his face. The protective way he said Molly's name hit Fran. She's a lot more to him than just a client, she decided. It was a tremendously reassuring thought. "Actually I'd like to go over a number of things with you," she said.

Mrs. Barry had finished preparing a tray for Molly. "Coffee, juice, and toast or a muffin is all she ever has," she explained.

Fran and Matthews helped themselves to coffee. Fran waited until Mrs. Barry had left to go upstairs with the tray before she asked, "Did you know that everyone at the hospital was surprised when they learned of Annamarie's affair with Gary Lasch, because they thought she was romantically involved with Dr. Jack Morrow, who was also on the staff of Lasch Hospital? And that Jack Morrow just happened to be murdered in his office two weeks before Dr. Lasch died? Did you know that?"

"No, I did not."

"Did you ever meet Annamarie Scalli?"

"No, the case was resolved before she was scheduled to testify."

"Do you remember if anything ever came up about a house key that was always kept hidden in the garden here?"

Matthews frowned. "Something may have come up, but it didn't amount to anything. Quite frankly, my feeling was that, because of the circumstances of the murder and the way Molly was covered with Dr. Lasch's blood, the investigation into his death began and ended with her.

"Fran, go upstairs and tell Molly I have to see her right away," Matthews said. "I remember she has a sitting room in her suite. I'll talk to her there before I let the police get near her. I'll get Mrs. Barry to have them wait down here somewhere."

Just then a distressed Mrs. Barry hurried into the kitchen. "When I went upstairs a moment ago with her breakfast, Molly was in bed, fully dressed and with her eyes closed." She paused. "Dear God, it's just like the last time!"

37

Dr. Peter Black invariably started his day with a quick check of the international stock market on one of the cable financial channels. He then ate a spartan breakfast—during which he insisted upon complete silence—and later listened to classical music on the car radio as he drove to work.

Sometimes when he reached the hospital grounds he would take a brisk stroll before settling down at his desk.

On Monday morning the sun was out. Overnight the temperature had risen almost twenty degrees, and Black decided a ten-minute walk this morning would clear his head.

It had been a troubled weekend. The visit to Molly Lasch on Saturday evening had been another failure, Cal Whitehall's stupid, ill-conceived notion of the way to win the woman's cooperation.

Peter Black frowned as he noticed a gum wrapper lying at the edge of the parking lot and made a mental note to have his secretary call the maintenance department and warn them about their sloppiness.

Molly's stubborn insistence on pursuing this idea of her innocence in Gary's death infuriated him. *"I didn't do it. The killer went thataway"*—Who did she think she was kidding? He knew what she was doing, though. He thought of it as Molly-strategy: Tell a lie loud enough, emphatically enough, often enough, and eventually some people will believe you.

It will be all right, he reassured himself. The mergers *will* go through. After all, they had the inside track to absorb the other HMOs, and the process already was underway. This is where we miss Gary, Black thought. I just don't have the patience for the endless socializing and glad-handing needed to keep key company executives on board with us. Cal can use business leverage to keep some of them in line, he told himself, but Cal's kind of aggressive power plays don't work with everyone. If we're not careful, some might switch to other health plans.

Frowning now, his hands in his pockets, Peter Black continued his walk around the new wing of the hospital, thinking back to his early days there, and remembering with grim admiration how Gary Lasch used to seem to thrive on all the socializing. He could turn on the charm and, when necessary, his solicitous demeanor, that look of concern that he had perfected.

Gary knew what he was doing when he married Molly too, Black reflected. Molly was the perfect Martha Stewart-type hostess, with her looks and money and family connections. Important people were actually flattered to be invited to her dinner parties.

Everything had been going so smoothly, just like clockwork, Peter Black thought, until Gary was fool enough to get involved with that Annamarie Scalli. Of all the sexy-looking young women in the world, he had to go and pick a nurse who also happened to be smart.

Too smart.

He had reached the entrance to the colonial style brick building that housed the offices of Remington Health Management Organization. He debated briefly about continuing his walk, but then decided to go in. The day was ahead of him, and he would have to deal with it sooner or later.

At ten o'clock he received a call from a nearly hysterical Jenna. "Peter, have you heard the news? A woman who was murdered last night in the parking lot of a diner in Rowayton has been identified as Annamarie Scalli, and the police are questioning Molly. On the radio they just about came out and called her a suspect."

"Annamarie Scalli is dead?! Molly is a suspect?!" Peter Black proceeded to ask rapid-fire questions, pressing Jenna for details.

"Molly apparently met with Annamarie at the diner," Jenna told him. "You'll remember she said on Saturday that she wanted to see her. The waitress said Annamarie left the diner first, but that Molly followed her out less than a minute later. When the diner closed a little later still, apparently somebody noticed that a car had been in the lot for some time, and they checked it out because they've been having trouble with teenagers parking there and drinking. But what they found was Annamarie, stabbed to death."

After Peter Black replaced the receiver, he leaned back, a contemplative look on his face. A moment later he smiled and heaved a great sigh, as though a great weight had been lifted off his shoulders. Reaching into one of the desk's side drawers, he extracted a flask. Pouring himself a shot of whiskey, he lifted the small cup in a toast. "Thank you, Molly," he said aloud, then drank.

38

On Monday afternoon, when Edna Barry arrived home from Molly's house, her neighbor and close friend Marta came running over before she was even out of the car.

"It's all over the news," Marta said breathlessly. "They say Molly Lasch is being questioned by the police, and that she is a suspect in that nurse's death."

"Come in and have a cup of tea with me," Edna said. "You just wouldn't believe the day I've had!"

At the kitchen table, over tea and her homemade coffee cake, Edna described her shock at seeing Molly lying fully dressed under the quilt on the bed. "I thought my heart would stop. She was fast asleep, just like the last time. And when she opened her eyes, she looked all confused, and then she smiled. I tell you I got such a chill. It really was like six years ago—I almost expected to see blood on her."

She explained how she had rushed downstairs to get that reporter, Fran Simmons, who'd shown up there first thing that morning, and Molly's lawyer. They had made Molly sit up, then they walked her around her sitting room and made her drink several cups of coffee.

"After a while, Molly started to get some color in her cheeks, even though her eyes still had that funny vacant look in them. And then," Edna Barry said, leaning closer to Marta, "Molly said, 'Philip, I didn't kill Annamarie Scalli, did I?' "

"No!" Marta gasped, her mouth a circle of amazement, her eyes wide behind her harlequin glasses.

"Well, let me tell you, the minute she said that, Fran Simmons took my arm and shoved me down the stairs so fast it would make your head spin. She didn't want me to be able to report anything I might overhear to the police."

Edna Barry did not add that Molly's question had taken a great load of worry off her mind. Clearly Molly was mentally unstable. Nobody who wasn't sick would kill two people and then not even know if they did it. All her secret worry about Wally had been for nothing.

Now, in the safety of her own kitchen, with her concerns about Wally removed, Edna freely dished up the events of the morning for her confidante. "We were no sooner downstairs than a couple of detectives showed up on the doorstep. They were from the state attorney's office. Fran Simmons took them into the family room. She told them Molly was in consultation with her lawyer, but I knew he really was just trying to get her to talk some sense. They couldn't have brought her out the way she was."

Her mouth set in a straight line of disapproval, Edna reached across the table to the coffee cake and helped herself to a second slice. "It was a full half-hour before Molly's lawyer came downstairs. He's the same one who handled her trial."

"Then what happened?" Marta asked eagerly.

"Mr. Matthews—that's the lawyer—said that he was going to make a statement on behalf of his client. He said that Molly had met Annamarie Scalli in the diner the night before because she wished to bring closure to the terrible tragedy of her husband's death. They were together for fifteen or twenty minutes. Annamarie Scalli left the diner while Molly paid the check. Molly went directly to her car and came home. She learned of Ms. Scalli's death on the news and

extends her sympathy to the family. Beyond that, she has no knowledge of what might have happened."

"Edna, did you see Molly after that?"

"She came down the minute the police left. She must have
been listening from the upstairs hallway."

"How did she act?"

For the first time in this exchange, Edna showed a hint of sympathy for her employer. "Well, Molly's always quiet, but this morning was different. She seemed almost like she wasn't in touch with
what was going on. I mean, it was like the way she wandered
around after Dr. Lasch died, as though she wasn't quite sure where
she was or what had happened.

"The first thing she said to Mr. Matthews was, 'They believe I
killed her, don't they?' Then that Fran Simmons said to me that
she'd like to talk to me in the kitchen, which was just a way of not
letting me hear what they were planning."

"So you don't know what they talked about?" Marta asked.

"No, but I can guess. The police want to know if Molly killed
that nurse."

"Mom, is somebody being mean to Molly?"

Startled, Edna and Marta looked up to see Wally standing in
the doorway.

"No, Wally, not at all," Edna said soothingly. "Don't you worry
yourself. They're just asking her some questions."

"I want to *see* her. She was always *nice* to me. Dr. Lasch was
mean to me."

"Now, Wally, we don't talk about that," Edna said nervously,
hoping that Marta would not read any significance into the anger in
Wally's voice, or notice the terrible scowl that distorted his features.

Wally walked over to the counter and turned his back on them.
"He stopped over to see me yesterday," Marta whispered. "He was
talking about wanting to visit with Molly Lasch. Maybe you should
take him over to say hello to her. It might satisfy him."

Edna was no longer listening. Her full attention was focused
on her son. She realized that Wally was fishing in her pocketbook.
"What are you doing, Wally?" she asked sharply, her voice thin and
high.

He turned to her and held up a key ring. "I'm just going to get
Molly's key, Mom. I promise, this time I'll put it back."

39

On Monday afternoon, waitress Gladys Fluegel willingly accompanied Detective Ed Green to the courthouse in Stamford, where she related what she had observed of the meeting between Annamarie Scalli and Molly Carpenter Lasch.

Trying to contain her pleasure at the level of deferential treatment accorded her, Gladys allowed herself to be led into the courthouse by Detective Green. There they were met by another youngish man who introduced himself as Assistant State Attorney Victor Packwell. He led them to a room with a conference table and asked Gladys if she'd like coffee or a soda or water.

"Please don't be nervous, Ms. Fluegel. You can be a great help to us," he assured her.

"That's why I'm here," Gladys responded with a smile. "Soda. Diet."

Fifty-eight-year-old Gladys had a face that was creased with wrinkles, the result of forty years of heavy smoking. Her bright red hair showed gray roots. Thanks to her slavish devotion to on-line shopping, she was always in debt. She had never married, never had a serious boyfriend, and she lived with her contentious elderly parents.

As her thirties had yielded to her forties, and then her forties blended almost unnoticeably into her fifties, Gladys Fluegel found her outlook on life souring. Eventualities no longer seemed to hold even possibilities. She was no longer sure that someday something wonderful would happen to her. She had waited patiently for excitement to enter her life, but it never had. Until now.

She genuinely enjoyed waitressing, but over the years she had become impatient and abrupt with customers, at least on occasion. It hurt her to see couples linking hands across tables, or to watch parents having a festive night out with their kids, knowing that she had missed that kind of life.

As her resentful attitude had deepened, it had cost her a number of jobs, until finally Gladys had become a fixture at the Sea Lamp, where the food was poor and the patronage sparse. The place seemed to fit her personality.

On Sunday evening she had felt particularly edgy, due to the fact that the other regular waitress had called in sick and Gladys had been forced to cover for her.

"A woman came in sometime around 7:30," she explained to the detectives, enjoying the feeling of importance it gave her to have these policemen pay such close attention, not to mention the clerk, who was taking down her every word.

"Describe her, please, Ms. Fluegel." Ed Green, the young detective who had driven her to Stamford, was being very polite.

I wonder if his parents are divorced, Gladys thought. If they are, I wouldn't mind meeting his father. "Why don't you just call me Gladys? Everybody does."

"If that's what you prefer, Gladys."

Gladys smiled, then touched her hand to her mouth as though she were thinking, trying to remember. "The woman who came in first . . . Let's see . . ." Gladys pursed her lips. She wasn't going to tell them that she'd been irritated at that woman because she'd insisted on a booth way in the back. "She looked like she was somewhere around thirty, she had short, dark hair, was maybe a size 14. It was hard to tell for sure. She was wearing slacks and a parka."

She realized that they certainly knew what that woman looked like and that her name was Annamarie Scalli, but she understood also that, step by step, they needed to nail down the facts. Besides, she was enjoying all this attention.

She told them that Ms. Scalli had ordered only coffee, not even so much as a roll or a piece of cake, which of course meant that the tip wouldn't be enough for Gladys to buy a stick of gum.

They smiled when she said that, but their smiles were benign, and she took them as encouragement.

"Then that really classy-looking lady came in, and right away you could tell there was no love lost between the two of them."

Detective Green held up a picture. "Is this the woman who joined Annamarie Scalli?"

"Absolutely!"

"What exactly was their attitude to each other, Gladys? Think carefully—this could be important."

"They were both nervous," she said emphatically. "When I brought the tea to the second lady, I heard the other one call her Mrs. Lasch. I couldn't hear what they said to each other, except little bits of talk when I brought the tea and when I tidied up a table near them."

Gladys could tell that this information had disappointed the detectives, so she rushed to add, "But business was real slow, and since I was just moping around and there was something about those two women that made me curious, I sat on a stool at the counter and watched them. Of course, later I realized I'd seen Molly Lasch's picture in the paper last week."

"What did you observe going on between Molly Lasch and Annamarie Scalli?"

"Well, the dark-haired woman, I mean the one named Annamarie Scalli, started looking more and more nervous. Honest to God, it was almost like she was afraid of Molly Lasch."

"Afraid, Gladys?"

"Yeah, I mean it. She wouldn't look her in the eye, and, actually, I don't blame her. The blonde, I mean Mrs. Lasch—well, believe me, as Annamarie Scalli talked, you should have seen the look on Mrs. Lasch's face. Cold, like an iceberg. She sure didn't like what she was hearing.

"Then I saw Ms. Scalli start to get up. You could tell she wanted to be a million miles away from there. So I headed over to see if they wanted anything more—you know, refills."

"Did she say anything?" Detective Green and Assistant State Attorney Victor Packwell asked in unison.

"Let me explain," Gladys said. "Annamarie Scalli got up. Mrs. Lasch grabbed her wrist so she couldn't leave. Then Ms. Scalli broke away from her and rushed to get out. Practically knocked me down, she was in such a hurry."

"What did Mrs. Lasch do?" Packwell demanded.

"She couldn't leave fast enough either," Gladys said firmly. "I gave her the check. It was for a dollar thirty. She tossed five dollars down and went running after Ms. Scalli."

"Did she seem upset?" Packwell asked.

Gladys narrowed her eyes in a dramatic effort to remember and to describe Molly Lasch as she had appeared at that moment. "I would say she had a funny look on her face, kinda like she'd been punched in the gut."

"Did you see Mrs. Lasch get in her car?"

Gladys shook her head emphatically. "No, I did not. When she opened the door leading out to the parking lot, she seemed to be talking to herself, and then I heard her call out, 'Annamarie,' and I figured she still had something to say to the other woman."

"Do you know if Annamarie Scalli heard her?"

Gladys sensed that the detectives would be terribly disappointed if she said she couldn't be sure. She hesitated. "Well, I'm pretty sure that she must have gotten her attention, because Mrs. Lasch called her name again, and then called out 'Wait.' "

"She called for Annamarie to wait!"

It *was* like that, wasn't it? Gladys asked herself. I was half expecting Mrs. Lasch to come back looking for change, but then I could tell that all she cared about was to catch up with the other woman.

Wait.

Did Molly Lasch *say* that, or did that couple who had just taken a table call *Waitress?*

Gladys saw the excitement on the detectives' faces. She did not want this moment to end. This was part of what she had waited for. All her life. Finally it was *her* turn. She looked again at the eager faces. "What I mean is, she called Annamarie's name twice, then when she said 'Wait,' I got the feeling that she'd attracted her attention. I remember thinking that Annamarie Scalli had probably waited out in the parking lot to talk to Mrs. Lasch."

That was kind of the way it was, Gladys told herself, as the two men smiled broadly.

"Gladys, you're very important to us," Victor Packwell said gratefully. "I have to tell you that down the line you'll be needed for further testimony."

"I'm glad to help," Gladys assured him.

Within the hour, having read and signed her statement, Gladys was on her way back to Rowayton in Detective Green's car. The only thing that marred her happiness was Green's response to her probing about his father's marital status.

His parents had just celebrated their fortieth wedding anniversary.

At the same time, at the courthouse in Stamford, Assistant State Attorney Tom Serrazzano, was appearing before a judge to request a search warrant authorizing them to search Molly Carpenter Lasch's home and automobile.

"Judge," Serrazzano said, "we have probable cause to believe that Molly Lasch murdered Annamarie Scalli. We believe that evidence relevant to this crime may be found in these two locations. If there are bloodstains or hairs or fibers on her clothes or on a weapon or in her car, we want to seize them before she cleans or otherwise disposes of them."

40

On the drive back to New York from Greenwich, Fran systematically reviewed the events of the morning.

The media had arrived at Molly's house in time to catch the detectives from the state attorney's office as they were leaving. Gus Brandt had run file tape on Molly's release from prison, as Fran did a live voice-over by phone from Molly's house.

As the Merritt became the Hutchinson River Parkway, Fran replayed her report in her mind: "In a stunning development, it has been confirmed that the woman found stabbed to death last night in the parking lot of the Sea Lamp Diner in Rowayton, Connecticut, has been identified as Annamarie Scalli. Ms. Scalli was the so-called other woman in the Dr. Gary Lasch murder case, which was in the headlines six years ago and then again last week, when Molly Carpenter Lasch, the wife of Dr. Lasch, was released from prison where she had been serving time for killing her husband.

"Although details are sketchy at this time, the police have indicated that Mrs. Lasch was seen last evening at the Rowayton diner, apparently meeting with the murder victim.

"In a prepared statement, Lasch's lawyer, Philip Matthews, explained that Molly Lasch had requested a meeting with Ms. Scalli to bring closure to a painful chapter in her life, and that she and Scalli had an honest and frank exchange. Annamarie Scalli left the diner first, and Molly Lasch never saw her again. She extends her sympathy to the Scalli family."

After she'd completed the telecast, Fran had gotten in her car, planning to head immediately back to the city, but Mrs. Barry had come running out of the house to get her. Once she was inside, a grim-faced and disapproving Philip Matthews had asked her to come into the study. She had entered the room to find Molly sitting on the sofa, her hands clasped together, her shoulders drooping. The immediate impression Fran had gotten was that the jeans and blue cable-knit sweater Molly was wearing suddenly had jumped a size—she seemed so small inside them.

"Molly assures me that as soon as I leave she is going to tell you everything she told me," Matthews had said. "As her attorney, I can only advise her. Unfortunately, I can't compel her to take my advice. I realize Molly considers you a friend, Fran, and I believe you do care about her, but the fact is that if it came to a subpoena you might be forced to answer questions we may not want answered. It is for that reason I have advised her not to tell you the events of last night. But again, I can only advise her."

Fran had cautioned Molly that what Philip said was absolutely true, but Molly had insisted that she wanted Fran to know what happened anyway.

"Last night I met Annamarie. We spoke for fifteen or twenty minutes," Molly had said. "She left ahead of me, and I came home. I did not see her in the parking lot. A car was pulling out as I left the diner, and I called, thinking it might be her. Whoever was in the car, however, either didn't hear me call or didn't want to hear."

Fran had asked if it was possible that it *had* been Annamarie in that car, and suggested that perhaps she might have come back to the parking lot later, but Philip pointed out that Annamarie was found in her Jeep; Molly was sure that the vehicle she saw leaving the lot was a sedan.

Having heard about their leave-taking, Fran asked Molly what she and Annamarie had talked about. On that aspect of the meeting, Fran felt that Molly had been less forthcoming. Is there something she doesn't want me to know? she thought. If so, what was it, and why was Molly being secretive? Was Molly trying to use her somehow?

As Fran steered her car onto the Cross County Parkway, which would lead her to the West Side Highway in Manhattan, she reviewed a few other unanswered questions she had regarding Molly Lasch, among them: why did Molly go back to bed after she'd showered and dressed this morning?

A shiver of doubt ran up Fran's spine. Was I right in the first place? she asked herself. Did Molly really kill her husband?

And perhaps the biggest question of all: Who *is* Molly, and what kind of *person* is she?

It was the exact question Gus Brandt tossed at Fran when she got back to her office. "Fran, this looks like it's gonna turn into another O.J. Simpson case, and you've got the inside track with Molly Lasch. If she keeps knocking people off, by the time you feature her on the series, we'll need two episodes to tell the whole story."

"You're convinced that Molly stabbed Annamarie Scalli?" she asked.

"Fran, we've been looking at the tapes of the crime scene. The driver's window of the Jeep was open. Figure it out. Scalli heard Lasch call her and rolled it down."

"That would have to mean Molly went to that diner having planned it all out, including carrying a knife," Fran said.

"Maybe she couldn't find a sculpture that would fit in her purse," he said with a shrug.

Fran walked back to her office, her hands shoved in the pockets of her slacks. It reminded her suddenly of how her stepbrothers used to tease her about the habit. "When Franny's hands are quiet, her brain is working overtime," they would say.

It's going to be the same scenario as the last time, she thought. Even if they can't find a single shred of hard evidence to tie Molly to Annamarie Scalli's death, it won't matter—she's already been judged guilty of a second murder. Only yesterday I was thinking that six years ago nobody ever bothered to look for another explanation for Gary Lasch's death. The exact same thing is happening now.

"Edna Barry," she said aloud, as she entered her office.

"Edna Barry? What about her?"

Startled, Fran turned. Tim Mason was right behind her. "Tim, I just realized something. This morning, Molly Lasch's housekeeper, Edna Barry, came running downstairs to tell Philip Matthews and me that Molly had gone back to bed. She said, *'Dear God, it's just like the last time.'* "

"What do you mean, Fran?"

"There's something that has been bothering me. More than *what* Edna Barry said, it was *the way* she said it, Tim, like she was *glad* to find Molly that way. Why in the name of God would it please that woman to see Molly duplicate her reaction to Gary Lasch's death?"

41

"Molly's not answering the phone. Take me directly to her place, Lou."

Irritated and impatient that she had been unable to get away from her office due to a long-standing meeting scheduled for lunchtime, Jenna had caught the 2:10 train to Greenwich, where Lou Knox had been instructed to wait for her at the station.

Lou narrowed his eyes as he looked into the rearview mirror. Having noted her bad mood, he knew this was not the time to cross Jenna, but he had no choice. "Ms. Whitehall, your husband wants you to come directly home."

"Well, that's just too bad, Lou. My husband can wait. Take me over to Molly's house and drop me off. If he needs the car, you can come back for me later, or I'll call a cab."

They were at the intersection. A right turn would take them to Molly's house. Lou flicked on the left-turn indicator and got the reaction he'd expected.

"Lou, are you deaf?"

"Ms. Whitehall," Lou said, hoping he sounded sufficiently obsequious, "you know I can't cross Mr. Whitehall." Only *you* can get away with that, he thought.

When Jenna entered the house, she slammed shut the front door with such force that the sound reverberated throughout the entire structure. She found her husband seated at the desk in his second-floor office. Tears of outrage in her eyes, her voice trembling with emotion at being treated so cavalierly, Jenna walked up to the desk and leaned on it with both hands. Looking directly down into her husband's eyes, she said, "Since when do you have the absurd notion that toadying lackey of yours can tell me where I may or may not go?"

Calvin Whitehall looked at his wife, his eyes frosty. "That 'toadying lackey,' as you call Lou Knox, had no choice but to follow my orders. So your quarrel is with me, my dear, not him. I only wish that I could inspire the same devotion in all our help."

Jenna sensed she had gone too far and backed off. "Cal, I'm sorry. It's just that my dearest friend is alone. Molly's mother called me this morning. She'd heard about Annamarie Scalli, and she begged me to be with Molly. She doesn't want Molly to know, but Molly's dad had a slight stroke last week, and the doctors won't hear of him traveling. Otherwise they would fly up to be with her through all this."

The anger left Calvin Whitehall's face as he stood and came around the desk. He put his arms around his wife and spoke softly into her ear. "We do seem to be at cross-purposes, don't we, Jen? I didn't want you to go to Molly's now because an hour ago, I got a tip. The prosecutor's office has secured a search warrant for her house and will also impound her car. So, you see, it would be no help to her, and it could be a disaster for the Remington merger if someone as prominent as Mrs. Calvin Whitehall were to be publicly connected to Molly while the search is underway. Later, I want you to be with her, of course. Okay?"

"A search warrant! Cal, why a search warrant?" Jenna pulled out of her husband's embrace and turned to face him.

"For the very good reason that the circumstantial evidence against Molly in the death of that nurse is mounting up to the point that it's becoming overwhelming. My source tells me that more facts are coming out. Apparently the waitress at the diner in Rowayton has been talking to the prosecutors, and she's pretty much put the finger on Molly. She's the reason they got a search warrant so quickly. But my source also has other information. For example, Annamarie Scalli's pocketbook was clearly visible on the seat beside her. It had several hundred dollars in it. If the motive had been robbery, it certainly would have been taken." He pulled his wife toward him and put his arms around her again. "Jen, your friend still is the girl you went to school with, the sister you never had. Love that person, sure; but understand also there are forces working within her that have caused her to become a murderer."

The phone rang. "That's probably the call I've been expecting," Cal said as he released Jenna with a final pat on her shoulder.

Jenna knew that when Cal said he was expecting a call, it was her signal to leave him alone and to close the door behind her.

42

This isn't happening! Molly told herself. It's a bad dream. No, not a bad dream. It's a bad *nightmare!* Is there such a thing, she wondered, or is "bad nightmare" like saying "to reiterate again"?

Since that morning her mind had been a muddle of conflicting thoughts and half-remembered moments. Trying to concentrate on the question of grammatical redundancy seemed as practical an exercise as any she could imagine. As she considered the question of a "bad nightmare," she sat on the couch in the study, her back propped against the arm, her knees drawn up, her hands clasped around them, her chin resting on her hands.

Almost a fetal position, she thought. Here I am, huddled like this in my own home, while total strangers tear apart and examine everything in it. Her mind flashed to how she and Jen used to joke and say "Assume the fetal position" whenever something was just too overwhelming.

But that had been a long time ago, back when a broken fingernail or a lost tennis match was a big deal. Suddenly "overwhelming" had taken on a whole new meaning.

They told me to wait in here, she thought. I thought that once I was freed from prison, I'd never have to take orders about where I could come and go, never again. One week ago I was still locked up. But now I'm home. Yet even though this is my home, I can't make these terrible people go away.

Surely I'll wake up and it will be over, she told herself, closing her eyes. But of course it didn't help a bit.

She opened them and looked about her. The police had finished searching this room, had lifted the cushions of the couch and opened all the drawers of the side tables, had run their hands down the window draperies in case something was hidden in the folds.

She realized they were spending a long time in the kitchen, no doubt going through every drawer, every cabinet. She had overheard someone say they should collect any carving knives they found.

She had overheard the older investigator tell the younger officer to seize the outfit and shoes that the waitress had described her as wearing.

Now she could only wait. Wait for the police to leave, and wait for her life to return to normal—whatever that might be.

But I can't just sit here, Molly thought. I have to get out of here. Where can I go that people won't point fingers at me, won't whisper about me, and where the media will leave me alone?

Dr. Daniels. I need to talk to him, Molly decided. He'll help me.

It was five o'clock. Would he still be in his office? she wondered. Funny, I still remember his number, she thought. Even though it's been nearly six years.

When the phone rang, Ruthie Roitenberg was just locking her desk, and Dr. Daniels was reaching into the closet for his coat. They looked at each other.

"Do you want to let the service pick it up?" Ruthie asked. "As of now, Dr. MacLean is on call."

John Daniels was tired. He'd had a difficult session with one of his most troubled patients and felt every day of his seventy-five years. He was looking forward to getting home, thanking heaven that the dinner party he and his wife had planned to attend had been canceled.

Some instinct, however, told him he should take the call. "At least find out who it is, Ruthie," he said.

He saw the shock in Ruthie's eyes when she looked up at him and mouthed, "Molly Lasch." For a moment, he seemed unsure as to what to do and stood with his coat still in his hand as Ruthie said, "I'm afraid the doctor may already be gone, Mrs. Lasch. He just went out to the elevator. I'll see if I can catch him."

Molly Lasch. Daniels paused for a moment, then walked to the desk and took the phone from Ruthie. "I heard about Annamarie Scalli, Molly. How can I help you?"

He listened, and thirty minutes later Molly was in his office.

"I'm sorry to have taken so long getting here, Doctor. I went to get my car, but the police wouldn't let me take it. I had to call a taxi."

Molly's tone was one of bewilderment, as if she herself didn't believe what she was saying. Her eyes made Daniels think of the cliché of the deer caught in the headlights, although she was clearly more than merely startled. No, she seemed almost *haunted.* He realized immediately that she was in danger of slipping into the same lethargic state that had come over her after Gary Lasch's death.

"Why don't you rest on the couch while we talk, Molly," he suggested. She was seated in the chair opposite his desk. When she did not respond, he crossed to her and put his hand under her elbow. He could feel the rigidity of her body. "Come on, Molly," he coaxed as he urged her to stand.

She allowed herself to be guided by him. "I know how late it is. You're very kind to see me now, Doctor."

Daniels was reminded of the beautifully mannered little girl he had watched at the club. A golden child, he thought, the perfect product of breeding and quiet wealth. Whoever then would have dreamt that this moment was waiting in her future, suspected of a crime—a *second* crime—the police searching her home for evidence to use against her. He shook his head ruefully.

For the next hour she tried to explain aloud—for her own benefit as well as his—exactly why she had needed to talk to Annamarie.

"What is it, Molly? Tell me what you're thinking."

"It's that I realize now that when I ran away that week, up to Cape Cod, I went because I was angry. But I wasn't angry because I'd found out about Annamarie. In truth, Doctor, I wasn't at all angry because Gary was involved with another woman. I was angry because I had lost my baby and *she* was still pregnant. *I should have had that baby.*"

With a sinking heart, John Daniels waited for Molly to continue.

"Doctor, I wanted to see Annamarie because I thought that if I didn't kill Gary, then maybe she was the one who did. Nobody could prove where *she* was that night. And I knew she was angry with him; it was obvious from her voice when I overheard her talking to him on the phone."

"Did you ask her about that when you met her last night?"

"Yes. And I believed her when she said she didn't kill him. But she told me that Gary was glad I had lost the baby, that he was going to ask for a divorce, and that the baby would have complicated everything."

"Men often tell the other woman that they're planning to get a divorce. Much of the time it's not true."

"I know that, and maybe he *was* lying to her. But he wasn't lying when he told her that he was glad I'd lost my baby."

"Annamarie told you that?"

"Yes."

"How did that make you feel?"

"Doctor, that's what scares me so much. I think that at that moment I hated her with every drop of blood in my body, just for even saying those words."

With every drop of blood in my body, Daniels thought.

Molly suddenly started talking very rapidly. "You know what went through my mind, Doctor? That line from the Bible, *'Rachel mourned her lost children and would not be comforted.'* I thought of how I had mourned my baby. I had just felt life stirring in me, and then I lost it. In that moment I became Rachel, and the anger drained away and I was in mourning."

Molly sighed, and when she continued, all emotion had been drained from her voice. "Doctor, Annamarie left ahead of me. She was gone when I got to the parking lot. My very clear memory is that I came home and went to bed early."

" 'Very clear memory,' Molly?"

"Doctor, the cops are searching my house. The detectives tried to talk with me this morning. Philip ordered me not to tell anyone, not even Jen, what Annamarie Scalli told me."

Her voice became agitated again. "Doctor, is it like last time? Have I done something terrible and blotted it out again? If I have, and they can prove it, I'm not going to let them put me back in prison. I'd rather be dead."

Again, Daniels thought. "Molly, since you've been home, have you had any more feelings about someone else being in the house that night Gary died?"

He watched as the tension eased from her body and a measure of hope flickered alive in her eyes. "There *was* someone in the house that night," she said. "I'm beginning to be sure of it."

And I'm beginning to be just as sure that there was no one there, Daniels thought sadly.

A few minutes later, he drove Molly home. The house was dark. She pointed out that there were no cars parked outside, no sign of the police. Daniels would not leave until Molly was safely inside, until she had turned on the foyer lights. "Be sure to take that pill I gave you tonight," he cautioned. "We'll talk tomorrow."

Doctor Daniels waited until he heard the click of the front door lock before he walked slowly back to his car.

He did not believe that she had yet reached the point where she would harm herself. But if evidence was found to justify an indictment against her in Annamarie Scalli's death, he knew that Molly Lasch might choose another way to escape reality. Not dissociative amnesia this time, but death.

He drove home slowly, sadly, to his very late dinner.

43

When Fran reached the office on Tuesday morning, she found a message marked "urgent" from Billy Gallo. It stated simply that he was Tim Mason's friend, and he would like her to please call him on a very important matter.

When she called him back, Gallo picked up on the first ring and got directly to the point. "Ms. Simmons, my mother was buried yesterday. She died from a major heart attack that could and should have been prevented. I hear that you're doing a story on the murder of Dr. Gary Lasch, and I wanted to ask you to expand it to include an investigation into the so-called medical insurance plan he started."

"Tim told me about your mother, and I'm truly sorry for your loss," Fran said, "but I'm sure there is a procedure whereby you can register a complaint if you feel that she wasn't cared for properly."

"Oh, but you know the runaround you get when you try to register complaints, Ms. Simmons," Billy Gallo said. "Look, I'm a musician and I can't afford to lose my job, which unfortunately is with a show in Detroit. I've got to get back there soon. I talked to Roy Kirkwood, my mother's primary care physician, and he told me he had made an urgent recommendation that further tests be done. But guess what? The request was denied. He strongly believed that more could have been done for my mother, but they wouldn't even let him try. Please talk to him, Ms. Simmons. I went in to his office ready to bash his head in, and I came out feeling sorry for him. Dr. Kirkwood is only in his early sixties, but he told me he's closing his practice and taking early retirement. *That's* how disgusted he is with Remington Health Management."

Bash his head in, Fran thought. The wild thought went through her mind that there just might be one chance in a million that a relative of some patient might have felt that way about Gary Lasch.

"Give me Dr. Kirkwood's phone number and address," she said. "I'll talk to him."

At eleven o'clock that morning she was once again turning off the Merritt Parkway into Greenwich.

Molly had agreed to have lunch with her at one o'clock, but despite Fran's pleading, she would not leave the house. "I *can't,*" she said simply. "I feel too exposed. Everyone would just stare at me. It would be awful. I can't do it."

She accepted Fran's offer to pick up a quiche at the bakery in town and bring it with her. "Mrs. Barry isn't here on Tuesday," she'd explained, "and the police towed my car, so I can't get out to shop."

The only good news so far, Fran thought, is that Mrs. Barry won't be hanging around when Molly and I have lunch. It would be nice for once to talk to Molly without that woman marching in and out of the room every two minutes.

But she *did* want to see Edna Barry, and her first stop once she reached Greenwich was an unannounced visit to her home.

I'm going to be direct with her, Fran decided as she consulted her directions to Barry's house. For some unknown reason Edna Barry is hostile to Molly and afraid of me. Maybe I can find out what her problem is.

The best laid plans of mice and men, she thought as she stood on the narrow top step of Edna Barry's home and rang the doorbell. There was no answer, and Barry's red Subaru was not in the driveway.

Disappointed, Fran debated the wisdom of slipping a note under the door that stated that she had stopped by because it was important they talk. She knew such a message would upset Mrs. Barry, and that was fine. It was her intention to get the woman rattled.

Then again, would a note only serve to warn her and make her even more wary? she wondered. There's no question she's holding something back, and it could be terribly important. I don't want to risk scaring her off.

As Fran debated what to do, a call rang out:
"Yoo-hoooo."

She turned to see a woman in her fifties with a beehive hairdo
and harlequin glasses rushing across the lawn from the house next
door.

"Edna should be back soon," the woman explained breathlessly as she reached Fran. "Her son, Wally, was feeling pretty upset
today, so Edna took him to the doctor. When Wally doesn't take his
medicine, he's a real problem. Why don't you just wait for her in
my house? I'm Marta Jones, Edna's neighbor."

"That's very nice of you," Fran said sincerely. "Mrs. Barry
wasn't expecting me, but I really would like to wait for her." And I
would *love* to talk with *you,* she added to herself. "I'm Fran Simmons."

Marta Jones suggested they wait in the television room, which
obviously had originally been part of the porch. "It's so nice and
cheerful, and we'll be able to see Edna when she comes home," she
explained as she brought in steaming cups of freshly brewed coffee.

"I like coffee best when it's made in the old-fashioned percola-
tor," she explained. "Doesn't taste the same from all those new
machines." She settled back in the armchair opposite Fran. "It's just
too bad Edna had to take Wally to the doctor today. At least she
didn't have to take time off from her job. She works for Molly
Lasch three mornings a week—Monday, Wednesday, and Friday."

Fran nodded, happy to store that bit of information in her head.

"You may have heard about Molly Lasch," Marta Jones said.
"She's the woman who just got out of prison after serving time for
killing her husband, and now the rumor is that she's going to be
arrested for killing her husband's girlfriend. Have you heard of her,
Ms. . . . I'm sorry, I didn't get your last name."

"It's Simmons, Fran Simmons."

She saw the look in Marta Jones's eyes and knew what was
going through her head. *Fran Simmons. She's that television
reporter and the daughter of the man who stole the library fund
money and shot himself.* Fran braced herself, but Marta Jones's
expression changed to one of sympathy. "I won't pretend I don't
know about your father," she said quietly. "I was so sorry for you
and your mother at that time."

"Thank you."

"And now you're on television, and you're doing a program on Molly. So of course you know all about her."

"That's right."

"Well, maybe Edna will listen to you. Is it okay if I call you Fran?"

"Of course."

"I laid awake all last night, wondering if it isn't dangerous for Edna to work for Molly Lasch. I mean, it was one thing for her to kill her husband. That was temporary insanity, I'm sure. I mean, he was cheating on her that way and everything. But if less than a week after she gets out of prison she stabs her husband's girlfriend to death, I say she's out of control."

Fran thought of what Gus Brandt had said about Molly. The idea that she's a crazed, out-of-control killer is going to reach epidemic proportions, she realized.

"I'll tell you this," Marta continued. "I wouldn't want to be alone for hours in a house with that kind of person. This morning when I talked to Edna—when she was on her way to the doctor with Wally—I said, 'Edna, what would happen to Wally if Molly Lasch goes nuts and hits you over the head or stabs you to death? Who would take care of *him?*' "

"Does Wally require much care?"

"As long as he takes his medicine, he's pretty good. But when he *doesn't* take it and gets balky, well, Wally becomes a different person, sometimes a little out of control. Just yesterday he took the key to Molly Lasch's house off Edna's key ring. He wanted to go visit her. Of course Edna made him put it right back."

"He took the *key* to Molly Lasch's house?" Fran tried to keep her voice level. "Has he ever done that before?"

"Oh, I don't think so. Edna doesn't allow him to go there. Dr. Lasch was so fussy about his collection of early-American art. Some of it apparently was quite valuable. I do know though that Wally stopped in there once and picked up something he shouldn't have, and Edna was a wreck. He didn't break anything, but it was a valuable piece, and apparently Dr. Lasch just went on like a mad man about it, yelling and ordering him out of the house. Wally didn't like that at all . . . Oh look, there's Edna now."

They caught up with Edna Barry as she was opening her front door. The stricken look on Mrs. Barry's face when she saw Fran with Marta Jones was further confirmation to Fran that the woman had something to hide.

"Go inside, Wally," she snapped at her son.

Fran barely got a glimpse at the tall, good-looking man in his thirties before Edna shoved him into the house and pulled the door closed.

When she turned to face Fran, anger flushed her cheeks and made her voice tremble. "Miss Simmons," she said, "I don't know why you're here, but it's been a very difficult morning for me, and I can't talk to you now."

"Oh, Edna," Marta Jones asked, "isn't Wally any calmer?"

"Wally's *fine,*" Edna Barry said sharply, her voice registering a mixture of fear and anger. "Marta, I hope you haven't been filling Miss Simmons's ears with mean gossip about him."

"Edna, how can you say that? Nobody's a better friend to Wally than I am."

Tears filled Edna Barry's eyes. "I know. I know. It's just so hard . . . You have to excuse me. I'll call you, Marta."

For a moment Fran and Marta Jones stood on the steps, looking at the door Edna Barry had just closed in their faces. "Edna's not a rude person," Marta said quietly. "It's just that she's had a hard time of it. First Wally's father died, and then Dr. Morrow. Then right after that, Dr. Lasch was murdered, and—"

"Dr. Morrow?" Fran queried, interrupting Marta Jones. "What did he have to do with Edna Barry?"

"Oh, he was Wally's primary care physician and was really great at handling him. He was also real nice. If Wally started refusing to take his medicine, or made any kind of trouble, all Edna had to do was call Dr. Morrow."

"Dr. Morrow," Fran said. "You are talking about Dr. *Jack* Morrow?"

"Yes. Did you know him?"

"Yes, I did." Fran thought again about the kind young man who, fourteen years earlier, had embraced her when he broke the news of her father's death.

"If you remember, he was murdered in a robbery only two weeks before Dr. Lasch died," Marta said sadly.

"I imagine that upset Wally?"

"Don't ask. It was awful. And I guess it was right after that when Dr. Lasch yelled at him. Poor Wally. People don't understand. It's not his fault he's the way he is."

No, Fran thought as she thanked Marta Jones for her hospitality and got into her car. But people not only don't understand; they may not even *know* about the extent of Wally's problems. Could Edna Barry be covering up something? Is it conceivable that she allowed Molly to be convicted of a crime her son actually committed?

Was it possible that it had happened that way?

44

The sleeping pill Dr. Daniels had given Molly had been highly effective. She had taken it at ten o'clock the night before, and she'd slept until eight this morning. It had been a deep, heavy sleep, from which she emerged somewhat groggy, but refreshed.

She put on a robe and set out to get coffee and juice, which she would bring upstairs to bed; once settled in, she would try to put everything in focus. But even before she reached the kitchen, she realized that first she had to take care of the disorder she saw all about her in the house.

Though they had made an effort to put things right, the police had changed the whole *feeling* of the house. It was subtle, but Molly recognized all the changes. Everything they had touched or moved was askew, out of order, not right.

The harmony of her home, the remembrance of which had been her surcease in those days and nights in prison, was gone and had to be restored.

After a quick shower, she donned jeans, sneakers, and an old sweatshirt and was ready for work. The temptation to call Mrs. Barry and ask her to help came and went swiftly. It's *my* house, Molly told herself. Let me put it back together myself.

My life may be out of control, she despaired as she filled the sink with hot water and poured in liquid soap, but I can still get myself together enough to reclaim my house.

It isn't that there are terrible stains anywhere, just some finger marks and smudges, she thought as she rearranged the dishes they had moved and straightened the pots and pans so that they were again lined up just so.

Having the police run roughshod through the house was like a surprise inspection of my cell, she thought. She remembered the strident sound of feet marching down the cell block corridor, the order to stand against the wall, being made to watch as her bed was taken apart as they searched for drugs.

She did not realize that she had started crying until she rubbed her cheek with the back of her hand and a soap bubble got in her eye.

There's another reason for being glad Mrs. Barry is off today, she thought. I don't have to bury my emotions. I can let it out. Dr. Daniels would give me an A plus.

She'd been polishing the foyer table with butcher's wax when Fran Simmons called at 9:30.

Why did I agree to have lunch with her? Molly asked herself as she replaced the receiver.

But she knew why. Despite what Philip had cautioned, she wanted to tell Fran that for some reason Annamarie Scalli had seemed afraid.

And not of me, Molly thought. She wasn't afraid of me, even though she was convinced I killed Gary.

O God, O God, why are You letting this happen to me? she asked silently as she collapsed onto one of the bottom stairs.

Now she heard her own sobs. I am *so* alone, she thought, *so* alone. She remembered her mom on the phone yesterday: "Dear, you're right, it's better we don't come up yet."

I wanted Mom to say they were on their way to be with me, Molly thought. I need them here, *now.* I need someone to help me.

At 10:30 the doorbell rang. She tiptoed to the door, leaned against it and waited. I'm not going to answer it, she thought. Whoever is there has got to think I'm not home.

Then she heard a voice. "Molly, open up. It's me."

With a sob of relief, Molly unlocked the door and a moment later began crying uncontrollably as she was hugged by Jenna.

"Good friend, best friend," Jenna said, tears of sympathy in her eyes. "What can I do to help?"

Still sobbing, Molly nonetheless managed a laugh. "Turn the clock back a dozen years," she said, "and don't introduce me to Gary Lasch. Failing that, just be around for me."

"Philip isn't here yet?"

"He said he surely would be here at some point. He had to go to court."

"Molly, you've got to call him. Cal got a tip. They found a trace of Annamarie Scalli's blood on the ankle boots you were wearing Sunday night, and also in your car. I'm sorry. Cal hears that the prosecutor is going to have you arrested."

45

After Calvin Whitehall got a call tipping him off that traces of Annamarie Scalli's blood had been found on Molly Lasch's shoe and in her car, he went immediately to Dr. Peter Black's office.

"We've got a brand-new three-ring circus in the making," he announced to Black, then paused as he scrutinized him closely. "You don't seem that upset about it."

"Am I upset that Annamarie Scalli, a potential troublemaker, isn't out there anymore? No, I'm not," Peter said, a look of smug satisfaction on his face.

"You told me there wasn't a shred of proof of anything, and that if she had talked, she would have incriminated herself in the process."

"Yes, I did say that, and it's still accurate. Nevertheless, I find myself suddenly very grateful to Molly. Sordid as all this publicity will become, it has nothing to do with either one of us, or the hospital, or Remington Health Management."

Whitehall considered his partner's words.

Peter Black always had been intrigued by Cal's ability to sit both very still and very quiet when he was concentrating. It was as though his powerful body became rocklike in its stillness.

Finally, Cal Whitehall nodded in assent. "That's an excellent point, Peter."

"How is Jenna taking all this?"

"Jenna is with Molly right now."

"Is that wise?"

"Jenna understands that I will not tolerate photographs of her linked arm-in-arm with Molly showing up in the newspapers at this time. Once the merger is complete, she can be as helpful to Molly as she chooses. Until then, she's got to keep a certain distance."

"How much help *can* she be, Cal? If Molly goes to trial again, even that hotshot lawyer won't be able to get her the kind of deal he got from the prosecutor last time."

"I'm aware of that. But you must understand, Jenna and Molly are like sisters. I admire Jenna's loyalty, even while I have to keep it reined in at the moment."

Black looked at his watch impatiently. "When did he say he'd call?"

"It should be any minute now."

"It had better be. Roy Kirkwood is coming in. He lost a patient the other day and blames it on the system. The patient's son is on the warpath."

"Kirkwood is immune to a lawsuit. He did want extra tests. We can handle the patient's son."

"It isn't about money."

"Everything's about money, Peter."

Peter Black's private phone rang. He picked up the receiver, listened for a moment, then touched the conference button and lowered the volume. "Cal is here, and we're ready, Doctor," he said, his tone respectful.

"Good morning, Doctor," Cal's commanding voice had no trace of its customary arrogance.

"Congratulations, gentlemen. I believe we have achieved another breakthrough," the voice on the other end of the line said, "and if I'm right, all other accomplishments will pale by comparison."

46

When Fran arrived at Molly's home at one o'clock, it was immediately obvious to her that Molly had been crying. Her eyes were swollen, and even though she was wearing light makeup, there were traces of blotches on her cheeks.

"Come in, Fran. Philip got here a little while ago. He's in the kitchen, watching me make a salad."

So Philip's here, Fran thought. I wonder what brought him up here in such a hurry? Whatever it is, I bet he won't be happy to see me on the scene.

As they walked down the hall to the kitchen, Molly said, "Jenna was here this morning. She had to leave just a few minutes ago to meet Cal for lunch, but you know what she did, Fran? She pitched in and helped me get the house cleaned up. Maybe the police should have to take a course in how to execute a search warrant without leaving a mess."

Molly's voice was brittle. She sounds like she's on the verge of hysteria or a breakdown, Fran thought.

It was obvious that Philip Matthews had come to the same conclusion. His eyes followed Molly constantly as she moved about the room, as she took the quiche from the box and put it in the oven. The entire time, she continued to speak in the same rapid, edgy voice. "Apparently they found Annamarie's blood on the boots I was wearing Sunday night, Fran. And a trace of her blood in my car."

Fran exchanged a heartsick glance with Philip Matthews, certain that his expression of concern was a mirror of her own.

"Who knows? Maybe this will be my last meal in this house for a while—isn't that right, Philip?" Molly asked.

"No, it isn't," he replied, his voice tense.

"Meaning that after I'm arrested, I'll get out on bail again. Well, that's the nice thing about having money, isn't it? Lucky people like me can just write a check."

"*Stop* it, Molly," Fran snapped. She crossed to her friend and grabbed her shoulders. "I started my investigation with the premise that you killed your husband," she said. "Then I began to have doubts. I felt that the police should have done more digging in their investigation of Gary's death, perhaps considered a couple of other possibilities. But I admit I was troubled that you were so intent on finding Annamarie Scalli. And then you found her, and now she's dead. So while I'm still not *sure* if you're a pathological killer, I continue to have very real doubts. I think there is some crazy web of intrigue going on around here, and you've been caught in it, like someone trapped in a maze. Of course, I may be wrong. You *may* be what ninety-nine percent of the world seems to think you are, but I swear to you I'm in the one percent zone. I'm going to go for broke to prove you are innocent of the deaths of both Gary Lasch and Annamarie Scalli."

"And if you're wrong?" Molly asked.

"If I'm wrong, Molly, I'll do my best to see that you are placed in a facility where you can be comfortable and secure and be treated."

Molly's eyes brightened with unshed tears. "I will not get weepy again," she said. "Fran, you're the first and only person who has indicated any willingness to pursue the possibility that I may be innocent." She glanced over at Philip. "Including you, my dear Philip, who I know would slay tigers for me. And including Jenna, who would put her hand in the fire for me, and including my parents, who if they thought I was innocent would be here right now, raising hell. I think—and hope—I am innocent of these two deaths. If I'm not, I can promise you I won't be around to trouble people much longer."

Fran and Philip Matthews exchanged glances. By unspoken agreement they did not comment on what to both of them was an implied suicide threat.

Grace under pressure, Fran thought as Molly served the quiche from an exquisite Limoges plate with a slender stem and gold base. The delicately patterned floral place mats on the breakfast room table matched the wall hanging.

The wall facing the garden had a large bay window. A few green shoots visible outside hinted at the approaching end of winter. At the hilly end of the deep property, Fran noticed the rock garden and was reminded of something she wanted to discuss with Molly.

"Molly, I asked you something about house keys the other day. Did you say something about a spare key?"

"We always hid one back there." Molly gestured in the direction of the rock garden. "One of those rocks is a phony. Clever, don't you think? At least it beats having a ceramic Peter Rabbit with a detachable ear perched on the porch, in charge of the 'in case' key."

" 'In case'?" Philip queried.

"In case you forget the key."

"Did you ever forget your key, Molly?" Fran asked casually.

"Fran, you know I'm a good girl," Molly replied with a mock-serious smile. "I always do everything right. Why, everybody always said so. You must remember that from school."

"Yes, and they said it because it was true," Fran responded.

"I used to wonder what it would be like if the path hadn't been made so smooth for me. I understood that it was, you know. I knew that I had it easy, that I was privileged. I admired you so much when we were in school, because you worked for things you wanted. I remember that when you started playing basketball, you were still a runt, but you were so fast and determined, and you made the team."

Molly Carpenter admired *me!* Fran thought. I didn't think she even knew I was alive.

"And then, when your father died, I felt so terrible for you. I knew people always defer to my father, and they should—he naturally attracts and deserves respect; he was and is a wonderful father. But your dad was able to *show* how proud he was of you. It was both in him to do that, and you gave him the opportunity—which was never the case for me. God, I remember the look on your father's face when you scored the winning basket that last game of our senior year. It was great!"

Don't, Molly, Fran wanted to beg. Please don't.

"I'm sorry so many things went wrong for him, Fran. Maybe it was like it is for me. A chain of events that we can't control." Molly put down her fork. "Fran, the quiche is wonderful. I'm just not hungry."

"Molly, did Gary ever forget his key?" Fran asked. Without looking at him, she felt Philip Matthews's stare, his unspoken command to not pester Molly with questions.

"Gary? Forget? Heavens no. Gary was perfect. He used to tell me that one of the things he loved about me was that I was so predictable. Unlike most women, I was never late, never locked the keys in the car, never forgot my key ring. I got an A plus for that." She paused, then smiled faintly, as though remembering. "Funny, did you notice how today I'm thinking in school terms? Grades. Marks. Plus or minus."

Molly pushed back her chair and began to shiver. Alarmed, Fran rushed to her side. Just then the phone rang.

"It's got to be Mother and Dad, or Jenna." Molly's voice was almost too low to be understood.

Philip Matthews picked up the phone. "It's Dr. Daniels, Molly. He wants to know how you are."

Fran answered for Molly. "She needs help. Ask him if he can come over and talk to her."

After a few moments of a whispered exchange, Matthews hung up the receiver and turned to the two women. "He'll be right over," he promised. "Molly, why don't you lie down until he gets here. You look pretty shaky."

"I *feel* pretty shaky."

"Come on." Philip Matthews put an arm around Molly and pulled her against him as he led her from the breakfast room.

I might as well clean up, Fran thought as she looked at the mostly untouched meal. I'm certain nobody is going to want to eat anything now.

When Matthews came back, she asked, "What's going to happen?"

"If the lab tests on any of the items they took connect her in any way to Annamarie's death, she'll be arrested. We should know very soon."

"Oh, dear God."

"Fran, I bullied Molly into keeping back most of her conversation with Annamarie Scalli. Some of it was terribly hurtful and would sound like reason for her to hate Annamarie. I'm going to take a gamble now and tell you everything she told me, in hopes that you may help her. I believe you when you say you're out to prove her innocence."

"Which you yourself are not convinced of, right?" Fran said levelly.

"I'm convinced she isn't responsible for either death."

"That's not the same thing."

"Fran, first of all, Annamarie told Molly that Gary said he was relieved when she lost the baby; he said it would have just complicated things. Then she said she overheard Gary Lasch and Dr. Jack Morrow having a serious quarrel only a few days before Morrow was murdered. Dr. Morrow then talked to Annamarie about holding a very important file for him for safekeeping, but he died before he gave it to her. Molly told me that she had the distinct impression Annamarie knew something she wasn't telling, and that she was very fearful."

"Fearful for her *own* safety?"

"That's Molly's impression."

"Well, it's something to go on. And I've got something else I want to look into. Mrs. Barry's son, Wally, a young man with deep emotional and mental problems, was desperately upset by Dr. Morrow's death, and for some reason I haven't yet uncovered, he also was very angry at Gary Lasch. In addition he seems to have a particular interest in Molly. Only yesterday he took the key to this house off his mother's key ring."

The doorbell rang. "I'll get it," Fran said. "It's probably Dr. Daniels."

She opened the door to find two men holding out their shields and ID cards for her to read. The older one said, "We have a warrant for the arrest of Molly Carpenter Lasch. Will you take us to her, please?"

Fifteen minutes later the first cameramen were on the scene to record Molly Lasch, her hands cuffed behind her, her coat thrown over her shoulders, her head down, her hair falling forward over her face, as she was led from her house to a car from the state attorney's office. From there she was driven to the courthouse in Stamford where, in a replay of the events of nearly six years ago, she was booked on a charge of murder.

47

Feeling every day of her sixty-five years, Edna Barry waited for the evening news to come on as she sipped a cup of tea—her third in the last hour. Wally had gone to his room to nap, and she prayed that by the time he awakened the medicine would have kicked in, and he'd be feeling better. It had been a bad day, with the voices that he alone heard tormenting him. Driving home from the doctor's, he had slammed the car radio with his fist because he thought that the newsman was talking about him.

At least she had been able to make him go into the house before Fran Simmons could see just how terribly agitated he was this morning. But how much had Marta told Simmons about Wally?

Edna knew that Marta would never intentionally do anything to hurt Wally, but Fran Simmons was a smart cookie and already had begun asking questions about the extra key to Molly's house.

Yesterday, Marta had seen Wally take the key to Molly's house from Edna's pocketbook and heard him say that *this* time he would put it back. *Don't* let Marta have told that to Fran Simmons, Edna prayed.

Her mind flashed back to that terrible morning she had found Dr. Lasch's body, to the fear she had felt since, every time a key was mentioned. When the police asked me about keys to the house, I gave them the key I'd taken from the hiding place in the garden, Edna remembered. I hadn't been able to find my own key to the house that morning, and I was so afraid that Wally had taken it, a fear that she later found had been justified. She'd been terrified that the police would ask her more about the key, but fortunately they hadn't.

Edna focused on the television set as the news began. Shocked, she learned that Molly had been arrested on a charge of murder, arraigned in court, and minutes ago released on one million dollars bail under house arrest. The camera cut to Fran Simmons, live in front of the parking lot of the Sea Lamp Diner in Rowayton. The lot was still roped off with that yellow crime-scene tape.

"It is here that Annamarie Scalli was stabbed to death," Fran was saying, "a crime for which Molly Carpenter Lasch was arrested this afternoon. It has been reported that traces of Annamarie Scalli's blood were found on the sole of one of Lasch's shoes and in her car."

"Mom, is Molly all bloody again?"

Edna turned to see Wally standing behind her, his hair disheveled, his eyes bright with anger.

"Now don't say things like that, Wally," she said nervously.

"The statue of the horse and cowboy I picked up that time, remember that?"

"Wally, don't talk about it, please don't."

"I just want to tell you about it is all," he said petulantly.

"Wally, we're *not* going to talk about it."

"But *everybody's* talking about it, Mom. Just now, in my room, they were yelling in my head—all of them. They talked about the statue. It wasn't too heavy for me because I'm strong, but it was too heavy for Molly to lift."

The voices that tormented him were back, Edna thought with dismay. The medicine wasn't working.

Edna got up, went to her son, and pressed her hands to his temples. "Shhh," she said soothingly. "No more talk about Molly or the statue. You know how mixed-up your voices get you, dear. Promise me you won't say another word about the statue or about Dr. Lasch or Molly. Okay? Now let's get you one more pill."

48

Fran finished her segment of the broadcast and turned off her microphone. Tonight, Pat Lyons, a young cameraman, had come up from New York to tape her at the Sea Lamp Diner. "I like this town," he said. "Here by the water it reminds me of a fishing village."

"It *is* a nice town," Fran agreed, remembering how when she was younger she occasionally had visited a friend in Rowayton. Although it's a cinch the Sea Lamp isn't where the elite meet to eat, she thought as she looked at the somewhat seedy-looking diner. Nevertheless she intended to go in there for dinner. Despite the events of the last couple of days, and the presence of the crime scene tape and yellow chalk marks to indicate the location of Annamarie Scalli's car, the place was open for business.

Fran already had ascertained that Gladys Fluegel, the waitress who waited on Molly and Annamarie Scalli, was on duty tonight. She'd have to be sure to get one of her tables.

She was surprised to find the diner was half full, but then she realized it probably was because of the curiosity generated by the murder and all the ensuing publicity. She stood for a moment in the entrance, wondering if she was more likely to have a chance to chat with Fluegel if she sat at the counter. The problem was solved, however, by the waitress herself, who came rushing up to her. "You're Fran Simmons. We were watching you doing the broadcast. I'm Gladys Fluegel. I waited on Molly Lasch and Annamarie Scalli the other night. They were sitting right there." She pointed to an empty booth at the far end of the diner.

It was obvious to Fran that Gladys was more than anxious to tell her story. "I'd really like to have a few words with you," Fran said. "Maybe if I take that same table you can join me. Do you have a break coming up?"

"Give me ten minutes," Fluegel said. "I'll light a fire under them." She nodded to an elderly couple at a window table. "She's mad because he wants veal parmigiana, and she says it always gives him gas. I'll tell them to make up their minds; once I get their order in, I'll sit down with you."

Fran paced the distance as she walked to the end booth. About forty feet from the entrance, she decided. While she waited for Gladys to be free, she studied the interior of the diner. It was poorly lit to begin with, and the table was in the shadows, which made it a natural choice for someone who didn't want to be noticed. Molly had told Philip that Annamarie seemed fearful when they talked, but not of her. What was it she was afraid of? Fran wondered.

And why did Annamarie change her name? Was it just because she thought that the notoriety surrounding Gary Lasch's murder would follow her? Or did she have another reason for trying to drop out of sight?

According to Molly, Annamarie had left the diner first, then Molly paid the check and followed her. How much time did that take? It couldn't have been long, because otherwise it was logical for Molly to believe that Annamarie would have driven away already. But it had to be long enough for Annamarie to cross the parking lot and to get in her Jeep.

Molly says she called to her from the door, Fran thought. Did she catch up with her?

"Guess what they're both having?" Gladys said, pointing her thumb over her shoulder in the direction of the elderly couple. "Broiled flounder and spinach. She ordered for both of 'em. He's having a fit, poor guy."

She dropped a menu in front of Fran. "Specials tonight are fricasseed chicken breast and Hungarian goulash."

I'll have a hamburger at P. J. Clarke's when I get back to New

York, Fran decided, then murmured something about having a late dinner date and ordered a roll and coffee.

When Gladys returned with the order, she sat down. "I've got about two minutes," she said. "This is where Molly Lasch was sitting. That Annamarie Scalli was in your seat. As I told the detectives yesterday, Scalli was nervous—I swear she was *afraid* of Lasch. Then, when Scalli got up to go, Molly Lasch grabbed her wrist. Scalli had to pull away from her, and then she got out of here real fast, like she was afraid Molly Lasch would chase her, which of course is what she did. I mean how many women toss down a five-dollar bill to pay for a cup of tea and a coffee that cost a dollar thirty? I tell you, it gives me nightmares to think that just seconds after she left my table, that Scalli woman was dead." She sighed. "I guess I'm just going to have to face being a witness at the trial."

You're dying to testify, Fran thought. "Were there other waitresses here on Sunday night?" she asked.

"Honey, on Sunday night in this joint you don't need two waitresses. Actually I'm supposed to be off Sundays, but the regular girl called in sick, and guess who got stuck? On the other hand, it was very interesting to be here with so much going on."

"What about a chef or someone at the counter? There must have been that kind of help in here."

"Oh sure, the chef was around, although I tell you, it stretches the meaning of the word to call that bird a 'chef.' But he wasn't out here—he's always in the back. See no evil, hear no evil. If you get what I mean."

"Who was behind the counter?"

"Bobby Burke, a college kid. He works on weekends."

"I'd like to talk to him."

"He lives on Yarmouth Street in Belle Island. That's just over the little bridge down two blocks from here. He's Robert Burke, Jr. They're in the phone book. Did you want to interview me on television or something?"

"When I am taping the program on Molly Lasch, I would like to talk to you," Fran said.

"It will be my pleasure to oblige you."

I bet it will be, Fran thought.

Fran called the Burke residence from her car phone. At first Bobby Burke's father flatly refused to allow her to speak with his son. "Bobby has made a statement to the police that contained everything he had to say. He hardly noticed either woman come or go. He could not see the parking lot from the counter."

"Mr. Burke," Fran begged. "I'm going to be flat-out honest with you. I'm only five minutes away. I just spoke to Gladys Fluegel and I'm concerned that her interpretation of the meeting between Molly Lasch and Annamarie Scalli may be a little distorted. I'm a reporter, but I'm also a friend of Molly Lasch's. We went to school together. In the name of simple fairness, I appeal to you. She needs help."

"Hold on."

When Burke got back on the phone, he said, "Okay, Ms. Simmons, you can come over and talk to Bobby, but I insist on staying in the room with you. Let me give you directions to the house."

He's the kind of kid any parent would be proud of, Fran thought as she sat with Bobby Burke in the living room of his modest home. He was a skinny eighteen-year-old, with a shock of light brown hair and intelligent brown eyes. His manner was diffident, and he occasionally glanced at his father for guidance, but there was a hint of humor in his eyes when he answered some of Fran's questions, and especially when he spoke about Gladys.

"It wasn't busy, so I did see the two ladies come in," he said. "I mean, they came in separately, just a few minutes apart. It was kind of funny. Gladys always tries to put people at a table near the counter so she doesn't have to carry the order too far, but the first lady wasn't having any of that. She pointed to the back booth."

"Did you think she seemed nervous?"

"I really couldn't tell."

"You say you weren't busy?"

"That's right. There were just a few people at the counter. Although just before the women left, a couple came in and took a table. Gladys was back with the women when this couple showed up."

"Was she still waiting on them?"

"Writing the check. But she took her sweet time. She's naturally nosy and likes to know what's going on. I remember that the new couple started getting annoyed and called to her. That was just as the second lady was leaving."

"Bobby, did you think the first woman to leave—the one who then was killed in the parking lot—ran out as though she was nervous, or afraid?"

"She was moving pretty fast, but she wasn't really running."

"What about the second woman? You must know that her name is Molly Lasch?"

"Yes, I know that."

"Did you see her leave?"

"Yes."

"Was she running?"

"She was moving pretty fast too. But I got the impression it was because she was starting to cry, and I just figured she didn't want anyone to see her. I felt sorry for her."

She was starting to cry, Fran thought. That doesn't sound like a woman in a homicidal rage.

"Bobby, did you hear her call a name as she left?"

"I thought I heard her call out to someone, but I didn't catch the name."

"Did she call a second time? Did she call 'Annamarie, wait'?"

"I didn't hear her call a second time. But then I was pouring coffee, so maybe I didn't notice."

"I just left the diner, Bobby. The counter is near the door. Don't you think if Molly Lasch had called out loudly enough for someone in a car across the parking lot to hear her, you'd have heard her too?"

He thought for a moment.

"I guess so."

"Did the police ask you about this?"

"Not really. They asked if I heard Mrs. Lasch call to the other lady at the door, and I said I thought I did."

"Bobby, who was at the counter at that time?"

"By then it was just two guys who stop in once in a while. They'd been bowling. But they were talking to each other, not paying attention to anyone else."

"Bobby, who were the people who came in and took a table and called to Gladys?"

"I don't know their names. They're about Dad and Mom's age; I see them in there once in a while. I think they go to the movies, or something, and then eat on the way home."

"Bobby, if they come in again, will you get their names and phone number for me, or if they won't give you that information, will you give them my card and ask them to phone me?"

"You bet, Ms. Simmons," Bobby said with a smile. "I like your reports on the news, and I always watch the *True Crime* program. It's great."

"I just started working on *True Crime,* but thank you," Fran said. "The Lasch case will be the subject of my first program." She got up and turned to Robert Burke, Sr. "You've been very kind to allow me to talk with Bobby," she said.

"Well, the truth is, I've been watching the news some," he said, "and I get the feeling there's a terrible rush to judgment going on in this case; obviously you feel the same way." He smiled. "Of course, I may be prejudiced. I'm a public defender."

He walked Fran to the door and opened it. "Ms. Simmons, if you're a friend of Molly Lasch, you should know something else. Today, when the police questioned Bobby, I got the feeling that all they wanted to hear was a verification of what Gladys Fluegel had told them, and I can tell you that that woman is hungry for attention. I wouldn't be surprised if she doesn't start to remember all sorts of things. I know her type. She'll tell the police anything they want to hear, and you can bet that none of it will help Molly Lasch."

49

She'd been arraigned. Fingerprinted. Photographed. She heard Philip Matthews say, "My client pleads not guilty, Your Honor." The prosecutor arguing that she might disappear and requesting house arrest. The judge saying one million dollars bail and confining her to her home.

Shivering in the holding cell. The bail paid. Like an obedient child, Molly, listless and detached, did as she was told, until finally she was in the car with Philip, who was driving her home.

His arm around her, he half carried her into the house and to the family room. He made her lie down on the sofa, put one of the decorative pillows under her head, then went hunting for a blanket and tucked it around her.

"You're shivering. Where's the starter for the fire?" he asked.

"On the mantel." She was not aware she was answering a question until she heard her own voice.

A moment later the fire blazed up, warm and comforting.

"I'm staying," Philip said. "I have my briefcase; I can work on the kitchen table. You close your eyes."

When she opened them with a start, it was seven o'clock, and Dr. Daniels was sitting beside her. "You okay, Molly?"

"Annamarie," she gasped. "I was dreaming about her."

"Do you want to tell me about it?"

"Annamarie knew something terrible was going to happen to her. That was why she hurried out of the diner. She wanted to escape her fate. Instead, she ran into it."

"You think Annamarie knew she was going to die, Molly?"

"Yes, I do."

"Why do you think Annamarie knew that?"

"Doctor, that was part of the dream. You know the fable of the man who was told he was going to meet death that night in Damascus, so he rushed to Samara to hide? And a stranger came up to him in the street there and said, 'I am Death. I thought our appointment was in Damascus'?" She grasped Dr. Daniels's hands. "It was all so real."

"You mean there was no way Annamarie could save herself?"

"No way at all. I can't save myself either."

"Tell me about that, Molly."

"I don't really know," she whispered. "When I was in the holding cell today, and they locked that door, I kept hearing another door being locked or unlocked. Isn't that odd?"

"Was it a prison door?"

"No. But I don't know yet what door it is. The sound is part of what happened the night Gary died." She sighed and, pushing the blanket away, sat up. "Oh God, why can't I remember? If I could, maybe I'd have a chance."

"Molly, it's a good sign that you're retrieving specific incidents or sounds."

"Is it?" she said wanly.

The doctor studied Molly carefully. He could see the effects of the recent stress in her face: lethargic, depressed, withdrawn; sure that her own fate was sealed. Clearly she did not want to talk any longer.

"Molly, I'd like to get together with you every day for a while. All right?"

He had expected that she might protest, but she nodded indifferently.

"I'll tell Philip I'm leaving," he said.

"He should go home too. I'm so grateful to both of you. There're not too many people hanging around these days. My father and mother, for example. They've been noticeably absent."

The doorbell rang. Dr. Daniels saw the panic in Molly's eyes. Not the police? he thought, dismayed.

"I'll get it," Philip called.

Dr. Daniels watched the relief that washed over Molly as the click of heels and a woman's voice preceded Jenna Whitehall's arrival. Her husband and Philip followed her into the room.

Dr. Daniels watched approvingly as Jenna gave Molly a brief hug and said, "Your Rent-a-Chef service is here, ma'am. No housekeeper, alas, but the mighty Calvin Whitehall himself will serve and clean up, with the able assistance of Attorney Philip Matthews."

"I'm on my way," the doctor said with a brief smile, glad Molly's friends had come to her aid and anxious himself now to be going home. He instinctively disliked Calvin Whitehall, whom he'd met only a few times. His gut instinct was that the man was a natural bully, not remotely hesitant to use his immense power, not only to achieve his goals, but to manipulate people just so he could have the pleasure of watching them twist in the wind.

He was surprised and none too pleased when Whitehall followed him to the door.

"Doctor," Whitehall said, his voice low, as though he were afraid of being overheard, "I'm glad to see you're here with Molly. She's terribly important to all of us. Do you think there is any possibility of having her declared incompetent to stand trial, or failing that, to have her judged not guilty of this second murder by reason of insanity?"

"Your question leaves no doubt that you consider Molly guilty of the death of Annamarie Scalli," Dr. Daniels said coldly.

It was obvious Whitehall was both startled and offended by the implied rebuke.

"I would hope my question reflects the measure of the affection my wife and I hold for Molly and our awareness that a long prison sentence would be tantamount to a death sentence for her."

God help the person who tangles with you, Daniels thought, noting the flush of indignation on Whitehall's cheekbones and the chipped-ice glint in his eyes. "Mr. Whitehall, I appreciate your concern. I am planning to see or talk with Molly on a daily basis, and we will simply have to take all this one day at a time." He nodded and turned to the door.

As he drove home, Dr. Daniels thought, Jenna Whitehall may be Molly's best friend, but she is married to a man who tolerates no interference and who lets no one get in his way. It occurred to him that this renewed interest in the scandal surrounding the death of Gary Lasch, the founder of Remington Health Management, surely wasn't a welcome turn of events to Remington's chairman of the board.

Is Whitehall in Molly's home as the husband of her best friend, or is he there because he's trying to figure the best plan for damage control? Daniels wondered.

Jenna had brought asparagus au gratin, rack of lamb, tiny new potatoes, broccoli, and biscuits—all of the dishes prepared and ready to be served. With decisive haste she set the table in the kitchen, while Cal opened a bottle of wine that he let Molly know was a Château Lafite Rothschild Bordeaux, "from the best of my private stock."

Molly looked up in time to catch Philip's bemused expression, and Jenna's slight grimace at Cal's boasting, pretentious tone.

They *mean* well, she thought wearily, but I really wish they hadn't come. They're trying so hard to pretend it's an ordinary evening in Greenwich, and here we are, getting together at the last minute for an informal dinner in the kitchen. She remembered how, years ago, when Gary was still alive and she thought her life was happy, Jenna and Cal would occasionally drop in unannounced, invariably staying for dinner.

Domestic bliss—that was my life. I used to love to cook and thought nothing of whipping up a dinner in minutes. I enjoyed showing off the fact that I didn't need or want a cook or a live-in housekeeper. Gary used to seem so proud of me: *"She's not only gorgeous and smart, she can cook. How did I get so lucky?"* he would ask, beaming at her before their guests.

And all of it a charade, she thought.

Her head was aching so much. She pressed her temples with the tips of her fingers, massaging gently, trying to make the pain go away.

"Molly, would you rather just skip all this?" Philip asked quietly. He was sitting opposite her at the table, both of them ordered there by Jenna.

"As a husband and a doctor, he wasn't worth the price you paid for killing him, Mrs. Lasch."

Molly glanced up to see Philip staring at her.

"Molly, whatever do you mean?" he asked.

Confused, she looked past him. Jenna and Cal were staring at her too. "I'm sorry," she said haltingly. "I guess I'm at the point where I don't know the difference between what I'm thinking and what I'm saying. I just remembered that Annamarie Scalli said that to me when I met her at the diner Sunday night. What struck me at the time was that she was so sure I killed Gary, while I had gone to meet her harboring the hope that I might find out that she had been angry enough to have killed him."

"Molly, don't think about it now," Jenna urged. "Drink your wine. Try to relax."

"Jenna, listen to me," Molly said, her tone passionate. "Annamarie said that as a *doctor,* Gary wasn't worth the price I paid for killing him. What made her say that? He was a wonderful doctor. Wasn't he?"

There was a silence as Jenna continued her preparations. Cal just stared at her. "You understand what I'm getting at?" Molly said, her voice almost pleading. "Maybe there was something in Gary's professional life that we don't know about."

"It's something to pursue," Philip said quietly. "Why don't we talk to Fran about it?" He looked up at Cal and Jenna. "Initially I was against Molly cooperating in any way with Fran Simmons," he said, "but having been around her and seen her in action, I now honestly believe that she is in Molly's corner."

He turned to Molly. "By the way, she called while you were asleep. She's spoken to the boy who was working at the counter in the diner on Sunday night. He says he didn't hear you call out to Annamarie a second time, which is what the waitress is claiming. It's a small thing, but we should be able to use him to discredit her testimony."

"That's good—I know I didn't remember that," Molly said. "Sometimes, though, I wonder what is real and what I've imagined. I just told Dr. Daniels that something keeps coming into my head about the night Gary died—something about a door. He says it's a good sign that I'm starting to have specific memories. Maybe there are other answers to these deaths. I hope so. I do know that I can never go to prison again." She paused, then whispered more to herself than to the others, "That won't happen."

There was a long silence, which Jenna broke with cheerful determination. "Hey, let's not let this great dinner get cold," she said, taking her place at the table.

An hour later, on the way home in the car, sitting in the back as Lou Knox drove them, Jenna and Cal were silent until Jenna said, "Cal, do you think it's possible that Fran Simmons *will* uncover something that could help Molly? She *is* an investigative reporter, and maybe even a good one."

"But first you have to have something to investigate," Cal Whitehall said brusquely. "She doesn't. The more Fran Simmons digs, the more she'll find herself coming back to the same answer, which is the obvious one."

"What do you think Annamarie Scalli could have meant by criticizing Gary as a doctor?"

"My guess, my dear, is that Molly's little bursts of memory are highly unreliable. I wouldn't attach any importance to them, and I'm sure no jury would either. You heard her. She's threatening suicide."

"It's wrong for people to give Molly unreasonable hope. I wish Fran Simmons would stay out of it!"

"Yes, Fran Simmons *is* a terrible nuisance," Cal agreed.

He did not have to look at the rearview mirror to know that Lou Knox was watching him as he drove. With a barely perceptible nod, he answered Lou's unspoken question.

50

Did I detect a change in Tasha when I was there last week, or am I just imagining it now? Barbara Colbert asked herself as she stared out into the darkness on the drive to Greenwich. Nervously she clasped and unclasped her hands.

Dr. Black's call had come just as she was preparing to leave for the Met, where she had a subscription for the Tuesday night opera performance series.

"Mrs. Colbert," the doctor had said, his tone grave, "I'm afraid there's been a change in Tasha's condition. We believe that her systems may be shutting down."

Please let me get there in time, Barbara prayed. I want to be with her when she dies. They've always told me that she probably doesn't hear or understand anything we say to her, but I've never been sure of that. When the time comes, I want her to know that I am there. I want my arms around her when she draws her last breath.

She sat back and gasped. The thought of losing her child had the physical impact of a dagger in her heart. Tasha . . . Tasha . . . , she thought. How did this ever happen?

Barbara Colbert arrived to find Peter Black at Tasha's bedside. His countenance conveyed a kind of practiced grimness. "We can only watch and wait," he said, his voice solicitous.

Barbara ignored him. One of the nurses moved a chair close to the bed so that she could sit with her arm slipped around Tasha's shoulders. She looked into her daughter's lovely face, so serene, as though she were simply sleeping and might open her eyes at any minute and say hello.

Barbara stayed next to her daughter throughout the long night, unaware of the nurses in the background, or of Peter Black adjusting the solution that dripped into Tasha's veins.

At six o'clock, Black touched her arm. "Mrs. Colbert, it appears that Tasha has stabilized, at least to a degree. Why don't you have a cup of coffee and let the nurses attend to her? You can come back then."

She looked up. "Yes, and I must speak to my chauffeur. You're sure . . ."

He knew what she meant, and nodded. "No one can be sure, but I don't think Tasha is ready to leave us yet, at least not in the next little while."

Mrs. Colbert went out to the reception area. As she expected, Dan was asleep in one of the club chairs. A hand on his shoulder was enough to bring him to alert wakefulness.

Dan had been with the family since before Tasha was born, and over the years they had grown very close. Barbara answered his unasked question: "Not yet. They say she has stabilized for now. But it could be anytime."

They had rehearsed this moment. "I'll call the boys, Mrs. Colbert."

Fifty and forty-eight years old, and he still calls them the boys, Barbara thought, vaguely comforted by the realization that Dan was grieving with her. "Ask one of them to pick up a bag for me at the apartment. Call and tell Netty to have it ready."

She forced herself to go into the small coffee shop. The sleepless night had not affected her yet, but she knew it was inevitable.

The waitress in the coffee shop clearly knew about Tasha's condition. "We're praying," she said, then sighed. "It's been a sad week. You know, Mr. Magim died early Saturday morning."

"No, I didn't. I'm sorry."

"Not that it wasn't expected, but we were all hoping he'd make his eightieth birthday. You know what was nice, though? His eyes opened just before he died, and Mrs. Magim swears they focused right on her."

If only Natasha could say good-bye to me, Barbara thought. We were a very happy family, but never a particularly demonstrative one. I regret that now. So many parents end every conversation with their children by saying, "I love you." I always thought that was overdone, even silly. Now I wish I had never let Tasha out of my presence without saying that to her each and every time.

When Barbara went back to the suite, Tasha's condition appeared to be unchanged. Dr. Black was standing at the window of the sitting room, his back to her. He was using his cellular phone. Before Barbara could indicate her presence, she overheard him say, "I don't approve, but if you insist, then I don't have a choice, do I?" His voice was tight with anger—or was it fear?

I wonder who gives him orders, she thought.

51

On Wednesday morning, Fran had an appointment in Greenwich with Dr. Roy Kirkwood, who had been the primary care physician of Josephine Gallo, the mother of Tim Mason's friend, whose death Fran had been asked to investigate. She was surprised to find the doctor's reception room empty—not a usual situation for a physician these days, she thought.

The receptionist slid open the glass that separated her desk from the waiting area. "Miss Simmons," she said without asking Fran's name, "the doctor is expecting you."

Roy Kirkwood looked to be in his early sixties. His thinning silver hair, silver eyebrows, steel-frame glasses, lined forehead, and kindly, intelligent eyes all made Fran immediately think that this man *looked* like a doctor. If I were here because I was sick, I'd have confidence in him, she decided.

On the other hand, it occurred to her as he politely indicated the seat opposite his desk, she was here because one of his patients was dead.

"It's good of you to see me, Doctor," she began.

"No, I would say that it is *necessary* for me to see you, Ms. Simmons," he interrupted. "You may have noticed that my reception room is empty. Other than longtime patients, for whom I will care until I can transfer their records to other physicians, I am retired."

"Has this anything to do with Billy Gallo's mother?"

"It has *everything* to do with her, Ms. Simmons. Mind you, Mrs. Gallo might very easily have had a fatal heart attack in any circumstances. But with a quadruple bypass she also would have had a very good chance to live. Her cardiogram was within the normal range, but a cardiogram is not the only thing that can reveal that a patient is in trouble. I suspected she might be suffering from blocked arteries and wanted to do extensive testing of her. My request, however, was vetoed."

"By whom?"

"By management—Remington Health Management, to be specific."

"Did you protest the veto?"

"Ms. Simmons, I protested and continued to protest until there was no point. I protested that veto as I have many others in cases where my recommendations that my patients see specialists were denied."

"Then Billy Gallo was right—his mother might have had a longer life. Is that what you're saying?"

Roy Kirkwood looked both defeated and sad. "Ms. Simmons, after Mrs. Gallo had the coronary occlusion, I went to Peter Black and demanded that the necessary bypass surgery be done."

"And what did Dr. Black say?"

"He consented, reluctantly, but then Mrs. Gallo died. We might have saved her if that surgery had been authorized earlier. Of course, to the HMO she was just a statistic, and her death is a plus for the Remington profit line, so you have to wonder if they really care."

"You did your best, Doctor," Fran said quietly.

"Best? I'm at the end of my career and can retire comfortably. But God have pity on the new doctors. Most of them start out deep in debt and have to pay back loans for their education. Believe it or not, $100,000 is an average amount they owe. *Then* they have to borrow to equip an office and set up a practice. The way it stands today, they either work directly for a health maintenance organization, or have ninety percent of their patients enrolled in them.

"Today a doctor is told how many patients he must see. Some plans even go so far as to allot a doctor fifteen minutes a patient and require that he keep a time chart. It is not uncommon for doctors to work a fifty-five-hour week, for less money than they were making before the HMOs took over medicine."

"What's the answer?" Fran asked.

"Nonprofit HMOs run by doctors, I think. Also doctors forming their own unions. Medicine is making remarkable strides. There are many new medications and procedures available to doctors, some that enable us to prolong lives and give better quality of life. The incongruity is that these new procedures and services are being arbitrarily denied, as they were in Mrs. Gallo's case."

"How does Remington stack up with other HMOs, Doctor? It was, after all, founded by two doctors."

"By two doctors who inherited the sterling mantle of a great physician, Jonathan Lasch. Gary Lasch wasn't in the same class with his father—either as a doctor or a human being. As for Remington, it's as lean and mean as they get. For example, they've been systematically shaving services and personnel at Lasch Hospital as part of their ongoing cost-cutting campaign. I only wish Remington and the HMOs they're absorbing would be taken over by the plan that's headed by the former surgeon general. He's the kind of man the health system needs."

Roy Kirkwood stood up. "I apologize, Ms. Simmons. I realize I'm just letting off steam to you. But I do have a reason. I think you would be rendering a great service if you used the power of your program to wake up the public to this increasingly callous and alarming situation. Too many people are unaware of the fact that the lunatics have taken over the asylum."

Fran stood up as well. "Dr. Kirkwood, did you know Dr. Jack Morrow?"

Kirkwood smiled slightly. "Jack Morrow was the best. As smart as they come, a great diagnostician, loved his patients. His death was a tragedy."

"It seems strange that his murder has never been solved."

"If you think *I'm* upset with Remington Health Management, you should have heard Jack Morrow. I admit he probably went too far in pushing his complaints."

" 'Too far'?" Fran asked quickly.

"Jack could get hot under the collar. I understand that he actually referred to Peter Black and Gary Lasch as 'a pair of murderers.' That's going too far, although I confess it's the same way I felt about Black and the system when Josephine Gallo died. But I didn't *say* it."

"Who heard Dr. Morrow make that statement, Dr. Kirkwood?"

"Well, Mrs. Russo, my receptionist, for one. She used to work for Jack. If there were others who heard him, I'm not aware of it."

"Is she the lady outside?"

"Yes, she is."

"Thank you for your time, Doctor."

Fran went into the reception room and stopped at the desk. "I understand you worked for Dr. Morrow, Mrs. Russo," she said to the small, gray-haired woman. "He was so kind to me when my father died."

"He was kind to everyone."

"Mrs. Russo, you knew my name when I came in. Do you know that I'm investigating Dr. Gary Lasch's death for the *True Crime* television program?"

"Yes, I do."

"Dr. Kirkwood just told me that you heard Dr. Morrow refer to Dr. Lasch and Dr. Black as a 'pair of murderers.' That's pretty strong language."

"He'd just come back from the hospital and was terribly upset. I'm sure it had been the usual business of fighting for a patient who'd been denied a procedure. And then the poor man was shot to death only a few nights later."

"If I remember correctly, the police decided that a drug addict broke in and surprised him working late in his office."

"That's right. Every drawer of his desk was dumped on the floor, and the medical supply cabinet was emptied out. I understand that drug addicts can be desperate, but why did they have to shoot him? Why couldn't they take what they wanted and just tie him up or something?" Tears glistened in the woman's eyes.

Unless whoever broke in was afraid of being recognized, Fran thought. That's the usual reason a burglary becomes a homicide. She started to say good-bye, then remembered the other question she wanted to ask.

"Mrs. Russo, was anyone else around when Dr. Morrow called Drs. Lasch and Black a pair of murderers?"

"Only two people, thank goodness, Miss Simmons. Wally Barry, a longtime patient of Dr. Morrow's, and his mother, Edna."

52

Lou Knox lived in an apartment over the garage that sat to the side of the Whitehalls' residence. The three-room unit suited him well. One of the few hobbies he enjoyed was woodworking, and Calvin Whitehall had allowed him use of one of the storerooms in the over-sized garage for his tools and worktable. He also had permitted Knox to refinish the apartment to suit himself.

Now the living room and bedroom were paneled with bleached white oak. Shelves lined the walls, although one would not call them bookshelves, since Lou Knox was not a reader. Instead, his television, state-of-the-art stereo, and CD and video collections filled the shelves.

They were also excellent cover-ups for the large and ever-growing collection of incriminating evidence he had accumulated for possible use against Calvin Whitehall.

He was fairly certain that he would never need any of it, since he and Cal Whitehall had long ago reached an understanding on what his duties were to be. Besides, Lou knew that to use that evidence would be to incriminate himself as well. Therefore, that was a hand that Lou had no intention of ever showing except as a last resort. To do that would be to cut off your nose to spite your face, as the grandmother who raised him used to say when he complained about the butcher for whom he'd worked as a delivery boy.

"Does he pay you regular?" his grandmother would demand.

"Yes, but he asks his customers to put the tip on the bill," Lou used to protest, "and then he counts it as part of my salary."

All these years later it gave Lou satisfaction to remember how he had gotten back at the butcher. On his way to deliver an order, he'd open the package and take out part of it—a piece of the chicken, or a slice from the filet mignon, or enough chopped sirloin for a good hamburger.

His grandmother, who worked the four-to-midnight shift as a telephone operator at a motel ten miles away, would have left him a meal of canned spaghetti and meatballs, or something else he would find equally unappetizing. So on those days he had managed to filch some of the customers' meat, he'd come home from his after-school job and feast on beef or chicken. Then he'd throw out whatever his grandmother had left him, and no one was the wiser.

The only person who ever caught on to what Lou was up to was Cal. One evening when Cal and he were sophomores, Cal stopped over just as he was frying a steak he'd taken from a package the butcher had sent to one of his best customers.

"You're a jerk," Cal had said. "You broil steak, you don't fry it."

That night forged an alliance between the two young men: Cal, the son of the town drunks, and Lou, the grandson of Bebe Clauss, whose only daughter had eloped with Lenny Knox and returned to town two years later just long enough to deposit her son with her mother. That burden out of her life, she'd disappeared again.

Despite his background, Cal had gone off to college, helped by his cunning and a drive to succeed. Lou drifted from job to job, in between serving thirty days in the town jail for shoplifting, and three years in the state penitentiary for aggravated assault. Then, almost sixteen years ago, he'd received a call from Cal, now known as Mr. Calvin Whitehall, of Greenwich, Connecticut.

Gotta go kiss the feet of my old buddy, was the way Lou characterized the summons to Greenwich. Cal had made it eminently clear that their reunion was based solely on Lou's potential value to him as a kind of all-purpose handyman.

Lou moved to Greenwich that day, into a spare bedroom in the house Cal had bought. The house was far smaller than the one he lived in now, but it was definitely in the right location.

Cal's courtship of Jenna Graham was an eye-opener for Lou. Here was a classy, drop-dead beauty being pursued by a guy who looked like an ex-prizefighter. What on earth could she be expected to see in him?

Even as he asked the question, Lou figured out the answer. Power. Raw, naked power. Jenna loved the fact that Cal had it, and she was fascinated by the way he used it. He might not have had her pedigree, and he might not have come from her kind of world, but the guy could handle himself in any situation; her world was soon his home. And no matter what some of the old guard might think of Cal Whitehall, they knew better than to cross him.

Cal's parents were never invited to visit their son. When they died within a short time of each other, Lou was the one sent to make arrangements and to rush their bodies to the crematorium as fast as possible. Cal was no sentimentalist.

Over the years, Lou's value to Cal had increased significantly—he knew that. Even so, he had no doubt that if at any point it suited Calvin Whitehall to dispose of him, he, Lou Knox, would be thrown to the wolves. So it was with a certain degree of grim amusement that he remembered how jobs he had carried out for Cal were planned in such a way that Cal could wash his hands of any involvement. So if anyone was left holding the bag, guess who that would be?

Well, two could play that game, he thought with a sly smile.

Now it was up to him to see if Fran Simmons was going to be merely a nuisance, or if she was becoming dangerous. It should be interesting, he decided. Like father, like daughter?

Lou smiled as he remembered Fran's father, that eager-to-please jerk whose mother never taught him not to trust the Calvin Whitehalls of this world. So when he finally learned his lesson, it was a little too late.

53

Dr. Peter Black seldom made the trip to West Redding during the day. It was about a forty-minute drive from Greenwich, even when traffic was light, but more important, he made the trip frequently enough that he worried about becoming too familiar a face in the area. His destination was a remote farmhouse equipped with a state-of-the-art laboratory on its second floor.

On the tax rolls of the county, the structure was listed as a private home owned and occupied by Dr. Adrian Logue, a retired ophthalmologist. In fact, the property and the laboratory belonged to Remington Health Management, and when supplies were needed there, they traveled from the main lab in the trunk of Peter Black's car.

By the time he had pulled up in front of the farmhouse, Black's palms were sweating. He was dreading the inevitable argument ahead of him; moreover he knew it was one he would not win.

When he left less than half an hour later, he was carrying a package, the weight of which did not justify the strain he felt as he put it in the trunk of his car and started home.

54

Edna Barry could tell immediately that Molly had had company the night before. Even though the kitchen was tidy and the CLEAN signal was lit on the dishwasher, the subtle differences were there. Salt and pepper shakers were on the sideboard rather than on the counter, the fruit bowl was on the cutting board instead of the table, the coffeemaker was still out, uncovered, on the counter next to the stove.

The prospect of restoring the customary orderliness of the kitchen was a soothing prospect to Edna. I like my job, she thought as she hung her coat in the closet near the door. I'm going to hate having to give it up again.

It was inevitable, however. When Molly knew she was about to be released from prison, she had had her parents hire Edna to come in and spruce up the house and stock the kitchen. Now that she had been coming to Molly's house regularly again, Wally had started being a problem. He'd hardly mentioned Molly while she was in prison, but her return had done something to him, had set him off. He kept talking about her and Dr. Lasch. And each time he talked about them, he became angry.

If I'm not in and out of here three times a week, it won't be on his mind so much, Edna reasoned as she tied an apron over her matching polyester shirt and slacks. The apron was her own choice. Molly's mother had always furnished a uniform, but Molly had said, "Oh, Edna, that isn't necessary."

Again this morning there was no sign that Molly had made coffee for herself, no sign, for that matter, that she was even awake yet. I'll go upstairs and check on her, Edna decided. Maybe after all she's gone through, she's sleeping in. And she has gone through a lot. Why, since I was here Monday, Molly has been arrested again for murder and then released on bail. It's just like six years ago. As much as I hate to even think this, maybe she'd be better off if she were put away.

Marta thinks I should stop working here because Molly is dangerous, Edna thought as she climbed the stairs, once again reminded of the arthritis in her knees.

You're glad she thinks that, a voice whispered inside her head. Let the police focus on Molly and not think about Wally.

But Molly's always been so kind to you, another voice suggested. You *could* help her, but you won't. Wally was here that night—you *know* that. Maybe he could help her to remember what happened. But you can't risk it. You can't take a chance on what he might say.

Edna arrived upstairs just as Molly was getting out of the shower, and when she came into the bedroom in her thick terry bathrobe, her hair wrapped in a towel, she reminded Edna of the little girl Molly once had been, always so polite, who would say, "Good morning, Mrs. Barry," in her soft, low voice.

"Good morning, Mrs. Barry."

With a start, Edna realized that it was not an echo of memory; it was Molly, a grown woman, talking to her now.

"Oh, Molly, for just a moment there, I swear I was seeing you as a ten-year-old! Sounds like I'm losing it, doesn't it?"

"Not you," Molly said. "Me maybe, but surely not you. I'm sorry you had to come looking for me. I'm not as lazy as I look, though. I went to bed early enough, but then I didn't fall asleep until almost dawn."

"That's not good, Molly. Can't you get the doctor to give you something to help you sleep?"

"I did the other night, and it was a big help. I'll see if I can't get some more of the same. The trouble is that Dr. Daniels doesn't really believe in pills."

"I have some sleeping pills the doctor gave me to give to Wally in case he gets restless. They're not too strong. Would you want some to keep on hand?"

Molly sat at her dressing table and reached for the hair dryer. Then she turned and looked directly at Edna Barry. "I really would like that, Mrs. Barry," she said slowly. "Have you an extra bottle that I can replace?"

"Oh, you don't want a full bottle. There're about forty in the one I have in the medicine cabinet."

"Then split them with me, okay? The way things are going, I may need one a night for the next several weeks."

Edna had not known whether or not to let on that she knew Molly had been arrested again.

"Molly, I'm so sorry for everything that's happened. You know."

"Yes, I do. Thank you, Mrs. Barry. And now would you please bring me a cup of coffee?" She picked up the hair dryer and turned it on.

When she was sure Edna Barry was on her way downstairs, Molly turned off the dryer and let her damp hair fall on her neck. The warmth of the shower was gone, and the strands of hair felt cold and wet against her skin.

You don't really intend to take an overdose of pills, do you? she asked herself. She looked at the face in the mirror—it seemed to her someone she hardly recognized. Isn't it more like being in a strange place and looking for the exit, just in case you need to get out in a hurry? She leaned in closer to the mirror and stared into the eyes she saw there. Having asked the questions, she wasn't sure of the answers.

An hour later, Molly was in the study going through one of the boxes she had brought down from the attic. The prosecutors had two cracks at these papers, she thought. They confiscated them after Gary died, returned them after the trial, then went through them again yesterday. I guess now they've given up looking for anything interesting in them.

But what am *I* looking for? she asked herself.

I'm looking for something that might make me understand what Annamarie Scalli meant when she told me as a doctor Gary wasn't worth the price I paid for killing him. I don't even care anymore about his infidelity.

There were some framed pictures in the box. She pulled one of them out and looked at it closely. It was a photograph of her and Gary taken at the Heart Association Charity Ball the year they were married. She studied it dispassionately. She remembered how Gran used to say that Gary reminded her of Tyrone Power, the movie star who had been her heartthrob sixty years before.

I guess I never saw beyond the looks and the charm, she thought. Clearly at some point Annamarie did. But how did she find out? And *what* did she learn?

At 11:30, Fran phoned. "Molly, I'd like to stop by for just a few minutes. Is Mrs. Barry there?"

"Yes, she is."

"Good. See you in ten minutes."

When Fran arrived, she went directly to Molly and put an arm around her. "I gather you had a lovely afternoon yesterday."

"Never a better one." She managed a wan smile.

"Where's Mrs. Barry, Molly?"

"In the kitchen, I guess. She seems to be determined to fix lunch for me, even though I tell her I'm not hungry."

"Come on in with me. I have to talk to her."

Edna Barry's heart sank when she heard Fran Simmons's voice. Help me, please, dear Lord, she prayed. Don't let her go asking me about Wally. It's not his fault he's the way he is.

Fran came directly to the point: "Mrs. Barry, Dr. Morrow was your son's doctor, wasn't he?"

"Yes, that's right. He saw a psychiatrist as well, but Dr. Morrow was his primary physician," Edna replied, trying not to let her growing unease show in her face.

"Your neighbor Mrs. Jones told me the other day that Wally was very upset when Dr. Morrow died."

"Yes, that's right."

"I gather Wally was in a cast around that time?" Fran asked.

Edna Barry bristled, then nodded stiffly. "Toe-to-knee cast," she said. "He wore it for a week after they found poor Dr. Morrow."

I shouldn't have said that, she thought. She didn't accuse Wally of anything.

"What I was going to ask, Mrs. Barry, is if you or Wally ever overheard Dr. Morrow talk about either Dr. Gary Lasch or Dr. Peter Black, or maybe refer to the two of them as a pair of murderers?"

Molly gasped.

"I don't remember anything like that," Edna Barry said softly, her distress apparent in the way she kept wiping her hands on her apron. "What is that all about?"

"I don't think that if you had heard a statement like that it would be easily forgotten, Mrs. Barry. I know it certainly would make a lasting impression on me. On the way over in the car I called Mr. Matthews, Molly's lawyer, and asked him about the spare key to this house that is kept in the garden. According to his notes, you gave it to the police the morning Dr. Lasch was found murdered in his study, and you told them it had been in the kitchen drawer for a long time. You said that Molly had forgotten her house key one day and had taken the spare from the hiding place, and it had never been put back."

"But that is not *true*," Molly protested. "I never once forgot my house key, and I know the spare was in the garden the week before Gary died. I was out in back and happened to check on it. Why would you say it had been in the house for a long time because of me, Mrs. Barry? I don't understand."

55

On the evening news hour, Fran wrapped up her report on the latest developments in the Annamarie Scalli murder investigation with an appeal: "According to Bobby Burke, the counterman on duty in the Sea Lamp Diner the night of the murder, a couple came in the diner and took a table near the door moments before Annamarie Scalli hurried out. Molly Lasch's lawyer, Philip Matthews, is appealing to that couple to come forward and give a statement as to what they may have observed in the parking lot before they came into the diner or may have overheard in the diner itself. Attorney Matthews's number is 212-555-2800, or you can call me at this station at 212-555-6850."

The camera focused on Fran went dark. "Thanks for that report, Fran," Bert Davis, the news anchor, said crisply. "Coming up: sports with Tim Mason, followed by the weather with Scott Roberts. But first, some messages."

Fran unfastened the mike from her jacket and removed the earpiece. She stopped at Tim Mason's desk on the way out of the studio. "Can I buy you a hamburger when you're finished?" she asked.

Tim raised his eyebrows. "I was all set for a steak, but if it's a hamburger you want, then I still accept with pleasure."

"Nope. A steak is fine. I'll be in my office."

While she waited for Tim, Fran reviewed the events of the day. First there was the meeting with Dr. Roy Kirkwood, then her call to Philip Matthews, then Edna Barry's flustered reaction during the discussion of the spare key. Mrs. Barry had claimed that she was almost certain the spare key had been in the drawer for months, and when Molly denied it, Barry said, "Molly must be mistaken; but then, she *was* so confused at that time."

Driving back to the city, Fran had called Philip again and had told him that she had become more and more certain that Edna Barry had something to hide and that it had to do with that spare key. She certainly hadn't been forthcoming when Fran questioned her about it, however, so Fran suggested that Philip might have to lean on her to tell the truth.

Philip had promised to study every word of Edna Barry's statements to the police and testimony at the trial, then he had asked about Molly's reaction to Mrs. Barry's statement.

Fran told him that it clearly startled her, maybe even unsettled her. After Mrs. Barry went home, Molly had said something like, "I guess I must have been out of it even *before* the shock of finding out about Annamarie. I would have *sworn* that key was in the garden a few days before I overheard her call to Gary."

And I bet you're right, Molly, Fran said to herself angrily as Tim knocked, then poked his head around the door. She waved him in. "Let's go," he said. "I've made a reservation at Cibo's on Second Avenue."

"Good choice. I love it there."

As they walked down Fifth Avenue to Forty-first Street, Fran lifted her arms in a salute to the buildings and the bustle around them. "My town," she said with a sigh. "I love it. It's so good to be back."

"Me too," Tim agreed, "and I'm also glad you're back."

In the restaurant they chose one of the private booths.

Once the waiter had poured their wine and left to place their dinner orders, she said, "Tim, I believe you said your grandmother died in Lasch Hospital. When was that?"

"Let's see. It's just over six years ago, I think . . . Why do you ask?"

"Because when I first met you last week, we discussed Gary Lasch. Didn't you say that he took excellent care of your grandmother before she died?"

"Yes, I did. Why?"

"Because I'm starting to hear from some quarters that there was another side to Gary Lasch as a doctor. I spoke to the physician who treated Billy Gallo's mother—a Dr. Kirkwood. He told me he fought for her to see a specialist but couldn't get approval from the HMO for further treatment; then she had the major heart attack and died before anything could be done. Of course, Gary Lasch is long dead and had nothing directly to do with this, but Dr. Kirkwood said that this tightfisted approach to health care goes back some time. He's only in his early sixties, and he says he's packing it in, doesn't plan to practice medicine anymore. He's been tied to the Lasch Hospital most of his career, and he was most definite in saying that Gary Lasch had been nothing like his father. He said the problems he encountered with Mrs. Gallo were nothing new, that putting the patient's welfare first hadn't been a priority with the people running Lasch Hospital and Remington for a long time." Fran leaned closer and lowered her voice. "He even told me that Dr. Morrow, the young doctor who died in a robbery two weeks before Gary Lasch was killed, once referred to Lasch and his partner, Dr. Black, as a pair of murderers."

"That's pretty strong language," Tim said, breaking off a piece of roll. "Still, I've got to say my own experience was much more positive. As I said, I liked Gary Lasch and thought my grandmother got darn good care. I did think of one coincidence I may not have mentioned. Did I tell you that Annamarie Scalli was one of the nurses who took care of her?"

Fran's eyes widened. "No, you didn't tell me that."

"It didn't seem significant. All the nurses were excellent. I remember Annamarie as dedicated and very caring. When we got the call that my grandmother had died, we went straight to the hospital, of course. Annamarie was sitting by her bed, sobbing. How many nurses react like that, especially when it's a patient they've known only a short time?"

"Not too many," Fran agreed. "They couldn't last if they got emotionally entangled with all their patients."

"Annamarie was a very pretty girl, but she also struck me as kind of naïve," Tim recalled. "She was only in her early twenties, for heaven sake. When I found out later that Gary Lasch was carrying on with her, I was disgusted with him as a man, but as a doctor I can't remember a single thing about him to criticize.

"We joked that my grandmother had a crush on Lasch," Tim reminisced. "He was a really handsome and charming guy, but he also made you feel that he cared about his patients deeply. The guy just inspired confidence. I remember my grandmother saying sometimes he'd look in on her as late as eleven o'clock at night. How many doctors do *that?*"

"Molly Lasch quoted Annamarie Scalli as saying that as a doctor and as a husband, Gary Lasch wasn't worth the price she paid for killing him," Fran observed. "She said Annamarie was pretty positive about it."

"But Fran, isn't that the kind of talk you'd *expect* to hear from a woman in Annamarie's position?"

"Maybe as a woman she'd say that, yes. But it sounds to me as if she was also talking from the point of view of a nurse." Fran paused and shook her head. "I don't know, maybe I'm jumping to conclusions, but adding that to Dr. Jack Morrow's referring to Gary Lasch and Peter Black as murderers, I can't help but think there's something to all this. I sense that I'm onto something, and I suspect that an awful lot of this story has never come out."

"You're an investigative reporter, Fran. My bet's on you to get to the truth. I hardly knew Annamarie Scalli, but I was grateful for the care she took of my grandmother. I'd like to see her murderer caught, and it's a tragedy if Molly Lasch has been unfairly accused."

The waiter was placing the salads in front of them.

"Unfairly accused for the *second* time," Fran said pointedly.

"That may well be the case, but what's your next step?"

"I managed to get a meeting tomorrow with Dr. Peter Black. Should be interesting. I'm still trying to set up an appointment with my Cranden Academy fellow student, Jenna Whitehall, and her husband, the mighty Calvin Whitehall."

"Heavy-duty people."

Fran nodded. "I know, but they're all-important to the story, and I'm determined to get to them." She sighed. "How about let's give the subject a rest. So what do you think? Will my Yankees win the World Series again this year?"

Tim smiled. "Of course they will."

56

"This time I came alone," Jenna announced, as she phoned Molly from her car. "Just let me in for a few minutes."

"Jen, you're sweet, but I begged off from Dr. Daniels, and that took doing. I know it's only nine o'clock, but my eyes are closing. I really just want to go to bed."

"Fifteen minutes—that's all I ask for."

"Oh, Jen," Molly said with a sigh. "You win. Come on in. Just be careful. There were some reporters hanging around this afternoon, and I bet Cal wouldn't be happy to see his wife and the notorious Molly Lasch in the same picture on the front page of the tabloids."

She opened the door cautiously, and Jenna slipped in. "Oh, Molly," Jenna said as she hugged her. "I'm so sorry you're going through this."

"You're my *only* friend," Molly said, then quickly added, "No, that's not true. Fran Simmons is in my corner."

"Fran's called about setting up an appointment, but we haven't connected yet. Cal promised me he'd give her an appointment, and I understand she's already scheduled to come up here to talk to Peter tomorrow."

"I know she said she wanted to talk to all of you. I want you to feel free to say anything you want to her. I trust her not to hurt me."

They went into the family room, where Molly had a fire going. "I have something figured out," she said. "In this very large house, I live in three rooms—the kitchen, my bedroom, and here. When— and if—this is all over, I'm going to get a smaller place."

"I think that's a good idea," Jenna said, nodding in agreement.

"Of course, as you know, the State of Connecticut has other plans for me, and if they have their way, I'll be in a very small cell."

"Molly!" Jenna protested.

"I'm sorry." Molly sat back and studied her friend. "You look great. Basic black suit—an Escada, isn't it? Heels. Understated but gorgeous jewelry. Where have you been, or is it where are you going?"

"A business lunch. Corporate stuff. I took a late train home. I left my car at the station this morning, and tonight I came directly here. I've been feeling rotten all day. Molly, I'm terribly worried about you."

Molly attempted a smile. "I'm terribly worried about me too."

They were sitting side by side on the couch, a cushion-width apart. Molly leaned forward, her hands clasped. "Jen, your husband is convinced that I murdered Gary, isn't he?"

"Yes," Jenna said quietly.

"And he's also convinced I stabbed Annamarie Scalli to death."

Jenna did not answer.

"I know he is," Molly continued. "You know what you mean to me, but, Jen, do me a favor—don't bring Cal around anymore. The only place I can call a sanctuary is this house. I don't need enemies in it."

Molly glanced sideways at her friend. "Oh Jen, don't start crying on me. It has nothing to do with *us*. We're still the girls from Cranden Academy, aren't we?"

"You bet we are," Jenna said as she impatiently brushed her eyes with the back of her hand. "But Molly, Cal isn't the enemy. He wants to call in other lawyers, top-drawer criminal experts, to work with Philip in preparing an insanity defense for you."

"An insanity defense?"

"Molly," Jenna burst out, "don't you realize that a murder conviction could mean life imprisonment for you? Especially on top of the earlier conviction? We *can't* let that happen."

"No, we can't," Molly said, standing. "Jen, come into Gary's study with me."

The light was off in the study. Molly switched it on, then deliberately switched it off again. "Last night after all of you left, I went up to bed, but I couldn't sleep. About midnight, I came down here—and you know something? When I turned on the light, just as I did now, I could remember doing the same thing when I came home from the Cape that Sunday night. I'm sure now that the light in the study was out when I got here, Jenna. I would *swear* to that!"

"What does that mean, Molly?"

"Think about it. Gary was at his desk. There were papers on it, so he must have been working. It was nighttime. He must have had the light on. If I'm right about remembering that I came home, opened this door, and then turned the light on, it means that whoever killed Gary had turned it off. Don't you see?"

"Molly," Jenna murmured, her voice calm but protesting.

"Yesterday I told Dr. Daniels that I remembered something from that night about a door and a lock."

Molly turned to face her friend and saw the disbelief in her eyes. Her shoulders sagged. "Today, Mrs. Barry said that the spare key we hid in the garden had been in the house for weeks. She said it was there because one day I forgot my key. But I don't remember that either."

"Molly, let Cal bring in lawyers to assist Philip in preparing your defense," Jenna begged. "He spoke to a couple of the best of them today. They're both very experienced in presenting psychiatric defenses, and we really think they could help you." She saw the look of distress in her friend's face. "At least think about it."

"Maybe that's why I was dreaming about a door and a lock," Molly said grimly, ignoring Jenna's suggestion. "Maybe I have a choice: a locked prison cell or a locked room in an institution."

"Molly, come on," Jenna said, standing, "I'm going to have a cup of tea with you, then I am going to let you get to bed. You say you're not getting much sleep. Didn't Dr. Daniels give you anything to help you sleep?"

"He gave me something the other day, and Mrs. Barry came back this afternoon with a prescription that the doctor gave Wally."

"You shouldn't take anyone else's prescription!"

"The label was on it. I know it's okay. Don't forget, I *was* a doctor's wife, and I *did* pick up a little knowledge along the way."

When Jenna left a few minutes later, Molly double locked the front door behind her and stepped on the foot bolt. The sound that the bolt made—something between a click and a snap—made her pause.

Deliberately she repeated raising and lowering the bolt, listening carefully each time, willing her subconscious to supply the reason that familiar household sound was suddenly so chilling.

57

Dr. Peter Black began his day Thursday morning by going to visit Tasha. By any medical standards, she should be dead by now, he thought anxiously as he walked down the hallway to her suite.

Perhaps it had been a mistake to make her a part of the experiment, he thought. Normally this experiment would produce useful—and occasionally fascinating—clinical results, but it was proving to be difficult to carry out, due primarily to Tasha's mother. Barbara Colbert was much too alert and well connected. There were plenty of other patients at the residence who were more likely candidates for this extraordinary research, patients whose relatives would never suspect anything was amiss and who would take even the slightest sign of deathbed cognition as a gift from heaven.

I should never have mentioned to Dr. Logue that Harvey Magim seemed to recognize his wife at the end, Black thought, excoriating himself. But it was too late to stop now. He had to go on to the next step. That had been made clear to him. That next step was contained in the package he'd brought back from the laboratory in West Redding, and it was now safely tucked into his vest pocket.

When he entered the room, he found the duty nurse nodding by Tasha's bedside. That was good, he thought. A sleepy nurse was exactly what he wanted. It gave him an excuse to get her out of the room.

"I would suggest you get yourself a cup of coffee," he said sternly, waking her abruptly. "Bring it back here. I'll wait. Where is Mrs. Colbert?"

"She's asleep on the couch," the nurse whispered. "Poor woman, she finally dozed off. Her sons left. They'll be here again tonight."

Black nodded and turned to the patient as the nurse scurried out. Tasha's condition remained unchanged from last evening. She had stabilized, thanks, he knew, to the injection he'd given her when she started to sink.

He took the small package out of his pocket. It felt unnaturally heavy for its size. Last night's injection had had the expected results, but the one he was about to administer was totally unpredictable.

Logue is out of control, Black thought.

He lifted Tasha's limp arm and pinched it to find a suitable vein. Holding the syringe in place, he slowly pushed the plunger and watched as the liquid disappeared into her body.

He looked at his watch. It was eight o'clock. In about twelve hours it would be over, one way or the other. In the meantime, he was facing the unwelcome prospect of the meeting he had agreed to have with that snoopy newswoman, Fran Simmons.

58

After a restless night, Fran went to the office early Thursday morning to do some background work in preparation for her noontime interview with Dr. Peter Black. She had requested that the research department have whatever biographical information they could find waiting on her desk, and she was pleased to see that it was there already.

She read through it quickly, finding it surprisingly thin and not remotely impressive. Born in Denver of working-class parents; attended local schools; had mediocre to poor grades at medical school; did a residency in Chicago at an unrated hospital, then worked as a staff doctor there. Not much of a record, she said to herself.

Which has to lead one to ask the question, why did Gary Lasch seek him out? Fran thought.

Promptly at noon she was ushered into Dr. Black's office. She was immediately struck by the way the place was furnished. It impressed her as having a grandeur more suitable to a corporate executive than a physician, even if that physician *was* CEO of a hospital and health maintenance organization.

She did not know what she had expected Peter Black to be like. Maybe I anticipated something more akin to what I heard Gary Lasch was like, she thought as she shook his hand and followed him to a sitting area in front of a large picture window. A handsome leather couch, two matching armchairs, and a coffee table created a comfortable, living room atmosphere.

Gary Lasch by all accounts had been a handsome man with an engaging personality. Peter Black's complexion was sallow, and Fran was surprised at how nervous he seemed. Beads of perspiration glistened on his forehead and on his upper lip. There was a rigidity about him, especially in the way he sat on the edge of his chair. It was as if he were on guard against an anticipated attack. Although he was attempting to be courteous, there was no mistaking the stress in his voice.

He offered coffee. When Fran declined, he said, "Ms. Simmons, I have a particularly busy schedule today, and I assume you do as well, so why don't we get straight to the point. I have agreed to see you because I wanted to emphasize in the strongest possible terms that I think it's an outrage that in your quest for ratings you are exploiting Molly Lasch, a woman who is clearly mentally ill."

Fran looked back at him without flinching. "I thought I was *helping* Molly, not exploiting her, Doctor. May I ask if your diagnosis of mental illness is based on an actual medical evaluation, or is it merely the rush to judgment that seems to be the standard reaction of all her friends?"

"Ms. Simmons, it's clear we have nothing to say to each other." Peter Black stood up. "If you'll excuse me . . ."

Fran remained seated. "No, I'm afraid I *won't*. Dr. Black, you know I drove here from Manhattan because I have some questions for you. The fact that you allowed me to come was, in my opinion, a tacit acceptance of that understanding. I do think you owe me at least ten minutes of your time."

Grudgingly Peter Black sank back into his chair. "Ten minutes, Ms. Simmons. Not a second more."

"Thank you. I understand from Molly that you visited her Saturday night with the Whitehalls to ask her to delay my investigation because of your pending merger with other health maintenance organizations. Is that true?"

"That *is* true. I also had Molly's welfare in mind. I explained that to you."

"Dr. Black, you knew Dr. Jack Morrow, didn't you?"

"Certainly. He was one of our physicians."

"Were you friends?"

"Friendly. I'd say we were friendly. We respected each other. But did we socialize? No, we did not."

"Did you quarrel with him shortly before he died?"

"No, I did not. I understand he had words with my colleague Dr. Lasch. I believe it was over a denial of coverage of a procedure Dr. Morrow had recommended for one of his patients."

"Did you know that he referred to you and Dr. Lasch as 'a pair of murderers'?"

"I certainly did not, but it doesn't surprise me. Jack was a rash man and could get very hot under the collar."

He's scared, Fran thought as she studied Peter Black. He's scared, and he's lying.

"Doctor, did you know at the time that Gary Lasch was having an affair with Annamarie Scalli?"

"I did not. I was shocked when Gary confessed to it."

"That was only hours before he died," Fran said. "Isn't that true?"

"Yes, it is. It had been obvious all week that Gary was upset, and on that Sunday Cal Whitehall and I went to see him. That's when we heard about it." Peter Black glanced at his watch and shifted forward slightly.

He's ready to kick me out, Fran thought. I've *got* to get a couple more questions in first, though.

"Doctor, Gary Lasch was a close friend of yours, wasn't he?"

"Very close. We met in medical school."

"Did you see each other regularly after medical school?"

"I wouldn't say that. I was working in Chicago right after graduation. Gary came here as soon as he completed his residency and went into practice with his father." He stood. "Ms. Simmons, I really must insist on getting back to work." He turned and walked toward his desk.

Fran followed him. "Doctor, one last question. Did you ask Gary Lasch to bring you here?"

"Gary sent for me after his father died."

"Doctor, with all due respect, he invited you to join him as an equal partner in the institution his father founded. There were a number of excellent physicians already in the Greenwich area who surely would have bought into the practice, but he chose you, even though you had only worked as a staff doctor in a rather undistinguished Chicago hospital. What made you so special?"

Peter Black whirled to face Fran. "Get out, Ms. Simmons!" he barked. "You have extraordinary gall to come up here and make libelous insinuations when half the people in this town were victims of your father's thievery."

Fran winced. "Touché," she said. "Nevertheless, Dr. Black, I don't intend to stop looking for answers to my questions. You're certainly not providing me with any, are you?"

59

On Thursday morning, in Buffalo, New York, after a private funeral Mass, the remains of Annamarie Scalli were to be quietly interred in the family burial plot. No details of the service had been made public. There had been no wake. Her sister, Lucille Scalli Bonaventure, accompanied by her husband and two grown children, were the only people present for the private Mass and interment.

The lack of publicity had been a decision made and enforced by a grimly purposeful Lucy. Sixteen years older than Annamarie, she had always referred to her baby sister as her first child. Pleasant faced but plain herself, Lucy had delighted in the pretty little girl who grew up to be as smart as she was nice.

As Annamarie matured, Lucy and her mother frequently conferred about her choices in boyfriends and her possible career paths. They approved heartily when she chose nursing. It was a totally worthwhile career, and there was a good chance she would end up marrying a doctor. Who *wouldn't* want to marry a girl like Annamarie? they agreed.

When she accepted the job at Lasch Hospital in Greenwich, Connecticut, they initially had been disappointed to have her go so far away from home, but when she twice brought Dr. Jack Morrow with her to Buffalo for a weekend visit with her mother, it had seemed as if all their dreams for Annamarie were going to come true.

As Lucy sat in the front row of the chapel during the brief service, she thought back to that happier time. She remembered how

Jack Morrow would joke with Mama, telling her that even if Annamarie couldn't cook like she did, he'd put up with her. She remembered especially the night he had complained, "Mama, how am I going to make that girl of yours fall in love with me?"

She *was* in love with him, Lucy thought as scalding tears burned her cheeks—until that hateful Gary Lasch decided to go after her. She shouldn't be lying in that casket, Lucy thought angrily. She should have been married to Dr. Jack these past seven years. She could have been *both* a mother and a nurse—he wouldn't have wanted her to give that up. Nursing was as much in her soul as being a doctor was in his.

Lucy turned and looked with anguish at the casket, covered with the white cloth symbolizing Annamarie's baptism. You suffered so much because of that . . . that *bastard,* Gary Lasch, she thought. After he turned your head, you tried to tell me that you weren't ready to marry Jack. But that wasn't true. You *were* ready. You had just lost your way, Annamarie. You were a kid. He knew what he was doing.

"May her soul and the souls of all the faithful departed . . ."

Lucy was barely aware of the monsignor's voice as he blessed her sister's casket. Her grief and her anger were too great. Annamarie, look at what that man did to you, Lucy thought. He ruined your life in every way. You even gave up bedside nursing, and at one time that was all you wanted to do. You wouldn't talk about it, but I know you never forgave yourself for something that happened in that hospital. What was it?

And Dr. Jack. What about him? Poor Mama was so crazy about him, so impressed. She never called him Jack. Always Dr. Jack. You admitted that you never believed a drug addict killed him.

Annamarie, why were you so afraid for all those years? Even when Molly Lasch was in prison, you were afraid?

Little sister . . . Little sister.

Lucy became aware of raw, noisy sobs filling the chapel and knew they were coming from her. Her husband patted her hand, but she pulled it away. Right now the only person in the universe she felt connected to was Annamarie. The only consolation that came to her as the casket was wheeled down the aisle of the chapel was that maybe in a different world her sister and Jack Morrow might have a second chance at happiness.

* * *

After the interment, Lucy's son and daughter escaped to their jobs, and her husband went back to the supermarket where he was a manager.

Lucy went home and began going through the dresser that had been Annamarie's when she was growing up. It was kept in the bedroom in which she always stayed when she visited in Buffalo.

The top three drawers contained underwear, hosiery, and sweaters, left there so that Annamarie could use them when she came up for a weekend.

The bottom drawer was filled with pictures, framed and unframed, family albums, envelopes stuffed with snapshots, some letters and postcards.

It was when she was going through those pictures, tears blurring her vision and burning her eyes, that Lucy received a call from Fran Simmons.

"I know who you are," Lucy snapped, her voice charged with angry emotion. "You're that reporter who wants to air that dirty business all over again. Well, leave me alone, and leave my sister to rest in peace."

Speaking from Manhattan, Fran said, "I'm very sorry for your loss, but I have to warn you—Annamarie won't rest in peace if the case against Molly Lasch comes to trial. Molly's lawyer will have no choice but to portray Annamarie in the darkest possible terms."

"That's not fair!" Lucy wailed. "She was no home wrecker. She was just a kid when she met Gary Lasch."

"So was Molly," Fran said. "The more I hear, the sorrier I am for both of them. Mrs. Bonaventure, I'm flying to Buffalo tomorrow morning, and I want to meet you. *Please* trust me. I'm only trying to learn the truth about what happened, not just the night Annamarie died, but six or more years ago at the hospital where she worked. I also want to know why Annamarie was so frightened. She *was* frightened, you know."

"Yes, I know. Something happened at the hospital not long before Gary Lasch died," Lucy said dully. "I'm flying down tomorrow to clear out Annamarie's apartment in Yonkers. You don't have to fly up here. I'll meet you there, Miss Simmons."

60

On Thursday afternoon, Edna Barry called Molly and asked if she could come by and see her for just a few minutes.

"Certainly, Mrs. Barry," Molly said, her tone intentionally cool. Edna Barry had been positive about the spare key, and not only that, she also had been actually hostile in her insistence that Molly didn't remember what had transpired. I wonder if she wants to apologize, Molly thought, as she returned to sorting through the stacks of material she had laid out on the floor of the study.

Gary had been meticulously neat and precise in everything he did. Now, thanks to the police, his personal files and medical reference materials were scattered and mixed, having been taken apart and haphazardly replaced. What does it matter? she thought. I have nothing if not time.

She had already begun to put aside a stack of pictures that she was planning to send to his mother. None with me in them, of course, she thought wryly, just the ones of Gary with various VIPs.

I never was close to Mrs. Lasch, she thought, and I don't blame her for hating me. I'm sure I would hate the woman I believed murdered my only child. Hearing about Annamarie Scalli's death must have brought it all back to her, and chances are the media have been trying to get to her as well.

She flashed momentarily to Annamarie and to their conversation. I wonder who adopted Gary's son, she thought. I was so desperately hurt when I found out that Annamarie was pregnant. I hated her and I envied her. But even knowing what I do now, about how Gary scorned me, I long for the baby I lost.

Maybe someday I'll have another chance, she told herself.

Molly was sitting cross-legged on the floor as that last thought registered. She paused, almost shocked at the idea that perhaps someday a different life would be open to her. What a joke, she told herself, shaking her head. Even Jenna, my best friend, made it clear that she thinks my only options are a prison cell or an institution. How could I even imagine that this nightmare will ever end?

But still, she *did* have that hope, and she knew why. It was because bits of memory were breaking through; moments of the past buried deeply in her subconscious were starting to come to the fore. Something happened last night when I was locking the door, she thought, remembering the odd sensation that had coursed through her. I don't know what it was, but it was there.

She began to sort the medical and scientific journals and magazines that she remembered Gary had kept in careful chronological order on the bookshelves. The publications were varied, but Gary obviously had had a reason for keeping them. A glance inside a few of them showed that in virtually all he had checked at least one article in the table of contents. They all probably can be thrown out, Molly decided, but out of curiosity I'll at least glance through them when I get organized here. It will be interesting to see what Gary found worth saving and referencing.

The kitchen doorbell rang, and then she heard Mrs. Barry call. "Molly, it's me."

"I'm in the study," she called out as she continued to stack the magazines, then paused as she listened to the footsteps coming down the hallway. Hearing them, she remembered how often it had crossed her mind that Mrs. Barry had a heavy foot. She never wore anything except orthopedic, rubber-soled shoes, which always made a firm, squishing sound on the floors.

"Molly, I'm sorry." Edna Barry was barely inside the room before she began to speak.

Molly looked up and knew immediately that Mrs. Barry was not apologizing. Her expression was determined, her mouth set in a firm line. She was dangling the house key in her hand. "I know it's not a nice thing to do after all these years, but I can't work for you anymore. And I need to stop right away."

Bewildered, Molly pushed herself up from the floor and stood. "Mrs. Barry, you don't have to quit because of the thing about that key. We both think we're right about whether or not I brought it in from the garden, but I'm sure there's a reasonable explanation, and I'm confident that Fran Simmons will find it. You must understand why this point is so important to me. If somebody else used that key to come into the house, then it was *that* person and not me who left it in the drawer. Suppose someone who somehow knew about the key's hiding place out back came in that Sunday night?"

"I don't think anyone came in that night," Edna Barry said, her voice shrill. "And I'm not quitting because of the key. Molly, I'm sorry to say this, but I'm *afraid* to work for you."

"Afraid!" Stunned, Molly stared at the housekeeper. "Afraid of what?"

Edna Barry averted her eyes.

"You're not . . . afraid . . . of me? Oh dear God." Shocked, Molly reached out her hand. "I'll take the key, Mrs. Barry. Please leave. Now."

"Molly, you've got to understand. It's not *your* fault, but you *did* kill two people."

"Get out, Mrs. Barry!"

"Molly, get help. *Please get help.*"

With something between a groan and a sob, Edna Barry turned and rushed away. Molly waited until she saw the woman's car turn from the driveway and onto the road before she sank to her knees and buried her face in her hands. As she rocked back and forth, low whimpering sounds escaped from inside her.

She's known me since I was a baby, and *she* believes I'm a killer. What chance have I got? she asked herself. What chance have I got?

A few streets away, as she waited for the light to change, a distraught Edna Barry was reminding herself over and over that she had no choice but to give that reason to Molly for quitting. It strengthened her story about the spare key, and it kept people like Fran Simmons from getting too curious about Wally. I'm sorry, Molly, Edna thought, remembering the hurt she'd seen in Molly's eyes, but you've got to understand, *blood is thicker than water.*

61

Between bites of the lunch the housekeeper had served on a tray in his office, Calvin Whitehall barked orders to Lou Knox. He'd been in a foul mood all morning, partly, Lou suspected, because the Fran Simmons situation was getting under his skin. Lou knew that she was persistently calling for an interview and was refusing to be put off by Cal's vague promises of trying to set up something. From the talk he had overheard between Jenna and Cal, Lou also knew that Simmons had been scheduled to see Peter Black at noon that day.

When the private phone rang at 12:30, Lou had a feeling it would be Black, calling to report on the meeting. His instincts were right, and whatever it was that Black had to say sent Cal into a rage. "What did you say when she asked why Gary sent for you? If she picks up that scent . . . Why did you even see her in the first place? You know you can't do anything but hurt yourself. It doesn't take any brains to know that."

When Cal slammed down the phone, he looked almost apoplectic. It rang again almost immediately, and his sharp tone quickly softened when he realized who the caller was. "Yes, Doctor, I've spoken to Peter, as a matter of fact just a moment ago . . . No, he didn't tell me anything special. Should he have?"

Lou knew that the caller had to be Adrian Logue, the ophthalmologist, or whatever he claimed to be, who lived at the farmhouse in West Redding. For some reason that Lou didn't understand, both Whitehall and Black—and before that, Gary Lasch—always treated Logue with kid gloves. Over the years, Lou had occasionally driven Cal out to the farmhouse. It was never a long stay, though, and Lou always had waited in the car.

He'd seen Logue up close only once or twice—a skinny, mild-looking, gray-haired guy, who by now must be in his seventies. It was clear to Lou from watching his boss's expression that whatever the doctor was telling Cal was sending him over the edge.

It was always a bad sign when Cal went cold instead of exploding. As Lou watched, Cal's face froze into a tight, icy mask, and his eyes took on the veiled, slit-eyed look that reminded Lou of a tiger about to spring.

When Cal spoke, his voice was controlled but awesome in its confidence and authority. "Doctor, I have every respect for you, but you had absolutely no right to insist Peter Black go through with this procedure, and he had no right to follow your wishes. I can't think of anything more unnecessarily risky, particularly at this time. Under no circumstances can you be present when the reaction sets in. As usual, you will have to be satisfied with the videotape."

Lou couldn't hear what Dr. Logue was saying, but he could tell the pitch of his voice was rising.

Cal interrupted him. "Doctor, I guarantee that you will have the tape tonight." He hung up the phone abruptly and gave Lou a look that made him know he was in serious trouble.

"I believe I indicated to you that Fran Simmons was a problem," he said. "It's time to address that problem."

62

As soon as Fran left Peter Black's office, she placed a call to Philip Matthews. He was in his office, and from his tone of voice she could tell he was deeply concerned about something.

"Where are you, Fran?" he asked.

"In Greenwich. I'll be starting back to New York soon."

"Any chance you could come to my office this afternoon around three? I'm afraid that things are getting worse for Molly."

"I'll be there," Fran said, then pushed the END button on her car phone. She was approaching an intersection and braked as the traffic light changed. Left or right? She asked herself. She wanted to stop at the *Greenwich Time* office and try to catch Joe Hutnik.

But now a powerful need was compelling her to drive past the house in which she and her parents had lived for those four years. Peter Black's scornful reference to her father had hurt her deeply. The pain, however, was not for herself, she realized, but for her dad. She wanted to see the house again. It was the last place she had spent time with him.

Let's do it, she decided. Three blocks later she turned her car onto a tree-lined street that immediately seemed so familiar to her. They had lived in the middle of the block, in a Tudor-style brick and stucco house. She had intended simply to drive by it slowly, but instead she parked at the curb across the street from the house and stared at it with tear-filled eyes.

It was a lovely house, with leaded windows that gleamed in the sunlight. It looks pretty much the same, she thought, as she visualized the long, high-ceilinged living room with the handsome Irish marble fireplace. The library was small, she remembered. Her dad had joked that it was built to house ten books, but she thought it a great place to retreat to.

She was surprised to realize how many good memories were rushing through her mind. If Dad had only seen it through, she thought. Even if he had gone to prison, he would have been released years ago and been able to start over someplace else.

It didn't have to happen—that was what had haunted her and her mother. Should they have been aware of something about him that last day? Could they have prevented it?

If only he had talked to us, Fran thought. If he had only said *something!*

And where did the money go? she asked herself. Why wasn't there a trace of it, or at least some hint of an investment that hadn't worked? Someday I'll find the answer, she vowed as she started up the car.

She looked at her watch. It was twenty minutes of one. The odds were good that Joe Hutnik would be having lunch, but on the off chance that he might be in, she decided to stop by the *Time*.

Joe was, in fact, at his desk and was insistent that she was not interrupting; besides, he wanted to talk to her. "A lot of water under the bridge since last week," he said gruffly as he waved her to a chair and closed the door.

"I would say so," Fran agreed.

"The raw material for your program is expanding."

"Joe, Molly is innocent of both those crimes. I know it. I *feel* it."

Joe's eyebrows came together. "Level with me, Fran. You're kidding, right? 'Cause if you're not, then you're kidding yourself."

"Neither, Joe. I'm convinced she didn't kill either her husband or Scalli. Look, you have your finger on the pulse of the town. What do *you* hear?"

"Very simple. People are shocked, sad, but not surprised. They all think Molly is off her rocker."

"I was afraid of that."

"Then you'd better be afraid of something else. Tom Serrazzano, the prosecutor, is pressuring the parole board to revoke her parole. He knows he's stuck with her having bail on the new charge, but he's arguing that her statement when she got out of prison was inconsistent with her statement at her parole hearing that she had accepted responsibility for her husband's death. Because she's denying that now, he's arguing that she perpetrated a fraud on the parole board and should be required to finish serving the whole sentence. And he just may get his way."

"That means Molly could go right back to prison."

"My guess is that it's going to happen, Fran."

"It *can't* happen," Fran murmured, as much to herself as to Hutnik. "Joe, I met with Dr. Peter Black this morning. I've been doing some digging into the hospital and the Remington HMO. Something is going on there; just what it is, I haven't figured out yet. But I do know that Black was nervous when I got there. He almost broke out in hives when I asked why he thought Gary Lasch plucked *him* from a nondescript job to be his partner running Lasch Hospital and Remington Health Management, when his record was less than sterling and there were so many better-qualified candidates already in the area."

"That's odd," Joe said. "As I remember it, the impression we were given around here was that it was a coup to persuade him to come work at the hospital."

"Trust me, it wasn't." She stood up. "I'm on my way. Joe, I want to get copies of anything the *Time* wrote about the library fund drive my father was involved in, and anything written about Dad and the missing funds after he died."

"I'll see that you get it," he promised.

Fran was grateful that Joe didn't ask questions, but even so she felt she owed him an explanation. "This morning, when I was trying to pin Dr. Black down, he came up with a righteous-wrath defense. What right had I to question him? he asked. I was the daughter of a thief who stole the donations of half the people in town."

"That was a lousy dig," Hutnik said. "But I think it's easy enough to figure out the reason for it. He's got to be under a lot of pressure right now, and he doesn't want anything new to come along that might threaten the Remington acquisition of the smaller HMOs. The truth is, at least according to my sources, the deal is in trouble, Fran, lots of trouble. American National is getting the inside track. And from what I hear, things at Remington are a little shaky at the moment. These new HMOs, small though they may be, would bring in some extra cash and allow Remington to buy some time."

Joe opened the door for her. "As I told you the other day, the head of American National is one of the most respected physicians in the country, and he's also one of the biggest critics of the way HMOs are run. He thinks a national system is the only right answer, but until that day arrives, American National, under his leadership, is getting the highest HMO marks in the health field."

"So you think Remington may be losing out?"

"Looks that way. The smaller HMOs that were supposed to be a shoo-in to join Remington are huddling with American now. It seems incredible, but it could happen that Whitehall and Black, despite all the stock they own in Remington, may not be able to avoid a hostile takeover down the line."

It may be petty of me, Fran thought as she drove back to New York, but after that crack about Dad, nothing would give me more pleasure than to see Peter Black fail.

She stopped at the office, checked her mail, and then took a taxi down to Philip Matthews's office in the World Trade Center for their three o'clock meeting.

She found him seated at his desk, which was stacked high with papers; his expression was grim. "I just spoke to Molly," he said. "She's pretty shaken up. Edna Barry quit this morning, and you know what reason she gave? Get this: she's afraid of Molly, afraid to be around a person who killed two people."

"She didn't *dare* say that!" Fran stared at him in disbelief. "Philip, I'm telling you right now, that woman is *hiding* something!"

"Fran, I've been going through the statement Edna made to the police after she discovered Gary Lasch's body. It's absolutely consistent with what she told you and Molly yesterday."

"You mean the part where she says that Molly was the only one who had used the spare key, and that she didn't return it to the hiding place in the garden? Molly absolutely denies that ever happened. Philip, after Mrs. Barry discovered the body, when the police were questioning people, didn't they ask Molly about the key as well?"

"When Molly woke up covered with blood that Monday morning and learned what had happened, she became practically catatonic, and the condition lasted for days. I don't see any record of her being questioned about it. Don't forget, there was absolutely no sign of forced entry, and Molly's fingerprints were all over the murder weapon."

"Which means that Edna Barry's story will be believed no

matter how sure Molly is that she's lying." Fran paced the office in irritation. "My God, Philip, Molly can't get a break anywhere."

"Fran, I had a phone call this morning from the mighty Calvin Whitehall. He wants to bring on some big guns to help in Molly's defense. He's already checked and they're available. They've been given details of the case, and according to Whitehall, they all agree that the plea should be 'not guilty by reason of insanity.' "

"Philip, don't let that happen."

"I don't *want* it to happen, but there's another problem. The prosecutor is moving heaven and earth to get Molly's parole revoked."

"Joe Hutnik at the *Greenwich Time* tipped me off about that. So this is the way it stands: Molly's housekeeper is saying that she's afraid of her, and Molly's friends are trying to have her committed. That's what an insanity defense would amount to, wouldn't it? She would have to spend time in an institution of some sort, right?"

"No jury would let her walk after a second murder, so yes, she'd be locked up no matter what. We'll certainly never get another plea bargain, and I'm not at all sure the insanity defense would work."

Fran saw the misery in Philip's face. "This is getting personal for you, isn't it?" she asked.

He nodded. "It's been personal for a long time. I swear to you, though, that if I thought my feelings for Molly would interfere with my judgment in defending her, I'd turn her case over to the best criminal lawyer I could find for her."

Fran looked at Philip Matthews compassionately, remembering that her first impression of him at the prison gate was of his fierce protectiveness toward Molly. "I believe that," she said softly.

"Fran, it's going to take a miracle to keep Molly from going back to prison."

"I'm meeting with Annamarie's sister tomorrow," Fran said. "And as soon as I get back to the office today, I'm going to get the research department to find every scrap of background it can on Remington Health Management and everyone connected with it. The more I hear, the more I believe that those murders have less to do with Gary Lasch being a womanizer than with problems at Lasch Hospital and Remington Health Management."

She picked up her shoulder bag, and on her way out, she stopped at the window. "You have a spectacular view of Lady Liberty," she said. "Is that to encourage your clients?"

Philip Matthews smiled. "It's funny," he said. "That's exactly what Molly asked the first time she was here six years ago."

"Well, for Molly's sake, let's hope Lady Liberty proves to be Lady Luck as well. I've got a hunch about something, and if I'm right, it could be the break we've been hoping for. Wish me luck, Philip. See you later."

63

The dramatic change in Tasha began around five o'clock. Barbara Colbert could see it actually happening.

For the past two days the nurses had not used the light makeup that gave a hint of color to her ashen complexion, but now a pinkish glow was becoming evident.

The rigidity of her limbs, which had been held at bay by constant massage, seemed to be relaxing spontaneously. Barbara did not need to see the nurse tiptoe away from the bedside or hear her murmur on the phone in the sitting room to know that she was summoning the doctor.

It's better for Tasha this way, she tried to tell herself. Please, God, give me strength. And please let her live until her brothers are here. They want to be with her at the end.

Barbara got up from the chair and sat on the bed, taking care not to disturb the tangle of intravenous lines and oxygen equipment. She took both Tasha's hands in hers. "Tasha, Tasha," she murmured. "My only consolation is that you're going to be with Dad, and he loved you as much as I do."

The nurse was at the door. Barbara looked up. "I want to be alone with my daughter," she said.

The nurse's eyes were filled with tears. "I understand. I'm so sorry."

Barbara nodded and turned back. For an instant she thought she saw Tasha move, thought she felt a pressure on her hands.

Tasha's breathing quickened. Barbara felt her heart ripping as she waited for the final breath. "Tasha, Tasha."

She was vaguely aware of a presence at the door. The doctor. Go away, she thought, but she didn't dare turn away from this last moment of her daughter's life.

Suddenly Tasha opened her eyes. Her lips curved into a familiar smile. "Dr. Lasch, it was so stupid," she murmured, "I tripped on my shoelace and went flying."

Barbara stared. "Tasha!"

Tasha turned her head. "Hi, Mom . . ."

Her eyes closed, slowly opened again. "Mom, help me . . . *please.*" Her last breath was a quiet sigh.

"Tasha!" Barbara shrieked. "Tasha!" She whirled around. Peter Black was standing motionless in the doorway. "Doctor, you heard her! She spoke to me. Don't let her die! Do something!"

"Oh, my dear," Dr. Black said soothingly, as the nurse rushed in. "Let our dear girl go. It is over."

"She *spoke* to me!" Barbara Colbert screamed. *"You heard her!"*

Frantically she pulled Tasha's body into her arms. "Tasha, don't go. You're getting better!"

Strong arms were embracing her, gently compelling her to release her daughter. "Mother, we're here."

Barbara looked up at her sons. "She *talked* to me," she sobbed. "As God is my witness, before she died, *she talked to me!*"

Lou Knox was watching television when he received the summons he was expecting. Cal had warned him that he'd be driving a package out to West Redding, but he hadn't been sure what time he would have to leave.

When he got to the house, he found Cal and Dr. Peter Black in the library. It was instantly apparent to him that they had just had a major row. Cal's mouth was a narrow, mean line, and his cheeks were flushed. Dr. Black was holding a large glass of what appeared to be straight scotch, and from the glazed look in his eyes it was obvious it wasn't his first drink of the night.

The television was turned on, but the screen showed the deep blue of the video setting. Whatever they had been watching was no longer playing. When Cal saw that Lou was there, he snapped at Black, *"Give* it to him, you fool!"

"Cal, I'm telling you—" Dr. Black protested, his voice a dull monotone.

"Just *give* it to him!"

From the table next to him, Black picked up a small box, loosely wrapped in brown paper. Mutely he held it out to Knox.

"Is this the package I'm to take to West Redding, sir?" Lou asked.

"You know damn well it is, Lou. Now hurry up."

Lou remembered the phone call Cal had made this morning. This had to be the tape he was talking about with the ophthalmologist, Dr. Logue. Cal and Black must have been looking at it, because it was obvious the package had been opened and then rewrapped. "Right away, sir," he said crisply. But not until I see what this tape is all about, he thought as he left.

He hurried back to his apartment and carefully double locked the door. It wasn't difficult to open the package again without tearing the wrapping. As he'd expected, there was a videotape inside. Quickly he inserted it in the VCR and then pushed the PLAY button.

What was this about? he wondered as he studied the screen. He saw a hospital room—a pretty fancy one—with a young woman asleep or unconscious in bed, and a classy-looking old lady sitting next to her.

Wait a minute, Lou thought, I know who that woman is. She's Barbara Colbert, and that's her daughter, the one who has been in a coma for years. The family gave so much money for the long-term care building at Lasch that they named it after the girl.

The time the tape was made showed on the lower right corner of the screen: 8:30 this morning. Did this record the whole day? Lou wondered. Surely he didn't have twelve hours on this one tape.

He fast-forwarded to the end of the tape, rewound a short way, then pressed PLAY again. The picture now showed the old lady sobbing, while two men held on to her. Dr. Black was bending over the bed. The girl must have died, Lou thought. He checked the time again at the bottom of the picture: 5:40 P.M.

Just a couple of hours ago, Lou thought. But this *can't* be just about the girl dying, he reasoned. She's been out of it for years, so they knew she was going to die some time.

Lou knew that at any moment Cal might come up the steps, demanding to know what was keeping him. His senses straining to hear Cal approaching, he again rewound the tape, this time going further back.

What he saw made him shiver. It was hard to believe, but there it was: the girl who had been out of it for years, waking up, turning her head, talking clearly, talking about Dr. Lasch. Then she closed her eyes and died. And then there was Black, telling the mother he hadn't heard the girl say anything.

It was spooky. Whatever this was about, it was big stuff. Lou knew that. He also knew the chance he was taking when he spent precious time duplicating the last fifteen minutes of the tape and hiding it in the compartment behind the shelves in his apartment.

He was just getting in the car when Cal came out. "What kept you? What have you been up to, Lou?"

Lou was sure the naked fear he felt was visible in his face, but he forced himself to control it. He knew what he had in that tape, and the power it gave him. Long years of making deception an art form served him well.

"I was in the bathroom. My stomach isn't so good."

Without waiting for a response, he closed the car door and started the engine. An hour later he was at the farmhouse in West Redding, handing the package to the man he knew as Dr. Adrian Logue.

Almost feverish with excitement, Logue grabbed the package from Lou's hand and slammed the door in his face.

65

"It was one of the hardest things I did in my entire life," Edna Barry explained on the telephone to Marta Jones. She had just finished tidying up the kitchen after dinner, and it seemed a good time to have a final cup of tea and get her story across to her friend.

"Yes, it must have been dreadful for you," Marta agreed.

Edna had no doubt that Fran Simmons would be nosing around again, asking more questions, and she might very well drop over to see Marta. Well, if she did, Edna wanted to be sure her neighbor got the story right. *This* time, Edna vowed, Marta was going to pass on information that *wouldn't* hurt Wally. She took another sip of tea and moved the phone to her other ear. "Marta," she continued, "you were the one who put the idea in my head that Molly might be dangerous, remember? I tried not to think about it, but she *is* acting strange. She's very quiet. Sits for hours, just by herself. Doesn't want anyone around. Today she was on the floor, going through boxes. There were stacks of pictures of the doctor."

"No!" Marta gasped. "I would think she'd have gotten rid of them long ago. Why would she hold on to those? Would *you* want to look at a picture of a man you killed?"

"That's what I mean about her acting so strange," Edna said. "Then yesterday, when she said she never took the key from the hiding place in the garden—well, Marta, I realized then that all that business about forgetting everything started *before* the doctor died. I think it all began when she had the miscarriage. Depression must have set in then, and after that Molly was never the same."

"Poor woman," Marta said with a sigh. "It would be a lot better for her if they put her someplace where she can get real help, but I'm glad you're staying away from her, Edna. Don't forget, Wally needs you, and he has to be your first priority."

"That's the way I feel. Marta, it's good to have a friend like you I can talk to. I've been so upset, and I had to get it off my chest."

"I'm always here for you, Edna. Get to bed early and get a good night's sleep."

Satisfied at having accomplished her purpose, Edna got up, turned off the kitchen light, and went into the den. Wally was watching the all-news channel. Edna's heart sank when she saw a tape of Molly at the prison gate. The anchorman was saying, "It was only ten days ago that Molly Carpenter Lasch was released from Niantic Prison after serving five and a half years for killing her husband, Dr. Gary Lasch. Since then she has been arrested for the murder of her husband's lover, Annamarie Scalli, and Prosecutor Tom Serrazzano is pressing to have her parole revoked."

"Wally, why don't you switch channels?" Edna suggested.

"Are they going to put Molly back in prison, Mom?"

"I don't know, dear."

"She looked so scared when she found him. I was sorry for her."

"Wally, don't say that. You don't know what you're talking about."

"Yes, I do, Mom. I was there, remember?"

Panicked, Edna grabbed her son's face with both hands and forced him to look up at her. "Do you remember how the police scared you when Dr. Morrow was killed? How they kept asking you questions about where you were on the night he died? Do you remember, before they came I made you put your walking cast back on and use your crutches so they'd leave you alone?"

Afraid, he tried to pull away. "Mom, let go of me."

Edna held eye contact with her son. "Wally, you must *never* talk about Molly or that night. Not ever again, do you understand that?"

"I won't."

"Wally, I'm not going to work for Molly anymore. In fact, you and I are going on a trip. We'll drive far away somewhere, maybe to the mountains, or maybe even to California. Would you like that?"

He looked doubtful. "I think so."

"Then swear you'll never talk about Molly again."

There was a long pause before he said quietly, "I swear, Mom."

66

Even though Molly tried, Dr. Daniels would not let her put him off a second day. He told her he was coming over at six o'clock, and promptly at six he rang the bell.

"You have such courage to be alone with me," she murmured as she closed the door. "But if I were you, I'd be careful. Don't turn your back on me. I might be dangerous."

The doctor was taking off his coat as she said this. He paused, one arm still in the sleeve, and he studied her carefully. "What's *that* supposed to mean, Molly?"

"Come inside. I'll tell you about it." She brought him into the study. "Show and tell," she said, indicating the stacks of files and magazines on the floor, the pictures and albums on the sofa. "You can see I wasn't just sitting here brooding."

"I'd say you were housecleaning," Dr. Daniels observed.

"Housecleaning in a way, yes, but it's actually a little more than that, Doctor. It's called 'a fresh start,' or maybe 'a new chapter,' or 'bury the past.' Take your pick."

Daniels crossed to the sofa. "May I?" he asked, indicating the photographs.

"Look at any of the photos, Doctor. The ones on the left, I'll send to Gary's mother. The ones on the right go into the circular file."

"You're throwing them out?"

"I think that's healthy, Doctor, don't you?"

He was flipping through them. "There seem to be quite a few with the Whitehalls."

"Jenna's my best friend. As you know, Cal and Gary and Peter Black ran Remington together. There are a fair number of photos of Peter and his two ex-wives in there somewhere."

"I know you're very fond of Jenna, Molly. What about Cal? Are you fond of him too?"

He looked up and saw the hint of a smile on her lips.

"Doctor, Cal isn't likable," she replied. "I doubt if anybody really likes him, including his schoolmate-chauffeur-general facto-tum, Lou Knox. People don't *like* Cal so much as they are fascinated by him. He can be marvelously amusing. And he's very smart. I remember we once were at a dinner in his honor attended by some six hundred impressively important people. You know what Jenna whispered to me? 'Ninety-nine percent of them are here out of fear.' "

"Do you think that bothered Jenna?"

"Heavens no. Jenna *loves* Cal's power. Although, of course, she's strong herself. Nothing stands in *her* way. That's why she's already a partner in a prestigious law firm. She did that on her own." Molly paused. "I, on the other hand, am a cream puff. I always have been. Jenna has been great. Cal, on the other hand, would love to see me disappear off the face of the earth."

I agree with that, John Daniels thought. "Is Jenna coming by tonight?" he asked.

"No. She had a dinner to attend in New York, but she called this afternoon. I was glad she did. After Mrs. Barry left I really needed a lift."

Daniels waited. As he watched, Molly's expression changed. A look of sorrow mixed with disbelief came over her face. Her voice was even, her tone almost a monotone, as she told him about Edna Barry and her parting words.

"I called my mother this afternoon," Molly said. "I asked her if she and my father were afraid to be with me too; I asked if that was why they were staying away when I needed them. You see, I didn't want anyone around last week. When I got home, I felt the way I guess a burn victim must feel: 'Don't touch me! Leave me alone!' But after Annamarie's body was found, I wanted them. I *needed* them."

"What did they say?"

"That they can't come. Dad will be all right, but he had a ministroke. That's why they're not here. They called Jenna and told her about it, and they asked her to be with me. And of course she has been. You saw that."

Molly looked past Dr. Daniels. "It was important that I talk to them. I needed to know they were there for me. They've suffered so much over all this. After Mrs. Barry left today, if I thought *they* had abandoned me too, I would have . . ." Her voice trailed off.

"Would have *what,* Molly?"

"I don't know."

Yes, you do, Daniels thought. Rejection by your parents would have pushed you over the edge.

"Molly, how do you feel *now?*" he asked gently.

"Embattled, Doctor. If my parole is revoked, and they send me back to prison, I don't think I can handle it. I need more time, because I swear to you: I am going to remember exactly what happened after I came back to the house from the Cape that night."

"Molly, we could try hypnosis. It didn't work before, but that doesn't mean it wouldn't work now. It may be that the memory block is like an iceberg and is breaking up. I could help you."

She shook her head. "No, I have to do it myself. There's—" Molly stopped. It was too soon to tell Dr. Daniels that all afternoon, one name kept coming up over and over in her head: *Wally*.

But *why?*

67

Barbara Colbert opened her eyes. Where am I? she wondered blearily. What happened? Tasha. Tasha! She remembered that Tasha had spoken to her before she died.

"Mom." Walter and Rob, her sons, were standing over her, sympathetic, strong.

"What happened?" she whispered.

"Mom, you know that Tasha is gone?"

"Yes."

"You passed out. Shock. Exhaustion. Dr. Black gave you a sedative. You're in the hospital. He wants you to stay here for a day or two. For observation. Your pulse wasn't that great."

"Walter, Tasha came out of the coma. She talked to me. Dr. Black must have heard her. The nurse too; ask her."

"Mom, you'd sent the nurse into the other room. *You* talked to Tasha, Mom. She didn't talk to you."

Barbara fought against sleepiness. "I may be old, but I am not a fool," she said. "My daughter came out of her coma. I know she did. She spoke to me. I remember clearly what she said. Walter, *listen* to me. Tasha said, 'Dr. Lasch, it was so stupid, I tripped on my shoelace and went flying.' Then she recognized me, and she said, 'Hi, Mom.' And then she begged me to help her. Dr. Black heard her asking for help. I *know* he did. Why didn't he do something? He just stood there."

"Mom, Mom, he did everything he could for Tasha. It's better this way, really."

Barbara tried to struggle to a sitting position. "I repeat—I am *not* a fool. I did not imagine that Tasha came out of the coma," she said, her anger giving her voice its customary tone of authority. "For some terrible reason Peter Black is lying to us."

Walter and Rob Colbert grasped their mother's hands as Dr. Black, who had been standing out of the range of her view, stepped forward and pricked her arm with a needle.

Barbara Colbert felt herself sinking into warm, enveloping darkness. She fought against it momentarily, then succumbed.

"The most important thing is that she rest," Dr. Black assured her sons. "No matter how prepared we think we are to lose a loved one, when the moment of saying good-bye comes, the shock can be overwhelming. I'll look in on her later."

When Black got to his office after making rounds, there was a message waiting from Cal Whitehall. He was to call him immediately.

"Have you convinced Barbara Colbert that she was hallucinating last night?" Cal demanded.

Peter Black knew the situation was desperate and that it would do no good to lie to Cal. "I had to give her another sedative. She's not going to be easily convinced."

For a long minute Calvin Whitehall did not respond. Then he said quietly, "I trust you realize what you've brought on all of us."

Black did not answer.

"As if Mrs. Colbert is not a big enough problem, I just heard from West Redding. Having endlessly reviewed the tape, the doctor is demanding that his project be disclosed to the media."

"Doesn't he know what that will mean?" Black asked, dumbfounded.

"He doesn't care. He's nuts. I insisted he wait until Monday, so we can agree on a proper presentation. I will have taken care of him by then. In the meantime, I suggest you make Mrs. Colbert *your* responsibility."

Cal hung up the phone with a bang, leaving no doubt in Peter Black's mind that he expected to be obeyed.

68

Lucy Bonaventure took an early morning plane from Buffalo to New York's La Guardia Airport and by ten o'clock was entering Annamarie's garden apartment in Yonkers. In the nearly six years that Annamarie had lived there, Lucy had never seen the place. Annamarie had told her the apartment was small—it had only one bedroom, and besides, it was always more convenient for Annamarie to drive to Buffalo for visits.

Lucy knew that the police had searched the apartment after Annamarie died, and she understood that was why it had a disheveled appearance. The bric-a-brac on the coffee table was shoved together; books were piled haphazardly on the shelves, as if they'd been pulled out and replaced at random. In the bedroom it was obvious that the contents of drawers had been examined, then just tossed back carelessly by uncaring hands.

She had arranged for the manager of the condo units to handle the sale of the apartment. All Lucy had to do was to clear it out. She would like to get that done in one day, but realistically she knew it would be at least an overnight job. It was painful for her even to be there, to see Annamarie's favorite perfume on the dresser, to see the book she'd been reading still on the night table, to open the closet and see her suits and dresses and uniforms, and to know she would never wear them again.

All the clothing, as well as the furniture, would be picked up by charities. At least, Lucy reasoned, some needy people would be helped. It was small comfort, but it was something.

Fran Simmons, the reporter, was due to arrive at 11:30. While she waited for her, Lucy began clearing out Annamarie's dresser, folding the contents neatly, then placing them in cartons the handyman had given her.

She wept over the photographs she found in a bottom drawer, showing Annamarie holding her infant son, pictures obviously taken minutes after he was born. She looked so young in the photos and was looking at the baby so tenderly. There were other pictures of him, each marked on the back, "first birthday," "second birthday," until the last one, the fifth. He was a beautiful child, with sparkling blue eyes, dark brown hair, and a warm merry smile. It broke Annamarie's heart to give him up, Lucy thought. She deliberated over whether to show the photos to Fran Simmons, then decided she would. They might help her to understand Annamarie and the terrible price she had paid for her mistakes.

Fran rang the doorbell promptly at 11:30, and Lucy Bonaventure invited her in. For a moment the two women took each other's measure. Fran saw a buxom woman in her mid-forties, with swollen eyes, even features, and skin that seemed blotched from weeping.

Lucy saw a slender woman in her early thirties with collar-length, light brown hair and blue-gray eyes. As she explained to her daughter the next day, "It wasn't that she was all dressed up—she had on a dark brown pants suit with a brown and yellow and white scarf at her neck, and simple gold earrings—but she looked so New York. She had a nice way about her, and when she told me how sorry she was about Annamarie, I knew it wasn't just talk. I'd made coffee, and she said she'd like a cup, so we sat down at Annamarie's little dinette table."

Fran knew it would be wise to get straight to the point. "Mrs. Bonaventure, I began to investigate Dr. Lasch's murder because Molly Lasch, whom I knew from school, asked me to do a show on the case for the *True Crime* program I work with. She wants to uncover the truth about these murders as much as you do. She has spent five and a half years in prison for a crime she doesn't remember and, I have come to believe, she did not commit. There are far too many unanswered questions about Dr. Lasch's death. No one ever really investigated it at the time, and I'm trying to do it now."

"Yes, well, her lawyer tried to make it look as if Annamarie killed Dr. Lasch," Lucy said with remembered anger.

"Her lawyer did what any good lawyer would do. He pointed out that Annamarie said she was alone in her apartment in Cos Cob the night of the murder, but that she had no one who could corroborate it."

"If that trial hadn't been stopped, he was going to cross-examine Annamarie and try to make her out to be a murderer. I know that was his plan. Is he still Molly Lasch's lawyer?"

"Yes, he is. And a good one. Mrs. Bonaventure, *Molly did not kill Dr. Lasch. She did not kill Annamarie.* She *certainly* did not kill Dr. Jack Morrow, whom she hardly knew. Three people are dead, and I believe the same person is responsible for their murders. Whoever took their lives should be punished, but it was not Molly. That person is the reason Molly went to prison. That person is the reason she has been arrested for Annamarie's murder. Do you want Molly Lasch sent to prison for something she didn't do, or do you want to find your sister's murderer?"

"Why did Molly Lasch track down Annamarie and ask to meet her?"

"Molly had believed she had a happy marriage. Obviously she did not, or Annamarie wouldn't have been in the picture. Molly was trying to find the answer to why her husband was murdered, and to why her marriage failed. Where better than to start with the woman who had been her husband's lover? This is where you can help. Annamarie was *afraid* of someone, or of something. Molly saw that when they met that night, but you must have seen it long before then. Why did she change her name and take your mother's maiden name? Why did she give up hospital nursing? From everything I hear she was a marvelous bedside nurse and loved doing it."

"Yes, she was," Lucy Bonaventure said sadly. "She was punishing herself when she gave it up."

But what I need to know is *why* she gave it up, Fran thought. "Mrs. Bonaventure, you said that something had happened in the hospital—something that was terribly upsetting to Annamarie. Have you any idea what it was, or when it happened?"

Lucy Bonaventure sat silently for a moment, obviously struggling with her desire to protect Annamarie versus the fervent need to punish her murderer.

"I know it was not long before Dr. Lasch was murdered," she said, speaking slowly, "and it was over a weekend. Something went wrong with a young woman patient. Dr. Lasch and his partner, Dr. Black, were involved. Annamarie thought Dr. Black had made a terrible mistake, but she didn't report it because Dr. Lasch begged her to keep quiet, saying that if word of the mishap got out, it would destroy the hospital."

Lucy held up the coffeepot and gave Fran a questioning look. Fran shook her head, and Lucy poured more coffee into her own cup. She replaced the pot on the burner and sat staring into her coffee cup a few moments before speaking again. Fran knew she was trying to choose her words carefully.

"Honest mistakes do happen in hospitals, Ms. Simmons. We all know that. According to what Annamarie told me, the young woman had been running when she was injured and was dehydrated when they brought her in to the hospital. Dr. Black gave her some kind of experimental drug instead of the normal saline solution, and she slipped into a vegetative state."

"How awful!"

"It was Annamarie's duty to report it, and she didn't, having been asked not to by Dr. Lasch. But then a few days later, she overheard Dr. Black say to Dr. Lasch, 'I gave it to the right person this time. It took her right out.' "

"You mean they were deliberately experimenting on patients?" Fran asked, shocked at this revelation.

"I can only tell you what I've put together from the little bit Annamarie told me. She wouldn't talk about any of it much, and usually only if she had a couple of glasses of wine and needed to unburden herself." Lucy paused and sat once more staring into her cup.

"Was there something else?" Fran asked gently, anxious to get the woman to talk, but not wanting to prod her too hard.

"Yes. Annamarie told me that the very next night after the young woman was given the wrong drug, an old lady who'd had a couple of heart attacks and had been in the hospital for a while, died. Annamarie told me she couldn't be sure, but she suspected the old lady was given that experimental drug and apparently was the one who was *'the right person'* she had heard Dr. Black refer to, because she was the only one who died in the hospital that week, and because Dr. Black was in and out of the room and didn't mark the chart."

"Wasn't Annamarie even tempted to report that death?"

"She had absolutely no proof of anything being wrong in the second incident, and when tests were done on the young woman, the results indicated no trace of a suspicious substance. Annamarie *did* talk to Dr. Black, and she asked him why he hadn't marked the old woman's chart when he treated her. He told her she didn't know what she was talking about and warned her that if she started spreading such unfounded rumors, she would be sued for slander. When she asked him about the young woman who was now in a coma, he said she'd gone into cardiac arrest in the ambulance."

Lucy paused and once more filled her coffee cup. "Try to understand. Annamarie originally believed that the first incident was an honest mistake. She was in love with Gary Lasch and at that point even knew she was pregnant by him, although she hadn't yet told him. She didn't want to believe that he would have anything to do with hurting someone, and she didn't want to cause him or the hospital any trouble. But then, while she was agonizing over what she should do, Jack Morrow was murdered, and suddenly she became frightened. She believed that he had begun to suspect something was going wrong at the hospital, but it was only a suspicion. He apparently had wanted to give her something to hold for him for safekeeping, a file or papers or something, but he never got the chance. He was murdered first. Then, two weeks later, Gary Lasch was murdered. By then, Annamarie was terrified."

"Did Annamarie ever fall out of love with Gary Lasch?" Fran asked.

"At the end. He was avoiding her, and she had started to fear him. When she told him she was pregnant, he told her to get an abortion. If it weren't for DNA testing, she was sure he would have sworn it wasn't his child.

"Jack Morrow's death was a terrible blow to Annamarie. Even though she had gone into an affair with Dr. Lasch, I think she always loved Jack. Afterwards, she showed me Dr. Lasch's picture. She said, 'I was obsessed with him. He does that to women. He *uses* people.' "

"Did Annamarie think that things at the hospital were still going wrong, even after Gary Lasch was killed?"

"I don't think she had any way of knowing. And besides, her energies were soon focused on taking care of the child she was carrying. Ms. Simmons, we *begged* Annamarie to keep her baby. We would have helped her raise it. She gave it up because she didn't think she was worthy of it. She said to me, 'What do I tell my child—that I had an affair with his father, who was then murdered because of our affair? When he asks me to tell him what his father was like, do I tell him he was a danger to his patients and betrayed the people who trusted him?' "

"Annamarie told Molly that as both a doctor and a husband, Gary Lasch wasn't worth going to prison for," Fran said.

Lucy Bonaventure smiled. "That sounds like Annamarie," she said.

"I can't tell you how grateful I am to you, Mrs. Bonaventure," Fran said. "And I know how hard this is for you."

"Yes, it is. But let me show you something before you go." Lucy Bonaventure went into the bedroom and picked up the photographs she had placed on the dresser top. She showed them to Fran. "This is Annamarie with her baby. You can see how young she was. The adoptive family sent her a birthday picture of him for the first five years. This is the little boy she gave up. She paid such a terrible price for her mistakes. I hope, if Molly Lasch is innocent, that you can prove it. But tell her that in her own way, Annamarie was in prison too, a self-imposed one perhaps, but still one filled with pain and deprivation. And if you want to know who she was afraid of, you're right, I don't think it was Molly Lasch. I think the person she really feared was Dr. Peter Black."

69

"Cal, what *is* the matter with you? You've done nothing but bark at me, when the worst thing I seem to have done is suggest you get away from here for a few days and maybe get some golfing in."

"Jenna, I should think that simply reading the daily papers with all the coverage about that nurse's death and Molly's arrest might help you understand why I'm on edge. You should realize, my dear, that a fortune will slip through our fingers if American National gets these HMOs and then proceeds with a hostile takeover of Remington. We *both* know you married me for what I could give you. Are you willing to scale back your lifestyle?"

"I'm willing to concede that I'm very sorry I took the day off," Jenna snapped. She had followed Cal into his office, alarmed by the obvious tension he had displayed at the breakfast table.

"Why don't you visit your friend, Molly?" he suggested. "I'm sure *she* will be delighted to be comforted by you."

"It really is bad, isn't it, Cal?" Jenna asked quietly. "But I'm going to tell you this, not as a wife, but as another fighter—I *know* you; no matter how bad it is, you'll figure out how to make it pay off for you."

Calvin Whitehall's laugh was a short, mirthless bark. "Thank you, Jenna, I really needed that. However, I believe you're right."

"I *am* going to go over to see Molly. I was really concerned when I saw her Wednesday night. She was terribly down. Then when I spoke to her yesterday, after Mrs. Barry quit, she was positively reeling from the blow."

"You told me about that."

"I know. And I know you agree with Mrs. Barry. You wouldn't want to be alone with Molly either, would you?"

"Precisely."

"Cal, Mrs. Barry brought Molly some twenty sleeping pills that were from a prescription for her son. I'm very worried about that. I'm afraid that as depressed as she is, she might be tempted to—"

"To commit suicide? What a perfectly wonderful idea. That would be just what the doctor ordered." Cal looked past Jenna. "It's all right, Rita, you can come in with the mail."

As the maid entered, Jenna went around the desk and kissed the top of her husband's head. "Cal, don't joke, please. I honestly think that Molly *is* considering suicide. You heard her the other night."

"My opinion stands. She'd be doing herself a favor if she exercises that option. And she'd be doing a favor for a lot of other people too."

70

Marta Jones knew that only Wally would ring her doorbell with such persistence. When the ringing began, she was upstairs, straightening out the linen closet; with a patient sigh, she hurried down the stairs, her arthritic knees protesting every step of the way.

Wally's hands were jammed in his pockets, his head was down. "Can I come in?" he asked, his voice flat.

"You know you can come in anytime, dear."

He stepped inside. "I don't want to go."

"*Where* don't you want to go, dear?"

"To California. Mom is packing. We leave tomorrow morning. I don't like to be in the car a long time. I don't want to go. I came to say good-bye."

California? Marta wondered. What is *that* about? "Wally, are you sure your mom said California?"

"Yes, California. I'm sure." He fidgeted, then grimaced. "I want to say good-bye to Molly too. I won't bother her, but I don't want to leave without saying good-bye. Do you think it's all right if I say good-bye to Molly?"

"I certainly don't see why not."

"I'll go see her tonight," Wally muttered.

"What did you say, dear?"

"I have to go. Mom wants me to go to my meeting."

"That's a good idea. You know you always enjoy those meetings, Wally. Listen, isn't that your mother calling you?" Marta opened the door. Edna was standing on the steps of her house, her coat on, looking for her son.

"Wally's in here," Marta called out. "Come on, Wally." Curiosity made her run across the lawn without bothering to get a coat. "Edna, is it true you're driving to California?"

"Wally, get in the car," Edna Barry pleaded. "You know you're late." Reluctantly he obeyed, slamming the passenger door behind him.

Edna turned to her neighbor and whispered, "Marta, I don't know if we'll end up in California or in Timbuktu, but I know I've got to get out of here. Every time I turn on the news I seem to hear something else bad about Molly. The latest is that there's going to be a special meeting of the parole board on Monday. The prosecutor wants her parole revoked. If that happens, she'll have to serve the rest of her original sentence for killing Dr. Lasch."

Marta shivered. "Oh, Edna, I know. I heard that on the news this morning, and I think it's just terrible. That poor girl should be in an institution, not in a prison. But you mustn't get so upset about it that you let it drive you away from here."

"I know. I've got to go now. I'll talk to you later."

When she got back to her house, Marta was chilled and decided she needed a cup of tea. Once it was ready, she sat down at the table, sipping it slowly. Poor Edna, she thought. She's feeling guilty about quitting her job with Molly, but of course she had no choice. Wally has to be her main concern.

When you think about it, she reminded herself with a sigh, it just goes to show that money *doesn't* buy happiness. All that Carpenter family money behind her couldn't keep Molly out of a prison cell.

Marta thought of the other prominent and wealthy Greenwich family that had been in the news this morning. She had read about Natasha Colbert, who had been in a coma over six years. She had finally died, and her poor mother, prostrate with grief, had suffered a heart attack, and it looked like she might not survive. Maybe God would be doing her a favor if he took her, poor woman, Marta mused, shaking her head. All that grief . . .

She pushed back her chair and went back upstairs to finish tidying the linen closet. As she worked, a nagging feeling of worry would not leave her. Finally she realized what was causing it. Edna would have a fit if she knew that I told Wally that it would be all right for him to say good-bye to Molly Lasch, Marta thought. Oh well, she decided, it was probably just rambling, like he does so much of the time. Anyway, tomorrow he'll be gone. No use upsetting poor Edna by mentioning it to her. She's got enough on her mind as it is.

71

When she left Annamarie's sister, Fran Simmons sat in her car for a few minutes, considering which might be her best course of action. It was one thing if doctors Gary Lasch and Peter Black had given a patient the wrong medication, something that had put her in an irreversible coma, and then had covered up their mistake. Terrible as that was, it did not compare with deliberately using an experimental drug to end a patient's life. But that apparently was what Annamarie Scalli believed had happened.

And since she had been there at the time but knew she couldn't prove her suspicions, how can *I* possibly hope to prove anything now? Fran wondered.

According to Lucy Bonaventure, Annamarie had said that Peter Black was the one who not only made the mistake, but possibly went on to kill an elderly patient as well. Would that have given Black a sufficient motive for killing Gary Lasch? Lasch's death did eliminate a credible witness to his crime.

It was possible, she decided. If you believed a doctor could kill in cold blood. *But why?*

The car was cold. Fran started the engine and immediately pushed the temperature control up to the highest setting and turned on the fan. It's not just the air that's chilled me, she thought, I'm cold *inside* too. Whatever evil was set in motion at that hospital, it certainly has caused many people a great deal of pain. But why? *Why?* Molly has been punished for a crime I am now sure she did not commit. Annamarie gave up her child and the work she loved just to punish herself. A young woman was put into a vegetative state because of an experimental drug. An elderly woman may have died prematurely as part of the experiment.

And those are just the ones I know about, she thought. How many others might there be? Why, this could still be going on, Fran thought with a start.

But I swear that the key to all this is the relationship or the bond or whatever it was that existed between Gary Lasch and Peter Black. There *has* to be a reason why Lasch brought Black to Greenwich and literally handed him a partnership in a family-owned hospital.

A woman walking her dog passed the car and looked at Fran curiously. I'd better get moving, she thought. She knew where she had to go next—to talk to Molly and see if she could shed any light on what was behind the Gary Lasch and Peter Black connection. If she could determine what it was that bound them together in the first place, then she might finally start to understand what was going on at the hospital.

On the way to Greenwich, she called her office for messages and learned that Gus Brandt wanted to talk to her, having said it was urgent. "Before you put me through to him, check and see if the research department material on Gary Lasch and Calvin Whitehall came through yet," she told her assistant.

"It's on your desk, Fran," she was told. "You won't be looking for reading material for a week with that pile to wade through, especially all the stuff on Calvin Whitehall."

"I can't wait to get at it. Thanks. Now put me through to Gus, please."

Her boss had been about to go out to lunch. "Glad you caught me, Fran," he said. "It looks as if you'll be visiting your friend Molly Lasch in the slammer by Monday afternoon. The prosecutor was just quoted as saying that he had no doubt that her parole would be revoked. And the minute he gets the official word, she'll be on her way back to Niantic Prison."

"They can't *do* that to Molly," Fran protested.

"Oh yes they can. And my guess is, they *will.* She got off light in the first place because she acknowledged that she had killed her husband, and then the moment she was free, she started claiming she didn't do it. That in itself is parole violation, baby. With a new murder charge against her, how would you vote if you were deciding whether or not she belongs behind bars? Anyhow, do a piece on it tonight."

"All right, Gus. See you later," Fran said with a sinking heart.

She had been planning to call Molly next and tell her that she needed to see her, but Gus's mention of going out to lunch had given her an idea. Susan Branagan, the volunteer in the coffee shop at Lasch Hospital, had mentioned that she had earned her ten-year pin for service there, which means she was around when a young woman went into an irreversible coma more than six years ago, Fran thought. That isn't the kind of event that happens often. She might remember who the young woman was and what had become of her.

Talking to that young woman's family and trying to get details of her accident might be a tangible way to start checking on the story Annamarie had told her sister, Fran thought. Perhaps it was a long shot, but not an implausible one. But I hope I don't run into Dr. Peter Black, Fran thought. He'd have a fit if he knew I was asking more questions about the hospital.

It was 1:30 when she reached the hospital coffee shop. The lunch hour was in full swing, and the volunteers were hard at work. There were two women bustling about behind the lunch counter, but to her intense disappointment, Fran saw that Susan Branagan wasn't one of them.

"There's a seat at the counter, or if you wait for just a minute, a table is being cleared right now," the hostess told her.

"I guess Mrs. Branagan isn't on duty today," Fran said.

"Oh, yes. She's here. She's waiting tables today. There she is, coming out of the kitchen now."

"Could I possibly wait for one of her tables?"

"You're in luck. The one being cleared is in her area. It seems to be about ready."

The hostess led her through the room, deposited her at a small table, and handed her a menu. A moment later a cheery voice addressed her. "Well, good afternoon. Have you decided what you'd like, or do you need a little more time?"

Fran looked up and immediately could see that Susan Branagan not only remembered her but now knew who she was. Keeping her fingers crossed that she wouldn't be rebuffed, she said, "It's nice to see you again, Mrs. Branagan."

Susan Branagan beamed with pleasure. "I didn't know I was talking to a famous person when you and I were chatting the other day, Ms. Simmons. As soon as I found out, I started watching you on the evening news. I *love* your reports on the Molly Lasch case."

"I can see you're busy now, but I'd love to speak to you for a few minutes later if you're willing. You were very helpful to me the other day."

"And since we talked, that poor girl you asked me about, that nurse, Annamarie Scalli, was killed. I can't believe it. Do you think Molly Lasch really did it?"

"No, I don't. Mrs. Branagan, are you off duty soon?"

"At two o'clock. This place clears out by then. Speaking of which, I guess I better take your order."

Fran glanced at the menu. "A club sandwich and coffee would be fine."

"I'll put your order in right away, and if you don't mind waiting, I'll be glad to have a chat with you again later."

Half an hour later, Fran looked about the coffee shop. It's exactly as she said, she thought. You'd think there'd been a fire drill. The place was suddenly three-quarters empty. Both the clatter of dishes and the hum of voices had sharply diminished. Susan Branagan had cleared the table and promised to be back in a flash.

When she returned she was no longer wearing her volunteer's apron, and she carried a cup of coffee in each hand. "Much better," she said with a sigh, as she put the coffee down and settled into the chair opposite Fran. "As I told you, I love this job, but my feet don't love it as much as the rest of me does. But you didn't come here to talk about my feet, and I just remembered I'm due at the hairdresser in half an hour, so how can I help you today?"

I like this lady a lot, Fran thought. She doesn't mind getting down to business. "Mrs. Branagan, you said the other day that you have your ten-year service pin?"

"That's right. And, God willing, some day I'll have my twenty-year pin."

"I'm sure you will. I'd like to ask you about something that happened in the hospital a good while ago. It was actually a short time before Dr. Morrow and Dr. Lasch were murdered."

"Oh, Ms. Simmons, so much happens here," Mrs. Branagan protested, "I'm not sure I'll be of any help."

"You might remember this incident, though. Apparently a young woman was brought in after an accident she suffered while she was running, and she went into an irreversible coma. I'm hoping you might know something about her."

"Something *about* her," Susan Branagan exclaimed. "You're talking about Natasha Colbert. She was in our long-term care residence for years. She died just last night."

"She died *last night!* "

"Yes. It's so sad. She was only twenty-three when she had the accident, you know. She fell while she was jogging and went into cardiac arrest in the ambulance. You know the Colbert family; they're the ones who own the big newspaper chain, so they are *very* wealthy. After the girl had the accident, her mother and father donated the money for the long-term care residence and named it after her. Look across the lawn—it's that lovely two-story building there."

Cardiac arrest once she was in the ambulance, Fran thought. Who was the ambulance driver? Who were the medics? She'd need to talk to them. They shouldn't be too hard to track down, though.

"Her mother collapsed when Tasha died last night. She's here right now, and I understand she's had a heart attack as well." Susan Branagan dropped her voice. "See that good-looking man over there? He's one of Mrs. Colbert's sons. There are two of them. One of them is with her every single minute. The other one was down here for a bite to eat about an hour ago."

If Mrs. Colbert dies from the strain of her daughter's death, then she's one more victim of whatever it is that's going on here, Fran thought.

"It's so painful for the sons," Susan Branagan said. "Of course, for all intents and purposes, they lost their sister over six years ago, but still, it hits hard when the end really comes." She dropped her voice. "I hear Mrs. Colbert went a little crazy after Tasha died. The nurse said she was screaming that Tasha had awakened from her coma and had spoken to her—which, of course, was absolutely impossible. She claimed Tasha had said something like, 'Dr. Lasch, I tripped on my shoelace and went flying,' and then, 'Hi, Mom.' "

Fran felt her throat close. She could barely force out the words. "Was the nurse in the room with Mrs. Colbert at the time?"

"Tasha had a suite, and Mrs. Colbert had sent the nurse into the sitting room. She wanted to be alone with her daughter. But when Tasha died, Mrs. Colbert wasn't alone. At the last minute the doctor got there. He says he heard nothing, and that Mrs. Colbert was hallucinating."

"Who was the doctor?" Fran asked, although she was sure she already knew.

"The head of the hospital, Dr. Peter Black."

If Annamarie's suspicions were valid over six years ago, and if Mrs. Colbert was right about what happened last night, it sounds as if, after destroying Tasha, Black has continued experimenting on her, Fran thought.

Helplessly she looked across the room at the man Susan Branagan had pointed out to her. She wanted to rush over to him, to warn him that his mother was a danger to Dr. Peter Black, and that he should get her out of the hospital before it was too late.

"Oh, there's Dr. Black now," Susan Branagan said. "He's going over to Mr. Colbert. I do hope it isn't bad news."

As they watched, Peter Black spoke quietly to the man, who nodded, got up, and began to follow him out of the room.

"Oh dear," Mrs. Branagan said, "I just *know* it's bad news."

Fran did not respond. As he was leaving, Peter Black had spotted her, and they stared at each other. His eyes were cold, angry, menacing—certainly not the eyes of a healer.

I'll get you, Fran thought. If it's the last thing I ever do, I'll get you.

72

Whenever a troubling situation reached crisis level, Calvin White-hall had the enviable ability to eliminate every trace of frustration and anger from his mind. That ability was put to the test by the call he received from Peter Black at 4:30 that afternoon. "Let me understand," he said slowly. "You are telling me that Fran Simmons was sitting in the coffee shop of the hospital, gossiping with one of the volunteers, when you went there to tell Barbara Colbert's son that his mother had died?"

It was a rhetorical question.

"Did you then speak to the volunteer and ask her the exact nature of her discussion with Fran Simmons?"

Peter Black was calling from his library at home and holding his second scotch in his hand. "Mrs. Branagan was gone by the time I could decently leave Mrs. Colbert's sons. I phoned her home every fifteen minutes until I got her. She had been at the hairdresser."

"I am not interested in where she had been," Whitehall said coldly. "I am interested in what she told Simmons."

"They were talking about Tasha Colbert," Peter Black said bleakly. "Simmons had asked her if she knew about a young patient at the hospital who had been in an accident and gone into an irreversible coma more than six years ago. Apparently Mrs. Branagan identified the patient for her and filled Simmons in on whatever knowledge of the events she had."

"No doubt including Barbara Colbert's statement that she had heard her daughter speak before she died?"

"Yes. Cal, what are we going to *do?*"

"*I* am going to save your skin. *You* are going to finish your drink. *We* are going to talk later. Good-bye, Peter."

The click of the receiver being replaced was barely audible. Peter Black gulped down the remaining contents of his glass and instantly refilled it.

Calvin Whitehall sat nearly motionless for several minutes while he considered and rejected possible avenues to follow. After some time, he reached a decision, analyzed it thoroughly, and was satisfied that it would eliminate two of his problems—West Redding and Fran Simmons.

He dialed West Redding. The phone rang a dozen times before anyone answered.

"Calvin, I've been watching the tape." The excitement in the doctor's voice made him sound almost youthful. "Do you *realize* what has been achieved? What arrangements have you made for press interviews?"

"That's exactly why I'm calling, Doctor," Cal said smoothly. "You don't watch television, so you wouldn't know who I'm talking about, but there is a young woman who is achieving national prominence as an investigative reporter, and who I am arranging to have come out and do a preliminary interview with you. She understands we have to maintain absolute secrecy, but she will immediately begin plans for a thirty-minute special that will be aired within seven days of now. You must realize that it is essential to whet public interest so that when this stunning scientific achievement is unveiled, the show will be watched by a huge national audience. It's all got to be carefully planned."

Whitehall got the response he anticipated. "Calvin, I am very pleased. I realize that we may have some minor legal problems to contend with, but that is of little importance given the significance of what I have achieved. At seventy-six years of age, I want to see my accomplishments recognized before my own time runs out."

"And you shall, Doctor."

"I don't think you've told me the name of the young woman."

"It's Simmons, Doctor. Fran Simmons."

Calvin hung up the phone and pressed the button on the intercom that connected him to the garage apartment. "Get over here, Lou," he said.

Even though Cal had announced no plans to go out that evening, and Jenna had left earlier, taking her own car, Lou Knox had been waiting for the summons. He had seen and heard enough to know that Cal was having serious problems and that, sooner or later, he would be called in to help solve them.

He was right on the money, as usual.

"Lou," Cal said, his manner almost genial, "Doctor Logue in West Redding has become a serious problem, as has Fran Simmons."

Lou waited.

"Believe it or not, I am setting up an appointment for Ms. Simmons to interview the good doctor. I think you should be in the vicinity when it takes place. Now I should tell you that Doctor Logue has a good many combustibles in his laboratory at the farmhouse. I know you've never been inside, so let me explain. The laboratory is on the second floor, but quite accessible thanks to an outside staircase to a back porch that leads directly to it. The window onto the porch is always left slightly open for ventilation. You're following me, aren't you, Lou?"

"Yes, Cal."

"Mr. Whitehall, Lou, please. Otherwise you might forget yourself in front of others."

"Sorry, Mr. Whitehall."

"There is a clearly marked oxygen tank in the laboratory. I am sure that a fellow as clever as you are could toss a flaming object into that room and be down those steps and clear of the house before the tank explodes. Don't you agree?"

"Yes, I do, Mr. Whitehall."

"This mission may take you away from here for several hours. Of course, any overtime service you do for me is always suitably rewarded. You know that."

"Yes, sir."

"I have been turning over in my mind the best way to persuade Ms. Simmons to visit the farmhouse. Naturally the utmost secrecy about her trip there must be maintained. Therefore I think she should receive a tip she can't resist, preferably from an anonymous source. You get my drift?"

Lou smiled. "Me."

"Exactly. How say you, Lou?"

"How say you?" was Cal's habitual touch of humor when he was satisfied that a good plan was about to be executed.

"You know me," Lou said, swallowing Cal's name before he uttered it, "I love to play Deep Throat."

"You've done it so well before. This time I think it should be *particularly* interesting. And *rewarding,* Lou. Don't forget that."

As they smiled at each other, Lou thought back to Fran Simmons's father and to the hot tip Lou had passed along to him, telling him he'd heard Cal talking of overnight riches to be made in a stock that was about to go public. The $40,000 Simmons had hastily borrowed from the library fund, thinking he would replace it in a few days. What led Simmons to take his own life was that a second withdrawal, under his forged signature, had been made that raised the deficit to $400,000. He knew that after he admitted the first illegal withdrawal, nobody would believe that he wasn't guilty of the second.

Cal had been particularly generous that time, Lou remembered. He'd been allowed to keep the original $40,000 Simmons had eagerly pressed into his hand and the worthless stock certificates that Simmons had trustingly put in Lou's name.

"Given our history, it seems only fitting that I be the one to make the call to Fran Simmons, sir," Lou said to his former school chum. "I look forward to it."

73

As soon as Fran left the hospital, she phoned Molly from the car. "I really need to see you," she said urgently.

"I'm certainly here," Molly told her. "Come by. Jenna is with me, but she has to leave soon."

"I hope I don't miss her. I've been trying to set up a date to talk with both her and her husband. I'll be there in a couple of minutes."

I'm cutting it close, Fran thought, checking her watch and calculating that she had to start back to New York in the next half hour, but I do want to see for myself how Molly is doing. She has to have received the notice for the special meeting of the parole board scheduled for Monday. It occurred to her that if Jenna was still there, she couldn't ask Molly about Gary Lasch's inviting Peter Black to join him in running the hospital. She'd be sure to tell her husband. Of course, Fran realized that given their history, Molly might tell Jenna what they talked about anyhow.

At ten minutes to three, Fran turned into Molly's driveway. There was a Mercedes convertible parked in front of the house, which she knew had to be Jenna's car.

I haven't seen her in so many years, Fran thought. I wonder if she's still as great looking as she was back then? For a moment the old sense of inadequacy enveloped her as she thought of the years she had lived in Greenwich and gone to school there.

When they were at Cranden Academy, it was generally known that Jenna's family didn't have money. Jenna herself used to joke, "My great-great grandfather made big bucks, and his descendants spent it all!" But there was no debating her blue-blood lineage. Like Molly's ancestors, Jenna's had been late-seventeenth-century settlers from England who came to Boston as wealthy appointees of the Crown, not like most who arrived, hoping to scrape together a living in the New World.

Molly opened the door as Fran came up the walk. She obviously had been watching for her. Fran was startled at Molly's appearance. She was ghostly pale, and her eyes were heavily circled. "Reunion time," she said. "Jenna waited to see you."

Jenna was in the study, looking through a stack of photographs. She jumped up when she saw Fran. "We'll meet again," she sang as she swooped across the room to embrace her.

"Don't remind me of that idiotic class history I wrote," Fran begged with an exaggerated grimace. After the quick embrace, she stepped back. "Come on, Jenna, isn't it about time you started to lose your looks?"

Jenna did look spectacular. Her dark brown hair fell with casual elegance to a point just above the collar of her jacket; her enormous hazel eyes positively glowed; her slender body moved with a seemingly unconscious air of careless elegance, as if the beauty she possessed and whatever compliments she received for it were no more than her due.

For an instant, Fran felt as though the clock had spun backwards. The closest she had been to Molly and Jenna during those four years at the academy was the time they all spent working on the yearbook. Today, this room reminded her of the yearbook office, with the piles of papers and files, the scattered photographs, the stack of old magazines.

"It's been a useful day," Molly said. "Jenna got here at ten and hasn't let up since. We've been going through everything that was in Gary's desk and on the shelves of this room when it was his study. We got rid of a lot of stuff."

"Not a fun day, but there's time for that later, isn't there, Fran?" Jenna asked. "When this nightmare is over, Molly is coming into the city and staying in the apartment with me. We're going to spend days in the marvelous new salon I've found, just being pampered. We're going on a shopping spree that will make the term 'excessive' seem inadequate, and then we're going to dine our way through the best restaurants in New York. Le Cirque 2000 will be our kickoff."

She spoke with such confidence that Fran suspended reality for a moment and actually believed her, even to the point of experiencing the feeling of being left out and a longing to be included in the plans. Again, shades of yesterday, she thought.

"I've given up believing in miracles, but if that miracle should happen, then Fran is definitely one of the celebrants," Molly said. "Without you two in my corner, I wouldn't have made it this far."

"You'll make it, I promise, on my honor as the wife of Cal the Mighty," Jenna said with a smile. "Speaking of whom, Fran, I'm afraid that this merger business has him busy and cranky at the same time, which is an awesome combination. I can get together with you almost any day next week, but it would be better to hold off trying to make an appointment with him."

She hugged Molly. "I've got to run, and Fran may want to go over something with you. Fran, it's really good to see you again. Next week, right?"

Fran thought fast. If Molly's parole were to be revoked, it would happen on Monday, and Jenna would certainly want to be with her. "How about Tuesday, around ten, in your office?"

"Perfect."

Molly walked with Jenna to the door. When she came back to the study, Fran said, "Molly, I've got to get back to New York on the double, so I'll be quick. I'm sure you heard about the special meeting of the parole board on Monday."

"Oh, yes, I've not only heard about it, I've received a notice to attend." Molly's face and voice were calm.

"I know what you're thinking, but hang in there, Molly. Something's going to break, I swear to you. I spoke to Annamarie's sister today, and she told me some shocking things about Lasch Hospital. They involve your husband and Peter Black."

"Peter Black didn't kill Gary. They were close."

"Molly, if even half of what I suspect about Peter Black is true, he's a thoroughly evil man, capable of committing just about any crime. This is what I need to know from you, and hopefully you'll have the answer: Why did your husband invite Peter Black to move here and share his practice? I've done research on Black. He was no great shakes as a doctor, and he didn't have a nickel to contribute to the operation. Nobody just gives away half a hospital to an old buddy—which, in fact, I don't believe Black really was to Gary Lasch. Do you know the reason Gary brought Black here?"

"Peter was already in place at the hospital when I started dating Gary. The subject never came up."

"I was afraid of that. Molly, I don't know what I'm looking for, but do me a favor and let me come back and go through all Gary's files before you discard anything. Maybe I'll find something helpful."

"If you want," Molly said indifferently. "I've got three full garbage bags already in the garage. I'll put them in the storage closet for you. How about the photos?"

"Hold on to them for now. We may want some of them for the program when we do it."

"Oh yes, the program!" Molly sighed. "Was it really just ten days ago that I asked you to start an investigation that I thought would prove my innocence? Oh, the naïveté of the lamb," she said with a wan smile.

She's given up hope, Fran thought. She knows in all likelihood that on Monday she's on her way back to prison to serve the remaining time from her original ten-year sentence, and that's even before the new trial for the murder of Annamarie Scalli. "Molly, look at me," she commanded.

"I *am* looking at you, Fran."

"Molly, you've *got* to trust me. I believe Gary's murder is only one of a series of murders that you certainly *could not* and *did not* commit. Believe me, I'm going to prove that, and when I do, you're going to be completely exonerated."

She's got to believe that, Fran thought, hoping she had sounded sufficiently convincing. It was apparent to her that Molly was sinking into listless depression.

"And then I'll get a makeover and dine my way through the best restaurants in New York." She paused and shook her head. "You and Jenna are great pals, but I think you're both mixing fact and fiction. I'm afraid my fate is sealed."

"Molly, I'm on the air tonight, so I have to go and get prepared. Please don't get rid of anything here." Fran glanced down at the couch. The photographs were spread out, and she could see that Gary Lasch seemed to be in just about all of them.

Molly noticed Fran looking at the old photos. "Jenna and I were reminiscing before you came. The four of us did have some good times, or at least *I* thought we did. God knows what my loving husband was thinking back then. Probably something like, 'Oh boy, another night out with the Stepford wife.' "

"Molly, *stop* it! Stop hurting yourself," Fran begged.

"Hurting myself? Now why would I need to do that? The whole world is already in on that act. They don't need any help from me. Fran, you've got to get back to New York, so go on. Don't worry about me. Oh, wait—one quick question. Do you have any use for these old magazines? I glanced at them, but they just contain medical articles Gary was reading. I thought I'd try to read them, but I'm fresh out of intellectual curiosity."

"Did he write any of the articles?"

"No. He just marked the ones that interested him."

What interested Gary Lasch as a doctor sure interests me, Fran thought. "Let me take the magazines with me, Molly. I'll glance at them, then get rid of them for you." She bent down and picked up the heavy stack from the floor.

Molly held the front door open for her. Fran stood for a moment, torn between the need to be on her way and her reluctance to leave Molly in her obviously despondent frame of mind. "Molly, any memory breakthroughs?"

"I thought I was having some, but like everything else, they seem to be sound and fury, signifying nothing. My brave talk about memory certainly was a mistake, wouldn't you say? It looks as though on Monday it's going to buy me four and a half years more of free room and board, and that's separate from when they convict and sentence me for Annamarie's murder."

"Molly, don't give up!"

Molly, don't give up. It was a refrain that ran through Fran's head, as with frequent worried glances at the clock on the dashboard, she drove through the heavier than usual traffic on her way back to New York.

74 _____

"Mom, I don't want to go to California." Wally Barry's tone had become increasingly belligerent throughout the day.

"Wally, we're simply not going to talk about it anymore," his mother responded firmly.

Edna watched helplessly as her son slammed out of the kitchen and stomped up the stairs. All day he had absolutely refused to take his medicine, and she was getting concerned.

I've got to get him away from here, she thought. I'll put some of his medicine in a glass of warm milk when he goes to bed. That will help him to sleep and calm him down.

She looked at Wally's untouched dinner plate. Wally's appetite was usually very good, and tonight in an effort to appease him, she had prepared a favorite meal—veal chops, asparagus, and mashed potatoes. But instead of eating, he'd sat at the table, muttering to himself, his attitude surly. The voices inside his head were talking to him tonight. Edna could tell, and it worried her.

The phone rang. She was sure that it was Marta; she had to make a quick decision. It would have been nice to have a quiet cup of tea with Marta, but it wasn't a good idea tonight. If Wally started talking again about the key, and about the night Dr. Lasch died, Marta might start taking him seriously.

It's probably all just his imagination, Edna told herself, an assurance she had made every time Wally mentioned the night of the murder. And if it isn't "just his imagination"? she wondered fleetingly, then dismissed the thought. Even if he *was* there, what happened that night surely wasn't his fault. The phone was ringing for the fourth time, so she finally picked it up.

It had been a struggle for Marta Jones to dial Edna's number. She had decided that she'd better warn Edna about her telling Wally that it was okay for him to say good-bye to Molly Lasch. She was going to suggest that maybe tomorrow morning on the way out of town, Edna could drop by Molly's house and let Wally speak to her. That would satisfy him, Marta was sure.

When Edna answered the phone, she said, "I just thought I'd run over and say good-bye to you and Wally, if that's all right."

Edna had her answer prepared. "Marta, to tell you the truth

I'm so far behind on getting packed and organized that I'd better not even let you in the door right now. The minute I take a break and sit down, I know I'll be useless to do anything more tonight. How about coming over in the morning and having some breakfast with us?"

Well, I can't *force* myself on her, Marta thought, and she *does* sound tired. I do hate to upset her. "Sounds good," she said with forced cheerfulness. "Is Wally helping you, I hope?"

"Wally's already upstairs in his room, watching television," Edna said. "He's had one of his difficult days, so I'm going to put an extra dose of his medicine in warm milk and take it up to him now."

"Oh, then he'll be sure to get some rest," Marta agreed. "I'll see you in the morning."

She hung up, relieved to think that Wally was safely in his own room and would soon be asleep. I guess he gave up on the notion of seeing Molly tonight, Marta decided. One less thing for her to worry about.

75

Among the lead stories for that night's evening news was the death of Natasha Colbert after six years in an irreversible coma, followed by the death, less than twenty-four hours later, of her mother, socialite and philanthropist Barbara Canon Colbert.

Fran sat at her desk in the studio and watched with somber eyes as the pictures flashed on the screen—Tasha, radiant and alive, with flaming red hair; her handsome, elegant mother. Peter Black killed *both* of you, Fran thought, although realistically, I may never be able to prove it.

She had spoken to Philip Matthews and heard his grim prediction that Molly almost certainly would be back in prison by Monday afternoon. "I spoke to her shortly after you left, Fran," Philip said. "Then I called Dr. Daniels. He's going over to see her this evening; he agrees that if she's taken into custody at the parole board meeting on Monday, she'll probably have a complete collapse. I'll be with her, of course, and he wants to be there as well, just to be on the safe side."

This is one time I hate my job, Fran thought as she received the signal that she was on air: "The Connecticut parole board has called an emergency session for Monday afternoon, suggesting the strong probability that Molly Carpenter Lasch will be returned to prison to finish serving the time left on her original ten-year sentence in the death of her husband, Dr. Gary Lasch."

She ended her report by saying, "In the past year in this country, three convicted killers have been exonerated of the crimes for which they were imprisoned, because of either new evidence or the confession of the real culprit. Molly Lasch's attorney has vowed a ceaseless fight to overturn or vacate her plea, as well as to prove that she is innocent of the charge of murder filed against her in the death of Annamarie Scalli."

With a sigh of relief, Fran unhooked her microphone and got up. She had reached the station barely in time to go into makeup and put on a fresh jacket. She hadn't had time to do more than wave to Tim as she rushed onto the set. A commercial was running between their spots, and he called out to her, "Fran, wait for me. I want to talk to you."

On her way into the studio she had dropped the magazines Molly gave her on her desk, and she hadn't done more than merely glimpse at the material on Lasch and Whitehall that she'd requested from the research department. Now, while she waited for Tim, she reached for it, eager to get started.

Skimming through the research material, she could see that the pages on both Calvin Whitehall and Dr. Gary Lasch seemed detailed and extremely thorough. It looks like research has pulled out all the stops in this one, she thought gratefully. I have a hunch I'll be doing a lot of reading tonight.

"You must plan to do a lot of reading."

Fran looked up. Tim was at the door. "Make a wish fast," she told him. "You just said exactly what I was thinking, and when that happens, you get whatever you wish for."

"I never heard that one, but anyhow it's easy to do. Here goes: I wish you'd have a hamburger with me. How's that?" he asked with a laugh. "I was on the phone with my mother earlier today, and when I told her I let you pay for dinner the other night, she yelled at me. She said she doesn't agree with this business of men and women splitting checks unless it's a business appointment or a case of dire financial necessity. She said that with my paycheck and total lack of responsibilities, I shouldn't be so chintzy." He grinned. "I think she was right."

"I'm not sure about that, but yes, I'd love to have a ham-burger—if you don't mind making it a fast one." Fran pointed to the stack of files and magazines. "I need to start working my way through all this stuff tonight."

"I was sorry to hear about the parole board emergency session. That's not good for Molly, is it?"

"No, it isn't."

"How's the investigation going?"

Fran hesitated. "There's something terribly wrong, even bizarre, going on at Lasch Hospital, but in all fairness, since I don't have a shred of proof yet, I shouldn't even talk about it."

"Maybe you should take a break from it anyhow," Tim suggested. "P.J.'s okay with you?"

"You bet, and I'll be home in two minutes from there."

With an easy motion, Tim picked up the magazines and research data from her desk. "You want all this stuff?"

"Yes. I'll have the whole weekend to wade through it."

"Sounds like fun. Let's go."

Over hamburgers at P. J. Clarke's they discussed baseball—the start of spring training and the strengths and weaknesses of the various players and teams. "I'd better be careful. You could take over the sports desk," Tim told her as he paid the check.

"I might do a better job there than I'm doing right now," Fran responded wryly.

Tim insisted on seeing Fran to her apartment. "I'm not going to let you carry all this stuff," he said. "You'd break your arm. But I assure you I'll get right out."

As they left the elevator on her floor he mentioned the deaths of Natasha and Barbara Colbert. "I jog in the morning," he said. "And today, while I was enjoying a run, I started thinking how Tasha Colbert went out one morning to jog, just like I do, and she tripped and fell and never had another thought."

Tripped on a loose shoelace? Fran thought as she turned her key in the lock and pushed the door open. She switched on the light.

"Where do you want these?" Tim asked.

"Right on that table, please."

"Sure." He laid them down and turned to go. "I guess the reason Tasha Colbert was on my mind so much was that she went into the hospital while my grandmother was there."

"She *did?*"

Tim was stepping into the hall. "Yes. I was visiting when she was brought in one afternoon in cardiac arrest. She was only two rooms away from Gran. Gran died the next day." He was silent for a moment, then he shrugged. "Oh, well. Goodnight Fran. You look tired. Don't work too late." He turned and headed down the hall too soon to see the stricken look on Fran's face.

She closed the door and leaned against it. With every fiber of her being, she was sure that Tim's grandmother must have been the elderly woman Annamarie Scalli had referred to, the one with a heart condition who was the original intended recipient of the experimental drug that destroyed Tasha Colbert and, a night later, was also given to her.

76

"Molly, before I leave I'm going to give you a sedative that will ensure that you sleep tonight," Dr. Daniels told Molly.

"If you like, Doctor," Molly said indifferently.

They were in the family room. "I'll get you a glass of water," Dr. Daniels said. He stood to go into the kitchen.

Molly thought of the bottle of sleeping pills she'd left out on the counter there. "The bar sink is closer, Doctor," she said quickly.

She knew he was watching her closely as she put the pill in her mouth and swallowed it with water. "I'm really all right," she said, as she put the glass down.

"You'll be more all right after you have a good sleep. You go right upstairs to bed."

"I will." She walked with him to the front door. "It's past nine. I'm sorry. I certainly have ruined your evenings this week, haven't I?"

"You haven't ruined anything. I'll talk to you tomorrow."

"Thank you."

"Remember. Straight upstairs to bed, Molly. You're going to start feeling groggy pretty soon."

Molly waited until she was sure he was driving away before she double locked the door and stepped on the foot bolt. This time the sound it made—something between a click and a snap—seemed to be familiar and nonthreatening.

I made it all up, she thought dully—that sound, the feeling that someone was in the house that night. I remember it that way because that's the way I wanted it to be.

Had she turned off all the lights in the study? She couldn't remember. The door to the study was closed. She opened it and leaned inside, reaching for the light switch. As light flooded the room, something caught her eye. Something was moving outside the front window. Was someone out there? Yes. In the glow from the study light, she could see Wally Barry, standing on the lawn, just a few feet from the window, staring in at her. With a startled cry she turned away.

And suddenly the study was different. It was paneled again, as it had been . . . before . . . And Gary was there, his back to her, at his desk—he was slumped over, his head soaked in blood.

Blood was running down from the deep gash in his head, soaking his back, pooling on the desk, dripping onto the floor.

Molly tried to scream but could not. She turned back and looked beseechingly to Wally for help, but he was gone. The blood was on her hands, her face, her clothes.

Dazed by terror, she staggered out of the room, up the stairs, and fell into bed.

When she awoke twelve hours later, still groggy from the sleeping pill, she knew that the vivid, bloody horror she had remembered was only part of the unendurable nightmare that her life had become.

77 _____

Fran knew that if she tried to read in bed, she would fall asleep, so she opted instead to change into a pair of comfortable old pajamas and then settled in her leather chair, her feet on the hassock.

She tackled Gary Lasch's file first. It reads like a slightly sophisticated Beaver Cleaver profile, she thought. He attended a good prep school and a good college, but not Ivy League. Couldn't make one, I'll bet, she told herself. He finished college with a B minus average, then went to Meridian Medical School in Colorado. After that he joined his father's practice. Soon thereafter his father died, and Gary was made head of the hospital.

And here we start to shine, Fran noticed. Engagement to socialite Molly Carpenter. More and more articles about Lasch Hospital and its charismatic CEO. Then stories about Gary and his partner, Peter Black, starting Remington HMO with financier Calvin Whitehall.

Next came his dazzling wedding to Molly. Then clippings about the beautiful couple—Gary and Molly at benefits and charity balls and other top-drawer social events.

Interspersed there were more items about the hospital and the HMO, including pieces about Gary being invited to make speeches at medical conventions. Fran read some of them. The usual fluff, she decided, putting them to one side.

Everything else in the Gary Lasch folder had to do with his death. Reams of newspaper articles about the murder, the trial, Molly.

Reluctantly, Fran decided that there was absolutely nothing in all the material on Gary Lasch to indicate that he was anything more than an average doctor who was smart enough to marry well and to get in on the health maintenance organization circus. Until he was murdered, of course.

Well, on to the almighty Calvin Whitehall, Fran told herself with a sigh. Forty minutes later, her eyes burning with fatigue, she said aloud, "Now *this* guy is a horse of a different color. I think the proper adjective to describe him would be 'ruthless,' not 'almighty.' It's a miracle he's stayed out of jail."

The list of lawsuits filed against Cal Whitehall over the years took up pages. The notations showed that a few were settled "for an undisclosed sum," while most were dismissed or resulted in a favorable verdict for Whitehall.

There were many recent articles about the proposed acquisition by Remington Health Management of smaller HMOs, and there was mention as well of the potential for a hostile takeover of Remington itself.

That merger deal really *is* in trouble, Fran reflected, as she continued to read. Whitehall has big bucks, but according to these articles, some of the biggest stockholders of the competing American National are powerhouses too. From what I see here, they all believe that the future of medicine in this country calls for the guidance of American National's president, the former surgeon general. If these quotes are accurate, they're willing to make sure that happens.

Unlike Gary Lasch's, Whitehall's file contained no long list of charities or sponsorship of charitable events to his credit. There was one civic trusteeship, however, that drove the sleepiness from Fran. Calvin Whitehall had been a member of the library fund committee with her father! His name was mentioned in newspaper articles in the file about the theft. I never knew he was part of that, Fran thought. But how would I? I was just a kid then. Mom wouldn't talk about the theft, and she and I left Greenwich soon after Dad committed suicide.

The articles included a number of blurry photostated pictures of her father. The captions weren't flattering.

Fran got up and walked to the window. It was after midnight, and even though there were lights still on in many of the apartments, it was clear that the city was settling into sleep.

When I do finally get to meet Whitehall, I'm going to ask him some hard questions, she thought angrily. For example, how did Dad manage to steal that much money from the fund without it being noticed? Maybe he can tell me where I can find records to show whether Dad took the money over a period of time, or if he went for it all at once.

Calvin Whitehall is a financier, she thought. Even all those years ago he was successful and wealthy. He should be able to give me some answers about my father, or at least tell me how I can find them.

She was tempted to go to bed, but decided to at least skim a few of the magazines she had taken from Molly. First she glanced at the dates on the covers. Molly had said they were old, but Fran was surprised to see that the earliest one went back over twenty years. The most recent were dated thirteen years ago.

She looked at the oldest one first. An article entitled "A Plea for Reason" was checked on the index page. The author's name seemed vaguely familiar, but perhaps not. Fran began to read. I don't like the way this guy thinks, she thought, horrified at what he had written.

The second magazine, eighteen years old, had an article by the same author. It was entitled "Darwin, Survival of the Fittest, and the Human Condition in the Third Millennium." Accompanying this entry was a picture of the author, a professor of research at Meridian Medical School. He was shown in the laboratory with two of his most promising student assistants.

Fran's eyes widened with shock as she matched the face of the professor to his vaguely familiar name, then recognized the two students.

"Bingo!" she said. "That explains it all."

78

At ten o'clock on Saturday morning, Calvin Whitehall set his plan in action. He had summoned Lou Knox to his study so that Lou could make the call to Fran Simmons in his presence. "If she isn't in, you'll try every half hour," he said. "I want to get her to West Redding today, or at the latest, tomorrow. I can't keep our friend Dr. Logue under control much longer."

Lou knew he was not expected to comment or respond in any way. At this stage of an action, Cal tended to think out loud.

"You have the cell phone?"

"Yes, sir." The cell phone would be used for this call because not only would it show up as ANONYMOUS CALL if Fran had Caller

I.D., but as a fail-safe, the number was billed to a phony name at a mail drop in Westchester County in New York.

"Go ahead and try her. And make sure you do a good job of convincing her. Here's the number. I'm happy to say it was listed." If it had been unlisted, Cal thought, it would have been simple enough to ask Jenna to get it from Molly, claiming that I wanted to set up the appointment Simmons had been requesting. But he was glad that step had not been necessary. It would have violated his cardinal rule: In any plan, the fewer people involved, the better.

Lou took the scrap of paper and began to press the numbers on the cell phone. There were two rings, and then he heard the receiver being lifted. He nodded to Cal, who watched him intently.

"Hello," Fran said.

"Ms. Simmons?" Lou asked, employing his late father's slight German accent.

"Yes, who is this, please?"

"I can't tell you on the phone, but I overheard you yesterday at the hospital coffee shop, talking to Ms. Branagan." He paused for effect. "Ms. Simmons, I work at the hospital, and you're right. Something terrible *is* going on there."

In her living room, still in her pajamas, the portable phone in her hand, Fran frantically looked for her pen, spotted it on the hassock, and grabbed the message pad from the table. "I *know* there is," she said calmly, "but unfortunately I can't prove it."

"Can I trust you, Ms. Simmons?"

"What do you mean?"

"There's an old man who has been creating drugs that they use in experiments on patients at Lasch. He's afraid that Dr. Black wants to kill him, and he wants to tell the story of his research before they are able to stop him. He knows it will get him in trouble, but he doesn't care."

He *has* to be talking about Dr. Adrian Lowe, the doctor in those articles, Fran thought. "Has he spoken to anyone else about this?" she asked.

"I know for a fact he hasn't. I deliver packages from him to the hospital. I've been doing this for some time, but I didn't know what they were until yesterday. He confided in me about the experiments. He was practically bursting with excitement. He wants the world to know what he did to make the Colbert girl come out of the coma before she died." He paused and lowered his voice to a harsh whisper. "Ms. Simmons, he even has it on tape. I know; I saw it."

"I'd like to talk to him," Fran said, trying to keep her voice calm.

"Ms. Simmons, he's an old man and practically a hermit. He may say that he wants people to know about him, but he's still scared. If you bring a bunch of people with you, he'll clam up, and you'll get nothing."

"If he wants me to come alone, I'll come alone," she said. "Actually I prefer that."

"Would tonight at seven be okay?"

"Of course. Where should I go?"

Lou circled his index finger and thumb in a victory symbol to Cal. "Do you know where West Redding, Connecticut, is, Ms. Simmons?" he asked.

79

Edna called Marta early Saturday morning. "Wally is still sleeping, so we're getting a late start," she said, trying to sound matter-of-fact. What she really wanted to do was to tell Marta not to worry about coming over to say good-bye, but she knew that would sound terrible, especially after putting her off last night.

"I'll make a coffee ring," Marta said. "I know how Wally enjoys my baking. Just give me a ting-a-ling when you're ready, and I'll be over."

For the next couple of hours, Marta fretted over Edna's phone call. She strongly suspected that there was trouble at Edna's house. The stress in her friend's voice this morning was even deeper than it had been last evening. Then too, she'd noticed Edna's car backing out of the driveway last night, just before nine, and she knew that was unusual as well. Edna hated night driving. Yes, something *definitely* was wrong.

Maybe it will be good for them to get away, Marta decided.

March is such a dreary month, and there's so much bad news around—that nurse being murdered in Rowayton; Molly Lasch probably going back to prison, not that she shouldn't be restrained somewhere, of course; Mrs. Colbert and her daughter Natasha, both dead within hours of each other.

At 11:30, Edna phoned. "We're ready for that coffee cake," she said.

"I'm on my way," Marta replied with relief.

From the moment she walked in the door of Edna's kitchen, Marta could see that she'd been right about trouble—and it wasn't over. It was clear that Wally was in one of his really dark moods. His hands were shoved deep in his pockets; he looked disheveled; he kept casting angry glances at his mother.

"Wally, look what I have for you," Marta told him. She unwrapped the cake from the aluminum foil. "It's still warm."

He ignored her. "Mom, I just wanted to *talk* to her. What's so bad about that?"

Oh dear, Marta thought. I bet he went over to see Molly Lasch on his own.

"I didn't go inside. I just looked in. I didn't go inside the *other time* either. You don't believe me, do you?"

Marta caught the frightened expression on Edna's face. I shouldn't have come, she thought, glancing around as if looking for some means of escape. Edna hates for me to be around when Wally gets upset. Sometimes his tongue runs away with him. Why, I've even heard him insult her.

"Wally dear, have some of Marta's cake," Edna pleaded.

"Molly did the same thing last night she did last time I was there, Mom. She turned on the light and got scared. But I don't know why she was scared last night. Dr. Lasch wasn't all bloody the way he was last time."

Marta put down the knife she was about to use to cut the coffee cake. She turned to her friend of thirty years. "What is Wally talking about, Edna?" she asked quietly, pieces of a very confused puzzle slowly falling together in her mind.

Edna burst into tears. "He's not talking about anything. He doesn't know what he's talking about. Tell Marta that, Wally. *Tell her. You're not talking about anything!*"

The outburst obviously startled him. "I'm sorry, Mom. I promise I won't talk about Molly anymore."

"No, Wally, I think you *should*," Marta said. "Edna, if Wally knows *anything* about Dr. Lasch's death, son or no son, you have to take him to the police and let them hear what it is. You can't let that woman go before that parole board and be sent back to prison if she didn't kill her husband."

"Wally, get the bags out of the car." Edna Barry's voice sounded flat and resigned as she looked at Marta with pleading eyes. "I know you're right. I have to let Wally talk to the police, but just give me till Monday morning. I have to have a lawyer with me to protect him."

"If Molly Lasch spent five and a half years in prison for a crime she didn't commit, and you *knew* it, I would think *you* need a lawyer to protect *yourself*," Marta said, sadness and distress in her eyes as she looked across the kitchen at her friend.

There was silence between them, as Wally noisily munched a piece of Marta's coffee cake.

80

Fran spent the rest of Saturday morning studying the articles that Dr. Adrian Lowe had either written, or which had been written about him. He makes Dr. Kevorkian look like another Albert Schweitzer, she thought. Lowe's philosophy was starkly simple: Thanks to advances in medicine, too many people were living for too long. The elderly were consuming financial and medical resources better used elsewhere.

One article stated that much of the elaborate treatment of chronically ill people was wasteful and unnecessary. That decision should be reached by medical experts and carried out without family involvement.

Another article expounded Lowe's theory that the incompetent were a useful—perhaps even necessary—resource for the study of new or untested drugs. They might be helped dramatically by the drug, or they might die. In either case they would be better off.

Following his career through the various articles, Fran learned that Lowe became so outrageous and outspoken in his theories that he was fired from the medical school where he taught and was even condemned by the AMA. At one point he was indicted for deliberately killing three patients, but the case wasn't proved. After that, he dropped out of sight. Fran finally remembered where she had heard of him before—he had been discussed in an ethics course she had taken in college.

Did Gary Lasch set up Dr. Lowe in West Redding so that he could carry on his scientific research there? Did he also bring Lowe's other dedicated student, Peter Black, to Lasch Hospital to help him conduct experiments on unsuspecting patients there? It was certainly beginning to look that way.

It also makes sense, Fran thought. It makes terrible, logical, brutal sense. This evening, God willing, I'll have proof. If this crazy doctor wants his so-called accomplishments known, then he's come to the right person. Boy, let me *at* him! I can't wait.

Her unidentified caller had given her specific directions to Lowe's location. West Redding was about sixty miles north of Manhattan. I'm glad it's March, not August, Fran thought. She knew the Merritt Parkway in the summer could be packed with vacationers on their way to the beaches. Even so, she intended to leave with plenty of time to spare. She was due there at seven o'clock—well, it couldn't come soon enough for her.

She debated about how much recording equipment to take with her. She didn't want to scare Lowe into clamming up about his work, but she prayed he would let her tape the interview, perhaps even videotape it. In the end she decided to bring both her recorder and video camera. Both would easily fit into her shoulder bag, along with her notebook.

The articles written about Lowe after he had granted interviews were both specific and expansive. I hope he still likes to let everyone in on his theories, Fran thought.

At two o'clock she had finished preparing the questions she wanted to put to Dr. Lowe. By a quarter of three, she was showered and dressed. She called Molly to check on her and was alarmed by the despondent tone of her voice.

"Are you alone, Molly?"

"Yes."

"Is anyone coming over?"

"Philip called. He wanted to come up tonight, but Jenna is going to be here. I asked him to wait until tomorrow."

"Molly, I can't talk about it yet, but a lot is happening, and it's all promising. It looks like I'm onto something that may be of real help to you and to Philip in handling your case."

"Nothing like good news, is there, Fran?"

"Molly, I have to be in Connecticut this evening, and if I left now, I could stop and visit with you for a few minutes on the way there. Would you like that?"

"Don't bother about me, Fran."

"I'll be there in an hour," Fran said, immediately hanging up before Molly could say no.

She's given up, Fran thought as she impatiently pressed the button for the elevator. In that condition, she shouldn't be left alone for even one minute.

81

It's *my* fault, Philip Matthews told himself over and over again. When Molly got out of prison, I should have dragged her into the car. She didn't know what she was doing when she talked to the media. She didn't understand that you can't admit to the parole board that you accept responsibility for your husband's death, then go out and say you didn't do it. Why didn't I get that across to her?

The prosecutor could have asked to get her parole revoked the minute she made that statement, Philip reasoned. That means that he's going after her now only because of the second charge.

My one chance to keep Molly out of prison when we appear before the board on Monday is to make them accept that there's a legitimate possibility that she's been wrongly accused of Anna-marie Scalli's death. Then I have to beg the members to understand that she didn't actually intend to retract her admission but rather that she just wanted to regain her memory of that night so she could fully face what had happened. He thought about it. The argument *might* work. *If* he could persuade Molly to stick to that story. . . . *If,* however, was the operative word.

Molly told the reporters that she had the impression there was someone else in the house the night Gary Lasch was murdered, he recalled, and she also said that in her heart, she did not believe she was capable of taking a human life. I might be able to persuade the parole board that this statement came from someone consumed with grief and despair, not from someone trying to trick them into granting parole. I could plead that it's a matter of record that she was suffering from clinical depression in prison.

Still, all my arguments about her mental state will amount to nothing if I can't create doubt about Annamarie Scalli's death, he thought. It all comes down to that.

That was why, late on Saturday afternoon, Philip Matthews drove to the Sea Lamp Diner in Rowayton. The parking lot where Annamarie Scalli had died was no longer cordoned off. Badly in need of repaving and with the white lines that delineated parking spaces almost invisible, it was in use again. There was no indication that a young woman had been brutally murdered there, no hint that Molly Lasch might have to spend the rest of her life in prison because traces of blood from the dead woman had been found on her shoe and in her car.

Philip had brought in a trusted investigator to work with him on the case, and together they were beginning to shape the defense he would offer in court.

Molly said that she had seen a medium-sized sedan pulling out of the parking lot as she left the diner that night. Philip's investigator had already established that no other customer had left the diner for at least several minutes before Annamarie ran out.

Molly said she had gone directly to her own car. She had noticed a Jeep parked in the lot when she first arrived at the diner to meet Annamarie, but she had no way of knowing that it was Annamarie's vehicle. The investigator had concluded that Molly must have stepped in the blood that was found on her shoe, and then the blood on the shoe had left a mark on the carpet in her car.

All the evidence is circumstantial, Philip fumed as he went into the diner. The blood on her shoe is the only tangible evidence they have to connect her with the murder. If the killer was in that sedan, it meant he had been parked in the lot, because Molly saw him pull out of the lot. What must have happened, Philip concluded, was that after the killer stabbed Annamarie, he ran back to his own car, then drove away as Molly exited the diner. The murder weapon hasn't been found. What I can argue is that a few drops of blood may have dripped from the knife onto the tarmac, and Molly stepped in it accidentally, not even noticing it.

But there's another major problem that we can't yet explain, Philip thought as he took one last look around the parking lot: a motive for this anonymous killer. Why would someone follow Annamarie Scalli to the diner, wait for her to leave, and kill her? Nothing in her personal life—other than her affair with Molly's husband years ago—would indicate a motive; he'd had her thoroughly checked out. I know that Fran Simmons is pursuing some theory about the hospital that may connect to Annamarie, he thought. I can only hope she comes up with something—*soon!*

When Philip entered the diner, he was pleased to see that Bobby Burke was at the counter. He was also relieved to see that Gladys Fluegel *wasn't* in sight. His detective had warned him that her story about Molly restraining Annamarie from leaving the diner and then rushing out after her had become increasingly more sensational every time she repeated it.

Philip took a seat at the counter. "Hi, Bobby," he said. "How about a cup of coffee?"

"Boy, you made it quick, Mr. Matthews. I guess Ms. Simmons called you right away."

"What are you talking about, Bobby?"

"I phoned Ms. Simmons an hour ago and left a message for her."

"You did? *What about?*"

"That couple you've been looking for, the ones who were here Sunday night? They happened to come in for lunch today. They're from Norwalk. Turns out they flew up to Canada Monday morning and just got home last night. Can you believe they didn't even *know* what had happened? They said they'll be glad to talk to you. Their names are Hilmer. Arthur and Jane Hilmer."

Bobby lowered his voice. "Mr. Matthews, just between us, when I told them what Gladys told the cops, they said she was full of baloney. They said they didn't hear Mrs. Lasch call 'Annamarie' twice. According to them, she called her *once*. And they're sure she didn't yell 'Wait!' It was Mrs. Hilmer who yelled *'Waitress,'* trying to get Gladys's attention."

Over the years, Philip Matthews knew he had become cynical. People were predictable and never failed to disappoint you. At that moment, however, he felt like a child in Wonderland. "Give me the Hilmers' number, Bobby," he said. "This is *great!*"

Bobby smiled. "There's more, Mr. Matthews. The Hilmers say that when they came in that night they saw a guy sitting in a medium-sized sedan in the parking lot. They even got a good look at his face, because they caught him with their headlights when they parked. *They can describe him.* I'm sure that guy never came in here, Mr. Matthews. It was a slow night, and I'd remember."

Molly has said since the beginning that she saw a medium-sized sedan pulling out of the lot, Philip thought. Maybe this is our break at last.

"The Hilmers said they won't be home until nine o'clock tonight, Mr. Matthews. They said if anyone wants to see them after that time, though, he should just be at their house. They understand how important this could be to Mrs. Lasch and are anxious to help."

"I'll be on their doorstep," Philip Matthews said. "Oh God, will I be on their doorstep!"

"The Hilmers said they parked right next to a brand-new Mercedes that night. They remembered because it was cold and that was as near to the entrance as you could get. I told them that must have been Mrs. Lasch's car."

"Obviously I hired the wrong person to help me with the investigation, Bobby. Where did you learn about all this?" Philip asked.

Bobby smiled benignly. "Mr. Matthews, I'm the son of a public defender, and he's a good teacher. I plan to be a public defender too."

"You've got a hell of a start," Philip told him. "Let me have that coffee, Bobby. I need it."

As he sipped, Philip debated whether to call Molly and tell her immediately about the Hilmers, then decided against it. I'll wait until I've actually seen them myself, he decided. Maybe there's even more they can tell that will help her. And I've got to get a sketch artist up here—tomorrow, if possible—so we can get an idea of the guy they saw in the parking lot. This could be our salvation!

Oh, Molly, Philip thought yearningly as the image of her face, haunted and sad, filled his mind. I'd give my right arm to see you free from this nightmare. And I'd give anything in the world to see you smile.

82

With methodical care, Calvin Whitehall prepared Lou for his assignment in West Redding. He explained that the element of surprise was essential to the plan if it was to work.

"Hopefully, the window from the porch to the laboratory will be open so you can quietly toss in the gasoline-soaked rags; otherwise you will have no choice but to break a pane," Cal said. "Now I realize that the fuse connected to our little device is short, but it should give you enough time to be down the steps and away from the building before the explosion."

Lou listened attentively as Cal went on to tell him that Dr. Logue had called, all excited about meeting the press. It was clear he was eager to show Fran Simmons his laboratory, so Lou could count on the two of them being upstairs in the lab when the bomb went off. "It will appear much more likely to be an unfortunate accident if what's left of them is found in the lab," Cal said casually, "to say nothing of the fact that if they were downstairs, they might have time to make it out.

"Escape will be impossible from upstairs," he went on. "The door from the laboratory to the porch has two separate locks, and it's kept bolted at all times because Dr. Logue is fearful that attempts may be made on his life."

He's right to be fearful, Lou thought, but then admitted to himself that, as usual, Cal's attention to detail was remarkable and no doubt would prove to be a safeguard for him.

"Unless you botch the job completely, Lou—and need I say, *don't!*—the fire and subsequent explosion will take care of the dual problems of the doctor and Fran Simmons. The farmhouse is over one hundred years old, and the interior staircase is very narrow and steep. There is no way, assuming the explosion is as great as I anticipate, that either or both of them could get out of the laboratory, run down the hall, and then get down those stairs in time to escape. However, you should be prepared for that eventuality, of course."

"Be prepared" was Cal's way of telling him to carry his gun. It had been seven years since he had fired it, but some skills never got rusty. Like riding a bike or swimming, Lou thought—you never forget how to do it. His most recent weapon of choice had been a good, sharp knife.

The farmhouse was in an isolated, wooded area, and although the explosion might be heard, Cal had assured him he would have enough time to be out of the immediate area and back on a main road before the police and fire departments appeared. Lou tried not to show his impatience at all the information Cal was throwing at him. He'd been to the farmhouse often enough to get the lay of the land, and he certainly knew how to take care of himself.

At five o'clock Lou left the apartment. It was unnecessarily early, but here again, Cal believed in being ahead of the game, and anticipating potential delays like traffic tie-ups was important if all was to go according to plan. "You ought to allow yourself more than enough time to park the car out of view of the farmhouse before Fran Simmons arrives," Cal had cautioned.

As Lou got in the car, Cal came around the side of the garage. "Just want to see you off," he said with a friendly smile. "Jenna is spending the evening with Molly Lasch. When you get back, come over to the house and have a drink with me."

And after assignments like this, it's okay if I call you Cal, Lou thought. Thanks a *lot,* old buddy. He started the car and headed to the Merritt Parkway north, on the first leg of his important trip to West Redding.

83

It seemed to Fran that Molly's state had worsened overnight. There were dark crescents under her eyes; her pupils were enormous; her lips and skin, ashen. When she spoke, her voice was low and hesitant. Fran almost had to strain to hear her.

They sat in the study, and several times, Fran noticed Molly looking around the room as if she were surprised at what she was seeing.

She seems so damn *alone,* so forlorn, Fran thought; she seems so worried. If only her mother and father had been able to be with her. "Molly, I know it's none of my business, but I have to ask you," she said. "Can't your mother possibly leave your father and get up here? You need her to be with you."

Molly shook her head, and for an instant the passivity left her voice. *"Absolutely not,* Fran. Had my father not had a stroke, both of them would have been here; I know that. I'm afraid that the stroke was a lot more serious than they admit. I've spoken to him, and he sounds pretty good, but with all the misery I've caused them, if something were to happen to him while she was up here, I would go absolutely mad."

"How much misery will it cause them if they lose you?" Fran asked bluntly.

"What do you mean?"

"I mean I'm worried sick about you, and so is Philip, and so, I'm sure, is Jenna. Let's say it straight—there's a damn good chance you'll be taken into custody again on Monday."

"Ah, we finally say it straight," Molly said with a sigh. "Thank you, Fran."

"Hear me out. I believe there's a very good chance that even if you do have to go back to Niantic, you'll be out again very soon— and not on parole, but completely exonerated!"

"Once upon a time," Molly murmured dreamily. "I didn't know you believed in fairy tales."

"Stop it!" Fran begged. "Molly, I hate to leave you here like this, but I can't stay with you right now. I have an appointment that is desperately important to a lot of people, including you especially. Otherwise I wouldn't leave your side. You know why? It's because I think you've already given up; I think you've decided that you're not even going to *appear* before that parole board."

Molly raised her eyebrows quizzically, but did not contradict her.

"Trust me, Molly, *please.* We're getting to the truth. I know we are. Believe in me. Believe in Philip. It may not even be important to you, but that guy loves you, and he won't rest until he proves you're the real victim in all this."

"I loved that line in *An American Tragedy,*" Molly murmured. "I hope I'm remembering it properly: 'Love me till I die and then forget me.' "

Fran got up. "Molly," she said quietly, "if you really decide to end your life, you'll find a way to do it whether you're alone or with 'the Pope's standing army,' as my grandmother used to say.

"I'm going to tell you something: I am angry at my father for committing suicide. No, I'm more than angry—I'm *furious*. He stole a lot of money, and he would have gone to prison. But he also would have come out of prison, and I would have been there with bells on to greet him."

Molly sat silently, staring at her hands now.

Impatiently, Fran brushed tears from her eyes. "Worse comes to worst," she said, "you serve out your term. I don't think you will, but I'll concede the point. You still would be young enough when you got out to enjoy—and I mean really enjoy—another forty years or so. You didn't kill Annamarie Scalli. We all know that, and Philip will blow the case apart. So for God's sake, girl, pull yourself together. You blue bloods are supposed to be classy. *Prove it!"*

Molly stood at the window and watched Fran as she drove away. Thanks for the cheery words, but it's too late, Fran, she thought. There's nothing left about me that's classy.

84

The doctor had been anxiously waiting for Fran Simmons to appear for a full half hour before the headlights of her car signaled her arrival. It was virtually on the stroke of seven when she rang his bell, an attention to promptness that he found gratifying. He—a scientist—was punctual himself and expected it in others.

He opened the door, and with a courtly greeting expressed his delight at meeting her. "For nearly twenty years I have been known in this area as a retired ophthalmologist," he said. "Dr. Adrian Logue. In fact, my real name, and the one which I now happily resume, is Adrian Lowe. As you already know."

The pictures she had seen of Adrian Lowe in the magazines

were almost twenty years old, and they depicted a decidedly more robust man than the one who was standing before her.

He was just under six feet tall, lean, a little stooped. His thinning hair was more white than gray. The expression in his pale blue eyes could only be described as kindly. His overall manner was deferential—even a little shy, as he invited her into the small living room.

Overall, Fran thought, he's not at all the kind of person I'd expected him to be. But then, what *did* I expect? she asked herself as she chose a straight-backed chair rather than the rocker he offered. After reading all that stuff he wrote, and knowing what I do about him, I guess I thought he'd look like some kind of zealot, with wild eyes and flailing arms, or like some goose-stepping Nazi doctor.

She had been about to ask him if he would permit her to record him, when he said, "I do hope you brought a recorder with you, Miss Simmons. I do not want to be misquoted."

"Indeed I did, Doctor." Fran opened her shoulder bag, slipped out the recorder, and turned it on. Don't let him guess how much you know already about what he's been up to, she warned herself. Ask all the important questions. This tape should make valuable evidence later on.

"I will be taking you upstairs to my laboratory directly, and we'll do most of our talking there. But first let me explain why you are here. No, in point of fact, let me explain why *I* am here."

Dr. Lowe rested his head against the back of his chair with a sigh. "Ms. Simmons, you must have heard the old cliché, 'For every positive there is a negative.' That premise is especially true in the practice of medicine. Therefore choices—sometimes *difficult* choices—must be made."

Fran listened without comment as Adrian Lowe, his voice sometimes soft, sometimes animated, explained his views about the advances in medical care and the need to redefine the concept of "managed care."

"There should be a cutoff of treatment, but I'm not talking merely about life-support systems," he began. "Let us say a person has had a third heart attack, or is past seventy and has been on dialysis for five years, or has been granted the enormous financial outlay needed to cover a heart or liver transplant that has failed.

"Isn't it about time to let that person cash in his or her chips,

Miss Simmons? Clearly it's God's will, so why should we keep fighting the inevitable? The patient might not agree, of course, and no doubt the family might sue for continuing coverage. Therefore, there should be another authority enabled to hasten this inevitable outcome without discussion with either the family or the patient, and without the incurring of further expense on the hospital's part. An authority capable of a clinical, objective, *scientific* decision."

Fran listened in astonishment at the almost unimaginable philosophy he was articulating. "Do I understand, Dr. Lowe, that you are actually saying that neither the patient nor the family should have anything to say or even know about the decision that is being made to terminate the patient's life?"

"Exactly."

"Are you also saying that the handicapped should be unknowing and unwilling guinea pigs for any experiments you and your colleagues might wish to conduct?"

"My dear," he said condescendingly, "I have a videotape I want you to see. It may help you understand why my research is so important. You may have heard recently of Natasha Colbert, a young lady from a very prominent family."

My God, he's going to admit what he did to her, Fran thought.

"Due to a most unfortunate accident, the terminal treatment that was about to be given to a chronically ill elderly woman was administered to Ms. Colbert instead of the routine saline solution that she required.

"This resulted in an irreversible coma, in which state she had existed for over six years. I have been experimenting to find a drug that would reverse that deep coma and last night, for the first time, enjoyed success, if only for a few moments. But that success is the beginning of something magnificent in science. Allow me to show you the proof."

Fran watched as Dr. Lowe placed a cassette into the VCR attached to a wide-screen television.

"I never watch television," he explained, "but for research purposes, I have this unit. I will show you only the final five minutes of the last day of Natasha Colbert's life. That is all you will need to understand what I have accomplished in the years that I have spent here."

In disbelief, Fran watched the tape and saw Barbara Colbert murmuring her dying daughter's name.

She knew her audible gasp when Natasha stirred, opened her eyes, and began to speak delighted Dr. Lowe.

"You see, you see," he exclaimed.

Shocked, Fran watched as Tasha recognized her mother, then closed her eyes, opened them again, and pleaded with her mother to help her.

She felt tears well in her own eyes at the agonizing sight of Barbara Colbert pleading with her daughter to live. With something approaching hatred, she witnessed Dr. Black denying to Barbara Colbert that Natasha had regained consciousness.

"She could only last a minute. The drug is that powerful," Dr. Lowe explained as he stopped and rewound the tape. "Someday it will be routine to reverse comas." He slipped the tape into his pocket. "What are you thinking, my dear?"

"I am thinking, Dr. Lowe, that with your obvious genius, it is incredible that all your efforts are not devoted to the preservation of life and to improving the quality of life, not to the destruction of lives whose quality you deem to be less than acceptable."

He smiled and stood up. "My dear, the number of thinking people who agree with me are legion. Now let me show you my laboratory."

Feeling a mixture of horror and growing uneasiness that she was alone with this man, Fran followed Lowe up the narrow staircase. Natasha Colbert, she thought angrily. She was put in that condition by one of his "highly effective drugs." Also Tim's grandmother, who had hoped to celebrate her eightieth birthday. And Barbara Colbert, who was too intelligent to be told she was hallucinating by Lowe's murderous disciple, Peter Black. He may even be talking about Billy Gallo's mother. How many others? she asked herself.

The upstairs hall was gloomy and dimly lit, but when Adrian Lowe opened the door to his laboratory, it was like stepping into another world. Knowing little about research laboratories, Fran could still see that this one appeared to be the epitome of technical perfection.

The room was not large, but the limited space was more than made up for by the careful arrangement of equipment so that every inch was put to practical use. In addition to the latest in computer technology, Fran recognized some of the equipment she had seen in her own, very high-priced doctor's office. There was also a rather substantial oxygen tank, with valves and tubes attached. Many of the machines appeared to be geared to testing chemicals, with others more suited to testing live subjects. Rats, I hope, Fran said to herself with a sinking feeling. Most of the lab equipment meant nothing to her, but what she did find impressive was the extreme cleanliness and orderliness of the place. It is both impressive and absolutely terrifying, she thought as she advanced into the room.

Adrian Lowe's face glowed with pride. "Miss Simmons, my former student Gary Lasch brought me here after I had been hounded out of medicine. He believed in me and my research and was devoted to lending me the support I needed to carry out my tests and experiments. Then he sent for Peter Black, another of my former students, and one who had been Gary's classmate. That proved not to be the wisest move, in retrospect. Possibly because of his problem with alcohol, Black has turned out to be a dangerous coward. He has failed me on a number of occasions, although most recently he has helped to hand me the greatest achievement of my career. In addition, there is Calvin Whitehall, who was kind enough to arrange our meeting, and who has been an ardent supporter of my research, both financially and philosophically."

"Calvin Whitehall did *what?*" Fran asked, a shiver of alarm running down her back.

Adrian Lowe looked puzzled. "Why, he arranged this meeting, of course. He suggested you would be the appropriate media contact. He made the arrangements with you and verified with me that you would be coming."

Fran chose her next words carefully: "Exactly *what* did Mr. Whitehall tell you I would do for you, Doctor?"

"My dear, you are here because you are going to produce a thirty-minute interview with me that will then allow me to share my achievements with the world. The members of the medical establishment will continue to excoriate me. But even they over time, as well as the general public, will come to embrace the wisdom of my philosophy and the genius of my research. And you, Miss Simmons, will lead the way. You are going to publicize that program in advance and place it on your own prestigious network."

Fran stood silent for a moment, both dumbfounded and horrified by what she had heard. "Dr. Lowe, you *do* realize that you will be exposing yourself, *and* Dr. Black, *and* Calvin Whitehall to possible criminal prosecution?"

He bristled. "Of course I do. Calvin has willingly accepted that as a necessary part of our important mission."

Oh dear God, Fran thought, he's become dangerous to them. And so have I. This laboratory is also dangerous to them. They've got to get rid of it—and *us*. I've walked into a trap.

"Doctor," she said, trying to sound calmer than she felt, "we've got to get out of here. Immediately. We've both been set up. Calvin Whitehall would never let you go public with all this, especially on television. You *must* realize that!"

"I don't understand . . ." the doctor responded, an almost child-like confusion crossing his face.

"Trust me. *Please!*"

Dr. Lowe was standing next to her by the laboratory's center island, his hands on the Formica surface. "Miss Simmons, you're not making sense. Mr. Whitehall—"

Fran grabbed his hand. "Doctor, it isn't safe here. We have to get out."

She heard a faint noise and felt a sharp draft. At the far end of the room the window was being raised. "Look!" she screamed pointing to the shadowy figure, barely visible against the night.

She saw the flicker of a tiny flame, watched as an arm lifted it, then seemed to pull back. Suddenly she realized what was happening. Whoever was outside that window was going to throw a fire-bomb into the room. He was going to blow up the laboratory—and both of them with it.

Doctor Lowe pulled his hand from her tight grasp. Fran knew it was useless to run, but she also knew she had to try. "Doctor, please."

But in a lightning movement he reached below the counter of the island, pulled out a shotgun, racked back the slide with a loud, ominous click, then aimed and fired. The noise deafened her. She saw the arm holding the flame disappear, then heard the thud of a body. An instant later flames shot up from the porch.

Dr. Lowe pulled a fire extinguisher off the wall and thrust it at her. Then he ran to a wall safe, opened it quickly, and frantically began to search through it.

Fran leaned out the window. Flames were licking at the shoes of their would-be assailant, who lay on the porch. He was groaning and clutching at his shoulder, trying to stem the gushing flow of blood. Fran pressed down with her finger, and a stream of foam sprouted from the extinguisher, putting out the flames directly around him.

But the fire had spread already to the railing of the porch and was seconds away from reaching the steps. Some of the flaming liquid from the firebomb had also flowed between the floorboards of the porch, and she could see flames already licking underneath. It was clear to Fran that no extinguisher could save this house. She knew also that if she opened the door to the porch, the flames would sweep through the laboratory and engulf the oxygen tank.

"Doctor, get out," she shrieked. He nodded, and with his arms full of files, he ran out of the laboratory and down the hall. She could hear the clatter of his feet on the stairs as he descended.

She looked back out onto the porch. There was only one way to try to save the life of the injured man, which she was determined to try to do. She could not leave him to be blown up when the laboratory went. Holding the extinguisher, Fran squeezed herself out of the narrow window and onto the small porch. The flames had returned, inching closer to the wounded man and threatening soon to climb the house's outside wall. Spraying foam from the fire extinguisher in the space between the window and the stairs, she created a temporary path. The would-be killer was lying almost at the top of the steps. Fran set the extinguisher down, put her hands under the man's right shoulder, and with all her strength, she lifted and rolled him. For an instant he teetered at the top step, then in an end-over-end motion that brought agonized cries from his lips, he tumbled down the stairs.

Fran tried to straighten up but lost her balance in the slippery foam and fell, her feet going out from under her. Her head struck the top step, her shoulder banged against the sharp edge of the next one, her ankle twisted as she finally dropped to the ground.

Dazed, she managed to scramble to her feet just as Dr. Lowe came around the side of the house. "Grab him," she shouted. "Help me to get him clear before the whole place explodes."

Their assailant had fainted during his tumble, and was now a deadweight. With superhuman strength, Fran assumed most of the burden but still managed, with Dr. Lowe's help, to pull Lou Knox nearly twenty feet before the explosion Calvin Whitehall had planned so carefully took place.

They headed for safety as flames leaped skyward and debris rained around them.

85

After Fran left, Molly went upstairs and into the bathroom, where she stood in front of the mirror, studying her face. It looked unfamiliar, as if she were looking at a stranger—one she didn't particularly care to meet. "You used to be Molly Carpenter, didn't you?" she asked her mirror image. "Molly Carpenter was a very lucky person, privileged even. Well, guess what? She's not here anymore, and you can't go back to pretending to be her. You can only go back to being a number who lives in a cell block. Doesn't sound like a lot of fun, does it? And maybe it's not such a great idea."

She turned on the taps to fill the Jacuzzi, tossed in scented bath salts, and walked into the bedroom.

Jenna had said she was going to stop at a cocktail party before coming over. Her housekeeper would deliver dinner. Jenna will look gorgeous, Molly thought. Then she made a decision. I'll surprise her—tonight I'm going to have my one last fling at being Molly Carpenter.

An hour later, her hair washed and shining, makeup camouflaging the circles under her eyes, dressed in pale green silk slacks and a matching cowl-neck shirt, Molly waited for Jenna to arrive.

She got there at 7:30, looking every bit as beautiful as Molly had expected. "I'm late," she wailed. "I was at the Hodges'. They're clients of the firm. All the big guns came from New York, so I just couldn't get away any faster."

"I wasn't going anywhere," Molly said quietly.

Jenna stood back and looked at her. "Molly, you look *terrific*. Molly, you're wonderful!"

Molly shrugged. "I don't know about that. Hey, does your husband expect us to get blotto? When dinner arrived, it was accompanied by three bottles of that great wine he brought the other night."

Jenna laughed. "That's Cal. If one bottle would be a pleasant remembrance, three bottles will remind you what an important guy he is. Not the worst trait, I'd say."

"Not at all," Molly agreed.

"Let's test it," Jenna suggested. "Let's get a buzz on. Let's pretend that we're still the girls who set the tone for this town."

"We *did*, didn't we?" Molly thought. I'm glad I got dressed up.

It may be my last hurrah, but it will be fun, I know what I have to do tonight. No more will I be the prisoner in the dock. Fran had a nerve to come in here and make me feel guilty. What does *she* know about it? She remembered Fran's words: "*I am angry at my father . . . I'm furious . . . Believe in Philip. It may not even be important to you, but that guy loves you . . .*"

They stood at the bar built into an alcove in the hallway that ran between the kitchen and family room. Jenna rummaged in the drawer, found the corkscrew, and opened a bottle of the wine. She scanned the shelves and selected two delicate crystal glasses. "My grandmother had these glasses as well," she said. "Remember how our grandmother's wills read? You got this house and God knows what else. I got six glasses. That's about what Gran was down to when she departed this earth."

Jenna poured the wine, handed one glass to Molly and said, "Bottoms up."

As they clinked glasses, Molly had the disturbing sensation that she was seeing something in Jenna's eyes that she didn't quite understand, something new and entirely unexpected.

She couldn't imagine what it meant.

86

Lou should have been back by 9:30. As he did with everything, Calvin Whitehall had calculated the precise amount of time it would take for his henchman to go to West Redding, take care of business, and return. As he watched the clock in his library with intense awareness, he acknowledged to himself that unless Lou returned soon, something must have gone terribly wrong.

Too bad, because this was an all-or-nothing game. There was no such thing as cutting his losses if he failed.

By ten o'clock he had begun to consider how quickly he could distance himself from his aide-de-camp, Lou Knox.

At ten minutes after ten the front doorbell rang. He had told the housekeeper to take the night off, something he frequently did. It annoyed him to have household help around all the time. Cal understood that, of course, this feeling was the product of his origins. In most cases, no matter how much you achieve in life, humble beginnings trigger humble responses, he thought.

He headed down the hall toward the door, catching his reflection in a mirror along the way. What he saw was a barrel-chested man with a ruddy complexion and thinning hair. For some reason a remark he had heard about himself when he was fresh out of Yale flashed into his mind. The mother of one of his Yale friends had whispered, "Cal does not look comfortable in his Brooks Brothers suit."

He was not surprised to find not one but four people at the door. The spokesman said, "Mr. Whitehall, I'm Detective Burroughs from the prosecutor's office. You are under arrest for conspiracy to murder Frances Simmons and Dr. Adrian Lowe."

Conspiracy to murder, he thought, letting the phrase echo in his mind.

It was worse than he expected.

Cal stared at Detective Burroughs, who cheerfully returned his gaze. "Mr. Whitehall, for your information, your coconspirator, Lou Knox, is singing like a bird from his hospital bed. And another piece of good news—Dr. Adrian Lowe is making a statement at the police station right now. It seems he can't praise you enough for all you did to make his criminal research possible."

87

At seven o'clock, Philip Matthews was parked in front of the Hilmers' house, hoping that perhaps they'd get home early.

However, it was ten minutes past nine when they pulled into their driveway. "I'm so terribly sorry," Arthur Hilmer said. "We knew there was a good chance that someone would be waiting for us here, but our granddaughter was in a play, and . . . well, you know how that is."

Philip smiled. A nice man, he thought.

"Of course you don't know how it is," Hilmer corrected himself. "Our son is forty-four. You're probably about that yourself, I'd say."

Philip smiled. "Do you read tea leaves?" He then introduced himself, explaining briefly about Molly's being in danger of having to return to prison, and how they could be important to him in defending her case.

They went into the house. Jane Hilmer, an attractive, well-preserved woman in her mid-sixties, offered Philip a soft drink, a glass of wine, or coffee, all of which he refused.

Arthur Hilmer obviously understood that he needed to get down to business. "We talked to Bobby Burke at the Sea Lamp today," he said. "You could have bowled the two of us over when we heard what had happened there that Sunday night. We'd caught a movie at the mall and then gone to the diner for a sandwich."

"We left first thing the next morning to visit our son in Toronto," Jane Hilmer volunteered. "We only just got back last night. Today, we stopped at the diner for lunch on our way to Janie's play, and that's when we heard." She looked at her husband.

"As I said, we were bowled over. We told Bobby that of course we wanted to help in any way we could. Bobby probably told you that we got a pretty good look at the guy in the sedan in the parking lot."

"Yes, he did," Philip confirmed. "I'm going to ask you to make a statement to the prosecutor's office tomorrow morning, and then I want you both to get together with the police artist. A sketch of the man you saw in that sedan would be very helpful."

"Glad to do that," Arthur Hilmer said. "But I can be even more help to you, I think. You see, we paid particular attention to both of the women when they left. We'd seen the first woman go by our table, and it was obvious that she was upset. Then that classy-looking blond lady, who I now understand is Molly Lasch, left. She was crying. I heard her call out, 'Annamarie!' "

Philip tensed. Don't give me bad news, he silently begged.

"It was obvious the other woman didn't hear her," Arthur Hilmer said flatly. "There's a little oval window over the cashier's desk. From where I was sitting I could see out clearly into the parking lot, or at least to the part closest to the diner. The first woman must have crossed the lot over to the darker side—I couldn't see her. But I'm certain I saw that second lady—I mean Molly Lasch—go straight to her car and take off. I can swear there's no way in heaven or hell she could have walked across the parking lot to that Jeep and plunged a knife into the other woman, not in the time between when I saw her walk out the diner and when she drove away in her car."

Philip didn't know that his eyes had moistened until he brushed them with the back of his hand in a reflex gesture. "I can't begin to find words," he said, then stopped. He sprang up. "I'll try to find the right words to thank you tomorrow," he said. "Right now, I've got to get to Greenwich."

88

Dr. Peter Black stood at the window of his upstairs bedroom, a glass of scotch in his hand. He watched with blurring eyes as two unfamiliar cars pulled into his driveway. He did not need to observe the businesslike manner in which the four large men emerged, and came walking up his cobblestone walk to know that it was all over. Cal the Mighty has finally crashed, he thought with a trace of humor. Unfortunately, he's taking me with him.

Always have a contingency plan—that was one of Cal's favorite mottoes. I wonder if he has one now? Peter Black thought. Truthfully, though, I never liked the guy, so I really don't care.

He crossed to his bed and opened the drawer of his night table. Then he took out a leather case and extracted a hypodermic needle, already filled with fluid.

With a look of suddenly personal curiosity, he studied the instrument. How many times had he, with compassion in his face, given that injection, knowing that the trusting eyes gazing up at him would soon lose their focus and then would close forever?

According to Dr. Lowe, this drug not only left no trace in the blood, there was also no pain attached to its effect.

Pedro was knocking at the bedroom door, to announce the uninvited guests.

Dr. Peter Black stretched out on his bed. He took a final sip of scotch and then plunged the needle into his arm. He sighed as he briefly thought that at least Dr. Lowe had been right about there being no pain.

89

"I am all right," Fran insisted. "I know there's nothing broken." She had refused to go to the hospital, and was taken instead in a squad car to the prosecutor's office in Stamford as was Dr. Lowe. From there she'd called Gus Brandt at home, filling her boss in on the events of the evening. Using the phone hookup, he'd gotten Fran's breaking story on the air, with file-tape footage providing the background.

When the police—both state and local—had arrived at the scene of the explosion, Dr. Lowe announced that he wanted to surrender to the authorities and make a full statement about the medical breakthroughs his research had achieved.

Standing in the field, the fire still burning fiercely behind him, his files clutched in his arms, he apologized to Fran. "I could have died tonight, Miss Simmons. Everything I have accomplished would have gone with me. I must go on record immediately."

"Doctor," Fran had said, "I can't help observing that while you yourself are well into your seventies, you certainly were less than philosophical when somebody tried to end your life."

The state troopers had transported them to the state attorney's office in Stamford. Fran had made her statement to an assistant prosecutor, Rudy Jacobs. "I had Dr. Lowe on tape," she told him. "If only I had thought to grab my recorder before the place blew up . . ."

"Ms. Simmons, we won't need it," Jacobs told her. "They tell me the good doctor is talking his head off. We're getting him on camera and on tape."

"Have you identified the man who tried to kill us?"

"We sure have. His name is Lou Knox. He's from Greenwich, where he lives and works as Calvin Whitehall's chauffeur, and apparently takes care of a whole variety of other jobs."

"How badly was he hurt?"

"He took a few pellets in his shoulder and arm, and he's got some burns, but he'll be okay. I hear he also is spilling his guts. He knows we have him cold, and his only hope for some kind of break is full cooperation."

"Has Calvin Whitehall been arrested?"

"They've just brought him in. He's being processed as we speak."

"Could I get a look at him?" Fran asked with a wry smile. "I went to school with his wife, but I've never met him. It would be interesting to see the guy who tried to have me blown to bits."

"I don't see why not. Follow me."

The sight of the barrel-chested, balding, coarse-featured man in a wrinkled wool sports shirt surprised Fran. Just as Dr. Lowe had not looked anything like the pictures she had seen of him, there was nothing in this rumpled man to suggest "Cal the Mighty," as Jenna called her husband. In fact, it was hard to picture Jenna—beautiful, elegant, refined—married to someone so coarse in appearance.

Jenna! How awful this is going to be for her, Fran thought. She was supposed to be with Molly tonight. I wonder if she has even heard?

Jenna's husband would surely go to prison, Fran thought as she considered the immediate future. Molly may still be headed back to prison too. Unless, of course, some of what I've uncovered tonight about misdeeds at Lasch Hospital can help her somehow. My father killed himself rather than face prison. What a strange bond for us Cranden Academy girls to have—all three in some way impacted by the reality of prison.

She turned to the assistant prosecutor. "Mr. Jacobs, I'm starting to feel all my aches and pains. I guess I will take you up on that ride home now."

"Sure, Ms. Simmons."

"But first could I use the phone again for a minute? I'd like to check my messages."

"Of course. Let's go back to my office."

There were two messages. Bobby Burke, the counterman at the Sea Lamp Diner, had phoned at four o'clock to tell her he had located the couple who'd been in the diner Sunday night at the same time that Molly was meeting with Annamarie Scalli.

Great news, Fran thought.

The second call was from Edna Barry and had come in at six o'clock: "Ms. Simmons, this is very hard for me, but I feel like I have to make a clean breast of everything. I lied about the spare key to Molly's house because I was afraid my son might have . . . might have been *involved* in Dr. Lasch's death. Wally is very troubled."

Fran pressed the receiver more firmly against her ear. Edna Barry was sobbing so much it was hard to understand her words.

"Ms. Simmons, sometimes Wally tells wild stories. He hears things in his head and thinks they're true. That's why I was so afraid for him."

"Are you okay, Ms. Simmons?" Jacobs asked, noting her look of concerned concentration.

Fran raised her finger to her lips as she strained to hear Edna Barry's faltering voice. "I wouldn't let Wally talk. I've kept shushing him when he tried. But he said something just now that, if it's true, might be very, very important.

"Wally claims he saw Molly come home the night Dr. Lasch died. He says he saw her go in the house and turn on the light in the study. By then he was standing at the study window, and when she turned on the light, he saw Dr. Lasch was covered with blood.

"This next part is what is so important, if it's true, and Wally's not just imagining things. He swears he saw the front door to the house open, and a woman start to come out. She spotted him, though, and jumped back inside. He didn't see her face and doesn't know who she is, and he ran as soon as he saw her."

There was a pause and more sobbing before she began again: "Ms. Simmons, I should have let him be questioned, but he never told me about this woman before. I didn't mean to hurt Molly—I was just so afraid for my son." The sound of sobbing filled Fran's head for several long moments. Then Mrs. Barry composed herself enough to continue; "That's all I can tell you. I guess you or

Molly's lawyer will want to talk to us tomorrow. We'll be here. Good-bye."

Stunned, Fran replaced the receiver in its cradle. Wally says he saw Molly come home, she thought. Of course, he's not well. He may not be a reliable witness. *But,* if he is telling the truth, and if he did see a woman coming out of Molly's house . . .

Fran thought back to what Molly had told her of her memory of that night. Molly had said she was sure there was someone else in the house. She had talked about hearing a clicking sound . . .

But *what* woman? Annamarie? Fran shook her head. No, I don't believe that . . . Another nurse he was fooling around with . . . ?

A clicking sound. I've heard a clicking sound in Molly's house myself, Fran realized. I heard it yesterday when I stopped by and Jenna was there. It was the click her high heels made in the hallway.

Jenna. *"Good friend. Best friend."*

Oh my God, was it possible? There was no forced entry, no struggle. Wally saw a woman leaving the house. Gary had to have been killed by a woman he knew. Not Molly. Not Annamarie. All those pictures. The way Jenna looked at him in them.

90

"No more, Jenna, that's definitely enough. I swear to you I'm getting a buzz on."

"Oh for heaven's sake, Moll, you've had a glass and a half."

"I thought this was at least my third." She shook her head as if trying to clear it. "You know, this wine is potent."

"What's the difference? With all you have on your mind, you might as well relax. You hardly touched dinner."

"I ate plenty, and it was good. I'm just not very hungry." She raised her hand in protest as Jenna poured more wine into her glass. "No, I can't drink any more. My head is spinning."

"Let it spin."

They were seated in the study, both with their heads back, their bodies sunk into comfortable, overstuffed chairs that faced each other across a small, low table. For several minutes they sat in silence, while a jazz piano CD played softly in the background.

In a pause between songs, Molly spoke. "You know what, Jen? Last night I had a nightmare. It was very unsettling. I thought I saw Wally Barry at the window."

"Good Lord!"

"I wasn't scared, just startled. Wally would never hurt me; I know that. But after seeing him at the window, I turned back and all of a sudden this room looked the way it did that night when I came home and found Gary dead at his desk. And I think I've figured out why I made that connection—I believe Wally really was here that night."

Molly had kept her head back while she spoke. She was starting to feel so sleepy. She tried to keep her eyes open and to raise her head. What had she just said? Something about finding Gary.

Finding Gary.

Suddenly her eyes were fully open, and she sat forward.

"Jen, I just said something important!"

Jenna laughed. "Everything you say is important, Molly."

"Jen, this wine tastes funny."

"Well, I won't tell the mighty Cal you said that. He would be insulted."

"Click, snap. That's another sound I heard."

"Molly, Molly, you're getting hysterical." Jenna stood and crossed to her friend. Standing behind the chair, she put her arms around her and bent her head forward so that her cheek was resting against Molly's head.

"Fran thinks I'm going to commit suicide."

"Are you?" Jenna asked calmly, relaxing her embrace and standing back, then moving to sit on the table in front of Molly.

"I thought I was. I planned to. That's why I got all dressed up. I wanted to look classy when they found me."

"You *always* look classy, Molly," Jenna said softly. She slid Molly's wineglass closer to her. Molly reached for it and knocked it over.

"Not classy to be clumsy," she murmured, slumping back in

her chair. "Jen, I *did* see Wally at the window that night. I'm sure of it. It may have been a dream last night, but it wasn't before. Call him, okay? Ask him to come over and talk to me."

"Molly, be reasonable." Jenna chided. "It's ten o'clock." Grabbing their cocktail napkins, she mopped the spilled wine from the tabletop. "I'll get you a refill."

"Noo . . . no . . . no. I've had enough."

My head hurts, Molly thought. *Click, snap.* "Click, snap," she said.

"What are you talking about?"

"The sound I heard that night. Click . . . snap . . . click, click, click."

"You heard that, dear?"

"Uh-huh."

"Molly, I swear you *are* getting your memory back. You should have gotten a buzz on sooner. You just sit there and relax. I'll get you that refill."

Molly yawned as Jenna picked up the empty glass and hurried to the kitchen.

"Click, click, click," Molly said aloud, in synch with the clicking sound Jenna's high heels made on the hallway floor.

91

As he drove to Greenwich, Philip decided that he should at least give Molly a few minutes' warning before he arrived on her doorstep. He dialed her house and waited in anticipation for either her or Jenna to answer.

He listened with growing concern as the telephone rang seven, eight, ten times. Either Molly was in such a dead sleep that she couldn't hear the phone, or she had turned off the ringer.

But she wouldn't turn it off, Philip decided. Very few people have her number, and she surely wouldn't want to be out of touch with any one of us at this point.

He remembered his conversation with her that afternoon. Molly had sounded so listless, so depressed then—maybe she is already asleep. No, Jenna is with her, Philip reminded himself as he turned into Molly's street at the intersection.

But maybe Jenna left early. He glanced at the clock on the dashboard: ten o'clock. It's not that early, he thought. Maybe she's finally getting a decent night's sleep. Should I just turn around and go home? he wondered.

No. Even if he had to rout Molly out of bed to tell her about the Hilmers' testimony, he was going to do it. Nothing short of a miracle would ease her mind more than that news. It would be worth waking her up for.

As he neared Molly's house, a squad car with its lights flashing sped past him. Horrified, he watched as it turned into Molly's driveway.

92

Jenna came back to the study with a fresh glass of wine for Molly. "Hey, what are you up to?" she asked.

Molly had moved to the sofa, where she had spread out all the photographs they had been going through earlier.

"Memory lane," she replied, her words slurred. She took the glass and lifted it in a mock toast. "Lord, look at the four of us," she said, tossing a photo on the coffee table in front of the sofa. "We were happy then . . . or at least, I thought so."

Jenna smiled. "We were happy, Molly. The four of us made quite a showing for ourselves. It's too bad it had to end."

"Uh-huh." Molly took a sip of wine and yawned. "My eyes are closing. Sorry . . ."

"The best thing in the world for you right now is to finish that wine and get a good, long sleep."

"*The four of us,*" Molly said, her tone groggy. "I like to be with you, Jenna, but not with Cal."

"You don't like Cal, do you, Molly?"

"You don't like him either. In fact I think you hate him. That's why you and Gary . . ."

Molly was vaguely aware of the glass being taken from her hand, then of Jenna's arm around her, of Jenna holding the glass to her lips, of Jenna whispering soothingly, "Swallow, Molly, just keep swallowing . . ."

93

"There's Jenna's car," Fran Simmons said to Assistant Prosecutor Jacobs as they pulled into the driveway in front of Molly Lasch's house. "We have to hurry—she's in there with Molly!"

Jacobs had ridden in the squad car with Fran and two police officers. Even before the vehicle had come to a complete stop, Fran had the door on her side open. As she jumped out, she saw another car racing up the driveway behind them.

Unmindful of the steady throb of pain emanating from her ankle, she ran up the steps to the house and pressed her finger on the bell.

"Fran, what's going on?"

Fran turned to see Philip Matthews racing up the steps. Was he afraid for Molly too? she wondered fleetingly.

Inside, she could hear chimes echoing through the house.

"Fran, did something happen to Molly?" Philip was beside her now, flanked by the police officers.

"Philip! It's Jenna. It was her! It's got to be. She was the other person here the night Gary Lasch was murdered. She doesn't dare let Molly get her memory back. She knows Molly heard her running out of the house that night. She's desperate. We've got to stop her! I know I'm right."

"Break in the door," Jacobs ordered the policemen.

The door, made of solid mahogany, took a precious full minute before their battering ram dislodged it from its hinges and crashed to the floor.

As they ran into the entrance hall, a new sound echoed through the house—Jenna's hysterical screams for help.

They found her kneeling beside the couch in the study, where Molly was slumped over, her head partially covering a picture of her murdered husband, Gary Lasch. Molly's eyes were open and staring. Her hand dangled limply over the side of the couch. A wineglass lay on the carpet, its contents soaking into the deep pile.

"I didn't know what she was doing!" Jenna wailed. "Every time she left the room she must have been putting sleeping pills in the wine." She threw her arms around Molly's supine body, weeping as she rocked her. "Oh, Molly! Wake up, wake up . . ."

"Get away from her." With abrupt force, Philip Matthews grabbed Jenna and shoved her aside. Roughly he pulled Molly up. "You can't die, now! Not now!" he shouted. "I won't *let* you die."

Before anyone could move to assist him, he had lifted her in his arms. Moving swiftly he plunged through the door that led from the study into the downstairs guest bathroom. Jacobs and one of the officers followed him inside.

Within seconds Fran heard the sound of the shower running, followed moments later by the retching, gagging sound of Molly emptying her stomach of the wine that Jenna had laced with the sleeping pills.

Jacobs emerged from the bathroom. "Get the oxygen from the car!" he ordered one of the policemen. "Send for an ambulance," he told the other.

"She kept saying over and over again that she wanted to die," Jenna babbled. "She kept going into the kitchen and refilling her glass. She was imagining weird things. She said you were angry, that you wanted to kill her, Fran. She's crazy. She's out of her mind."

"If Molly was ever crazy, Jenna, it was when she trusted you," Fran said quietly.

"Yes, I was." Molly, supported by Philip and one of the policemen, was being helped back into the room. She was soaking wet from the shower and still heavily sedated, but there was no mistaking the total condemnation in her eyes and voice.

"You killed my husband," she said. "You tried to kill me. It was you I heard that night. Your heels running down the hall. I had locked the front door. I had pushed the bolt down. That was the sound I heard. The click of your heels in the hallway. You pushing up the bolt, unlocking the door."

"Wally Barry saw you, Jenna," Fran said. He saw a *woman,* she thought. He didn't see Jenna's face, but maybe she'll believe me.

"Jenna," Molly cried, "you let me spend five and a half years in prison for the crime you committed. You would have let me go back to prison. You wanted me to be convicted of Annamarie's death. Why, Jenna? Tell me why."

Jenna looked from one to the other, at first with almost pleading eyes. "Molly, you're wrong," she began.

Then she stopped, knowing it was useless. Knowing she was trapped. Knowing it was over.

"Why, Molly?" she asked. "Why?" Her voice began to rise. "WHY? Why did your family have money? Why did Gary and I need to marry what you and Cal could offer us? Why did I introduce Gary to you? Why all the foursomes? So that Gary and I could be together as much as possible, never mind all the times we were alone together over the years."

"Mrs. Whitehall, you have the right to remain silent," Jacobs began.

Jenna ignored him. "From the time we laid eyes on each other, we were in love. And then you told me that Sunday afternoon that Gary had been having an affair with that nurse and that she was pregnant." She laughed bitterly.

"I was now the *other* other woman. I came here to have it out with Gary. I parked down the street so you wouldn't see my car if you were early. He let me in. We quarreled. He kept trying to make me get out before you got home. Then he sat at his desk and turned his back to me and said, 'I'm beginning to think that I didn't do so badly marrying Molly. At least when she's angry, she goes to Cape Cod and refuses to talk to me. Now go home and leave me in peace.' "

The anger left her voice. "And then it happened. I didn't plan to do it. I didn't mean to do it."

The shriek of the approaching ambulance broke the silence that followed as Jenna's voice trailed off. Fran turned to Jacobs and said, "For the love of God, don't let that ambulance take Molly to Lasch Hospital."

94

"Ratings for last night's show are great," Gus Brandt said, six weeks later. "Congratulations. It's the best *True Crime* episode we ever aired."

"Well, you can thank yourself for setting it in motion," Fran told him. "If you hadn't assigned me to cover Molly's release from prison, none of this would have happened, or if it had, it would have happened without me."

"I especially like what Molly Lasch said in the wrap-up, the part about having faith in yourself and hanging in when you feel overwhelmed. She credits you with keeping her from committing suicide."

"Jenna almost did that for her," Fran said. "If her plan had worked, we would have all assumed that Molly really had killed herself. Still, I think I would have had my doubts. I don't believe that when push came to shove, Molly would actually have taken those pills."

"It would have been a loss—she is one beautiful woman," Gus said.

Fran smiled. "Yes, and she always has been—on the inside as well as the outside. That's much more important, don't you think?"

Gus Brandt returned Fran's smile, and he gradually shaped his expression into one of benevolence. "Yes, I do. And speaking of important, I think it's time you gave yourself a little break. Go ahead, take a day off. How about Sunday?"

Fran laughed. "Is there a Nobel Prize for generosity?"

Hands in her pockets, her head down, in what her stepbrothers called "Franny's thinking position," she went back to her office.

I've been traveling on reserve ever since that day I waited for Molly to come out of Niantic Prison, she admitted to herself. It's all behind me now, she thought, but I'm still licking my wounds.

So much had happened. In his effort to escape a possible death sentence, Lou Knox had willingly volunteered whatever information he could about Cal Whitehall and the mysterious doings at Lasch Hospital. The pistol he had in his pocket when he was arrested at the farmhouse had been the weapon used to kill Dr. Jack Morrow. "Cal told me that Morrow was one of those guys who always make trouble," he had told the cops. "He was asking too many questions at the hospital about some dead patients. So I took care of him."

The Hilmers had positively identified Lou as the man they had seen sitting in the sedan in the parking lot of the Sea Lamp Diner. Knox explained the reason for Annamarie's death: "She could have been a big-time troublemaker," he said. "She heard Lasch and Black talking about getting rid of the old lady with the bad heart. She also went along with covering for Black when he messed up the Colbert girl, but Cal got cold feet when he saw on Molly's calendar that she was meeting Annamarie Scalli in Rowayton. He was sure that next Annamarie would shoot off her mouth to that Fran Simmons. An inquiry by her might have led her to the ambulance attendants who'd been paid off to say Tasha Colbert went into cardiac arrest on the way to the hospital. Then I'd have to take care of them. So it was just simpler to get rid of Scalli."

When you start counting the people who were murdered in cold blood because they were perceived as threatening, and add to that the ones who died in the name of research, it's pretty chilling, Fran said to herself. And when I put what happened to Dad in the same context, I realize that he was a victim as well. His weakness compounded it, of course, but Whitehall actually caused his death.

Assistant Prosecutor Jacobs had shown Fran the worthless stock certificates that Lou had kept as a reminder of a profitable little scam on her father. "Cal had Lou Knox give your father a hot tip to buy $40,000 worth of this stock," Jacobs told her. "He was sure your father would fall for it, because he apparently practically worshiped Whitehall's financial success.

"Cal Whitehall counted on your father to borrow the money from the library fund. He was on the committee with your father and had access to the account as well. The $40,000 withdrawal became $400,000, thanks to Cal's manipulations, and your father knew he could neither replace it nor prove that he hadn't taken the entire amount."

He still took money that wasn't his, even if he only meant it as a kind of loan, Fran thought. At least Dad must be smiling, since Lou's other "hot tip" didn't blow me to kingdom come as intended.

She would cover the trials of Dr. Lowe, Cal Whitehall and Jenna for the network. Ironically, Jenna's defense was apparently going to be passion provocation manslaughter, the exact charge to which Molly had earlier pleaded guilty.

Evil people, all of them. But, she reflected, they're going to pay for what they did with many years in prison. On the bright side, though, Remington Health Management will be taken over by American National Insurance, with a good and decent man at the helm. Molly is selling the house and moving to New York, where she'll start a magazine job next month. Philip is crazy about her, but Molly needs a lot of time to heal and sort out her life before even thinking about a commitment. What is to be will be, and he knows it.

Fran reached for her coat. I'm going home, she decided. I'm tired and I need to regroup. Or maybe it's spring fever setting in, she thought, as she looked out at the flowers on display below at Rockefeller Center.

She turned to see Tim Mason standing in her doorway. "I've been watching you today," he said. "I have decided you look kind of down. My prescription is to come with me to Yankee Stadium immediately. The game starts in forty-five minutes."

Fran smiled. "A perfect solution for the blues," she agreed, making a quick decision.

Tim linked her arm in his. "Dinner will be a hot dog and beer."

"Your treat, remember," Fran interjected. "Think of your mother's feeling on the subject."

"Absolutely. However, a small bet on the outcome of the game would enhance my enjoyment."

"I'll take the Yankees, but I'll give you a three-run spread," Fran offered.

They stepped into the elevator and the door closed behind them.